MEDIUM ÆVUM

EDITORIAL COMMITTEE

K. P. Clarke, A. J. Lappin,
N. F. Palmer, P. Russell, C. Saunders

EDITOR FOR THIS VOLUME

A. J. Lappin

MEDIUM ÆVUM
MONOGRAPHS XXXIV

L'ENTRÉE D'ESPAGNE

CONTEXT AND AUTHORSHIP AT THE ORIGINS OF THE ITALIAN CHIVALRIC EPIC

CLAUDIA BOSCOLO

THE SOCIETY FOR THE STUDY OF MEDIEVAL
LANGUAGES AND LITERATURE

OXFORD · MMXVII

THE SOCIETY FOR THE STUDY OF MEDIEVAL
LANGUAGES AND LITERATURE
OXFORD, 2017

http://aevum.space/monographs

© 2017 Claudia Boscolo

ISBN:
978-0-907570-34-9 (PB)
978-0-907570-33-2 (HB)
978-0-907570-35-6 (E-BK)

British Library Cataloguing in Publication Data
A catalogue record for this book is available
from the British Library

CONTENTS

Abbreviations   vii
INTRODUCTION   ix

1. GENRE
L'Entrée d'Espagne in the context of Romance studies   1
Notions of the hybrid and the Romance epic   7
L'Entrée d'Espagne as an example of hybridism   14

2. LITERARY INFLUENCES
Traces of the Breton romance   17
L'Entrée d'Espagne and the classical tradition   51

3. THE MAIN CHARACTERS
Elements of characterisation   95
Roland in *L'Entrée d'Espagne* and in the *Chanson de Roland*: a portrait of the hero   110
Roland and the Saracens   117
Charlemagne in the *Chanson de Roland*   120
Charlemagne in *L'Entrée d'Espagne*   124
The question of authority   140
Roland returns to Spain   151

4. REPRESENTATIONS OF ISLAM

Islam, Europe and the *Chanson de geste*	155
The Saracen Pantheon	166
Saracens in *L'Entrée d'Espagne*	178
Roland in Syria	206

5. HISTORICAL CONTEXT AND TEXTUAL MATTERS

Current hypotheses	215
The second prologue	222
Ferragu's birth	229
The question of authorship	238
The question of language	245
Is the poem really unfinished?	249

BIBLIOGRAPHY	259
INDEX OF NAMES	281

ABBREVIATIONS

AIV *Atti dell'Istituto Veneto di Scienze, Lettere ed Arti (Classe di Scienze Morali, Lettere ed Arti)*

INTRODUCTION

L'Entrée d'Espagne is a Franco-Venetian poem that has been variously dated to between the first and third decades of the fourteenth century. It is divided into 681 laisses of differing lengths, giving a total of 15805 verses, on the model of the *Chanson de Roland* (290 laisses; 4002 verses).[1] It was composed about a decade before the invention of *ottava rima* in Italian literature, in the second quarter of the fourteenth century. The first and only edition of the *Entrée* was published by Antoine Thomas in 1913, in two volumes with an introduction, and is based on the sole extant manuscript in Venice.[2]

We know next to nothing of this anonymous poet except that he was from Padua. This simple piece of biographical information is given by internal elements in the text, which also suggest that he may have lived and worked far from his native city. Beyond this, all is open to speculation. His cultural background, profession and the identity of the patron to whom his work was addressed remain a mystery. Thus is a subject lending itself to much speculation, with two different approaches offering solutions: on the one hand, a more traditional, philological approach emphasises that the text contains a great deal of information needing interpretation; on the other, a historical-sociological approach indicates both events and social

---

[1] All references to the text of the *Chanson de Roland* are made to *Chanson de Roland - Canzone di Orlando*, ed. by A. M. Finoli, transl. by F. Pozzoli (Milan: Mursia, 1984).

[2] *L'Entrée d'Espagne. Chanson de geste franco-italienne, publiée d'après le manuscrit unique de Venise*, ed. by A. Thomas, 2 vols (Paris: Firmin-Didot, 1913). Unless otherwise stated, all references to the text of the *Entrée* are to this edition. Venice: Biblioteca Nazionale Marciana, fr. Z. 21 (=257). For a study of the manuscript see S. Marcon, 'L'*Entrée d'Espagne*, manoscritto marciano Fr. Z. 21 (=257). La storia e l'aspetto materiale', in *La Entrada en España. Poema épico del siglo XIV en franco-italiano* (Valencia: Ediciones Grial, 2003), pp. 291-318.

factors relating to the poem's time of composition, capable of narrowing the range of answers to the most obvious questions: Who was the author? Where was it written? For whom? Does it contain elements of polemic against the establishment of the age or is it perfectly in line with the patron's wishes and tastes?

This book aims to redefine the role of the *Entrée* in the history of Italian literature by answering these questions as accurately as possible, keeping the text as the focus, and extracting from it all possible information. Specifically, it interprets the *Entrée* no longer as the last of the *chansons de geste*, or one of Ariosto's main sources, but as an independent work of art whose potentialities were exploited by its Italian readers in the following two centuries, and whose hybrid form prevents its classification as a work of one particular genre. I also argue that the *Entrée* is not left accidentally unfinished but that the author deliberately stopped writing when he had articulated his point of view.

Description

This book is divided into six chapters. Chapter one deals with the existing state of research and introduces the text as an example of late medieval hybridisation, discussing romance epic as resulting from major modifications of the *chanson de geste*. Chapter two investigates the presence of Breton romances in the *Entrée* through citations of names and resemblances between the structures in the poem and in the *matière de Bretagne*. It aims at establishing a strong link between the *Entrée*'s second section and the matter of Britain. It also describes the classical influence on the *Entrée*, taking into consideration the matter of Aeneas in Italy, the matter of Troy, the circulation of Ovid's works, and the tradition of Alexander the Great. It includes references to and comparisons both with classical heroes, and themes and motifs borrowed from what was available of classical literature in medieval times. Chapter three deals with issues of the characterisation of the poem's main personages and provides bases for a theory of characterisation (direct and indirect), referring specifically to Roland and his transition from epic to chivalric hero. Through different uses of the word *desmesure*, this concept gradually assumes a negative connotation and can no longer be connected to

INTRODUCTION

Roland. It also discusses Charlemagne's authority as resulting both from his characterisation and his relationship with Roland. It follows the process leading to the rupture in the relationship of Charlemagne and Roland, and relates the problem of authority to contemporary discussions on the Italian political situation during the fourteenth century. Chapter four describes knowledge and misconceptions of Islam in Europe during the Middle Ages and their reflection in the treatment of the Saracen religion. An analysis of the theological dispute between Roland and the Saracen giant Ferragu shows how the latter is a multifaceted character, whose role can be interpreted in the light of a range of influences that may have been part of the author's background. A study of the Eastern episode of the *Entrée* provides further evidence that the poet was more interested in matters of chivalry than in geographical descriptions, positioning the *Entrée* even closer to the Breton romance. It deals with the characterisation of the Saracens and their relationship with the Christian world. A number of Saracen characters have been taken into consideration, divided into good and evil, except for Ferragu who has been treated on his own due to his significance in the poem. Chapter five contains my contribution to the two most important problems, still unsolved to date. It tries to answer the issue of the poem's ending. I suggest the poem is not unfinished and provide evidence to support this idea. I also engage with the question of authorship and patronage; I find strong evidence to suggest that the unknown author resided outside his native city of Padua, and possibly lived and composed the *Entrée* in the area under Visconti rule.

The *Entrée* offers almost unlimited material for study, connecting it with the tendency to encyclopaedism very much in fashion in the thirteenth and fourteenth centuries. Therefore, while this book seeks to survey the material as broadly as possible, it does not isolate and exhaustively consider all of the intriguing elements emerging from a close analysis of the text.

Despite the excellence of Thomas' edition from many perspectives, more recent scholarship has offered revised findings and alternative *lectiones*, showing it to be outdated[3]; nonetheless, it

---

[3] M. Infurna, 'Note sull'edizione Thomas dell'*Entrée d'Espagne*', in C. Montagnani, ed., *Miscellanea Boiardesca* (Novara: Interlinea, 2010), pp.

remains the only edition to date and of such quality that in recent years a new anastatic reprint has been issued.[4] A facsimile of the Venetian manuscript has also been printed by Ediciones Grial of Valencia, under the direction of Carlos Alvar. This expensive reproduction is indeed a major development, allowing one to conveniently consult what is both the only extant manuscript and a masterpiece of fourteenth-century illumination. It also contains an interesting study of the history and features of the manuscript.[5]

Recent translations of parts of the *Entrée d'Espagne* have been published. One by Marco Infurna stops at line 279 and resumes the narrative only from line 9018, an interruption not due to the large lacuna occurring later, from line 13991. In fact, the foreword gives no explanation as to why the translator decided to cut out parts of the text or, in some instances, to anthologize whole passages. Overall this edition omits about nine thousand verses, which is very disappointing for those awaiting a complete Italian translation.[6] Furthermore, Infurna's translation narrowly follows the original text, separating the sentences as per the lines of the *Entrée* – even though it is virtually impossible to render the typical rhythmic cadence of this Franco-Italian poem in modern Italian. This results in what is essentially a prose text unnecessarily split into lines. Infurna's translation was also more preoccupied with fidelity to the original text than with pleasing the reader, to the extent that his version sounds somewhat artificial.

Moreover, it was expected that this edition would contain the text of the fragments held in the libraries in Reggio Emilia and Châtillon which were discussed by René Specht.[7] These fragments

---

25–37. M. Infurna, 'Rolando dall'eremita. Su un verso dell'*Entrée d'Espagne*', *Medioevo Romanzo*, 30 (2006), 167–75.

[4] *L'Entrée d'Espagne. Chanson de geste Franco-italienne. Ristampa anastatica dell'edizione di Antoine Thomas*, ed. by M. Infurna (Florence: Olschki, 2007).

[5] Marcon, 'L'*Entrée d'Espagne*, manoscritto marciano Fr. Z. 21 (=257)'.

[6] *L'Entrée d'Espagne. Rolando da Pamplona all'Oriente*, ed. and transl. by M. Infurna (Rome: Carocci, 2011).

[7] R. Specht, 'La tradition manuscrite de l'*Entrée d'Espagne*. Observations sur le fragment de Châtillon', in A. Limentani, M. L. Meneghetti, R. Brusegan et al., eds, *Essor et fortune de la chanson de geste dans l'Europe et*

INTRODUCTION

partially reconstruct the lost section of the story contained in the approximately five thousand missing lines of the lacuna. While informing the reader that the fragments 'presentano versi collocabili nella grande lacuna',[8] Infurna does not try to bridge the gap in the text, nor does he address Léon Gautier's first attempt at resolving the question of the lacuna.[9]

More interestingly, Paolo Gresti published a prose translation of lines 1-548, 806-920 and 1150-4180. This translation also contains an introduction and a commentary to the selected text. This is an admirable enterprise in that Gresti chose to render excerpts of the *Entrée d'Espagne* into modern Italian prose, showing more consideration for the contemporary Italian reader than fidelity to the assonance of the Franco-Italian text. I personally appreciate this choice because the *Entrée d'Espagne* bears the characteristics of a prose narrative, despite respecting the typical assonance of epic poetry.[10]

---

l'Orient latin. Actes du IXe Congrès international de la Société Rencesvals pour l'Étude des épopées romanes (Padoue-Venise, 29 août –4 september 1982) (Modena: Mucchi, 1984), II: 749–55; R. Specht, 'Il frammento reggiano dell'*Entrée d'Espagne*. raffronto filologico col codice marciano francese XXI (257)', *AIV*, 136 (1977–78), 407–24.

[8] *L'Entrée d'Espagne*, ed. Infurna, p. 38.
[9] L. Gautier, *Les Epopées françaises*, 5 vols (Osnabrück: Zeller, 1878).
[10] *Duello tra Rolando e Feragu nell'Entrée d'Espagne*, transl. into prose by P. Gresti (Mantua: Arcari, 2012).

GENRE

L'Entrée d'Espagne in the context of Romance Studies

The legacy of the French *chansons de geste* in Italy has been widely debated over the past decades. A great variety of studies share the view that the Franco-Italian tradition is either a corruption of the original themes and motifs of French epic, as well as of its language, or that its poetic value is irrelevant next to its marking a literary threshold between the end of the feudal world and the beginning of the bourgeois. However, acceptance of the literary stature of the Franco-Italian corpus is now growing. For this reason, the time is ripe to draw some conclusions from the mass of dispersed articles which have discussed different aspects of *L'Entrée d'Espagne*, and completed the arguments sketched within the only two existing books on it. For those unfamiliar with Franco-Italian, the *Entrée* is the sole work of appreciable literary importance written in this hybrid language. For its more expert readers, it is the poem that best embodies the societal thinking, aspirations and self-awareness of the emerging social class which was to dominate the Po Valley for centuries to come. Viewed as a snapshot of its times, the *Entrée* contains a number of features that help today's reader to form an idea of a long-faded and otherwise inaccessible era. While Dante Alighieri was creating the *Divine Comedy*, a literary model for the Italian language and epitome of the Italian fourteenth century, the French language and especially its Italian variant remained obscure even as Franco-Italian poems fed the roots of the Renaissance. This fertile environment is the Franco-Italian corpus and particularly its most magnificent poem, *L'Entrée d'Espagne*.

L'Entrée d'Espagne is commonly classified as a romance epic. However, since the term 'romance epic' is used slightly differently by Italianists to other romance language specialists, its usage in this book needs to be defined. While non-Italianists call 'romance epic' all poems of a certain length conveying the matter of Charlemagne in a romance language, regardless of the period of composition, I follow the normal usage of Italianists who define 'romance' as epic texts belonging to a late stage of development of the *chanson de geste* in Italy, starting from the age of Humanism.

Scholars debating the *Entrée* have provided two main perspectives. From the French viewpoint, the *Entrée* is largely a late *chanson de geste*, containing remarkable although not entirely unique characteristics. Insistence on the unoriginality of some of the *Entrée*'s main features has led French scholars to overlook the impact of these modifications on Italian literature. From the Italian perspective, the *Entrée* is an early chivalric poem, and mainly serves to illustrate Italy's cultural situation between the full establishment of the Italian language and the redaction of the Italian late-medieval and Renaissance masterpieces. Nevertheless, it is possible to approach the legacy of the French *chansons de geste* in Italy from the viewpoint of what was overcome rather than perpetuated by the Italians, and of what was invented rather than anticipated in the *Entrée*. By way of a critical analysis and close reading of this Franco-Italian poem, the intention of this book is to place it in a framework that can explain its many peculiarities.

Ever since Dionisotti's groundbreaking study,[1] the *Entrée* has been regarded with the sort of reverential respect usually paid to works of art that do not fall into any pre-established category. Entailing as it does distance and detachment, this kind of attitude in no way guarantees involved analysis. It has taken much consideration of the nature of the romance epic, and effort in establishing the transitional nature of the fourteenth century, to reach the conclusion that the *Entrée* really is a poem that best represents the spirit of that age in Italy. This was not an easy process. Above all, the language barrier has created confusion, disorientation, and a rather entertaining dispute as to this masterpiece's identity: is it Italian literature? Or French? Is the strange phenomenon termed 'Franco-Italian' a conspiracy to confuse posterity? How can academia appraise this *congerie* of works of differing styles and genres if the correct perspective has yet to be

---

[1] C. Dionisotti, '*Entrée d'Espagne, Spagna, Rotta di Roncisvalle*', in G. Gerardi Marcuzzo et al., eds, *Studi in onore di Angelo Monteverdi*, 2 vols (Modena: Mucchi, 1959), I: 207–41.

established? Is the end-of-an-epoch perspective the right one,[2] or would it be more appropriate to view it as new and innovative, establishing a rupture with the past at the same time as it does new criteria for composition and entertainment?

All these questions did not arise at once, nor have the answers been easy to find. The present state of research into the *Entrée* suggests that scholars have finally reached a form of compromise, whereby the endeavour to define the romance-epic genre more precisely has strengthened the one to create a suitable academic environment in which the composition of a linguistic and generic hybrid such as the *Entrée* could be more wholly explained. Scholars have frequently pointed out the signal injustice of considering the *Entrée* as merely a source for what was to come, or an endpoint for the multifaceted experience of the *chansons de geste*. It must indeed be looked at diachronically as 'an important component in our understanding of the developmental process of literature'[3] – both as the product of an environment with unique qualities and a milestone in the creation of a range of typically Italian *topoi*. With that said, the *Entrée* (and Franco-Italian literature as a whole) had a space and a public of its own. It may be extracted from the general context of medieval literature and considered solely within the historical and highly local circumstances of fourteenth-century northern Italy. Genres and style no longer exist save for some general rules on the writing of epic which are still followed in the first part of the poem. Viewed in this way, the *Entrée* would be neither the natural progression of a pre-existing movement nor the conscious anticipation of one to come. It would be the artistic work of a single genius who, while acknowledging the legacy of the whole European *koinè*, refuses to follow a given pattern, to compose in a given language, or to wholly please a given audience.

[2] As in M. Bakhtin, *The Dialogic Imagination. Four Essays*, ed. by M. Holquist, transl. by M. Holquist and C. Emerson (Austin: University of Texas Press, 1981), pp. 3–40.

[3] Bradley-Cromey, *Authority and Autonomy in "L'Entrée d'Espagne"* (New York: Garland, 1993), p. 5. On this point see also G. Holtus, 'Quelques aspects de la technique narrative dans l'*Entrée d'Espagne*', in Limentani et al., eds, *Essor et fortune*, II: 703–16.

Fifteen years ago, suddenly and also paradoxically, two studies[4] overturned the long-existing lack of research on the *Entrée*. The books of Limentani and Bradley-Cromey books gather different opinions on the *Entrée* and discuss what very little had been said before. They organise these scattered points of view into thorough investigations, with different aspects of the Franco-Venetian poem analysed in depth and interesting theories put forward. The most complete bibliography on the *Entrée*, containing everything published up to 1992, is in Bradley-Cromey. In her Introduction, she tackles some questions that needed revisiting and clarifies her approach to the *Entrée*, focussing on the problem of Roland's autonomy. This is viewed as a result of the circumstances in which the poem was produced, and it is indeed a source of information internal to the text, on which a profile of the author can be based. While providing an original insight into a number of open questions, Bradley-Cromey aims at situating the *Entrée* in a certain time and location, transforming it into a means of understanding that particular point in history. This is certainly an interesting way of proceeding and succeeds in treating the *Entrée* as a poem of a distinct importance and relevance within the history of literature.

Limentani's aim was different. Lacking a book's unity and structure, his study collects articles published over three decades which were indeed the first to throw some light on the *Entrée*, their framework lifting the poem clear of an indistinct background. His suggestions as to the author's origins and culture, and learned discussion of some of the poem's major motifs, have laid the foundations for future research.

More recent studies dealt with several other issues, such as date and style, most of which may be considered as answered. Yet a number of questions are still open to further analysis; for example, the conclusions reached by André de Mandach on the identity of the author are not convincing.[5] While his premises are acceptable and

---

[4] Alberto Limentani, *L'"Entrée d'Espagne" e i signori d'Italia*, ed. by M. Infurna and F. Zambon (Padua: Antenore, 1992) [published posthumously]; Bradley-Cromey, *Authority and Autonomy*.

[5] A. de Mandach, 'L'*Entrée d'Espagne*. Six auteurs en quête d'un personnage', *Studi medievali*, 30 (1989), 163–208; A. de Mandach, 'Sur les traces de la cheville ouvrière de l'*Entrée d'Espagne*. Giovanni

his argument meticulous, de Mandach's desire to assign an identity to the Paduan author led him to select the first available name, whereas a number of elements in- and outside the text may suggest a different conclusion. Limentani has certainly succeeded in convincing his readers, including Bradley-Cromey, that the *Entrée* is an entirely Paduan product, perfectly justified by the spirit of the Paduan environment. However, while he suggested a Paduan education for the author, he never corroborated Dionisotti's first claim that the *Entrée* had been created at the court of the Visconti by an anonymous Paduan writer[6] and preferred to avoid the question by broadly accepting that the author might have moved far from his native city. Dionisotti also suggested that Franco-Italian is indeed the correct name for the collection of texts produced in the hybrid and purely literary form in which the French language circulated in northern Italy;[7] by doing so he insisted on considering the work in this language as generally northern Italian without reference to any particular environment.[8]

All the work to date is enlightening as to the poet's Paduan upbringing and his cultural background. Yet very little has been done to clarify another issue, of patronage, which could add a further level of detail and help to identify the author. It is indeed in Padua and Treviso that he completed his apprenticeship as a young poet and met masters such as Lovato Lovati, Albertino da Mussato, and Pietro d'Abano. But what did he read away from Padua? Whom did he meet? Who did he become in his maturity, very possibly spent far from home? All this is perhaps more relevant to the understanding of the *Entrée*'s structure and significance. The *Entrée* is the product of a mature intellectual and so it is his maturity that

---

Nono', in G. Holtus, H. Krauss and P. Wunderli, eds, *Testi, cotesti e contesti del franco-italiano. Atti del I simposio franco-italiano (Bad Homburg, 13–16 aprile 1987)* (Tübingen: Niemeyer, 1989), pp. 48–64.

[6] Dionisotti, '*Entrée d'Espagne, Spagna, Rotta di Roncisvalle*', pp. 213–14.

[7] See also L. Renzi, 'Il francese come lingua letteraria e il franco-lombardo. L'epica carolingia nel Veneto', in Folena, ed., *Storia della Cultura Veneta*, III: 563–89.

[8] This idea was argued for by Renzi, 'Il francese': 'c'è un francese di Lombardia e un franco-lombardo (denominazione forse preferibile a franco-italiano e al più comune franco-veneto)' (p. 574).

must be the object of research. The pre-humanist background that so vividly emerges from a close reading of the poem should be seen in a different context: that of the satellite centres of the Visconti court with their contradictions, political strife and literary influences, mostly coming from abroad and shaping a more stratified reality than we used to believe the case, from which much can be deduced.

Corrado Bologna[9] placed the *Entrée* within the vibrant framework of fourteenth century northern Italy, delineating a highly accurate profile of the historical circumstances contemporary with the poem's composition. Although he does not advance any original theories as to how the author might have profited from the turbulent political situation in the Visconti dominions in the first half of the century, he provides sufficient data to evoke an image of a lively circulation of people and works in the area under the influence of the powerful family.

A number of disparate articles tackle different aspects of the masterpiece of Franco-Italian literature. As established by Leslie Zarker-Morgan, the presence of an omniscient narrator creates the conditions for the adoption of a prose narrative mode.[10] This corroborates the argument that the *Entrée* belongs to romance rather than epic. This conclusion is also reached via a very different approach by Bradley-Cromey, whose study on forest and voyage in the *Entrée* demonstrates how intertextuality modifies the narrative structures in this late epic.[11]

All current opinions seem to converge on one point: the *Entrée*, while having been traditionally viewed from the perspective of late *chansons de geste* – that is, of what it has *lost* – can be seen from the

---

[9] C. Bologna, 'La letteratura dell'Italia settentrionale nel Trecento', in A. Asor Rosa, ed., *Letteratura italiana. Storia e geografia* (Turin: Einaudi, 1987), I: 511–600.

[10] L. Zarker-Morgan, 'The Narrator in Italian Epic. Franco-Italian Tradition', in *Aspect de l'epopée romane. Mentalités, idéologies, intertextualités* (Groningen: Egbert Forsten, 1995), pp. 481–90.

[11] Bradley-Cromey, *Authority and Autonomy*, pp. 215–48 (originally published as 'Forest and Voyage. Signs of Sententia in the *Entrée d'Espagne*', in H.-E. Keller, ed., *Romance Epic. Essays on a Medieval Literary Genre* (Kalamazoo: Western Michigan University Press, 1987), pp. 91–101.

totally opposite angle – namely, of what it has *gained* from this process of 'degeneration'. However, a degeneration it is not, whether one views it diachronically as a moment of transition or cast in the synchronicity of the early Trecento in Lombardy. It is not a matter of choice but rather of discussing Italian culture as a nascent phenomenon, no longer depending on France, although admiring that foreign culture from which much inspiration was still drawn.

To decide whether or not the *Entrée* belongs to the genre of *chanson de geste*, it is necessary to consider as a major issue the hero's shifting identity, due to the impossibility on the one hand of the knight co-existing with an epic structure, and on the other of the epic hero co-existing with romance purposes. The poem acquires the status of a hybrid once it is proven that the two facets of the same character are represented in the *Entrée*.

The figure of Charlemagne as an emperor under challenge from his lords, and Roland's independence of thought and action, as discussed by Bradley-Cromey, patently reflect a modified historical backdrop; these modifications clearly do not leave any space for the celebration of other nations' heroes. This is the century when epic and romance heroes acquire an Italian identity, and their stories reflect entirely Italian matters such as the struggle for autonomy from the emperor, or the necessity of an imperial intervention, lamented by Dante and others, to end the political disorder within the communes. The issue of the rise of the Italian lordships plays a central role in the creation of a hybrid genre in which the old no longer fits and the new has not yet become canonical. 'Hybrid', however, is not necessarily tantamount to transitional nor it is a synonym for accidental. Hybridism can be a genre in itself, which is also the subject of this study.

Notions of the hybrid and the Romance epic

In order to discuss a literary work that is a hybrid of *chanson de geste* and romance, it is first necessary to stress that a *chanson de geste* is a notion distinct from and not to be confused with classical epic.

Classical epic persisted throughout the disintegration of the Roman Empire, being kept alive and acquiring a didactic role in *scriptoria* during the Carolingian Renaissance. Although in the

Middle Ages it necessarily lost its original political meaning, it still maintained a high artistic value and achieved an eminent literary status through the many reworkings imbuing it with Christian culture. Thus, the *Aeneid* shifted its original political significance to that of an allegorised epic of the soul's journey towards perfection and salvation, through the interpretation of Christian commentators from Fulgentius in the sixth century to John of Salisbury in the twelfth.[12] The reading of the *Aeneid* as an allegorical journey and the perception of pathos in Aeneas' epic led to the inclusion of the matters of Troy and Rome in the genre of *romans d'antiquité* – medieval French romances that reworked major classical epics such as the *Roman de Troie* and the *Roman d'Eneas*,[13] and that up until the end of the fourteenth century were considered the most suitable vehicles for this matter. The classical epic hero, the quintessentially complex character, became the ideal protagonist of a romance. Thus, classical epic and *roman* started being closely associated in that both engaged with the representation of the complexities of human nature. Fulgentius provided medieval readers with an allegorical interpretation of classical epic so that the *Aeneid* could be understood as a quest for Aeneas' own identity, and this reading provides the most comprehensive justification for Dante's choice of Virgil as his guide.[14] Additionally and in opposition to Virgil's 'canonic' epic, Ovid's *Metamorphoses* has been described as a human epic[15] since the fusion of elegiac and epic styles inspired the insertion

[12] On this point see F. Mora-Lebrun, *L'Enéide' médiévale et la chanson de geste* (Paris: Champion, 1994).

[13] Benoît de Saint-Maure, *Le Roman de Troie*, ed. by L. Constans (Paris: Société des Anciens Textes Françaises, 1904–12); *Enéas*. Unless stated otherwise, all references to the text of the *Enéas* are to *Enéas. Roman du XIIe siècle*, ed. by J. J. Salverda de Grave (Paris: Champion, 1964).

[14] Dante, discussing the four stages of the voyage of the soul toward its union with God, refers directly to Fulgentius: 'lo figurato che di questo diverso processo dell'etadi tiene Virgilio nello Eneida' (*Convivio*, IV, XXIV, 9). D. Alighieri, *Convivio*, ed. by F. Brambilla Ageno, 3 vols (Florence: Le Lettere, 1995), II: 416–17. See B. J. Bono, *Literary Transvaluation. From Virgilian Epic to Shakespearean Tragicomedy* (Berkeley: University of California Press, 1984), p. 51 and n. 17.

[15] A. J. Boyle, ed., *Roman Epic* (London: Ruthledge, 1996). See also B. Otis, *Ovid as an Epic Poet* (Cambridge: Cambridge University Press, 1970).

of the theme of love into the treatment of war, which anticipates the most distinctive trait of the Italian chivalric epic. Thus, the rewriting of epic in the light of Ovid led readers after the twelfth century to consider content before genre.[16]

In the fourteenth century, classical epic was under re-evaluation by Italian intellectuals: Dante and then Boccaccio lamented the lack of epic in Italian literature ('arma vero nullum latium adhuc invenio poetasse', *De vulgari eloquentia*, II, 2, 8).[17] By *arma* Dante refers to epic in the classical sense and not to the *chansons de geste*. He had a clear idea of the difference between classical and romance epic, and so too did the anonymous author of a translation of Ovid's *Metamorphoses* into French (which circulated with the name of *Ovide moralisé* between 1308 and 1328)[18] who defended Homer against the versions of Benoît, Dares and Dictys. This view can be considered representative of the state of the reception of epic in the fourteenth century, when classical epic and *chanson de geste* were considered quite distinct.

Even though Dante's statement referred specifically to classical epic, *chansons de geste* had never held an especially important position in vernacular Italian literature either. While in the fourteenth century the *chanson de geste* remained *mutatis mutandis* the preferred entertainment of those curious about the subject of Charlemagne and all its implications, the Italian form of epic is the product of a fusion between *chanson de geste* and romance. Specifically, the *Entrée* preserves textual aspects of a *chanson* but contains particular traits of a Breton romance, such as the themes of love, voyage and chivalry; one aspect of this is the solitude of the epic hero,[19] who seeks an ideal as he would the Holy Grail but must

---

[16] Mora-Lebrun, *L'"Eneide" médiévale*, p. 11.

[17] D. Alighieri, *De vulgari eloquentia*, in *Opere minori*, ed. by P. V. Mengaldo and B. Nardi, 6 vols (Naples: Ricciardi, 1995–96), III/1: 3–237 (p. 154).

[18] *Ovide moralisé. Poème du commencement du quatorzième siècle publié d'après tous les manuscripts connus*, (Amsterdam: Johannes Müller; Uitgave van de N. V. Noord-Hollandsche Uitgeversmaatschappij, 1915–1938; repr. Wiesbaden: Verhandelingen der Koniklijke Academie van Wetenschappen to Amsterdam, 1966).

[19] The solitude of the epic hero is paralleled by the fourteenth-century Ulysses of *Inferno*, who indeed recalls the hero of a chanson: the one

face hostility in the secular world.[20] In the *Entrée*, Roland must consequently suffer departure from Charlemagne and solitary adventure,[21] which rather than symbolizing heroic stature serves as a period for reconsidering his ideals. While solitude in the Breton romance is associated with an allegorical forest, the symbolic voyage is often rather undertaken on the sea;[22] the forest, the ocean and indeed the desert thus become corresponding concepts.[23] In *chansons de geste* there are no allegorical forests whereas the *Entrée* hero's

---

    who inspires great actions and is to be held responsible for failure: see M. Corti, 'Percorsi dell'invenzione', in *Scritti su Cavalcanti e Dante* (Turin: Einaudi, 2003), pp. 178–298.

[20] W. Calin, *The Epic Queste* (Baltimore: The John Hopkins Press, 1966), p. 108. William Calin made some interesting remarks on the motif of quest in the Christian epic. He explains that while the Exodus myth serves as the prime source and a literary example of how life for all men is a pilgrimage and exile, the true Christian does not wander idly but seeks perfection and salvation. The Christian hero must seek a spiritual *terra repromissionis* prefiguring the literal Heavenly City, imitating the example of Moses and Joshua who wandered for years seeking the highest good, symbolised by the Promised Land. The pilgrimage may serve as an act of penance, and the hero must suffer before admittance to the highest mysteries. The voyage may also manifest a desire to merit grace which, having descended upon the Christian, may spur him to wander (p. 107). 'In archetypal terms, quest and adventure imply a departure. The hero leaves home, family, friends, the world of ordinary mortals behind. He is exalted by the concept of travel and movement, a search for the unknown' (p. 185).

[21] Roland's solitude is highlighted by his being the only Christian amidst the Saracens.

[22] See, for example, Brendan, *Navigatio sancti Brendani*, ed. by Carl Selmer (Notre Dame, IN: University of Notre Dame Press, 1959).

[23] However, although the concepts of sea and forest correspond in both being metaphors for withdrawal and isolation, Ulysses drowns in Dante's epic sea, whereas Dante the Pilgrim, in his non-epic, challenging and obscure forest, experiences isolation but eventually returns 'a riveder le stelle', that is out into the mundane world. Corti, 'Percorsi dell'invenzione', explains Ulysess' drowning as a 'naufragio filosofico' and considers this episode the most outstanding example of how Dante consigned to the bottom of the sea the entire philosophical system supporting medieval thought until the start of the fourteenth century. Ulysses' drowning is thus a metaphor for failure, while Dante's exit marks the transition to a post-Aristotelian age (p. 268).

isolation begins precisely with a voyage by sea. It is evident that the *Entrée* lies outside the realm of pure *chansons de geste*.

The transformation of the *chanson de geste* into a romance epic, through the embodiment in the Christian epic of *roman* elements, is a process that requires a reflection on the nature of the epic itself. In a paper published in 1987, R. H. Webber advanced four statements which, as she wrote, should be read as 'a tentative beginning to the morphology of the romance epic'[24] (as opposed to, or rather completing, the morphology of folktale established by Propp)[25]. These read as follows:

1. The Romance epic hero is a redoubtable warrior-knight whose mission may be noble or ignoble, productive or fatal.
2. The Romance epic hero's fate is death if his heroism is tainted with pride or if his mission is unworthy.
3. The Romance epic story is frequently made up of two moves, which may be linked in either one of two ways: by a hero who is killed and then avenged by a second hero; or by a single hero who undertakes two separate missions in succession that involve different epic actions.
4. The backdrop of the Romance epic story is usually the wars between Roland and the infidels.[26]

It is unclear whether the four statements were designed to include late *chansons de geste*, some indeed being so late that they fall into a borderline category neither in- nor outside the *chanson de geste* genre. This is the case of the *Entrée*. Examining Webber's statements closely, however, one notices that with the exception of the third they could be expanded.

The definition of the romance epic hero as a redoubtable warrior knight suits the twelfth century protagonist of a *chanson de geste*, Roland above all. Yet could it be applied as easily to a fourteenth century hero? Wisdom is not a feature of the romance epic hero as described in Webber's statements, which refer to the model of the

---

[24] R. H. Webber, 'Towards the Morphology of the Romance Epic', in H.-E. Keller, ed., *Romance Epic*, pp. 1-9 (p. 8).
[25] V. Propp, *Morphology of the Folktale* (Austin: University of Texas Press, 1968).
[26] Webber, 'Towards the Morphology', p. 8.

désmesuré hero of the earlier *chansons*.[27] From a strictly sociohistorical viewpoint, the conglomerate of territories forming central-south-western Europe not least shared concepts of production, utility and convenience which were newly formed as the feudal contract gradually gave way either to primitive nationalism or membership of a network of city states. Considering the type of audience addressed by the late *chansons de geste* and the social backdrop to its reception, it is not surprising that the formidable former warrior-knight should be made to ask himself if he is doing the right thing, or indeed what the right thing to do may be, according to his society's new standards. Roland in the *Entrée* represents one hero who questions his own mission and considers if it is truly noble or productive without necessarily dismissing it as ignoble or fatal. Does this still make him a romance epic hero?[28]

If the Romance epic hero's fate is death when his heroism in tainted with pride or his mission is unworthy, can we conversely say that his fate is survival if his *desmesure* is overcome and his mission worthy? Examples from late *chansons de geste* of the hero's survival (understood very broadly) are the *Poema del mio Cid* and indeed the *Entrée*, which represent instances of how the heroes overcome their excessive pride. One may argue that the Cid and Roland in the *Entrée* are very different characters in that the former represents the mature hero, a generation older than the latter. However, they both represent the spirit of their own age, and thus we can put them on the same level. It is Webber's statement, in reverse, that can be applied to late *chansons*. Furthermore, the question of the *Entrée*'s incompleteness is strictly related to that of Roland's survival: as the end of the story does not coincide with that of the account of the

---

[27] It must be said that according to Webber, however, Roland 'does not represent the ideal knight'. The hero's pride, his *desmesure*, and 'his insistence on heroism above all else' harm more than help the cause that the hero is defending: Webber, 'Towards the Morphology', p. 2.

[28] Let us consider one entirely Italian character, Dante the Pilgrim. Assuming that Dante's poem can conveniently be defined as an epic, Dante the Pilgrim's voyage leads him from the perdition and moral darkness of the philosophical forest where he found himself in his mid-age crisis to the brightness of supreme knowledge. Many times he doubts his own worth and certainly does not display the features of the Christian knight.

seven years before Rencesvals (which as stated by the author himself is the poem's subject), was the purpose of the whole poem to rescue the tragic epic hero? What did the Paduan mean when he inserted the hermit episode as a sort of *mise en abyme* of Roland's life at the end of the *Entrée*; was it that Roland deserved to be rescued because he had finally managed to shed his unjustified and excessive pride; or did he mean to impute an injustice to the Rencesvals tradition by underlining the abuse Roland had still to suffer from an emperor whose role was no longer appreciated in the *Entrée*? Matters of autonomy deeply influence the treatment of events to the extent that when setting a standard for the identification of the romance epic hero, the matter of *desmesure* must not be taken for granted.

The final statement lends itself to discussion. It is true that all epics are set against backdrop of war and Webber's romance epic specifically within the framework of the clash between Christians and Saracens. However, different aspects of warfare are depicted in different phases of the epic. The representation of history for propagandistic purposes guarantees no fidelity to historical facts. Both epic and *chansons de geste* must therefore be taken as fiction. For example, the *Aeneid* merges legends with history to create a foundation myth. To give shape to a national hero, the *Chanson de Roland* offers a fictionalised account of an historical event which took place centuries before the poem was written. With that said, fictional works provide a very good understanding of the socio-economic environment in which they were produced and convey the authors' societal thinking.[29]

On the one hand, a twelfth century *chanson de geste* is based on the celebration of feudal relations between a king and his vassals, set in a context of war. On the other, it depicts the conflict between Christians and Saracens as a paradigm of good versus evil. Fourteenth-century Italian society was no longer based on feudal organisation. In this new system, the *chanson de geste* could not possibly perform any specific social function, least that of helping to form a national identity. The end of the crusades, moreover,

---

[29] See for example D. Quint, *Epic and Empire* (Princeton: Princeton University Press, 1993); D. Quint, *Origin and Originality in Renaissance Literature. Versions of the Source* (New Haven: Yale University Press, 1983).

followed by trade and cultural exchange originating with pilgrimage, made the Saracens a less exotic category of human beings and their customs more familiar to the Italian public. Due to the early medieval circulation of apologists' works and the complete failure of the great Franciscan and Dominican dreams of conversion, the Saracens were to remain solely the personifications of error – to such an extent that in later *chansons* they tend simply to be literary counterparts to the Christian heroes, aiding the latter's fully rounded characterisation. This is exactly what happens in the *Entrée* in which an extended section is dedicated to the confrontation between Roland and the Saracen Ferragu, developing into a theological dispute and terminating with the exotic giant's death, due only to his inability to counter Roland's theological explanations. As to the other Saracen characters, they are all complex figures who either befriend Roland or die more like tragic heroes than impersonal generic enemies.

L'Entrée d'Espagne as an example of hybridism

It appears that a general definition of the most distinctive traits of the *chanson de geste* does not entirely apply to a fourteenth-century product such as the *Entrée*. The attempt to set the foundations for a morphology of the romance epic in fact provides a morphology of the twelfth-century *chanson de geste*. From Italianists' point of view there is a need to distinguish between the different types of epic in the Middle Ages. As late as the end of the thirteenth century one can envisage at least three: the *chanson de geste* (the matter of France, to which the four statements apply very well); the reworking of classical epic into the form of *romans d'antiquité* (the matter of Rome); and the romance epic (a hybrid of *chanson* and the matter of Rome, with a strong influence from the matter of Britain). Paradoxically, it is only by establishing the nature of the hybrid that one can proceed to define the quintessential Italian genre, namely the chivalric poem. By treating the hybrid synchronically as its own genre, a long-term perspective can be acquired and the landscape of Italian literature more fully emerge.[30]

[30] On the importance of the *Entrée*'s hybrid nature see A. Roncaglia, 'La letteratura franco-veneta', in E. Cecchi and N. Sapegno, eds, *Storia*

Elements of hybridism in the *Entrée* are numerous. First, Roland's characterisation shows how he is orientated towards a rejection of all excesses. This is evident in the two episodes of the theological dispute and his flight to the East. A result of his interaction with other characters in these two pivotal episodes is his gradual acquisition of wisdom. Roland represents the ideal fourteenth-century knight. He also displays an open-minded and mercantile attitude towards the Saracen world, so much so that the reader will doubtless recognise a fourteenth-century man beneath the armour of a twelfth-century hero. The changed socio-economic conditions of the environment in which later *chansons* are produced may be held responsible for the gradual creation of this new type of hero. Among the surviving heroes, Webber distinguishes between 'the noble hero-leaders (Charlemagne, the Cid, Fernàn Gonzalez) and heroes with a worthy mission (Guillaume, Bernardo del Carpio, Rodrigo, Mudarra)',[31] but there does not seem to be any space for those heroes such as Roland who undergo modification. His long literary history spans two centuries, finally producing the Italian Orlando who no longer bears any of the distinguishable traits of the character from which he originated. Before Roland is transformed into Orlando, he has to survive a change of social and political climate which causes several adjustments in his priorities. For example, his autonomy clashes with that of Charlemagne;[32] his narrowly-conceived mission is replaced by a curiosity about the East which he fulfils by his flight from Charlemagne's camp; his interaction with the Saracens produces interesting cultural exchanges; his interest in a woman different from Aude adds complexity to his character.

---

della letteratura italiana, 9 vols (Milan: Garzanti, 1987), II: 727–59 (pp. 741–42): 'Il rapporto di ibridismo che si profila dietro il piccolo, compatto corpus della letteratura franco-veneta appare quindi marchiato da un'ineliminabile ambiguità, scaturendo dalla natura stessa della mediazione coscientemente (e si vorrebbe dire quasi "metodologicamente") ricercata dagli autori che rielaborano l'antico epos carolingio'.

[31] Webber, 'Towards the Morphology', p. 7.
[32] This point is treated extensively in Bradley-Cromey's study.

Dionisotti and Limentani insisted on the *Entrée* being a kind of *summa* of all fourteenth-century knowledge, and that this encyclopaedic nature in some way connects the *Entrée* to Dante and is indeed symptomatic of the spirit of that century.[33] Fourteenth-century epic, as well as Dante's poem, converges upon the model of the quest. The question is whether Roland mirrors the protagonist of a *queste* more than he retains his role of an epic hero. To answer this it is necessary to shift the focus from Roland's tragic fate to his experience of all the many choices and characters confronting him throughout the narrative.

---

[33] 'Quella consistenza di poema stacca *l'Entrée* dalle *chansons* post-rolandiane, e le consente di accostarsi al gruppo delle opere poetiche tardo-medievali a carattere di summa, quali innanzitutto il Roman de la rose e la Commedia: restando beninteso, entro i suoi limiti, visibili innanzitutto nella precarietà della soluzione linguistica: e il problema aperto più interessante rimane appunto quello dell'eventuale disponibilità, per il Padovano, del modello dantesco, e della misura dell'apprezzamento che egli, eventualmente, ne seppe dimostrare' Limentani, *L'Entrée d'Espagne e i signori d'Italia*, p. 33.

LITERARY INFLUENCES

Traces of the Breton Romance

The second part of the poem is strongly inspired by the narrative modes of the matter of Britain, but elements derived from romances can also be found in the more obviously epic first section.

At first the author displays a lack of appreciation for the *fables d'Artu*, an attitude close to that of the early Humanists in Padua who for the sake of philology dismissed Arthurian literature in favour of the classical world: Lovato Lovati is the most noteworthy such case.[1] The author of the *Entrée* makes a clear distinction between *chanson* and *fables*: with the word *cançons* he means a higher literary genre, whereas *fables* is used negatively (ll. 365–67):

> Segnors, car escoltez, ne soit ne criz ne hu,
> Gloriose cançons, c'onques sa pier ne fu;
> Ne vos sambleront mie de les fables d'Artu.

This is supported by another two instances in the poem where the author uses the word in a negative sense. The first is that of Ferragu's annoyed reply to Estout, who excessively praised Roland: "'Tei toi" – dist il – "que trop le m'ais loé; | Je croi qe soies uns fablaors prové'" (ll. 1570–71). In this case the word *fablaors* means someone who makes up stories – a liar. In a second instance the poet

---

[1] His polemical attitude was aimed against jongleurs whose storytelling activity deformed the original narratives and language to render them accessible to a popular audience. On the letter by Lovati see Roncaglia, 'La letteratura franco-veneta', p. 754; G. Folena, 'La cultura volgare e l'"Umanesimo cavalleresco" nel Veneto', in V. Branca, ed., *Umanesimo europeo e Umanesimo veneziano* (Florence: Sansoni, 1963), p. 142; Renzi, 'Il francese come lingua letteraria', pp. 569–70. Later, Petrarch, in *Trionfo d'Amore* III, 79–81, maintained that the 'vulgo errante' aspires to imitate the model of Lancelot and Tristan, while the higher example of classical literature was reserved to the more sophisticated mind of the intellectual. F. Petrarch, *Rime e Trionfi*, ed. by R. Ramat (Milan: Rizzoli, 1971).

explains how the truth is the result of the accord between different versions, while the liar is the one who disagrees (ll. 2804–09):

> Une novelle que viegne de longor
> C'un home aporte o tri o quatre ancor,
> S'adonc s'acordent les dos al prim ditor
> El quart contraire, tenuz vient fableor,
> Car bien savomes que devant un rector
> Plus d'un sol home vienent creü ploisor.

From the context of the *Entrée* (another occurrence is in line 3273: *fablerie*) what emerges is that *fable* and its derivative words mean falsification. The tales of king Arthur would then falsify the historical truth, which is instead guaranteed by the genre of epic. It is interesting to notice that the poet's dismissive attitude is only really found in the initial part of the poem, while a great number of other features suggest a gradual change of mind. In fact, in the *Entrée* we find that there are many mentions of motifs and characters from the Breton romances. As will be demonstrated, the poet remembers Tristan's combat against the Morhault, *La Queste del Saint Graal*,[2] Galaad and the Knights of the Round Table, and Febus el Forte. It is the purpose of this chapter to analyse the influence of the Breton romances on the *Entrée* in detail, taking into consideration both quotations of names and the resemblance between the poem's general structure and some of the structures of the *matière de Bretagne*.

A limitation of the *Entrée*'s plot is that the end of the hero is already known. The plot is in a sense rigid, since the reader is aware that no adventure or duel can alter the destiny of Roland, who to be faithful to the traditional finale must die in Rencesvals. Thus, the poet is all the more original in that he entertains his audience with an old story, elaborating and adding new elements to the plot. Late epic poems are often interlaced with themes and motifs inspired by the romances, which created possibilities for invention in an increasingly stereotyped genre.

---

[2] *La Queste del Saint Graal*, ed. by A. Pauphilet (Paris: Champion, 1984).

Where the epic hero conforms to the ideal and engages with the routine epic patterns, creation is not possible. It was then that interference from the Arthurian cycle (which itself gathered and re-elaborated themes and motifs from its Celtic background) modified the plot, enriching it with episodes that could cause ironic or comic effect – and indeed amazement and wonder – through contrast with the traditional pattern. In Italy the fusion of the two cycles was carried out with extraordinary fervour, and the *Entrée* represents the first step towards the creation of an entirely new Roland, from then on gradually transfigured into a knight of the Round Table.[3]

However, this is not the only feature of the poem suggesting a fusion between the epic and romance narrative modes. In the *chansons de geste* and in the Breton romance tradition, action is more important than description; the difference is that action in the epic is exclusively warlike and always justified by the imposition of the Christian faith upon the pagan, while in the Breton romances action is deprived of any ideological basis and unfolds according to the rules of adventure, which removes any flavour of war from armed performances such as duels. The symbolic meaning of the adventure is then left to the reader's discernment with the support of a hermit, wise man, or more supernatural figure like an angel.

In the *Entrée* the only similar occurrence is the encounter at the poem's end with the hermit, but interpretation of events does occur in the narrative in the form of discussion and analysis carried forward by the poems' characters After the great three-day duel between Roland and Ferragu, for example, the peers of France gather and begin an argument as to why Roland was the victor. From this a range of viewpoints emerge, with highly varied attempts to attach a symbolic meaning to the events most recently narrated in the poem and to find possible explanations for Roland's victory. The whole of laisse CLXXV contains such discussion, of which the following verses are an example (ll. 4276–78):

---

[3] A. Viscardi, 'Arthurian Influences in Italian Literature', in R. S. Loomis, ed., *Arthurian Literature in the Middle Ages* (Oxford: Oxford University Press, 1959; repr. 1979), pp. 419–29 (p. 425).

'Ne quitez mie qe por teran vigor
L'aie conquis le niés l'emperor;
Mais la puisance est venue de sor'.

In romances, it is through the dialogues that explanations of the various adventures are given, events take shape and characters reveal their nature, more effectively than by objective description.[4] In the *Entrée* dialogue plays a pre-eminent role. It is thus that Charlemagne and Roland express their own points of view and that the plot unfolds, especially in the Eastern section where Roland befriends and becomes necessary to the Muslims. It should be noted that the need both of Roland and Charlemagne to express opinions and to discuss their mutual behaviour originates in a range of major modifications to the social structure vis-à-vis feudalism. When the *Entrée* was written there no longer existed (or at least not in northern Italy) an idea of unquestionable authority[5] comparable to that of the Charlemagne in the *Chanson de Roland*. His point of view in that work was taken for granted and codified in a number of physical postures rather than expressed through opinions. Emotional tension in the *Chanson* is high because of the inner drama of the plot. In the *Entrée* the situation is different. A clash is perceived and expressed through dialogues, and at Charlemagne's court a few peers take up Roland's defence and will later try to convince the king of his own mistake. A need is felt to analyse Roland's behaviour and valour, with countless discussions spring from this necessity.

---

[4] See the case of Flamenca as discussed by I. Nolting-Hauff, 'La tecnica del dialogo', in M. L. Meneghetti, ed., *Il romanzo* (Bologna: Il Mulino, 1988), pp. 282–97.

[5] In 1355 Bartolo da Sassoferrato wrote that Guelphs and Ghibellins did not obey 'né alla Chiesa né all'Impero, ma solo a quelle fazioni che in una città o in una provincia si trovano': *Tractatus de guelphis et gebellinis*, in L. Simeoni, *Storia politica d'Italia. Le signorie* (Milan: Vallardi, 1950), p. 39, qtd in G. Tabacco, *Egemonie sociali e strutture del potere nel medioevo italiano* (Turin: Einaudi, 1974), p. 317. See also H. Baron, *The Crisis of the Early Italian Renaissance*, 2 vols (Princeton: Princeton University Press, 1955), II: 445 ff. The vacancy of Imperial power after the death of Frederick II allowed the two parties to consolidate their power independently of the conflict between the two higher authorities: Tabacco, *Egemonie sociali*, p. 318.

Given that the reader was acquainted with a portrait of Roland as hero and defender of Christendom before approaching the *Entrée*, the poet's presentation of the facts after Charlemagne's insult to Roland produces quite an impact, since he introduces the Roland of the second section as a completely new figure: a subject and faithful servant of the king of Persia (ll. 10945–51):

> Se vos vorois entendre, je vos dirai ancor
> Cum Rollant pasa mer en tere alïenor
> E com dou roi de Perse fu loial servior,
> Quant il fist la bataile en la loi Paienor
> Por la fille a Soudans, Dionés al frois collor,
> Vers le Turc qe de force estoit superior
> (Pelias oit a nom, mout avoit de valor);

Starting with Roland's flight from Charlemagne's camp and up to the Eastern episode, the reader is not made aware of how long the hero rides before reaching the sea or remains in the East. Even the visit to the hermit does not have a duration measured in real time; this is common in epic, in which major life events occur divorced from normal secular time. Time as a concept is a feature of the newborn bourgeois society and economy; it is found in the vernacular Venetian version of the *Navigatio*, for example, in which St. Brendan's odyssey becomes an exploration for marvellous goods.[6]

While it has no lack of realistic elements, the *Entrée* recounts a journey through the devices of rupture and expiation which cannot include elements relating to human time. When dealing with the soul's life and journey, rather, one deals with inner and eternal states of duration. The *Entrée* therefore still preserves an exquisite epic

---

[6] The problem of time in medieval literature is highly complex. Even within the epic significant variations are to be found: see Calin, *The Epic Queste*, p. 105. For divergent conceptions within the Lancelot – Graal Prose Cycle see P. Imbs, 'La Journée dans *La Queste del Saint Graal* et *La Mort le Roi Artu*', in *Mélanges de philologie romane offerts à Ernest Hoepffner* (Paris: Les Belles Lettres, 1949), pp. 279–93. General studies on the conception of time in medieval society are R. Barbieri, *Uomini e tempo medievale* (Milan: Jaca Book, 1986); J. Le Goff, *Tempo della Chiesa e tempo del mercante* (Turin: Einaudi, 1977); J. Le Goff, *I riti, il tempo, il riso. Cinque saggi di storia medievale* (Rome/Bari: Laterza, 2003).

flavour in that it deals with abstraction from time, just as the *chanson de geste*, traditionally set at the junction of history and myth, recounts events separated from their historical framework.

Textual References from Breton Romances

The influence of the Breton romance is especially strong in precise textual references in the *Entrée*. There was a well-established tradition of translating Arthurian romances into Italian vernaculars, particularly the different varieties of Venetian and Tuscan. The peak of this production occurred between the second half of the thirteenth century and first half of the fourteenth. In the later fourteenth century one distinct branch of the *volgarizzamenti* is the *cantari* in *ottava rima*, short compositions in which the adventures of the Knights of the Round Table are individually reprised and treated. However, despite the circulation of contemporary Italian texts relating to the Arthurian tradition it is possible that the author was influenced by his reading of the original French texts.

A reference to Chrétien's *Perceval* is found at the beginning of the *Entrée*: 'Mielz valt sovant taisir q'estre trop averbés' (l. 154). This line recalls the same idea expressed in Chrétien when the protagonist sees the Grail procession and does not dare to ask to whom the Grail was served, remembering the words of the wise man who first advised him not to ask too many inopportune questions. Chrétien comments as follows in the *Perceval* (ll. 3248–51):

> Si criem que il n'i ait damage,
> Por che que j'ai oï retraire
> Qu'ausi se puet on bien trop taire
> Com trop parler a la foie[e].

Compared to Chrétien's words, there is a modification in the phrasing in the *Entrée* although the meaning remains the same: the sentence in the *Entrée* is presented in the form of a proverb whereas in Chrétien the words appear as an explanation of Perceval's fear of being too intrusive. Chrétien's words are more delicate, conveying the subtle state of mind of a guest honoured to be seated at such a rich table and not wanting to appear arrogant. In the *Entrée* the context is different: Roland intervenes in the debate about whether the French army should defy Marsile. Gales de Vormendois, the wisest of Charlemagne's men, has just spoken against the enterprise. Roland obviously speaks in favour and opens his intervention by reproaching Gales for his pusillanimity.

It is in this context that Roland tells Gales that it is better not to speak at all than to say too much. The sentence is used here in the form of an accusation of foolishness and a suggestion to keep one's mouth shut rather than speak unwisely. The situation somewhat recalls the scene in the *Perceval*, except that the king was expecting Perceval to speak. The question Perceval never asked has a profound meaning that goes to the very heart of his quest, one for identity signified by the quest for the Grail. Perceval's silence causes him to lose the Grail and to have to continue his wandering. It can be assumed that here the poet had read the sentence, memorising and using it out of context although with a similar meaning. The same idea is repeated in another place, again formulated as a proverb although this time Cato is mentioned as the author of the original phrase: 'Por ce dit voir Caton li Roman: | Gran vertus est a metre a la lengue le fran' (ll. 11562–63). Although Cato is reported to have said these words the verse can be regarded as a quotation from Chrétien's *Perceval*.[7] The allusion to Cato in the *Entrée* must not mislead us into incorrectly identifying the source of this reference since a third occurrence corroborates the fact that the *Entrée* poet knew *Perceval* well and quoted from it: Roland 'de trou parler a foulie tenue' (l. 12575).

---

[7] Viscardi, 'Arthurian Influences', p. 420. An echo of the episode of the question is also found in Guittone d'Arezzo's *Amor tant'altamente* (canzone XXI), where a clear reference is made to the *Perceval*. Guittone asserts that it is a fault when a good servant dares to ask a reward for his long service, but he hopes that what happened to Prezevallo, whose fault was not to ask, will not happen to him ('perché giá guiderdone | non dea cheder bon servo; | bisogna i' n'ho, che 'l chere 'l suo servire, | se no atendendo m'allasso; | poi m'avvenisse, lasso!, | che mi trovasse in fallo | sí come Prezevallo - a non cherere', ll. 70–76): Guittone d'Arezzo, *Rime*, ed. by F. Egidi (Bari: Laterza, 1940), pp. 47–49 (49). Guittone's reference testifies to the widespread knowledge of the *Perceval* in Italy.

A quotation from the *Queste* occurs when Charlemagne, full of rage against Roland for planning to besiege Noble without his approval, declares that he will take revenge for Roland's insubordinate behaviour and search for him through plains and forests as Galaad did for the Grail (ll. 9229–31):

> 'Par cil Dieux q'en la cros sofri paine et moleste,
> N'ala si Galaaz por le Graal en queste
> Con je ferai par lui en plains et an foreste';

This refers to the *Queste* where it is made clear for the first time that Galaad is the quest's paramount protagonist, surpassing all the other knights in purity of spirit and for this reason fully enjoying the sight of the holy vessel.[8]

The Grail is mentioned again in the following passage (ll. 8726–29):

> Cist estoit de bataile le mestre natural:
> N'avoit tiel en Espagne en la loi criminal;
> De peior n'oit asez a conquier le Graal.

Cist refers to *Grandonie l'emiral*, who was so powerful among all pagans ('en la loi criminal') that many of the knights who went in search of the Grail were greatly his inferiors. This implies that the knights of the Round Table are still the ideal yardstick when it comes to defining the limits of bravery and heroism, together with the most popular classical heroes.

A very interesting reference to the romance of Tristan and Ysolt is made when the author speaks about Ogier's sword (ll. 9711–16):

> Tient l'espee en son poing, que fist Gallaneüs,
> Qe fu al buen Tristans, le fiuz Meliadus,
> Dont oncist le Morot en l'isle de Carchus,
> Quant il vient au rois Mars demander le treüs:
> Par cil Tristans fu tot cil peïs asolus,
> Qe fust en grant servaje a toz temps remanus.

The author has used the *incipit* of the story of Tristan as an example of heroism, describing how the knight freed a country from the

---

[8] *La Queste del Saint Graal*, ed. Pauphilet, pp. 267–80.

slavery to which it was subjected by the Morhault, who expected a yearly tribute of money from the inhabitants. By killing the Morhault, Tristan became a hero in the eyes of king Mark, hence the beginning of the love story between Tristan and Mark's wife Ysolt.[9]

The character of Febus seems to have attracted the attention of the Paduan poet. In the *Entrée* the author mentions him three times (ll. 5427–29):

> Cil se defent con tante de vertu
> Qe s'il est voir de la force Febu,
> Mervoille fust se elle tornast en lu.

In the episode where Roland meets the hermit who tells him his story and how he fought against many Saracens to defend his hermitage, the poet includes Febus in the number of classical references quoted for comparison (ll. 14914–17):

> Tu bien avroies dit de croire les romans
> E de Rome e de Troie e dou tens ancians
> E qu'il fust verité la force des jaians,
> D'Erculés e d'Antheu e de Febus le grans.

However, Febus is not a classical figure at all but instead a knight belonging to the most primitive phase of chivalry preceding the Arthurian age. Febus first appears in the *Roman de Palamedés* on which Ariosto drew constantly when writing his own poem. He is mentioned in the episode of 'Brehus-sans-pitié', who fell into a cavern and there met a hermit who told him the story of his noble ancestor Febus, one of the founders of chivalry. In Italy this episode followed a literary pattern of its own: only the two chapters of the *Palamedés* about Brehus and Febus were partially translated into the Tuscan vernacular at the end of the thirteenth century and then

---

[9] As seen above, another reference to this story is made when the author characterises Dionés by her white hands. Although the reference is not explicit, the lady famous for her white hands is Tristan's wife Ysolt of the White Hands, not to be confused with Mark's wife, Ysolt the Blonde.

elaborated in a series of six *cantari* on Febus around 1340.[10] In both the prose version and *cantari* Febus deals with giants,[11] which might have been what attracted the poet in the first place. The numbering of Febus among the giants supports the hypothesis that the author was familiar with and inspired by the vernacular tradition of the *Palamedés* (or indeed the original French version).[12]

A third reference to Febus is made regarding his own time, when Roland's enterprises would have been regarded as miracles. Roland is therefore stronger and more valorous than Febus, who in his own age was looked up to as an exceptionally strong man (ll. 10087–89):

> Adonc se fist le seing ou Diex fu sospendus;
> Ja fera il tiel couse qe droit au tems Febus
> Seroit grant impossible e miracle tenus.

Despite the author not making a real comparison between Febus and Roland, an episode found in the second part of the Tuscan translation of *Palamedés* from chapter LXXV[13] suggests that the adventures of Febus might have somehow inspired the poet in his characterisation of Roland. Febus befriends a pagan and joins his company in a pagan festival of Venus. Febus' friend is characterised simply as *pagano*, leaving his exact religion unclear. In the *Entrée* (as in many other *chansons de geste* and romances featuring Muslims), the Saracens are often called pagans as well as receiving many other imprecise epithets which only confirm that they are not Christians

---

[10] The pattern that led from the episode of Brehus to the *cantari* of Febus is treated in detail by *Dal Roman de Palamedés ai cantari di Febus-el-Forte. Testi francesi e italiani del due e trecento*, ed. Alberto Limentani (Bologna: Commissione per i testi di lingua, 1962).

[11] *Palamedés*, in *Dal Roman de Palamedés*, ed. Limentani, pp. 139 ff., pp. 163 ff.; *Cantari*, in *Dal Roman de Palamedés*, ed. Limentani, IV, 17–31, 48–61, p. 243.

[12] It is worth noting that by an association of ideas the author transforms Hercules and Febus into giants, when really they were only meant to be strong men fighting against the giants. In fact, there is another place in the poem where a man is said to be a giant ('Si estoit son cuisins Henestor le jaiant', l. 11975). Henestor (cousin of Pélias, nephew of Malcuidant) is mentioned in the entourage of Pélias to strengthen the idea that not only was Pélias himself powerful but also surrounded by powerful people.

[13] *Palamedés*, in *Dal Roman de Palamedés*, ed. Limentani, p. 133.

but at the same time do not specify to what religion they belong. Whatever their religion, the important point is that the enemy is not a Christian. However, Febus' friend seems to be a pagan in the sense that he is a polytheist, worshipping many gods in the fashion of the ancient world. The pagan is nonetheless called Harsan in the *Palamedés* and Arsanne in the *cantare* which suggests he might as well be intended as an Arab. In the *Palamedés* he is described as a very good man:

> Quando Febus intese la buona volontà del pagano, elli lo tiene a troppo grande valore a grande bontade di lui: und'elli dice bene a sei medesmo ch'elli non puote essere che quelli non sia troppo homo da bene.[14]

The fourth *cantare* states how willingly Febus leaves his Christian armour to wear pagan clothes that Arsanne gives him (ll. 16–19):

> Disse Febus: 'O nobile signore,
> vostro pensiero mi piace molto lodo,
> e ho già tanto diletto al mio cuore,
> che dire non vel potrei quant'io ne godo'.

In the *Entrée*, Roland does not hesitate to abandon his Christian appearance when he travels in the East, and this happen not only for safety but because he finds pleasure in doing so, just as with Febus whose target was the pagan princess. It is when Febus is in the company of Harsan that he meets the giants and starts a fight with the strongest of them. Febus has the occasion to prove that his strength is superior to that of the giant. In this way, the pagan is completely bewitched by his Christian companion.

Both the prose version and the *cantare* tell us that stories of chivalry from this moment onwards will always be treated with a certain degree of detachment, with the element of wonder there to entertain rather than suggest a moral meaning. The plot excepted, this way of treating the subject no longer belongs to the Breton romances. This is a development belonging to a later age than the *Entrée*. However, the evolution of an epic plot into a romance is typical of Italian literature where, as we have seen, major

---

[14] *Palamedés*, in *Dal Roman de Palamedés*, ed. Limentani, p. 137, §1.

modifications lead in the direction of the *cantare*. In a way the *Entrée* represents the prehistory of this evolution both in terms of structure and content.

Besides the exotic and complex plot, the usage of such a device as *entrelacement* makes the *Entrée* stylistically closer to romance than epic. The main peculiarity of the *chanson de geste* is in fact that it usually focuses on one character whose belligerent life is described throughout the poem. The technique of *entrelacement* is typical of the structure of Breton romances, and it is a literary device that belongs with romances and not epic poems.[15] As a narrative technique it appears in the second part of the poem as Roland's *desmesure* diminishes. The two elements together suggest that the narrative loses its epic consistency in favour of romance. The *entrelacement* consists in a shifting from one story to another in such a way that the interference between the two influences the plot. The case analysed by F. Lot is that of the *Lancelot* in prose in which a countless number of adventures interweave the story of Lancelot with that of the other Knights of the Round Table, making the plot so complicated that it is almost impossible to disentangle. As F. Lot pointed out, *entrelacement* in the prose *Lancelot* allows the plot to become extremely intricate, and usually the adventures of Lancelot and of the other knights interlace with one another so as to influence the development of Lancelot's story. This does not happen in the *Entrée* where the type of interlacing adopted is less complicated (as in Chrétien's shifting from the story of Perceval to that of Gawain)[16] and consists only in the shifting of focus from one episode to another, as in the following example (ll. 4214–16):

> De cels lairomes qu'an Aragon s'en vont
> E canterons de cels qe remis sont
> Dedans la ville...

---

[15] See F. Lot, *Etude sur le Lancelot en prose* (Paris: Champion, 1918). See also Meneghetti, ed., *Il romanzo*, pp. 299–311.
[16] Chrétien leaves Gawain to return to Perceval ('De monseignor Gavain se taist | ichi li contes', ll. 6214–15) and then leaves Perceval again to take up the story of Gawain ('De Perceval plus longuement ne parole li contes chi', ll. 6514–15). Such phrases are indicative of *entrelacement*.

Chivalry in L'Entrée d'Espagne

While we are normally acquainted with a characterisation of Roland as an epic hero, in the *Entrée* he is frequently presented to the audience as a knight: 'Roland, par chi l'estorie et lo canter comanze, | Li melors chevalers que legist en sianze' (ll. 17–18). Not only is Roland said to be a knight and a *chevaler Jesu* (l. 3155), in the first place certainly implying that he is fighting for the cause of religion, but when he rides to Noble he puts Ogier in charge of guarding the *oriflame* and leaves five hundred knights with him: 'E .V.ᶜ chevalers avec vos remanra' (l. 9023); 'Cinquecent chevalers li Donois lui baila' (l. 9034). In these lines from the description of the final siege of Noble, the word *chevaler* is used primarily as a military rank to define the members of Charlemagne's army to which Roland also belongs. As it appears in this context the word is taken from military vocabulary and is not a reference to the Breton conception of knighthood. Although belonging to a very late era and containing a number of major modifications of the *chanson de geste* genre, this poem is still in some ways close to the *Chanson de Roland*. There, Turpin 'defines the rules of the knight's life'[17] as we can see from the following lines (1877–82):

> Itel valor deit aveir chevaler
> Ki armes portet e en bon cheval set:
> En bataille deit estre forz e fiers,
> U altrement ne valt .IIII. deners,
> Einz deit monie estre en un de cez mustiers,
> Si prierat tuz jurz por noz peccez.

In French epic, what is expected from a knight is that he be 'a man trained to fight on horseback, who does so with strength and the ferocity of a savage animal and with pride: the term proud, *fier*, derives from the Latin *ferus*, meaning wild, untamed, as with animal and beast'.[18] In the *Entrée*, Charlemagne speaks to his barons in this way after hearing the news about Nobles (ll. 8258–64):

---

[17] P. Haidu, *The Subject of Violence. The Song of Roland and the Birth of the State* (Bloomington: Indiana University Press, 1993), p. 53.

[18] Haidu, *Subject of Violence*, p. 54.

> 'A le nom Deus e de la Vergen pie,
> Tost vos aleç armer, ma baronie,
> Che la bataile quirent la jent ahie;
> Hui poroit estre nostre guere complie.
> Or i para chi ame civalerie,
> Che conquirons honor e signorie
> Et en aprés la parmanable vie'.

He incites his barons in the name of chivalry, implying that the defeat of the enemy is a matter of justice and that anyone who loves chivalry must admit the justice of the French defeating the pagans.

After Roland's true identity is discovered, however, Pélias says of him (ll. 12933–36):

> 'Cist n'est villain ne de foible lignaige,
> Mais voiremant civalers de paraige
> Que por mostrer proesche et vassalage
> Vait ensi soul por estrainge regnaige'.

A perception that the distinction of roles in society must not be blurred is found in many places in the poem and particularly in a proverb which signifies their acknowledgement by the poet: a villain is a villain and a nobleman a nobleman, and no confusion is allowed between social classes: '"Non doit villain porter pellice vaire, | E a gentil dame doit païsans desplaire"' (ll. 13459–60). It is clear that a nobleman has distinctive traits differentiating him from the people. Later Pélias addresses Roland in such a way (ll. 13086–94):

> 'Cevallers frere – ce a dit Pelliais –
> Si Sarracins, Crestians o Judais
> Is, nel sai; més par la loi que tu ais
> Et par cil ordre dont civaler te fais,
> Par tot l'amor de l'ami plus verais
> Ch'ais en ces mont, se tu le voies mais,
> Chuntente moi de voir dir, non de gais,
> De quel lignaze es tu nez et etrais,
> De roi, de quens, de duch ou de plus bais?'

Pélias recognises that Roland is of a high rank and calls him a knight; in this sense the word *civaler* no longer indicates a rank in the army but the social class Roland belongs to by birth. Pélias' words, 'Cist n'est villain ne de foible lignaige', imply that Roland is not only a valorous fighter but also a nobleman in deed and feeling. The word thus assumes a more complete sense here, combining capacity and valour on the battlefield with behaviour in the world. In brief, Roland is required to know how to fight, entertain and love.[19] In this sense the word reflects its broader meaning in the Arthurian world whereby Roland is recognised by his own natural qualities rather than the words of the spy who refers his information to the king of Persia. Roland's knightly behaviour is confirmed when Dionés wants to thank him for having freed her from the man who wanted to take her and he replies (ll. 13193–97):

'Dame – dist il – sol la belle achuntance
Que m'avois fait a merir me comance.
Petit hai fait, mais a le sustinance
De vostre peres moi met in oferance;
Jamais in moi non trovera falance'.

Roland speaks authentically chivalrous words to Dionés since he is happy with her friendship (*achuntance*) and wants nothing more in return for her defence. Roland's response to Dionés' feelings is relevant only in bringing to light his primary concern, which is the dissemination of chivalry. It is not a question of indifference to any amorous sentiment, but specifically because the transformation into a celestial knight has already begun Roland can only defend the lady without expecting reward. The ethos of the perfect knight is superior to the temptation of the worldly adventure. In the case of the *Entrée*, the motif of the lady's defence is inserted in the narrative within an elaborate network of relationships: the defence is a gesture due to Dionés in order to honour the friendship with her father.

In the *Entrée*, a reflection of the chivalric ethic applied to Roland is also found in a passage where forgiveness is granted to the one who repents ('Je me repant: le pardoner est droit', l. 3375). According to knighthood, forgiveness is a Christian and subsequently chivalric duty. This ethic, applied to Roland, is to be linked with the development of the plot: Charlemagne's offence

---

[19] The most exemplary of all knights in this respect is Lancelot, who besides winning all the duels entertains and wins over the most noble of all ladies, Queen Guenevre.

against Roland is followed by Roland's retaliation through his absence and Charlemagne's regret. Having purified himself while absent, Roland recovers a human dimension and is ready to return to Charlemagne who, through the pain caused by the loss of his nephew, is ready to plead for forgiveness. Only then, having been asked, is Roland ready for the most chivalric of actions, forgiveness.

The section dedicated to the duel between Roland and Ferragu contains the long dialogue from lines 3635 to 3984 in which Roland attempts to persuade Ferragu to embrace the true faith. At the end of the dialogue, Ferragu refuses to convert and consequently they resume fighting. Roland's frustration at seeing his words spoken in vain leads him to threaten the Saracen to either convert or die (ll. 3489–92):

> 'Che Diex vos dunt grace avant le vespree
> De pervenir a la loi batiçee,
> O voirement a ceste moie spee
> Vos soit enchué l'arme dou cors sevree'.

Roland's irritation with Ferragu gives way to a wiser attitude in the second part of the poem, the Eastern episode. There the poet adopts chivalry as a way of communicating openness to dialogue, to enforce the idea that violence is no longer acceptable as the means of bringing together two opposing cultures. Rather, conversion comes by demonstrating that the Christian faith is superior through valour, honour and especially chivalry. Roland thus insists on promoting chivalry among his Saracen hosts, advancing himself as a living *exemplum* of heroism and honour which he makes the enemy keen to imitate; he no longer uses violence to convert the pagans but the force of persuasion. The result is that the Saracens themselves will want to be baptised to honour the Roland who helped them defeat their enemy.

When Roland defeats Isorés and sends him to Charlemagne as a prisoner, the scene is reminiscent of the sending of knights, defeated in duel by a knight of the Round Table, to king Arthur's court (ll. 5501–34):

> Rollant a feit le valet desarmer
> En pur gambaus, a loi de presoner,
> E pués l'a feit sor un cheval monter.

A soi apelle .VI. de ses chevaler:
'Al roi mon sir le m'alez amener
E por m'amor le doiez deprïer
Q'il non li die ne li face engombrer,
Car c'est le fil dou roi son averser;
Por cist puet molt son honor avancier'.
[...]
Li .VI. François menrent le baceler
Devant le roi qi a France a garder,
Que ja son trief avoit fait redricier;
[...]
As piezs l'emperor estoit en jenoilon
Isorez en gambauz, bien resemble prison.
'Sire – dist il al roi – non seroit pas rason.
Se sui pris en bataille, deffendant ma mason'.

In Breton romances the idea (frequently depicted) is that the defeated knight would spontaneously submit himself to king Arthur's court.[20] The account varies from the Breton romance type, however, in that Isoré is an actual prisoner of war and guarded by six Frenchmen with the duty to take him alive to Charlemagne's court. Another difference is that king Arthur treats knights who surrender spontaneously as part of his court whereas Charlemagne would have had Isoré hanged were the prince not protected by Roland, who made it clear that the emperor should not touch him. As will emerge in the section of this study on the characterisation of Charlemagne, however, the emperor's behaviour in the case of Isoré was unjust and in fact Roland expected Charlemagne to treat the young Isoré with

---

[20] Episodes of this kind are found in Chrétien's *Lancelot* in which the protagonist sends many defeated knights to present themselves as prisoners to Guenevre. In Chrétien's *Perceval*, the protagonist sends three knights to king Arthur's court, Anguigueron (ll. 2314 ff.), Clamadeu (ll. 2682 ff.), and the Orgueillos (ll. 3930 ff.) The most interesting of these episodes is Clamadeu's, where it is said that it was a rule for a knight who had been defeated to go spontaneously to prison: 'Costume estoit a cel termine | Sel trovon escrit en la letre | Que chevaliers se devoit metre | En prison atot son atour | Si com il partoit de l'estour | Come il avoit conquis esté | Qu'il n'i eüst ja rien osté | Ne rien nule n'i eüst mise' (ll. 2722–29).

all honour. Charlemagne's refusal to co-operate is another cause of friction between uncle and nephew.

The theme of adventure and related motifs

The *Entrée* can be compared to the romances of the *matière de Bretagne* for a variety of reasons. Quotations as well as motifs borrowed from the most popular Breton romances are profusely disseminated in the text. Of these, the most important by far are motifs related to the theme of adventure.

In line 6965 the threat of the pagan army ready to give battle over the main tower is defined by the poet as a *paüreuse estrine*, which in this context should be understood as *aventure* (ll. 6966–68):

> Signor, quant cist signal est sor la tor perine,
> Ce est sinifiance de paürose estrine;
> N'i romant hom a armer ni dame ni mescline.

The same word is used to define the war in Spain: 'Or le condue Diex et sante Madeloine | E cil buen saint par cui il sont en tiel estroine!' (ll. 9062–63). The war is therefore nothing but a risky adventure! To define as an *aventure* what was historically a very harsh struggle for power, over a quite extended territory, is something that deserves a closer analysis.

In line 7211, speaking with the *maître des œuvres* in charge of the weapons, Charlemagne also defines the siege of Noble as an adventure: 'Nostre aventure proveruns da novel'. It is not a single occurrence. In line 8982, the return of the spy Bernard dressed as a pilgrim is likewise described: 'E Dieux! qeil aventure lor vient a gran destin!', and the same word occurs again in line 11146, when Roland leaves Charlemagne's camp after being humiliated by the emperor: 'Que aventure m'avient por bone ovragne!'.

Although this terminology must be understood as being evocative of the Breton romance genre, a close examination of the contexts and overtones of the word 'adventure' in the *chanson de geste* genre - a task that cannot be undertaken within this study - could suggest more than a generic reference to the Grail narratives, as the term appears to indicate a real understatement of warfare as such (i.e. as the result of political and economic struggles), approaching it rather as the quintessentially manly activity and a chivalric obligation which no noble man could possibly reject.

Another reference to the Grail romances is a mention of a wasteland, akin to the *queste*'s desert/forest. After the return of Bernard the spy Roland hears that the city of Noble is defenceless and so decides to lay siege without consulting the king. This is the cause of Charlemagne's harsh reaction and public humiliation of Roland, and of Roland's departure to the East; it is therefore central to the narrative. The French army led by Roland rides towards Noble. Many of the soldiers are unhappy with the decision to leave the emperor to follow Roland, hence the dark atmosphere of these verses. Leaving the plain behind they ride through a forest, descend into a dark valley and enter the wasteland: 'D'autre part descendirent en la scure valee; | Par une gaste lande s'est l'ost achaminee' (ll. 9070–71). The mood of the army is pessimistic, the enterprise very risky, and the barons ride with their heads lowered not knowing which way to go. They do not see the need to follow Roland's plan and so greatly risk losing the war (ll. 9073–80):

> Les baruns cevalcerent, cescuns teste basee;
> Ne savent en qual part soit lor voie adrecee;
> Li uns regardent l'autre coiemant, a celee.
> 'E Dieux!' – feit l'uns a l'autre – 'cum feite desevree
> Feit Rollant de son oncle, sainte Vergen loee!
> Par lui puet encui estre tote l'ost periliee.
> Quel part alomes nos? Ou est nostre oubergee?
> Ne troveromes tere ne soit deseritee'.

The march ends when they cross a stream (ll. 9081–83):

> Al trepaser d'un eive se fust l'ost arestee;
> Avant qe tote l'ost soit d'autre part pasee,
> I avroit maintes paroles dites e divisee.

The crossing of a stream is a significant *topos* in romances as is the *gaste lande* (l. 9071). The passage from one side of the water to the other is usually symbolic of a passage to the Otherworld or the entering or exiting of the wasteland. Thus, the entire passage contains all the elements that make a romance episode.

Oliver reproaches Roland for his decision to leave without discussing the matter with Charlemagne and his disapproval anticipates the emperor's ire (ll. 9105–17):

> 'Le partir qe vos feites resenble mout savage
> A cestor q'amenez, e laser l'anperage:
> Encui poroit le rois perdre par cist follage'.

Furthermore, when Oliver prays while Roland rides his horse through the night, there is a mention of a forest/desert situation: 'Li duc Rollant chevaiche por meis la desertine' (l. 11395). This is one of the poem's loftiest stylistic moments, suggesting that Roland is riding in a desert of loneliness and dismay. This line and those following recall the moment of dismay of the Breton knight who is alone, lost in the forest, and cannot see the direction of his *queste*. Thus Roland can be considered to be riding alone through the *gaste lande*. The army is mechanically following his lead but everyone is against him. Roland knows he is going against Charlemagne's will without making him aware of his plans, and in some way he realises that his decision will have severe consequences.

This powerful passage is evocative of the figure of the wandering knight. In fact, during his journey in the East Roland refers to himself as a wandering knight travelling the world to cause justice to triumph over evil (ll. 12756–58):

> 'Cant por droiture mantenir et ses non
> Vais travalant por estranges rouyon
> E prant bataille et trai a fenysson'.

The first episode that marks a noticeable difference between the first, epic section and the second, which is chivalric, is Roland's adventure of the fountain on his way to the coast. The poet dedicates two entire laisses (CCCCXCV and CCCCXCVI) to describing the fountain of master Clarïel, starting with the engineering work that makes it function (ll. 11400–408):

> Endroit primes sonans trova il, a cil traïne,
> Une place reonde dedens la gran gaudine
> E une fontanele plus cler qe eve de Rine,
> Adornee et encluse de fort piere mabrine
> E bien afiguree de l'ouvre Saracine.

LITERARY INFLUENCES

De la biauté de lei dirai vos la convine.
La fontaine sordoit por engine torneïs
En un piler de maubre qe est de mur voutis.
A .x. tüel de cobre fesoit ses giteïs;

The author then describes how the fountain is decorated with copper figures which move with the wind. Of these figures the most interesting is the Arab king swinging his sword as if he wanted to defend the fountains from attack (ll. 11409–18):

Sor ceschuns de tüels estoit un Arabis
De cobre, tuit armei, laboreis et stampis;
Ceschuns tenoit l'espie e l'eschu a son pis.
E sor l'autre piler, ce conte li escris,
Desor une cariere, sot un arbre floris,
Seoit un roy de cobre, ne troi gran ne petis;
Et ert si engignei sor lu un edifis,
Quand vent i fiert, brait cum fust asotis:
Entor l'arbre tornoit, corand tot escaris,
Con s'il vousist defendre le font el pleiseïs.

The poet then says that at the base of the fountain is a wide vessel containing clear water and in front of that a building (ll. 11419–29):

Au pié de la fontaine, ou colent li tüel,
D'une piere mabrine i avoit gran vasel
Tot plein d'une clere aigue deci qe en le orel.
Devant le cours de l'aigue oit un edifis bel;
Por force de cours fiert sor l'englume un martel;
N'i ousent aprochier ni beste ni oisel.
Environ la fontaine avoient mant pustel;
Por les chevaus liger estoient mis anel.
Le pere ou roy Marsille, quand estoit jovencel,
Fist la fontaine feire a un mestre, Clariel:
Ne avoit maudre en Espagne de labor de quarel.

Such descriptions are common in Breton romances; bridges and fountains are places where writings often appear that need to be interpreted by a hermit, who will make an entrance later in the narrative. Generally, the fountain in Breton romances is a landmark for encounters and it usually bears a great significance in the narrative. The most famous case is in Chrétien's *Yvain*[21] where a description of a fountain is given by two different characters, Yvain's cousin Calogrenant, and a creature which is half-villain and half-animal. At the court of king Arthur, Calogrenant starts telling how he was wandering in a forest in search of adventures and wonders, and met a half-man, half-beast which directed him to a fountain. The first description is the one given by the creature (ll. 378–405):

> La fontaine venras qui bout,
> S'est ele plus froide que mabres.
> Ombres li fait li plus biaus arbres
> C'onques peüst faire Nature.
> En tous tans le fueille li dure,
> Qu'il ne le pert pour nul yver.
> Et si pent .i. bachin de fer
> A une si longue chaaine
> Qui dure dusqu'en la fontaine.
> Les la fontaine trouveras
> Un perron tel com tu venras,
> Mais je te ne sai dire quel,
> Que je n'en vi onques nul tel,
> Et d'autre part ne chapele
> Petite, mais ele est mout bele.
> S'au bachin veus de l'iaue prendre,
> Et desus le perron espandre,
> La venras une tel tempeste,
> Qu'en chest bos ne remaurra beste,
> Chevreus ne dains ne chiers ne pors;
> Nis li oisel s'en istront hors,
> Car tu venras si fort froier,
> Venter, et arbres pechoier,
> Plovoir, toner, et espartir,
> Que se tu t'en pues departir
> Sans grant anui et sans pesanche,
> Trop seras de meilleur chaance
> Que chevalier qui i fust onques.

---

[21] Chrétien de Troyes, *Le Chevalier au lion ou Yvain*, ed. by D. Hult (Paris: Livres de Poche, 1994).

The fountain is made of marble and it has a hanging bowl to draw the water like the one in the *Entrée*. However, most interesting is that in both cases it includes devices to keep visitors away: in the *Entrée*, the moving king, a building of some kind ('un edifis bel', l. 11422), and a beating hammer; in the *Yvain* the water thrown on the stone, creating such a tempest that not a single animal could remain alive in the forest.

Following the beast's instructions, Calogrenant arrives at the fountain. He describes what he sees with his own eyes (ll. 420–33):

> De la fontaine poés croire
> Qu'ele bouloit com yaue chaude.
> Li perrons fu d'une esmeraude
> Perchie aussie com une bouz,
> S'avoit .iiii. rubins desous,
> Plus flamboians et plus vermaus
> Que n'est au matin li solaus,
> Quant il appert en orïent.
> Et sachiez, ja a enscïent
> Ne vous en mentirai de mot.
> La merveille a veoir me plot
> De la tempeste et de l'orage,
> Dont je ne me tieng mie a sage;
> Que maintenant m'en repentisse.

Composed of emeralds and rubies, the water of the fountain boils. Calogrenant is particularly intrigued by the tempest caused by the drawing of the water from the fountain.[22]

---

[22] Two other famous occurrences of adventures at a fountain are the combat of Lancelot with a knight, which is recounted by Chrétien as well as in the *Lancelot* in prose and was so popular that the *Novellino* portrays Lancelot fighting at a fountain as a cliché: *Il Novellino. Le ciento novelle antike*, ed. by G. Manganelli, 4th edn (Milan: Rizzoli, 1999), XLV, p. 56; the episode of Tristan and Ysolt meeting at the fountain beneath the pine can be found in the broad tradition of vernacular versions of Tristano, for example the so-called *Tristano Veneto. Il Libro di Messer Tristano*, ed. by A. Donadello (Venice: Marsilio, 1994), and is also found in the *Novellino*, ed. Manganelli, LXV, pp. 76–77. A useful study on Arthurian tradition in Italy is in Viscardi, 'Arthurian Influences'.

The fountain episode is of particular note not only for its resemblance to similar episodes in other romances but also and especially for its position in the narrative. According to Franco Cardini, the Fountain of Youth was in fact (together with the Amazons and the Earthly Paradise) one of the wonders which the East had to offer those knights longing for chivalric adventure once their role as fighters for feudalism had definitively lapsed.[23] The presence of the fountain seems to highlight the passage from the epic to the Eastern section, and in Roland's role from being the emperor's subordinate to that of a knight. The chivalric adventure was attempted by those knights who no longer fitted into the newly organised social structure of the late Middle Ages, which is a similar situation to that of Roland in the *Entrée*. His wandering in the East after the rupture of the feudal pact allows him to experiment with the realm of adventure.

The idea of adventure becomes a recurrent motif in the *Entrée*. In one case, it is clearly said that the episode carries a deeper meaning. The cruel Saracen Pélias (nephew of Malcuidant to whom Dionés had been promised in marriage) has been defeated by Roland. The poet explains that (ll. 13171–77):

> Mort est le Turch por sa desmesurance:
> Ce senefie que ceschuns fait infance
> Que contre droit motre orgoil ne bubance.
> Chant a ce fait le niés au roi de France,
> Non par orgoil, mais por senefiance,
> Dou brant essue sor le Païn le brance.

The poet replaces the traditional intermediary between the public and the text – in Breton romances generally a hermit or other character who serves to explain the connection between the literary levels of *semblance* and *senefiance*. An episode conceals a deeper meaning under the guise of a wondrous or mysterious event: for example, in the *Queste* the *aventure* is developed to its extreme limits, signifying the progressive acquisition of knowledge by

---

[23] F. Cardini, 'Il guerriero e il cavaliere', in J. Le Goff, ed., *L'uomo medievale* (Rome/Bari: Laterza, 1987), pp. 81–123 (pp. 118–19).

Galaad's own soul.[24] The terminology adopted by the author in the *Entrée* is clearly inspired by the language of the *Queste*, in which after every *aventure* (the *semblance*) a *senefiance* is provided:

> Et Galaad dist au preudome: 'Sire, ai je fet de ceste aventure quan que je en doi fere?' – 'Oïl, fet il; car ja mes la voiz dont tant de mal sont avenu n'i sera oïe'. – 'Et savez vos, fet Galaad, por quoi tantes merveilles en sont avenues?' – 'Sire, fet cil, oïl bien, et je le vos dirai volentiers; et vos le devez bien savoir come la chose ou il a gran senefiance'.[25]

In the *Entrée* the Saracen is dead because of his *desmesure*, a sin that Roland himself is trying to expiate. The meaning is that everyone who acts against the law (*contre droit*: in this case the celestial law) is to be punished. Roland did so *non par orgoil mais por senefiance* – not for pride but to demonstrate which side the law is on. When analysing the *Entrée* vis à vis the Breton romance influence, one should ask if Roland's voyage to the East can be considered a real *queste*.

It has been repeatedly said that the most important innovation of the *Entrée* is the theme of the journey and the similarity that it establishes with the Old French romances, which are constructed upon a complicated plot of adventures set in a realm of abstract time and space.[26] The voyage to the East establishes a tangible shift of genre from epic to romance and is moulded on the example of the many allegorical journeys to the Otherworld. Of great popularity throughout the Middle Ages were the *katabasis* of classical antiquity, the *echtrai* and *immrama* of the Irish tradition, and the traversing of the fog or the forest in Breton romances (but also in the *Navigatio sancti Brendani*). All the elements are in fact there: a land of sin; an offended king to be variously left, rescued and joined; a hero who half-unconsciously journeys towards an unknown destination; a guide who leads him there through an element of nature (water, fog,

---

[24] See E. Baumgartner, *L'Arbre et le Pain. Essai sur la Queste del Saint Graal* (Paris: SEDES, 1981).

[25] *La Queste del Saint Graal*, ed. Pauphilet, p. 37.

[26] On this point see C. Segre, 'Quello che Bachtin non ha detto. Le origini medievali del romanzo', in *Teatro e romanzo* (Turin: Einaudi, 1984), pp. 61–84; repr. in Meneghetti, ed., *Il romanzo*, pp. 125–45.

or forest); and an unknown and wondrous land with another king to rescue whose role is antithetical or corresponds to that of the offended king in the land of sin.

On the other hand, in the tradition of the *chanson de geste* the intrinsically Christian nature of the hero's enterprise makes of him both a crusader and a pilgrim. Akin to what happens in the Grail narratives the hero is seeking an ideal but must confront enemies in the secular world.[27] In the case of the *Entrée*, however, Roland does not encounter any personal enemies in his journey to the East, but the king of Persia's enemy becomes Roland's too since thanks to his superior strategic skills Roland is put in charge of defeating him. He fights against Pélias as a sign of friendship to the sultan and (as it emerges only at the end of the combat) because he believes in a general obligation to defeat evil.

Far from facing a hostile environment he is welcomed in the East, even being offered the governance of Persia and the hand of the young princess. Roland does not seem to be looking for any ideals there nor is he travelling as a pilgrim. He is certainly no crusader either and does not travel to the far-off land to defeat the enemy and impose the true faith, although his desire to bring chivalry to the Saracens does correspond to some extent with one to circulate ideals closely related to Christendom. In the final analysis, his journey is a temporary escape from a social order with which he no longer agrees. Roland's approach to reality is not only diametrically opposed to that of the *Chanson de Roland*; it also differs from the whole tradition of the Grail quest narratives in which a material object (the Grail) embodied the *queste*'s very essence as the symbol (*semblance*) of an ideal object (the perfection of faith and soul of the knight). In the *Entrée*, we witness neither the presence of an object nor indeed a striving for the truth, unless the truth is to be understood here as empirical rather than revealed.

It is not the truth of God that Roland goes seeking but the truth emerging from a comparison of two different experiences: subjection to Charles' authority and escape. Experience seems to be a key word in the *Entrée* in which Roland is not satisfied with the treatment he is receiving in exchange for his efforts to please the king and win

---

[27] Calin, *The Epic Queste*, p. 108.

Spain on his behalf. He is frustrated and thus sets forth only to return to Spain and his original role at the end of this temporary suspension of his martyrdom. His return to Charlemagne's camp is not entirely his choice: it can be read as the call of the cause and the subsequent re-appropriation of the role of hero of the Christian world; or it may just be that the *chanson de geste* is such a prevalent literary tradition that it acted as a catalyst upon the poet's imagination, superimposing its rules on any innovation deriving from the romances. Roland's return to Spain is nothing more than a conventional element which does not in any way diminish the innovative narrative found between the period of Roland's initial faithfulness to the emperor and his final return.

The figure of the hermit

It is important to notice that when Roland lands in Spain the poet chooses to indulge in one more Eastern-like episode, which suggests the desire for a further delay in returning to the epic narrative mode and perhaps a sense of loss of narrative freedom experienced during the Eastern episode. The episode of the hermit covers a quite extensive section of the poem's last part. Starting from laisse DCXXIX and up to laisse DCLIX, the account acquires an unmistakable flavour of Grail romances which persists until the end when Roland again meets Charlemagne.

The whole episode of the hermitage is inspired by the elaboration of the legend of the Grail. In this particular episode, the narrative acquires a novel flavour. Roland wears ornate costumes, eats celestial food, traverses a forest thanks to a path that opens miraculously in front of him, and while he talks to Samson the hermit his companions are convinced he is in front of them because an angel has replaced him. When Roland first makes contact with Samson the hermit, a wonderful perfume suddenly descends on the scene, transforming the setting into a sort of earthly paradise (ll. 14733–37):

> Non puet plus avant dir, q'il li est sorvenu
> Une oudor santisme de dous lou descendu:
> Se totes les espices qu'anch en Surie fu

I fusent asenblees et entor espandu,
Lor fleior contre cil seroit van e perdu.

This element of the wonderful scent surrounding holy men is also found in the *Navigatio sancti Brendani*,[28] one of the most famous accounts of voyage and hermitage of the Middle Ages.[29] Here, the monks recognise by the scent of his clothes that the holiest monk in the confraternity has visited the Promised Land and then inspired Brendan's journey.

In the *Entrée* Roland, Sansonet and Hugues eat incomparably delicious fruits in a wild orchard which suggests they have reached a kind of earthly paradise. This element has a parallel in the *Navigatio* where the monks undertaking a voyage to the Promised Land are fed in a miraculous way by heavenly figures. When led by Brendan they reach the *terra repromissionis*, the first thing they find is a wonderful orchard from which they harvest endless fruits. The motif of celestial food is very much present in the *Entrée* since the hermit is fed by an angel; again, this greatly resembles the *Navigatio* in which the aged St. Paul is fed by a sea creature. In the *Queste* not only are Galaad, Perceval and Bohort fed by the Holy Grail in the city of Sarraz but

---

[28] *Navigatio sancti Brendani*, ed. Selmer; *La navigazione di San Brandano*, ed. and transl. by A. Magnani (Palermo: Sellerio, 1992); *The Voyage of Saint Brendan*, ed. and transl. by J. J. O'Meara (Dublin: Dolmen Press, 1976).

[29] The *Navigatio* was mostly known in the Middle Ages through the Anglo-Norman translation by Benedeit: *Il Viaggio di San Brandano*, ed. and transl. by R. Bartoli and F. Cigni (Parma: Pratiche, 1994). It was also translated into the Venetian and Tuscan vernaculars: *Navigatio sancti Brendani - La navigazione di San Brandano*, ed. by M. A. Grignani (Milan: Bompiani, 1992). It is probably the most famous description of a journey to the Promised Land ever told in medieval literature. One instance of its circulation is the mention in Guido delle Colonne, *Historia,* ed. Meek, 10.211–20, which uses it as a source for the episode of the Leviathan. See also R. A. Bartoli, 'La *Navigatio* in Italia', in *La navigazione di San Brandano e la sua fortuna nella cultura romanza dell'età di mezzo* (Fasano: Schena, 1993), pp. 353–94; M. Davie, 'The *Voyage of Saint Brendan*. The Venetian Version', in W. R. J. Barron and G. S. Burgess, eds, *The Voyage of Saint Brendan. Representative Versions of the Legend in English Translation* (Exeter: University of Exeter Press, 2002), pp. 155–230.

Galaad is then left alone to experience the sight of the Grail;[30] in the *Entrée*, the fruits will cause Roland's companions to fall asleep. Sansonet and Hugues will awake when the hermit is dead and Roland has already buried him. The knights desire to eat more of those fruits but at that point they have a bitter taste. Their function was to put Sansonet and Hugues to sleep in order to leave Roland alone with the hermit.

The characterisation of the hermit in the *Entrée* conforms to the prototype hermit of the Breton tradition: 'Rolant voit de l'hermit le ancïen visaire | Qi senbloit de la barbe Abraant o Machaire;' (ll. 14687–88). A source for the characterisation of the hermit is a Life of St. Machaire containing an antecedent.[31] However, it is more likely that the author is referring generally to Abraham and St. Machaire with the purpose of conveying an idea rather than of using one precise source. Other examples, such as St. Paul in the *Navigatio* and Cato in *Purgatorio* I, testify to a general agreement that a long white beard and ancient features (as per the description of the prophets in the Bible) convey the image of a very wise man who has undergone pain and found knowledge through the examination of his own sufferings.

The detail of the crucifix the hermit wears around his neck, made of the wood of the true cross, is an element of some importance which follows the symbolic tradition of the Grail romances: 'Mout est cele cros digne, qant dou sante ligne fu | Ou le cor Nostre Sir fo mis et estendu' (ll. 14728–29). In the narrative of

---

[30] In the *Queste*, Galaad, who is in the East with his companions Perceval and Boort, is called by a bishop to leave his company and enjoy the vision of the Grail which is denied to the other two: 'Et voient un bel home vestu en semblance de evesque, et estoit a genolz devant la table et batoit sa coupe; et avoit entor lui si grant plenté d'angleres come se ce fust Jhesucrist meisme. Et quant il ot esté grant piece a genolz, si se leva et commença la messe de la glorieuse Mere Dieu. Et quant vint el segré de la messe, que il ot ostee la plateinne de desus le saint Vessel, si apella Galaad et li dist: "Vien avant, serjant Jhesucrist, si verras ce que tu as tant desirré a veoir". Et il se tret avant et regarde dedenz le saint Vessel. Et si tost come il i ot regardé, si comence a trembler molt durement, si tost come la mortel char commença a regarder les esperitex choses' (*La Queste del Saint Graal*, ed. Pauphilet, pp. 277–78).

[31] See F. Torraca, '*L'Entrée d'Espagne*', in *Studi di storia letteraria* (Florence: Sansoni, 1923), pp. 164–241.

the *Queste*, the wood of the tree of life that Eve brought out of the earthly paradise has a pivotal role since Galaad and his companions cross the sea on a boat containing a bed made of that very wood.[32] The cross upon which Jesus died was made of the same wood as the tree of life so that a continuity is established between the events of Genesis and the Gospels. The wood of the true cross is a relic as with the blood of Jesus contained in the Holy Grail and dripping from Longinus' spear, and its mention has a high symbolic value in establishing continuity between the Gospels and Grail legends. The fact that the hermit wears a cross made of that same wood may help to establish a close connection between this episode of the *Entrée* and the Grail cycle.

The hermit tells Roland the story of the horrible crime he committed when very young and that led him to undertake the hermit's life. He robbed his own father's house of all its goods. After the father discovered the robbery, he confronted his son and battered him. Blinded with rage Samson killed his father, and his mother and brother who had both witnessed the crime. He then fled and began to regret what he had done. He went to see the Pope in Rome and asked for clemency. After travelling a long time, to expiate his guilt he retired to the hermitage where Roland found him (laisses DCXXXVII–DCXL).

The account of the hermit tells the story of crime and redemption, bringing Roland back to his relationship with Charlemagne. On the eve of his encounter with his uncle, after a long absence which the French hero intended as punishment for the abuse he suffered, the story he hears helps him to clarify his feelings towards the emperor. In this sense the episode forms one example of *mise en abyme*.[33] The young Samson committed parricide and spent the rest of his life expiating his murder. Although the young Roland did not go as far as murdering his own uncle the relationship between Roland and Charlemagne can be regarded as effectively a

---

[32] *La Queste del Saint Graal*, ed. Pauphilet, pp. 222–26.
[33] Through the employment of another story's plot, this technique (which is typical of the matière de Bretagne) anticipates and signifies the story told in the text and offers the opportunity for elaborating an *exemplum* into a symbolic treatment of the story. There is at least another instance of this in the *Entrée*, in laisse DXXXVIII.

father-son bond for a variety of reasons: blood (he is a nephew, which establishes a continuity of lineage); fosterage (Roland was fostered by Charlemagne from birth); power (Roland is the king's only heir); and obedience (Roland is subjected to the king's authority). However, disobedience and the breaking of the feudal contract symbolised by Charles' blow create a rupture, akin to Samson's case. Roland's isolation in a foreign land and acquisition of a new identity, comparable to a voluntary annihilation of his previous self, corresponds to a form of eremitical life. He only encounters the hermit on his way back to his old self, which suggests that the stage of his expiation is complete.

The *Entrée* would not be the only case of a *chanson* embracing and merging with the genre of Grail romances. A highly atypical example in the history of the *chanson de geste* is *Huon de Bordeaux* which is subject to an Arthurian influence.[34] There, the fabulous Orient is derived from Arthurian romance and reflects the Celtic Otherworld – that mythological realm containing supernatural beings which from time to time is opened to selected members of humanity.

Calin suggests that 'Huon's most dangerous adventure, the sea voyage, partakes of an archetype we have seen in *Ami et Amile*: death and rebirth'.[35] This archetype, which is also present in epic,[36] is represented in Arthurian literature by the motifs of the desert-forest

---

[34] A. Adler, *Rückzug in epischer Parade* (Frankfurt am Main: Klostermann, 1986), pp. 270–71; D. D. R. Owen, 'The Principal Source of *Huon de Bordeaux*', *French Studies* 7 (1953), 129–39; Calin, *The Epic Queste*, pp. 189–90. Viscardi, 'Arthurian Influences', p. 424: 'French literature of the thirteenth century as represented in Huon de Bordeaux actually fused the Carolingian and Arthurian cycles, retaining the theme of strife between Charlemagne and the rebel barons as the main plot but interjecting characters and adventures reminiscent of the Matter of Britain.'

[35] Calin, *The Epic Queste*, p. 209. See also Adler, *Rückzug in epischer Parade*, p. 280.

[36] Calin, *The Epic Queste*, maintains that 'in so much of heroic literature – the myths of Jason and Moses, the Odyssey, Gilgamesh, and Lusiads – death and rebirth are intimately linked to the notion of withdrawal and return. The protagonist has left home to undertake certain adventures; his victory is consecrated by a triumphant return to the point of departure' (p. 210).

or the mist. The act of traversing a barrier leads the protagonist to explore the unknown and all its implications. The sea as an obstacle or boundary needing to be crossed signifies separation from the point of departure: physically from the land where the hero normally lives and acts, and psychologically from the hero's condition before the process of purification-rebirth. The land where this process happens represents a temporary interruption of reality in which the hero is provisionally suspended from his own identity, and that must necessarily be a foreign land where he does not naturally belong. In the *Entrée* the idea of an interruption of reality and suspension of identity is strengthened by Roland's assumption of a different identity altogether. Having then returned to the point of departure, Roland's process can be considered complete.

Roland asks the hermit to prophesy how many years he will live.[37] The hermit answers with a question which, as playful as it sounds, introduces the element of irony which is one of the most distinctive aspects of the *Entrée* (ll. 14944–47):

> Li hermit li regarde, puis li dist un sermon:
> 'Nen ais tu mie point lit le vers de cançon?'
> Li duc batu sa coupe dos fois soz le menton,
> E le hermit s'en veit e leisa lo baron.

The *cançon* he is referring to must surely be the *Roland*. How is Roland supposed to have read the *Chanson de Roland*, however, when it is the account of his own life and death and he is still alive? This point is wonderfully intriguing: the poet intertwines specific points in time, genres, and characters, making full use of the irony that permeates the whole of his work. Where his reader/audience by now expect a prophecy, they are instead presented with a rhetorical question, which generates initial disappointment. In the person of the hermit, however, the poet is entertaining a private dialogue with his own character, wondering how a fourteenth-century Roland can possibly not have read the mother of all *chansons de geste*. Of course, the reader of the *Entrée* is also assumed to have read the *Chanson*

---

[37] A parallel with Alexander can be made here: the Greek conqueror at the end of his life was obsessed with his future, and his fame as an extreme character also makes reference to his irrationality in the face of divinations and presages.

beforehand, or at the least to be acquainted with such a popular story. Not only does Roland thus become the reader of his own life story but also the representative young magnate of the fourteenth century; especially among the public audience of Charlemagne's epic were the magnates who towards the end of the thirteenth century aspired to a higher social status by investing capital in land and castles, and to nobility through the appropriation of the cultural background of which the epic of Roland was a great part.

The question therefore asked of Roland is, rather, one addressed to the reader: 'Have you not read what happens to Roland?' The myriad implications of this question would deserve a study of their own. Suffice it to say here that the reader finds himself tricked and is left with the perception that the poet is playing with the tradition – the roles as well as his sources.

While his companions are asleep from eating the heavenly fruits, the hermit prophesies for Roland that he will not live longer than seven years and will die as a martyr in the service of God (ll. 15126–31):

> 'Se tu por Deu travailes, bon merit en avrais,
> Car qant tu veus savor le jor de ton trepais,
> Donc te feit a savoir qe puis ke prix avrais
> Ceste cités asixe, .VII. ans plus non vivrais;
> En le servise Deu come martre morais
> E si serais traïs, con fu il por Judais'.

The strong mysticism and symbolism infusing the whole passage (seven are the years that Roland still has to live; an act of treachery is the cause of his death) very recalls strongly the latest representatives of Breton romances, in particular the *Queste*. Having predicted Roland's death Samson himself dies in Roland's arms, concluding his archetypal process of death and rebirth by leaving his legacy to the young hero yet to complete his own expiation. The death of the hermit follows a pattern most common to the Breton and Celtic tradition; after a holy man has accomplished his journey or duty, he no longer needs to add any other form of fulfilment to his life and therefore he dies. Galaad therefore dies after the vision of the Grail, St. Brendan after visiting the *terra repromissionis sanctorum*, and in the *Entrée* the hermit was only staying alive to prophesy Roland's destiny. This has an antecedent in the Bible, for example the death of Simeon after seeing the infant Christ. The scene of the hermit's death and burial has a strong biblical flavour. While Roland sits on a stone holding Samson in his arms, a picture which recalls the image of the Pietà, the French hero hears the song of angels, and a voice tells him where to bury the hermit (ll. 15207–18):

> Le duch Rolant s'asis sor une piere lee;
> En ses braç tient le cors dont l'arme en est sevree.
> Il vit environ lui l'eglixe aluminee,
> Si oï de cant d'angles une grant asenblee
> Qui ont l'arme benigne aveque aus portee.
> Le duch ne seit qe fere, ma si a escoutee
> Une vois qe lui dist: 'Porte sens detrïee
> Cil cors en cele roche dun la piere est crossee,
> Ou tu vois de clarté si tres grant brandonee.
> Quant tu l'avrais chouchié, va prendre cele spee
> Qui pant a cil piler qi est a cele entree:
> Quant l'ait mise ou flanch, si t'en vais a ta alee'.

As in the Bible, the voice of God speaks to the chosen one. Roland follows its instructions and buries the hermit in a sepulchre which he finds ready for the burial ceremony. It is noteworthy that the hermit is buried with his sword lying next to him, as a knight and not as a holy man (ll. 15231–36):

> Le ber garde in la roche, qi asés iert prochain;
> Un sercul vi overt, dunt la piere fu saine;
> Entor i oit de candoiles ardant une qincaine.
> L'ermite li choucha o tot l'espee vaine;
> Puis est la piere cluse en la roche anciaine;
> Dou cors ni dou sercuel ne vit pués rien certaine.

In conclusion, the long and articulated hermit episode plays a notable role in the transition between genres, as the hermit is a feature belonging exclusively to the *matière de Bretagne*.

L'Entrée d'Espagne and the Classical Tradition

The Matter of Aeneas in Italy

The *Entrée* is a work of art that deserves to be studied from numerous points of view due to the enormous breadth of sources on which it draws. It should be received by today's public as a sort of encyclopaedic overview of the cultural milieu of the fourteenth century. Physical proximity to the early humanistic centre of Padua might have influenced the author's readings. Yet even if the author tends to be identified with an eminent personality in the milieu of the Paduan humanists, there is insufficient evidence to prove that he resided in that area his entire life. One way to trace the author's movements is to identify his readings and thus determine the availability of manuscripts in the areas where he might have resided. As discussed in this chapter, it is possible to identify the sources of the *Entrée*'s classical citations and influences. The matter of Aeneas is derived from the *Aeneid* (possibly directly) although the commentaries played a pre-eminent role in the dissemination of the Latin text. There is also the possibility of an influence from the *Enéas*. The matter of Troy is derived from the Dares/Dictys tradition, filtered through Benoît and Guido delle Colonne, with some influence from the Franco-Italian *Hector et Hercule* and from the *Ovide moralisé*. There is stylistic evidence to suggest that the reading of Ovid in the Latin might have influenced some of the author's choices, while the matter of Alexander is based mainly on the version of Alexandre de Bernay.

Throughout the poem three identifications with classical figures contribute to the making of a new Roland; his multifaceted characterisation is built on comparisons with the greatest heroes of antiquity. Thus, the Roland/Aeneas link serves to introduce and clarify the motif of the journey and of the *katabasis*; the Roland/Hector connection implies the opposition between the Greeks and the Trojans, and the preference for the French/Trojans; the Roland/Alexander association suggests generosity and magnanimity, and establishes a parallel with the greatest traveller to the East. A remarkable number of references to classical heroes and myths make of the *Entrée* an attempt to encapsulate, in medieval epic, most of what had survived of classical literature. Through employing a great variety of associations and sources from the classical tradition, Roland in the *Entrée* starts his transformation into the perfect Italian humanistic lord: educated, well-travelled, magnanimous, and open to a foreign and ancient culture.

The discussion about classical influences and especially the presence of Virgil in the *chanson de geste* has been carried forward in some works of the foremost importance.[38] It is not the aim here to discuss in depth the question of whether in fact the author of the *Entrée* had seen a manuscript containing Virgil's text, or had attained a substantial knowledge of the poem's content by other means (perhaps by reading the *Enéas*). The solution would entail a different approach altogether to the matter. The aim of this study is rather to define the environment in which many influences merged, allowing such a variegated product to arise as part of fourteenth century literature and to contribute in shaping the *poema cavalleresco*.

In his commentary on the classical sources of the *Entrée*, Limentani very cautiously treats the question of whether a direct influence from Virgil can be hypothesised or whether intertextuality involves only texts reworking the matter of the *Aeneid*. He argues that while a mention of Aeneas is unusual in the *chanson de geste* genre, where it does occur this does not necessarily imply direct knowledge of the source; nor, however, does it imply the opposite.[39]

---

[38] First and foremost D. Comparetti, *Virgilio nel Medio Evo* (Livorno, 1872). Comparetti opened a discussion that interested J. Bédier, *Les Légendes épiques* (Paris: Champion, 1913). See also E. Faral, *Recherches sur les sources latines des contes et romans courtois du Moyen Âge* (Paris: Champion, 1913 ; repr. 1967); M. Wilmotte, *Le Français à la tête épique* (Paris: Renaissance du Livre, 1917); M. Wilmotte, *L'Épopée française. Origine et élaboration* (Paris: Boivin, 1939); G. Chiri, *L'epica latina e la chanson de geste* (Genoa: Orfini, 1936). Thomas discussed the question in the preface to his edition of the *Entrée* with reference to Curtius, who pointed out that a Virgilian model or one derived from Virgil was present in the *Chanson de Roland*. Bédier concluded that the *Aeneid* did have a great deal of influence on the *Chanson* but it was a hard task to isolate passages and find precise correspondences.

[39] '[…] la menzione di Enea è inconsueta alla tradizione delle chansons de geste. Ovvio che ciò non vuol dire nulla circa una conoscenza del testo virgiliano; ma ormai, dopo i sondaggi effettuati, sarebbe sciocco affrettarsi nel senso contrario ': Limentani, *L'Entrée d'Espagne e i signori*

Considering Léopold Constans' idea that elements of the *Entrée*'s classical mythology which are not derived from the *Roman de Troie* come from the *Histoire ancienne jusq'à César*,[40] Limentani takes into account the possibility that the *Histoire* could be the main source for references to the matter of the *Aeneid*, concluding that '*Fets des Romains* e *Histoire ancienne* non bastano a dar ragione di tutto'.[41] Limentani pointed out that the section in the *Histoire* dedicated to Aeneas is too fleeting to have imprinted details in the author's memory and influenced his knowledge of the subject. A passage from the Venetian manuscript of the *Histoire* reads as follows: 'qui le voudra trover, sou quiere [= l'enquiere?][42] ou romanz d'Eneas et de

---

d'Italia, p. 157. There is a mention of Aeneas in *Girart de Vienne*; see E. G. Parodi, 'I rifacimenti e le traduzioni italiane dell'Eneide prima del Rinascimento', *Studi di Filologia Romanza* 2–4 (1887), 97–368 (pp. 98, 99 n.1). *Girard de Viane*, ed. by F. G. Yeandle (New York: Columbia University Press, 1930).

[40] L. Constans, '*L'Entrée d'Espagne* et les légendes troyennes', *Romania*, 43 (1914), 430–32. Limentani, *L'Entrée d'Espagne e i signori d'Italia*, p. 153 n. 19, argues that Constans' conclusion is too hasty, as J. Monfrin noted in 'Humanisme et traductions au Moyen Âge', *Journal des savants*, 148 (1963), 161–90; repr. in *L'humanisme médiéval dans les littératures romanes du XIIe au XIVe siècles* (Paris: Fourrier, 1964), pp. 217–46 (218–19). Constans refers to a version of the *Histoire* that belongs to the end of the fourteenth century, which is impossible given that the *Entrée* dates to the century's first half. However, a section covering about six leaves of the Venetian manuscript of the *Histoire*, Venice: Biblioteca Nazionale Marciana, MS fr. Z. 2 (=223), originally in the Gonzaga library, is entirely dedicated to the adaptation of the *Aeneid* with some passages modelled on Servius: see M.-R. Jung, *La Légende de Troie en France au Moyen Âge* (Tübingen: Francke, 1996), p. 338. The *Histoire ancienne* was written for Roger IV before the siege of Lille dating to 1213: G. Raynaud de Lage, 'L'*Histoire ancienne jusqu'à César* et les *Faits des Romains*', *Le Moyen Âge*, 55 (1949), 5–13; G. Raynaud de Lage, 'Les "romans antiques" dans l'*Histoire ancienne jusqu'à César*', *Le Moyen Âge*, 63 (1957), 267–309. J. Monfrin, 'Les "Translations" vernaculaires de Virgile au Moyen Âge', in *Lectures médiévales de Virgile. Actes du colloque organisé par l'École française de Rome (Rome, 25–28 octobre 1982)* (Rome: École française de Rome, 1985), pp. 189–249, analyses in detail the section dedicated to Aeneas with indications of the sources, in particular Virgil (pp. 211–20).

[41] Limentani, *L'Entrée d'Espagne e i signori d'Italia*, p. 154.

[42] Perhaps to be understood as 'chercher'.

Virgile'.[43] The author/scribe is suggesting here that those wishing to learn more about the subject can find further information in the *Enéas* and *de Virgile*.[44] While discussing the possible sources for the matter of Aeneas, Limentani reports this passage without paying much attention to the phrase *de Virgile*. However, it seems that the author/scribe may be referring to the *Aeneid* itself.

It is important to stress that since the publication of Parodi's study on the Italian reworkings and translations of the *Aeneid* before the Renaissance,[45] it is accepted that 'Virgil's original poem was throughout the period one of the most read and studied of all texts, from school upwards; indeed in some circles, it was more popular even for leisure reading than the various rewritings of the Middle Ages'.[46] As the scholarly background of the *Entrée* poet allows for a great deal of speculation as to his knowledge,[47] could it be that he benefited from a wide circulation of the Virgilian epic?

---

[43] Venice: Biblioteca Nazionale Marciana, MS fr. Z. 2 (=223), f. 108 v.a.

[44] The Venetian manuscript dates to the years 1389–94, too late to have been read by the author of the *Entrée*. This does not imply that the same text did not circulate in an earlier manuscript dating possibly to the first half of the century. However, the question cannot be analysed without further evidence: Limentani, *L'Entrée d'Espagne e i signori d'Italia*, p. 153 n. 20.

[45] Parodi, 'I rifacimenti e le traduzioni'.

[46] J. E. Everson, *The Italian Romance Epic in the Age of Humanism. The Matter of Italy and the World of Rome* (Oxford: Oxford University Press, 2001), p. 45 and n. 31.

[47] The poet of the *Entrée* was 'un di quegli "uomini di corte" tra il pedagogo e il segretario dei Signori, de' quali conosciamo più d'un esempio; e rappresenta quella classe di mezza cultura, né laici né umanisti, che al pari di quella dei "notai" formò la "massa di manovra" nella conquista della nuova civiltà italiana': E. Carrara, *Da Rolando a Morgante* (Turin: Edizioni de 'L'Erma', 1932), p. 48. See also Limentani, *L'Entrée d'Espagne e i signori d'Italia*, p. 173. The *Entrée* is 'by a writer of some culture, who displays knowledge and incorporation of classical material into his work, even if these elements are still clearly viewed from a medieval perspective': Everson, *The Italian Romance Epic*, p. 31.

In fact, at a later stage of his discussion and by way of comparison between the *Entrée* and two passages of the *Commedia*, Limentani formulates the idea that there may be a direct influence from Virgil. His analysis of lines 12269–70 (in which Roland enters the tent of the Sultan and witnesses the dispute over Dionés' marriage), of the name of the Asian lake where Roland first arrives, and of some of the narrative's structures, convincingly shows that a contact between the *Entrée* and the *Aeneid* exists.[48]

Furthermore, Limentani states that 'resta fuori discussione la solidarietà dell'*Entrée* con l'ambiente padovano'.[49] The Paduan environment aimed primarily at rediscovering the original purity of the classical tradition and adopted a philological approach in doing so. The 'solidarietà con l'ambiente padovano' is an idea that is also widely accepted by Bradley-Cromey and supported by recent research,[50] although it is only after a more precise identification of the author that one can decide how close he was to that environment. Regardless of speculation on this last point, however, and in contrast with the matters of France and of Britain, the matter of Rome 'constitutes the most difficult area in terms of discerning the extent to which poems produced in humanist milieux really reflect direct classical culture as opposed to one mediated and refracted through medieval perspective'.[51]

Apart from Limentani's findings, I have come across another two elements that may suggest the *Aeneid*'s influence.[52] First, at the end of the episode of the duel between Ferragu and Roland, a discussion follows the latter's victory. In this context Gerard's speech concentrates on the giant's enormity and on how the difference in

---

[48] Limentani, *L'Entrée d'Espagne e i signori d'Italia*, pp. 170–71. This also anticipates his idea that the poet knew the *Commedia*, discussed by him in pp. 273–89.
[49] Limentani, *L'Entrée d'Espagne e i signori d'Italia*, p. 153.
[50] Bradley-Cromey, *Authority and Autonomy*, pp. 14–16. A. de Mandach, 'Sur les traces de la cheville ouvrière', identified the author based on textual evidence with the Paduan judge Giovanni di Nono.
[51] Everson, *The Italian Romance Epic*, p. 28.
[52] The edition consulted for this study is Publius Virgilius Maro [Virgil], *Aeneid*, in *Opera*, ed. by R. A. B. Mynors (Oxford: Oxford University Press, 1969).

size between the two contenders did not guarantee victory to the largest (ll. 4254–80, particularly ll. 4258, 4260):

> 'Seignor Paiens, vos parlez dou melor.
> Se je voloie estre mençoigneor,
> Veor poez l'impossible labor,
> Ch'ancué est mort por la quaile l'astor;
> Non merveilez, car je vi ja, seignor,
> Dui escoler de dui escrimaor:
> L'uns estoit grant e l'autre asez menor;
> Le uns vers l'autre se mirent par hiror,
> E bien disoient la plus partie d'entor
> Che le pitit en avroit la pejor;
> Ne savrent mot qu'il geta soi en sor,
> Li destre braz li detrença le jor;
> A grant mervoile li tindrent li plusor.
> Savez por quoi fu vencu li grignor ?
> Son cheitis mestre fu de chetis color,
> A soi fist onte et a cil mal e plor.
> Le meistre al mendre en oit joie et honor;
> Son escoler le fist clamer dotor.
> E por ce feit ceschuns home folor
> Ch'en le forz entre por trover la fredor.
> Mout par avoit Feragu grant valor,
> Longe stature vers le nostre contor.
> Ne quitez mie qe por teran vigor
> L'aie couquis le niés l'empereor;
> Mais la pusance est venue de sor'.

The duel is spoken of by way of comparison to the biblical episode of David and Goliath. However, some details suggest that the immediate source for the description of the two duellers may be the episode of Hercules and Cacus in *Aeneid* 8.193–272. The *Enéas* makes a very brief mention of Cacus ('Carus avoit li mostres non', l. 4638) in the context of Hercules' labours and refers to the mythical giant as a monster who devastated its region, but no reference is made there to its size. By contrast, book VIII of the *Aeneid* goes to great lengths to describe Cacus' size and strength. Secondly, in the *Entrée* there is a reference to the river Acheron ('Ainz voldroie estre en le flons d'Acheront', l. 5215). There is no mention of the Acheron in the *Enéas*; excluding the *Odyssey* the other sources where the Acheron is given are *Aeneid* 6.107 and 6.295, and *Metamorphoses* 5.538–41.[53]

It could also be suggested that the motif of *katabasis* in the *Aeneid* offers a parallel to the more profound meaning of the Eastern episode. Roland's punitive absence (the hero leaves following a violent altercation with Charlemagne) starts with the crossing of the sea, corresponding to Aeneas' crossing of the river Lethe and the subsequent oblivion of all sins (in the East Roland purifies himself from the sin of *desmesure*). Given the presence of a *nocchiero* (Baudor – a friendly one, as opposed to Dante's Charon in *Inferno* III), the episode of the sea-crossing, which divides the two parts of the poem, can be read like a journey from the world of the living to the Otherworld. Roland's journey culminates with the episode of the hermit in which Roland's complete solitude is an element of particular relevance. Like Aeneas' companions when the hero descends to the Otherworld, Roland's companions are completely cut out from the action when the French hero witnesses the prophecy and subsequent death of the hermit. Furthermore, the prophecy is the pivotal moment of both episodes.

Despite the three arguments of Limentani in support of a direct knowledge of Virgil and this other evidence, it remains wise to consider that this may not have been the case. Looking closely, the mention of Hector and Cacus is in fact in the *Enéas* as well as in the *Aeneid*, and the Acheron appears in Dante's *Comedy*. As suggested by Limentani, those passages of the *Aeneid* that influenced the poet may have been filtered through his reading of the *Inferno*, although this option considerably weakens the hypothesis of a learned background for the poet of the *Entrée* (which on the other hand, it must be said, is strengthened by other elements in the text).

While initially proposing that an intermediary text might have provided knowledge of the matter of Aeneas, Limentani does not favour one particular option but maintains that this 'ben difficilmente potrebbe essere stato il *Roman d'Enéas*',[54] which

---

[53] The edition consulted for this study is Publius Ovidius Naso [Ovid], *Metamorphoses*, ed. by W.S. Anderson (Leipzig: Teubner, 1977).

[54] Limentani, *L'Entrée d'Espagne e i signori d'Italia*, p. 157.

according to the Italian scholar circulated in another geographical area altogether. However, if one excluded the *Entrée* author from having direct knowledge of Virgil's text (which is open to debate since Limentani, following Constans, has convincingly argued that all information about the *Aeneid*'s plot was taken from the *Histoire ancienne*), there remain few texts on which the *Entrée* author could have based his knowledge of the matter of Aeneas. By contrast, the commentaries certainly ensured this knowledge.

As the Venetian manuscript of the *Histoire* to which Limentani refers[55] bears the clear influence of Servius' *glossae*, one possibility is that the *Entrée* author could have used this manuscript as a start; and given the scant narration of the events, he might have referred directly to Servius' *glossae*[56] which at the time were widely circulating.[57] The 'immense influence in succeeding centuries of Servius' commentary and the fact that every reader and scholar from the fourth to the fourteenth centuries became acquainted with Virgil largely through the eyes of Servius and his fellow commentators'[58] suggests that, if Virgil's original was not available to the poet, one intermediary text for the knowledge of the *Aeneid* could certainly have been Servius.[59] In considering this question we should also turn our attention to the other of the two major commentaries on Virgil's poem produced in the late empire, Claudius Donatus' *Interpretationes Vergilianae*. The commentaries both of Servius and Donatus are texts of fundamental importance, and notable (especially in the case of Servius) for the conservation and philological discussion of particular passages.

---

[55] Limentani, *L'Entrée d'Espagne e i signori d'Italia*, p. 153 and n. 20.
[56] Servius [Maurus Servius Honoratus], *Commentarius in Vergilii Bucolicon*, ed. by G. Thilo and H. Hagen (Leipzig: B. G. Teubner, 1887; repr. Hildesheim, Zürich, New York: Georg Olms, 1961).
[57] As F. Mora-Lebrun has demonstrated, Servius' commentary plays a seminal role in the process of the 'mise en roman': Mora-Lebrun, *L'"Eneide" médiévale*, p. 171 ff.
[58] Everson, *The Italian Romance Epic*, p. 52.
[59] We have two different versions of Servius' commentary, one shorter and the second much longer (the so-called *Servius Danielis*). Scholars have always considered the longer version as the more reliable. However, it now seems that the shorter is more precise whereas the second was lengthened by the scribal addition of parts.

Throughout the Middle Ages the tradition of the *Aeneid* was perpetuated by a number of reworkings. Dating to the early fourteenth century, the prose account of the matter of Aeneas by Guido da Pisa,[60] the *Fatti di Cesare*,[61] and the *Fiorita* by Armannino Giudice from Bologna[62] depend directly on Virgil's poem.[63] These versions were aimed at moderately well-educated readers and it seems quite unlikely that such a knowledgeable writer as the *Entrée* author would rely on the accounts of contemporary writers when they rather testify to the circulation of Virgil's text (since their versions and translations are based on Virgil), thereby made accessible by these *divulgatori* to those unable to read Latin.

It would also be natural to assume that the author of the *Entrée* was an avid reader of French works, especially in verse. It is true that 'although many of the tales based on Roman history and mythology did come into Italy from France and are often clearly rewritings of French originals, this is not invariably the case'.[64] However, given that the *Entrée* is written in French and qualifies as a *chanson de geste*, I suggest revisiting the discussion of the poet's possibly being influenced (at least in part) by the *Enéas*.[65] Limentani assumed that

[60] Guido da Pisa, *I fatti di Enea*, ed. by F. Ageno (Florence: Sansoni, 1957).

[61] *I fatti di Cesare*, ed. by L. Banchi (Bologna: Collezione di opere indite o rare, 1863).

[62] Dating to 1325 and edited partially by G. Mazzatinti, 'La *Fiorita* di Armannino giudice', *Giornale di Filologia Romanza*, 3 (1881), 1-51. Extant manuscripts are Florence: Biblioteca Nazionale Centrale, MS II. III. 139 (prov. Strozzi 1261 <e 308>) and Oxford: Bodleian Library, MS Canonici It. 2.

[63] Everson, *The Italian Romance Epic*, p. 45. See Parodi, 'I rifacimenti e le traduzioni'. A less known version is the *Compilazione della 'Eneide' di Virgilio fatta volgare in sul principio del secolo xiv da Ser Andrea Lancia*, ed. by P. Fanfani (Florence: Stamperia sulle logge del Grano, 1851).

[64] Everson, *The Italian Romance Epic*, p. 41.

[65] J. Monfrin, 'Les "Translations" vernaculaires', investigates the mode of reception and the perspective of those without access to the Latin texts. Although this is not the case for the author of the *Entrée*, it is interesting to note what he writes of the four classical romances: 'Il s'agit de créations littéraires originales, qui ne peuvent être considérées comme de vraies traductions; mais ils reprennent plus ou moins fidèlement les lignes générales d'un récit antique, ainsi que, parfois, des éléments de détail' (p. 192).

the *Enéas* circulated in a different area from the whereabouts of the *Entrée* author,[66] and as far as we are currently aware manuscripts of the *Enéas* were not disseminated in the north of Italy in the fourteenth century. However, the *Enéas* was certainly read up until the thirteenth century, as one manuscript was produced in Italy and dates to the end of the twelfth century or beginning of the thirteenth.[67]

I have found three elements in the text which I will analyse in detail, drawing from them several conclusions in support of the *Enéas*' influence upon the *Entrée*. Among the foremost of these justifying a comparison between the texts is the parallel between Dido and Dionés.[68] Although a large lacuna between lines 12520–13727 prevents the reader from fully enjoying the development of the relationship between Roland and Dionés, and prevents one from drawing any conclusions about the treatment of the princess' character by the author,[69] Dionés is fully delineated. The characterisation of the Arab princess is modelled upon queen Dido as depicted in the *Enéas*, where she is described as having white hands, as is Dionés later on. Although this is a *topos* of Breton romance that could be used to argue for the matter of Britain's pervasive influence on the *Entrée*,[70] it is possible that the author was keen on keeping one of Dido's physical characteristics in the *Enéas* (ll. 838–40):

---

[66] Limentani, *L'Entrée d'Espagne e i signori d'Italia*, p. 157. However, it must be said that Limentani's statement about the *Enéas* is not corroborated by a precise reference to the sources from which the scholar took this information.

[67] Florence, Biblioteca Laurentiana, Plut. XLI, 44.

[68] The name *Dionés* could be derived from *Didonis-Didonem*, with reduction to 0 of intervocalic -d-; and -é- from ĭ/ē. Furthermore, the Roland/Aeneas identification has a logical consequence in the Dionés/Dido parallel.

[69] Léon Gautier tried to join the two parts of the *Entrée* by using the prose versions of *La Spagna* and the *Viaggio* edited by M. Ceruti, although he did not take into account the rhymed version of *Spagna* which would have helped to better identify the content of the lacuna: Gautier, *Les Epopées françaises*, III: 446–47; see A. Thomas, *L'Entrée d'Espagne*, I: XVIII–XIX, n. I.

[70] Ysolt of the White Hands is Tristan's wife.

.I. bacin d'or ont aporté
a quoy la roÿne a lavé
ses mains qui moult par furent blances.

The second element suggesting the two texts' closeness is the question of wisdom. Dionés falls in love with Roland as Dido did with Aeneas. When witnessing the hero's great valour both Dionés and Dido are bewitched. Dido is deeply moved by the account of the siege of Troy and of how the Trojan had escaped the dangers, and although the element of magic somehow puts a limit to psychological insight, in the *Enéas* her feeling is clearly a passionate development of maternal willingness to protect the hero from further dangers. Furthermore, it is Aeneas' valour, strength, and manly attitude that move Dido to passion. In the *Entrée* the explanation for Dionés' passion is very similar: again, she is confronted with the figure of a hero who has escaped many dangers and who is now willing to fight once more to protect her. The element of manly valour is again dominant and is the real cause for the blossoming of such emotions. In Breton romances it is not a manly attitude to danger which makes a maiden fall in love with a knight, but usually his inner beauty, kindness, and chivalric behaviour as expressed in his fairness and the art of courting a lady following a well-defined code. St. Bernard condemned this excessive focus on aesthetics and the appearance of worldly knights as anti-masculine, and suggested that knights concentrate instead on the practice of battle.[71] The opposition between manly valour and aesthetics defines a precise border between epic and romance, and although the *Enéas* is better classified for a number of reasons as a romance (especially because of the courtly elements developed in the second part) it still reveals the great influence of the Latin *epos*. Thus, both the *Enéas* and the *Entrée* gravitate towards the example of the *Queste* in which aesthetics are supplanted by moral perfection, thereby fulfilling St. Bernard's request.

---

[71] Bernard of Clairvaux, *Liber ad milites templi de laude novae militiae*, intr. and transl. by C. D. Fonseca, in *Opere*, vol. I, *Trattati* (Milan: Fondazione di studi cistercensi, 1984), pp. 425–83 (pp. 50–53).

In the *Entrée* Roland is certainly impressed by Dionés but (in contrast to all the other men) does not desire her. In fact, her beauty disturbs him (ll. 12560–64):

> Soz ciel n'a home, tant ait chiere barbue,
> Ne la querist avoir en si braz nue.
> Roland la garde, trestot le sang li mue;
> Non la voudroit le ber avoir veüe;
> D'Audein li mambre, tot le vis li tresue.

Dionés reminds him of Aude, and in turn that he has a mission to accomplish in this world. It is interesting how the figure of Aude functions as a symbol in the *Chanson d Roland* and is always treated as such in the tradition, including the *Entrée*. The Aude-symbol serves as a reminder, not only for Roland but also for the reader, that Roland's escape to the East is not meant to be permanent and a complete abandonment of his responsibilities but is transitional and experimental, with the final goal of broadening his perception of the world. The sudden mention of Aude amidst Roland's exotic adventure brings the reader back to the story's main thread. Thus, while Dionés spends her nights sighing for love, Roland prefers to entertain himself with the other knights, explaining the art of chivalry (laisses DLXXX–DLXXXI) with the intention of fostering a positive legacy.

After the lacuna the narration takes up again with the celebration of the marriage between Dionés and Anseïs, who is made king of Jerusalem (to line 14022). A study of the tradition of Anseïs (especially in Italian) could provide hints as to what happened in the lacuna. The reader is not aware of how the plot unfolded and why Dionés in the end marries Anseïs. Hypotheses might be advanced: for example, Roland's indifference to Dionés could reflect his instinctive attraction for her, but upon the consideration that Roland cannot remain in the East. The *Entrée* tells the story of the seven years preceding Rencesvals. The hero is therefore meant to return home. The fact that Dionés accepts marriage to Anseïs rather than displaying symptoms of insanity leading to suicide (as in Dido's case) could be explained as a celebration of wisdom by both protagonists of the episode, Roland and Dionés. In fact, the first characteristic trait given for Dionés is the word *sage*. She is so wise that she accepts a different marriage without putting up much resistance (at least as far as we know). Besides her great wisdom, she is said to be a real beauty and expert in astrology (ll. 13580–82):

> A merveille fu sage la fille au roi Soudan
> Sa pere de beauté non fu Pollisenan[72]
> Plus savoit des estoille que nul ome mondan.

The final remark on her expertise in reading the stars, above that of all wise men (*ome mondan* to be understood possibly as 'scientist'), must be read as a positive quality that adds to her wisdom as well as her exotic status. A western woman depicted as an astrologer would have produced the impression of a sorceress, and by no means wise but rather dangerous. This recalls Angelica in the *Orlando Furioso* whose character seems to be a dark evolution of Dionés: bearing the same characteristics (she is the princess of Catai and an expert in magic and medicine), Angelica is not at all *sage* and indeed is the cause of all the havoc and of Roland's insanity.

The cruel ending to Dido's love and conversely the celebration of the healthy love of Lavinia for Aeneas,[73] which generates the foundation myth of the Italian people's ancestors, suggest that the kind of love preferred by the medieval reader was a more domestic sentiment, resulting in improvement of the household and celebrating the two lovers' social status. Dido's passion is described negatively in the *Enéas* as *raige* (l. 1343) and again a few lines later as *mortel raige* (l. 1351). Dionés thereby seems to result from the mergence of the two female characters, embodying the best of both. While on the one hand manly valour ignites her feelings, on the other her wisdom softens them until she finally accepts a different

---

[72] The reference to Polyxena's beauty can again be connected with *Metamorphoses* 13.439–45. Guido delle Colonne, following Dictys/Benoît, also insists on her beauty: Guido delle Colonne, *Historia*, ed. Meek, 5.73–74; 8.273–80; 23.95–109.

[73] J. Monfrin, 'Les "Translations" vernaculaires', points out that the third book of the *Aeneid* is condensed in the *Enéas* into four lines. He then gives other examples of how, while the plot remains the same, the balance between the parts of the poem is altered. The most striking of these shifts of symmetries is the long digression on the psychological insight into Lavinia's and Aeneas' passion in the *Enéas*, an innovation compared to the *Aeneid*.

marriage since her union with Anseïs results in the foundation of a Christian kingdom in the East. In other words, it has the same political and moral value as the union of Aeneas and Lavinia.

The third element for comparison between the two texts is the motif of the journey. What the *Entrée* author seems to be doing is comparable to what Fulgentius did with the *Aeneid*: in his *Expositio virgilianae continentiae*, Fulgentius proposes to read Virgil's epic as a journey through human life, from an early age, through all the mistakes of adolescence, to maturity.[74] There is the possibility that Fulgentius' interpretation had served intellectuals throughout the Middle Ages as a means of understanding Virgil's epic as a sort of *Bildungsroman*.[75] In order to understand the image that the medieval readers had formed of the *Aeneid*, it is helpful to re-read the *Enéas* in the light of Fulgentius' interpretation.[76] The same can be done for the *Chanson*. The author of the *Entrée* re-reads the epic as a celebration of the whole life of the hero, which leads to the introduction of an impressive number of modifications to the character of Roland.

The *Chanson de Roland* provides a synchronic portrait of the hero by capturing one moment of his life, namely that of youth and *desmesure*, which inevitably results in his death. After the hero's death a fairly long section of the poem (1559 lines out of 4002) narrates Charlemagne's retaliation against Ganelon; the narrative is not entirely about the life of Roland, in fact, but can be viewed as a celebration of one single episode in Charlemagne's long struggle against the Arabs. The *Chanson de Roland* does not imply a journey at all, let alone a symbolic one through the life of the hero. Conversely, the *Entrée*'s most important innovation is the insertion

---

[74] Mora-Lebrun, *L'Enéide' médiévale*, p. 19.
[75] Mora-Lebrun, *L'Enéide' médiévale*, p. 117.
[76] Mora-Lebrun, *L'Enéide' médiévale*: '[...] relire le *Roman d'Enéas*, point de fuite vers lequel nous semble converger toute une tradition, à la fois poétique et exégétique, trés dense, et "miroir déformant" destiné à modifier durablement, par la suite, l'image que les médiévaux se sont forgée de l'Enéide [...] lui [Virgile] permettant de jouer un rôle actif dans les représentations mentales des clercs et même des laïcs médiévaux, et de contribuer à la naissance du roman' (p. 22).

of the motif of the Journey in the East, during which Roland is turned into a knight wandering the world to make justice triumph.

In the *Enéas* the journey is developed in two different ways. On the one hand there is Aeneas' trip from Troy to Italy, on the other his *katabasis* to the underworld by which he purifies his soul and can becomes the pious founder of a new civilisation. The journey in the *Enéas* is therefore understood as a physical action – a movement from one country to another, from the land of sin (Troy, where Helen was brought to marry an enemy) to the land of renewal (Rome, where Aeneas finally finds a new land to start his own lineage) – as well as a spiritual change from the warrior's state to that of the forefather and role-model.

In essence, the similarity between the *Entrée* and the *Enéas* is that the Franco-Venetian poem can be sharply divided into two parts, the first covering the epic section (properly defined), and the second (of which circa 5000 lines are unfortunately missing) dedicated to Roland's journey. In the first part, there are many hints of a detachment from what may be identified as pure epic. Numerous elements in the text lend themselves to a reading of the poem in the light of Italy's major political and societal changes during the thirteenth and fourteenth centuries. As far as a possible definition of genre is concerned, however, the poem's second part is the most significant. This section opens (or rather merges into the first) with a marvellous, almost cinematic fading of the image of Charlemagne, shifting to an entirely new and introspective portrayal of Roland's emotions as he aimlessly wanders abroad after his last violent meeting with the emperor (ll. 11127–37):

> Del trief s'en ist honteus et sospirant,
> El destrer monte, l'escu et l'aste prant,
> Les laces ferme de son heume luisant
> Ensi des host belement galopant.
> Quant fu defors, si s'an veit speronant:
> En stragne guise veult fer son vengemant.
> Honte le maine et hiror si grant
> Ne lui remambre d'ami ne de parant;
> Anz q'il retort, par le mien esciant,
> De lui veoir seront plus desirant
> François et Carles qe mer de son enfant.

Full of anger, Roland forgets friends and family and rides away. His vengeance consists in disappearing from the sight of all so that the French and the emperor will finally long to see him again and put aside the sad, violent episode. He rides for three days and then meets two felons whom he kills for threatening Baudor, the owner of the ship on which Roland embarks and which will take him to Syria. The owner is very kind and grateful to Roland for the service he has performed. He reassures Roland, who had never sailed before and looks sick (ll. 11800–02):

> 'Cun este vos ?' – fait il – 'quel penser vos demaine?
> N'aiés paor dou mer, car plus est la nef saine
> Au besoing qu'ele fait que au chaut la funtaine'.

Yet even as Roland is comforted his real worry surfaces (ll. 11814–20):

> Vait s'an la nef, char molt ot bons oraje.
> Mais tant vos di qe plus contre corage
> Non s'an parti Eneas de Cartaige,
> Chant alla quere la grant Sibille saige,
> Come Rolant soi mis en cels voyage,
> Remembrant lui qu'en la tere sauvaige
> Laisoit son oncle et le amoros bernayge.

A comparison is made here between Aeneas' mood when he fled from Carthage and Roland's when he left his uncle and the beloved French barons alone in the foreign land of Spain, fighting against the Saracens, to sail for an unknown land. It is a noteworthy comparison that establishes a link between Aeneas and Roland more through the feelings they have in common than their status as epic heroes. The shared element of love (respectively, for Dido, and for Charlemagne and the barons of France) reinforces this comparison. Furthermore, it is said that Roland set out upon his own journey just as Aeneas left in search of the great and wise Sybil ('Chant alla quere la grant Sibille sage'), who could be read as a metonymy for the whole land of Italy. The Sibyl could also be understood as a synonym for *voyage*, rhyming with her epithet of *saige* in the following line. Aeneas' journey is thus a pilgrimage to the oracle in search of his personal future rather than a real expedition to the lands that were to become the country of his offspring.[77] While the future of Aeneas' people is here temporarily left aside, the journey becomes Aeneas' completely individual odyssey in which the hero is alone with himself in order to solve the issue of his own future, without regard for those he has left behind. Roland's position is the same: he is sailing in search of himself, not knowing where and grieving for what he has left but at the same time determined to experience something different.

In support of this idea there is a place in the *Enéas* where the sibyl of Cuma is said to be *saige* (ll. 2284–87):

> Sebilla te porra conduire,
> une feme qui set d'anguire;
> de Comes est devineresse,
> moult par y a saige prestresse.

Aeneas is in the Elysian Fields and his father Anchises foretells his destiny. Again, in these prophetic lines the voyage is the central element, and the Sibyl appears as the protector of Aeneas' journey to the Promised Land.

A short digression on the nature of the Promised Land itself is needed here. Line 555 of the *Enéas* says: *en Lombardie est notre cors*, 'our heart is in Lombardy'. It is difficult to believe that the Italian reader of the twelfth century would have ignored this line and failed to see in the Trojans' promised land a legitimisation of the land of

---

[77] Bearing in mind the idea of the journey as a sort of soul-rescuing enterprise inherited from Platonic literature: according to Mora-Lebrun's analysis of the possible causes of a re-reading of the *Aeneid* and subsequent creation of the *Enéas*, Plato's *Timeus* and Macrobius' commentary to Cicero's *Somnium Scipionis* must have led to a different approach to the reading of the Latin epic. The motif of the journey in particular is the thread that tightly binds together the *Aeneid*, the *Timeus*, Fulgentius' interpretation, Macrobius' commentary, and the *Enéas*. There is a discernible evolution towards approaching the Latin epic as a journey of the human soul. The theme of the journey through the various stages of human life is very much present in Macrobius as it was in Plato, and becomes the leading idea in the interpretation of Virgil's poem. In this sea especially plays a dynamic role, being a metaphor of both the lost soul and the journey through adversities leading to the final goal. See also R. Guénon, *Simboli della scienza sacra*, transl. by F. Zambon (Milan: Adelphi, 1997), p. 297.

Italy. The latter's identification with the northern Italian territory in the *Enéas* must certainly have caught the attention of the thirteenth- and (above all) fourteenth-century reader. Given that Paduan humanism justified further research into the classical sources on the grounds that Padua was founded by Antenor,[78] it is reasonable to suppose that the equivalence of Italy and Lombardy in the *Enéas* would flatter its early northern readers, and later increasingly so as identification with their ancestors was felt more strongly, above all due to political reasons. Furthermore the author of the *Entrée* identifies a particular region of Italian territory with the term *Lombardie* – precisely the one bordering France where the *Enéas* is most likely to have circulated at least in the earliest stage of its dissemination. The *Entrée* author gives the topographical identifiers of this region in a passage where he displays a quite precise knowledge of early medieval history (ll. 662–64):

> Un autre en envoia Disirer de Pavie,
> Qe tient Millans et Brisse et tote Lombardie,
> Qe la mer de Venese gard bien vers Sclavonie

Desiderius was the eighth-century king of Pavia and the father of Ermengarda, whom he married to Charlemagne to establish an alliance which eventually failed. There is also another mention of the Lombards towards the end of the *Entrée* ('Ne la prendroit por forche li Lombart de Pavie', l. 14660), referring again specifically to Pavia.

A connection between lines 11816–18 of the *Entrée* and 2284–87 of the *Enéas,* and the motifs that these lines convey (the reference to Lombardy as the Promised Land in the *Entrée* and the identity of Sibyl with Italy in the *Enéas*), suggest that the *roman* rather than any intermediary text could have been the *Entrée* poet's primary source. Indeed, Lombardy is the region where the author lived at least the second half of his life. After a fierce battle, Pavia was taken by Matteo Visconti in 1315. This was the first land subjected to the Visconti rule and the start of the military supremacy over Milan's

---

[78] Cfr. G. Billanovich, *La tradizione del testo di Livio e le origini dell'Umanesimo*, 2 vols (Padua: Antenore, 1986), I: 1st p.; G. Billanovich, 'Il preumanesimo padovano', in Folena, ed., *Storia della Cultura Veneta*, II: 19–110.

surroundings which eventually gave birth to the family's powerful lordship. Therefore, it is no wonder that the *Entrée* should mention and take such great account of Desiderius, the almost legendary king of Pavia. Through the mention of this historical figure the author seemingly wants to establish a direct connection between Charlemagne and the Visconti, since the French emperor married the daughter of the Lombard king and the Visconti having conquered the town succeeded to Desiderius' lineage.

As Jacques Monfrin and Limentani accepted, the dissemination of the *Enéas* involved different regions of Europe from the one where the author lived. However, it is quite difficult to deny that a romance with such a strong impact on its readers, mainly for its great innovation in matters of style, was completely forgotten at the time of the *Entrée*'s composition. Although it appears hard to argue with Limentani's work, it must therefore be said that details such as those analysed here permit a re-consideration of the nature of classical influences in the *Entrée*.

The matter of Troy

The *Entrée* reflects the fourteenth-century tendency to refer to the matter of Rome and Troy as *romans*, as line 14915 testifies. Having returned to Spain and on his way back to Charlemagne's campaign, Roland encounters Samson the hermit who tells him the story of his troubled life and of the Saracen assaults he had had to withstand. He describes the Saracens to Roland using expressions of wonder at their enormous size and strength, and by comparing them to the giants in the stories of Rome and Troy (ll. 14912–17):

> Se tu fuses venus por mi les mors gisans,
> En veor le mervoile des tostes caup tinans,
> Tu bien avroies dit de croire les romans
> E de Rome e de Troie e dou tens ancians
> E qu'il fust verité la force des jaians,
> D'Erculés e d'Antheu e de Febus le grans.

The hermit refers to the matter of Rome and Troy as *romans*, and through a synecdoche he calls them *romans d'antiquité*. The distinction between romance and classical epic (as discussed above) will explain the hermit's choice of term. The author's definition of the matter by its genre is also suggestive variously of its transmission, of how the author came to know it, or of his preference for reading it in the form of romances rather that in the original. His statement very much sounds a reflection of a twelfth-century attitude; and while the use of the word *roman* probably only signifies 'story', 'lengthy matter' or 'cycle' in a general sense not exclusive to epic,[79] the author both here and in many other parts of his poem displays an attitude halfway between medieval and humanistic. Elsewhere the poet specifically states that his information on the Trojan War is based on Dares, whether on his own text or Benoît's translation.[80]

In the passage seen above the poet generally refers to a number of *romans d'antiquité*, covering the matter of Rome, Troy, and more vaguely *dou tens ancians* (possibly the *Alexandre* and the *Thèbes*). In the second part of the quotation there is a mention of the giants with particular reference to *Erculés, Antheu* and *Febus le grans* (l. 14917). As the *Entrée* author makes only a very vague, general reference to a whole range of literature in which a reader could presumably find accounts of stories about the giants, it would be possible to include Ovid, Lucan, Statius, and Virgil (i.e. epic) alongside the twelfth-century *romans d'antiquité*. Certainly, of all the *romans d'antiquité* the one circulating most widely was the *Roman de Troie*.[81] Comparing the dissemination of the *Enéas* with that of the *Troie*, it is in fact striking that the *Troie* is found in five Italian manuscripts (two from the area dominated by the Gonzaga, one from Milan, one from Florence and one from Naples)[82] whereas

[79] In the same fashion, the word *latin/latiner* (ll. 5843, 6021) only means comprehensible language or to speak in/translate into a comprehensible language, and not what we mean and understand by this word today.

[80] See laisse DXXXVIII. Dares the Phrygian and Dictys of Crete claimed that they witnessed the Trojan war, and that Homer reported only a part of it and as second-hand information: *Dictis Cretensis ephemeridos belli Troiani libri*, ed. by W. Eisenhut (Leipzig: Teubner, 1958); *Daretis Phrygii de excidio Troiae historia*, ed. by F. Meister (Leipzig: Teubner, 1873). Benôit, although acknowledging that Homer was marvellous, wise, and a scientist, preferred to follow the Dares/Dictys tradition.

[81] Benoît, *Roman de Troie*, ed. Constans.

[82] Venice: Biblioteca Nazionale Marciana, MS fr. Z. 17 (=230); Venice: Biblioteca Nazionale Marciana, MS fr. Z. 18 (=231) (this also contains *Hector et Hercule*); Milan: Biblioteca Ambrosiana, MS D. 55. sup.; Florence: Biblioteca Riccardiana, MS 2433 (which also contains the

LITERARY INFLUENCES

only one Italian manuscript of the *Enéas* survives. This can be explained by the fact that the Italians were interested in the events of the Trojan War which led both Aeneas and Antenor to escape from it and become the respective founders of Rome and Padua.

In the *Troie*, a long section is dedicated to Hercules' part in Jason's expedition to Colchis, and a general reference to the Greek hero's many labours, particularly to his killing many a coward giant (ll. 805–10):

> Jason i fu e Herculés,
> Cil qui sostint maint pesant fés
> E mainte gran merveille fist
> E maint felon jaiant ocist
> E les bones iluec ficha
> Ou Alisandre les trova.

Yet there is no particular mention of his eleventh labour,[83] to fetch the golden apples of the Garden of the Hesperides. On the long and difficult journey to the garden, he had a number of adventures among which was wrestling with the giant Antaeus, whom he lifted high in the air and crushed to death.[84] By contrast, the single mention of giants in the *Enéas* is the episode of Hercules and Cacus.

A key to interpreting the following passage of the *Entrée* (ll. 4256–60) is offered by the word *labor*, used by the author as a metonymy for the duel. This suggests a comparison with Hercules' labours, although the word for labour in the *Troie* is *fès* (l. 806).

> Voer poez l'impossible labor,
> Ch'ancué est mort por la quaile l'astor;

Hector et Hercule); Naples: Biblioteca Nazionale Vittorio Emanuele III, MS XIII. C. 38.

[83] Cfr. L. Constans, '*L'Entrée d'Espagne* et les légendes troyennes', p. 431.

[84] Sources for this episode are Ovid (*Ibis* 393 ff.; a brief mention in *Metamorphoses* 9.183–84); Lucan (*Pharsalia*, 4.590 ff.); Statius (*Thebais*, 6.893 ff.). The editions consulted for this study are: Publius Ovidius Naso [Ovid], *Ibis*, ed. by A. La Penna (Florence: la Nuova Italia, 1957); Ovid, *Metamorphoses*, ed. Anderson; Marcus Annaeus Lucanus [Lucan], *Pharsalia - La guerra civile*, ed. by R. Badalì (Turin: UTET, 1988); Publius Papinius Statius [Statius], *Thebais*, ed. and transl. by G. Faranda Villa (Milan: Rizzoli, 1998).

> Non merveilez, car je vi ja, seignor,
> Dui escoler de dui escrimaor:
> L'uns estoit grant e l'autre asez menor.

The matter of Troy as told in Italy in the thirteenth and fourteenth centuries, both in Latin and the vernacular, depended principally on the *Troie*. The most important case is Guido delle Colonne's Latin prose version of the *Roman de Troie*.[85] Guido tells us how Hercules 'by his might slew an infinite number of giants in his day and crushed the very strong Antaeus, holding him up in the air in his arms and rendering him lifeless in an unbearable embrace'.[86]

A brief reference must also be made to the Franco-Italian *Cantare d'Hector et Hercule* dating to the beginning of the fourteenth century.[87] This text proves to be very interesting since a few details

---

[85] Guido delle Colonne, *Historia destructionis Troiae*, completed in November of 1287, as the author states in the epilogue. Guido bases his account on Benoît but abridges the *Troie* and inserts inventions of his own. He also refers several times to Ovid (*Metamorphoses* and *Heroides*) as a source. His work is representative of the medieval knowledge of the matter of Troy and was immediately accepted as history because based on the tradition of Dares and Dictys, at the time generally considered the most reliable sources.

[86] Guido delle Colonne, *Historia*, ed. Meek, 1.70–72.

[87] J. Palermo, *Le roman d'Hector et d'Hercule. Chant épique en octosyllabes italo-français* (Geneva: Droz, 1972); J. Palermo, 'L'Hector et Hercule franco-italien. Chant épique ou romans courtois?', in Limentani et al., eds, *Essor et fortune*, II: 729–36. This very short epic poem recounts the episode of the death of Hercules, not according to the classical version as found in the Dares/Benoît tradition but as an independent development in which Hector accomplishes the revenge desired by Priamus. In fact, this episode is unknown in the tradition of the Troy legend, and the theme of revenge was only anticipated in Dares (ed. Meister, pp. 8, 14–19) and then in Benoît (ed. Constans, ll. 3772–78). According to J. Palermo, the text bears a number of features which can help to date a French original on which the Franco-Italian version is supposedly based (pp. 49–51). E. Gorra, *Testi inediti* (Turin: Trevirio, 1869), on the other hand, maintains that there is enough textual evidence to suggest that this development is entirely an Italian invention (pp. 273–74). His argument is supported by the fact that all five extant manuscripts in which the poem is found were produced in Italy. In three of them it appears either before or after the *Roman de Troie*, ensuring its circulation and survival. A critical analysis of these

LITERARY INFLUENCES

recall the characterisation of Hector and Hercules in the *Entrée*. For example, Hercules in this *cantare* is referred to as a giant while he lays siege to the city of Termachi to punish Laomedon (ll. 31–36):

> Si vos dirai, se oïr voudrés,
> Com le jeiant, dan Herculés,
> Le fort, le fiers; le sourpouissant,
> A grant esfors de garnimanz,
> A force asigia Phyleminis,
> Dedans le murs de son päis.

Another occurrence is when Hector feels sorrow upon seeing the dead giant Hercules who was so valiant and strong (ll. 1411–13):

> Quant Hector vit le jeiant mort
> Qui tant fu ardiz, vaillanz et fort,
> A grant mervoille fist dur lament.

This recalls verse 14917 of the *Entrée* where the author refers to 'la force des jaians | D'Erculés e d'Antheu'. In this verse, he seemingly takes it for granted that Hercules was a giant just like those he fought. A mere association of ideas might have led the author to refer to both Hercules and Febus as giants although it is likely that he did so by the inspiration of this *cantare*.

Furthermore, in the *cantare* it is said that Hector's sword was called *Duranda*,[88] *Durindal*,[89] and *Durindarda*,[90] establishing a very clear connection with Roland. The tradition then continues in the *Aspromonte, Li fatti di Spagna, Libro di Troiam*, and *Troiano a stampa*, then in Boiardo and generally in the subsequent Italian tradition.[91] In the latter the direct correspondence of Roland with

---

> three manuscripts would help identify the manuscript of the Troie used by the *Entrée* poet. The *Hector et Hercule* is uniquely preserved in its Franco-Italian form which testifies to the strong tendency to value the Trojans over the Greeks, fashionable in thirteenth- and fourteenth-century Italy, as widely discussed in this chapter.

[88] Paris: Bibliothèque nationale de France, MS fr. 821, ff. 1r–12v; Venice: Biblioteca Nazionale Marciana, MS fr. Z. 18 (=231), ff. 143r–152v.

[89] Florence: Biblioteca Riccardiana, MS 2433, ff. 1r–13v.

[90] Oxford: Bodleian Library, MS Canonici Misc. 450, ff. 120v–171v.

[91] Jung, *La légende de Troie*, pp. 614–15.

Hector is therefore an established *topos* starting from this *cantare*, and the *Entrée* is no exception. Although in the poem there is no mention of Hector's sword, the comparison between the two heroes is implied in a different way.

Hector is characterised as *bon* in the following lines of the *Entrée*: 'Pires feit de vos homes, ou le brant q'il manoie, | Ne fesoit de Greçois le bon Hector de Troie' (ll. 8814–15). In the *Troie* there is a precise reference to his goodness with Hector many times said to be wise and brave (e.g. ll. 3760, 3771, 4138). Below are two examples of how Benoît displays such a great attachment to the figure of Hector that the hero appears the model of all virtues (ll. 5309–17):

> Hector ot non l'aynz né des fiz:
> Onques plus prouz ne fu norriz.
> Tant fist de sei, tant ot bonté,
> Toz jors en sera mais parlé.
> Des Troïens li pluz ardiz
> Esteit sans faille Hector sis fiz.
> Des Troiens? Voire del mont,
> De ceus qui furent ne qui sunt,
> Ne qui ja mais jor deivent estre

Guido delle Colonne refers to Hector as 'a knight of unheard-of valour, aggressive and courageous'[92] and provides a full physical and moral description outlining the profile of a hero.[93]

The character of Hector appears very frequently in the *Entrée* in which Roland is often compared with the Trojan, especially during the duel between Ferragu and Roland. Ferragu is there compared to Achilles, and this reinforces the idea of the two characters as worst enemies. When interrogated by Ferragu about his best friend, Oliver describes Roland's valour by way of a meaningful comparison (ll. 2062, 2412–3):

---

[92] Guido delle Colonne, *Historia*, ed. Meek, 5.55–56.
[95] Guido delle Colonne, *Historia*, ed. Meek, 8.212–21.

> Bien le poüt Hector tenire por frer.
> Ne fu si proz le bon Hector de Troie
> Com il se tint, par Dié que tot sorpoie.

Hector also appears later in the text in a more general reference: 'Le jor fu a François tiel ardimant creü | N'a cil ne se preisast Hector et Troylu' (ll. 8953–54).

It would seem that Priam and his sons are the author's favourite characters. Following a tendency common in Italy in that century (and also witnessed by Dante)[94] the author's preference is for the Trojans, which is explained by Aeneas being the mythic father of the land of Italy and founder of the Roman Empire. As we have seen, the Empire is identified by the *Entrée* author with the land of Lombardy, and the tradition of Antenor as the founder of Padua was highly influential in the early humanistic environment to which the poem is closely connected. The fact that Ferragu is characterised as Achilles draws an especial distinction between the two warring parties: the French are the Trojans and the Saracens are the Greeks. His open preference for the Trojans is seen in laisse DXXXVIII, for example, dedicated to the account of Troy as related by Dares (l. 12471). Here, Pélias' sword is compared to Achilles', who killed the good Troilus *villainement* (ll. 12464–82):

> Ce fu la spie dun Acilés tua
> Le bon Troillus, que Prian engendra;
> Villainement l'oucist et asauta:
> Paris, son frere, puis aprés le venja
> Qant il li darç au tenple li lança
> A celui jor que il parlamenta;
> Pollisinan a fame avor cuda:
> Daire le conte, qui ce autoriça.
> Cil cinst la spie, que plus non demora.
> Li roi, son oncle, un eume li laça:
> Le buens Hetor en beson le porta,
> Protesillas oncist et devia
> Q'al port de Troie primerament entra;

---

[94] See G. Padoan, *Il pio Enea, l'empio Ulisse* (Ravenna: Longo, 1977), pp. 170–99.

> De celle mort sa fame devina,
> Al departir assés le castoia;
> Non l'en veust croire, d'un mal in acheva;
> Hetor l'oucist et l'eume gaagna.
> Cist Pellias en son chief le ferma;
> Qant oit ce feit, son ceval demanda.

This episode is highly elaborate. The comparison between Pélias' and Achilles' swords establishes a parallel between the two characters. Its final comparison between the helmets of Pélias and of Protesilaus (which Hector gains when he kills him) not only reinforces the idea that the Saracen is a counterpart to the evil Greeks but also anticipates the fate of Pélias, who will be killed by Roland/Hector. The beauty of this laisse lies in its ability to render, via an articulated metaphor, the contrast between Pélias' arrogance and his final punishment.

In this laisse, the author states as clearly as possible that he gathered his knowledge of classical matter from Dares. One may read between the lines that he simply accepted the version of Benoît (who famously based his account on Dares); it has also been suggested that the author himself might have read a copy of the *Histoire ancienne*.[95] This idea was discussed by Limentani,[96] and the first option in fact seems more reasonable since Guido delle Colonne behaves in precisely the same way as the author of the *Entrée*[97], never mentioning Benoît.

Thus passage 12464–82 of the *Entrée* provides evidence of the author's preferring the Benoît/Dares tradition,[98] present also in

---

[95] Constans, '*L'Entrée d'Espagne* et les légendes troyennes', pp. 430–32.
[96] See p. 53.
[97] Guido has in fact been seen as a plagiarist by A. Joly, *Benoît de Saint-Maure et le 'Roman de Troie' ou les métamorphoses d'Homère et l'épopée gréco-latine au Moyen Âge*, 2 vols (Paris: Franck, 1870–71), I: 447–55 and Gorra, *Testi inediti*, p. 147. However, as M. E. Meek explains in the introduction to Guido delle Colonne, *Historia*, he never claimed to have translated Dares and Dictys (pp. xvii–xiv and n. 15). The prologue to his account is indeed quite obscure and only refers to his preference for the Dares/Dictys tradition.
[98] A negative portrait of Achilles is found in *Troie* XXV.

LITERARY INFLUENCES

Guido delle Colonne,[99] to the version found in book XII of the *Ovide moralisé*. The author of the *Ovide moralisé* inserted accounts from the Trojan cycle in books VII, XI, XII,[100] and (rarely for his time) refuted the Dares/Dictys tradition, claiming Homer as a more reliable source.[101]

The episode as described in *Ovide moralise* XII reads as follows (ll. 1710–35):

> Achilles, li vaillans de pris,
> Est ja venus à la bataille.
> Des or comenceront, sans faille,
> L'ocision et le martire,
> La grant estoire et la matire
> Que traist li clers de Saint More
> De Darès, mes ne m'en vueil ore
> Sor lui de gaires entremetre
> Là où bien translata la letre.
> Moult fu li clers bons rimoierres,
> Cortois parliers et biaus faigtierres,
> Et moult fu bien ses romans fais,
> Mes nequedent, sauve sa pais,
> Il ne dist pas en touz leuz voir,
> Si ne fist mie grant savoir
> Dont il Homers osa desdire
> Ne desmentir ne contredire
> Ne blasmer oeuvre qu'il feïst.
> Ne cuit c'onques Homers deïst
> Chose que dire ne deüst
> Et que de verté ne seüst.
> Ja nel deüst avoir repris,
> Quar trop iert Homers de grant pris,

---

[99] Guido delle Colonne, *Historia*, ed. Meek, 24, 25.

[100] For the developments in book XII the anonymous author of the *Ovide moralisé* used the *Ilias latina* as a source: *Baebii Italici Ilias latina*, ed. by M. Scaffai (Bologna: Pàtron, 1997); see Jung, *La Légende de Troie*, pp. 621 ff.

[101] On the defence of Homer by the author of the *Ovide moralisé* against Benoît's statement, see Benoît, *Roman de Troie*, ed. Constans, VI, pp. 262 ff. See also Jung, *La Légende de Troie*, p. 622 and n. 1.

> Mes il parla par metaphore.
> Por ce li clers de Sainte More,
> Qui n'entendoit qu'il voloit dire,
> Li redargua sa matire.

Apart from the two differing viewpoints as to Dares' reliability, it is notable that both passages begin by mentioning Achilles. This should be sufficient to clarify which version of the story of Troy the poet preferred; in the *Entrée* Achilles is a villain who killed the good Troilus, whereas for the compiler of the *Ovide moralisé* he is *vaillant* ('valorous').

Although Priam and his sons are the classical figures for whom the poet displays an open preference, comparisons between the characters of the *Entrée* and classical heroes occur quite often in a rather random way. There is no precise intent to allocate a classical character's distinctive traits to one in the *Entrée*, which would allow one to interpret the poem as resurrecting classical heroes in the guise of medieval knights. Rather, the author makes an occasional comparison between a trait or the behaviour of one character and the corresponding one of a classical hero. In this way Roland is sometimes compared with Aeneas, at other times with Hector (and occasionally with yet others), so that Roland's entire character seems to result from the fusion of signature traits of various heroes of the classical tradition.

Similarly, the author does not distinguish between historical and mythological figures, also typical of his sources such as the *romans d'antiquité* as well as of literature contemporary with the *Entrée*.[102] If one closely compares the two passages below, one finds that the Trojan War is treated by the *Entrée* author as a historical fact and its protagonists as real historical figures (ll. 5575–58, 8689–90):

> Non d'autre guisse al doloros estor
> Le mostra Anibal, quant il oit la pejor
> Encontre Scipion, de Rome condutor.

---

[102] A discussion of history and myth in Guido delle Colonne, for example, is found in Meek's introduction to Guido delle Colonne, *Historia*, pp. xv–xix. For a discussion of history and myth in Dante, see G. Brugnoli, *Studi danteschi*, 3 vols (Pisa: ETS, 1998–1999), I: 141 ff.; E. Paratore, *Nuovi saggi danteschi* (Rome: Signorelli, 1973).

> Deci au tens Ector et dou maine Alexandre
> Deüst estre proisez de lui un asez maindre.

Time based on historical events is confused with a vaguer idea of the past, in which figures who contributed to the making of the Roman and Hellenistic empires are placed on the same level as mythological characters. The effect is surreal. The two extremities of Greek history are given: on one side Hector, a representative of the remotest Greek past; on the other Alexander, symbol of Greece's ultimate supremacy. The author does not treat Hector as the hero of a tale but as an actual historical figure on a par with Alexander. This lends further support to the argument that the *Entrée* author used Benoît as a source, since the *Troie* is based on the account of Dares and therefore on a supposedly historically reliable source. Just as the poet makes no distinction between mythological heroes and historical figures, so he also considers the past as a whole without any sense of time as separating the lives of history's great figures: 'Jusque au tens Cesarie et dou magne Alexandre' (l. 9919).

In characterising Ferragu as Achilles, the author is also quite consistent. Before the episode of the duel, when the French are still considering Ferragu's strength and have not yet decided how they should proceed against him, Gerard clashes with him in the forest. He falls from his horse and Ferragu spares his life (ll. 1301–08):

> Le ber Gerarz lors chiet en mie l'erboi;
> Le chief oit nuz, dont il forment s'esfroie.
> Cil treit l'espee, sor le duc la paumoie.
> 'Rend toi', dist il, 'c'oncir ne te voldroie;
> Prodom me senbles; trop repris en seroie.
> S'ensi non fais, a noiant m'en teroie
> S'a uns seul colp – se je ma main t'envoie-
> Ne t'oncesis, se fus Hector de Troie'.

The closing line introduces the comparison of Feragu with Achilles, and of Gerard with Achilles' worst enemy, Hector. On offer is a double classical reference for the duel-episode: on the one hand, Ferragu's reportedly being a giant and the duel's definition as *labor* (l. 4257) allows the reader to make a connection with the episode of Hercules and Cacus; on the other, Ferragu resembles Achilles because of the physical vulnerability that likewise causes the Saracen to be defeated, and because of his fierceness in battle.

In *Metamorphoses* 12, Achilles is said to be *perosus* (l. 582), *ferox* and *populator* (ll. 592–93). At the end of the book Ovid also adds a touch of negative characterisation when he says that: 'iam cinis est, et de tam magno restat Achille nescio quid, parvam quod non bene compleat urnam' (ll. 615–16). Ovid's final judgment on Achilles is harsh. Ever since Homer's depiction of the hero, Achilles had been perceived as the strongest of the Greek warriors and the one essential for the victory against Troy; driven by his own rage he destroys the city. Virgil says that the son of Achilles kills men at the altars (referring to the great cruelty of Pyrrhus against the Trojans; *Aeneid* 2.662–63), although before that Pyrrhus lies utterly when he calls Achilles his father, because Achilles had respected the rights of the suppliant (ll. 540–43). In *Metamorphoses* 12, a difference is made between the two depicted aspects of Aeneas, *furor* and *pietas*, and a third, *saevitas*, belonging to many Greek heroes and gods but not Aeneas; '*Saevus* conveys a natural fierceness most commonly seen in battle'[103]. Although Virgil uses this adjective only once to describe Aeneas' cruelty in battle, *pius* and *ferox* are usually the two words that apply to the Trojan and by which he was known in the Middle Ages. Achilles is on the list of *saevi*, those heroes whose cruelty surpassed their fairness.

Ovid's depiction of Achilles probably functioned as a vehicle for the medieval reception of the hero's figure since his poem circulated widely and influenced much of the poetic production of the period. It is thus not unlikely that Achilles' personality was understood at the time of the *Entrée*'s composition as that of a fierce and vengeful man, principally motivated by rage and without pity for his enemies.[104]

---

[103] C. J. Mackie, *The Characterisation of Aeneas* (Edinburgh: Scottish Academic Press, 1988), p. 190.

[104] What remains of Achilles before the rediscovery of Homer's text is what the medieval reader could gather from Virgil, Ovid, Statius (author of an Achilleis of which only 1100 hexameters remain), the *Roman de Troie* by Benoît de Saint-Maure, and the *Ilias latina* by Baebus Italicus. Statius' work only describes the episode of Achilles at Skyros, and his education: O. A. W. Dilke, *Statius' 'Achilleis'* (Cambridge: Cambridge University Press, 1954).

In the *Troie*, the depiction of Achilles is contained in a short sketch, and little is said in the romance about his fierceness in battle (ll. 5157–70):

> Achillés fu de grant biautié:
> Gros ot le piz, espés e lié,
> E les menbres granz e pleniers,
> Les oilz el chief ardiz e fiers;
> Crespes cheveus ot, s'iert aubornes.
> Ne fu mie pensis ne mornes;
> La chiere aveit liee e joiose,
> Envers son enemi irose.
> Larges esteit e despensers
> E mout amez de chevaliers.
> Grant pris aveit d'armes porter:
> A peine trovast hon son per.
> Mout iert hardiz e corajous
> E de victoire coveitos.

The *Ovide moralisé* and the *Troie* differ as far as their positions on the facts of Troy are concerned. Further evidence suggests that in most cases the *Entrée*'s author drew his inspiration from the *Troie*. For example, there are two mentions of Penthesileia in the *Entrée*, both referring to the aid given Priam by the Amazon in the Trojan War as an obligation for having purified her from the bloodguilt of killing a fellow Amazon, Antiope. The single brief mention of Penthesileia in *Metamorphoses* is in 12.611, referring to her slaughter by Achilles and which is not mentioned in the *Entreé*. Rather, the *Entrée*'s first mention focuses on Penthesileia's sword: 'Çante oit l'espee que fu Pantasilie, | Cele qi vint as Troiens en aÿe' (ll. 8499–500). Benoît dedicates a long paragraph to Penthesileia's intervention in the Trojan war (ll. 23357–24376). Two passages in this long section of the *Troie* are relevant to the analysis of the references found in the *Entrée* (ll. 23449–51, 23621–23):

> [...] Sans plus targier
> A ceint le brant forbi d'acier
> Dom el ferra granz coups maneis.
> Merveilles fet Panteselee:

> Ja n'i ferra coup de l'espee
> Q'un n'en ocie. [...]

The emphasis here is on the strength of her sword; Guido delle Colonne also refers twice to Penthesileia's sword.[105]

The second passage focuses on what is either Penthesileia's slowness or loyalty in going to help the Trojans (ll. 9686–88):

> Unques plus leement ne vint Pantesillan,
> la dame de Maçonie, an aider li Troian,
> Com il vint en Espaigne por trover Carleman.

If *leement* is to be read as *lentement*, the extreme slowness of the queen's intervention can only be explained by the fact that it came only when the war was almost lost, after Hector's death. However, *leement* could also be read as *loiaument* (loyally), in which case Guido delle Colonne can again be of help. Guido says that Penthesileia went to fight in Troy and help king Priam because of her great love for Hector.[106] Furthermore, the passage from the *Entrée* is taken from a dialogue in which Ogier assures an Arab that the Sultan will come to rescue the Saracens of Spain within a year; thus, the comparison would make little sense if *leement* were understood as 'slowly'.

Benoît says that the Amazons had Arab horses ('De bons chevals arrabiens', l. 23373) and that the queen rode a good Spanish horse ('un cheval d'Espagne bei', l. 23440). Apart from the absurd anachronism of Amazons riding Arab or Spanish horses, this detail also suggests a link with the Arab world through the exotic nature of Penthesileia, being a warrior and from a strange land. This is reinforced when the poet defines her as a *dame de Maçonie*, which could be understood as a corruption of *Amazonie*[107] but also as deriving from Maçon, the Saracen idol. As the Amazons become women of the land of Maçon, a linguistic link is thus established

---

[105] Guido delle Colonne, *Historia*, ed. Meek, 28.113; 28.119.
[106] Guido delle Colonne, *Historia*, ed. Meek, 28.26–29.
[107] Guido delle Colonne, following Benoît, says that Penthesileia lived in a region called 'Amazonia' (Guido delle Colonne, *Historia*, ed. Meek, 28.10).

between these extraordinary creatures and the Arab world.[108] At the close of feudalism, the Amazons were in fact among the many attractions for historical knights in undertaking the great adventure in the East (and were still believed to be located there as late as the sixteenth century). Despite the *Entrée*'s invaluable acknowledgments of its population and customs, its East thus remains populated by strange creatures like the Amazons, experts in magic and astrology like Dionés, or giants possessing exaggerated physical characteristics. Whatever belongs with wonder belongs with the Saracen world.[109]

While Limentani attributed the *Entrée*'s restitution to a milieu of highly culturally committed scholars and poets, it seems that by indicating the extent and quality of classical citations the *Entrée* preserves an anti-humanistic approach; its author follows the Dares/Dictys tradition, regardless of the discussion provoked by the author of the *Ovide moralisé*.[110] Thus it would appear more likely

[108] *Machonerie* (*Entrée*, l. 2148), meaning 'all the Saracen gods', is the hostile definition of the Saracen Pantheon. Differing from Old French *maçon* ('stoneworker' or 'brick-layer'), *Macon* and *Maçon* are found throughout the *Entrée* as corruptions of *Machon*, which is derived from *Machomet*, an alternative name for Mohammed (Mahomet): see ll. 2149, 2242, 2950, 4324, 4411, 11855, 12790, 12845, etc.

[109] The sources from which Benoît takes his information about the Amazons were texts also used for the same episode in the *Alexandre*, namely Julius Valerius' *Historia* and the *Historia de Preliis*: Faral, *Recherches sur les sources latines*, pp. 372–78; A. Petit, 'Le Traitement courtois du thème des Amazones d'après trois romans antiques: *Enéas*, *Troie* et *Alexandre*', *Le Moyen Âge*, 89 (1983), 63–84. The name of Penthesileia only occurs in classical sources that the *Entrée* author is very unlikely to have read, i.e. The Epic Cycle, Proclus' summary of the Aethiopis, Apollodorus' *Epitome*, Diodorus Siculus, Pausanias, Quintus of Smyrna: J. March, ed., *Dictionary of Classical Mythology* (London: Cassell, 2000), p. 310. Moreover, apart from the quotation in *Aeneid* 11.659 and the brief mention in *Metamorphoses*, very few of the classical sources mention the Amazons. It seems reasonable to conclude, once again, that information about Penthesileia could have reached the author through his reading of Benoît and of the *Alexandre*.

[110] It is well known that Petrarch and Boccaccio were the first two poets to display a deep interest in reading Homer in the original, and Boccaccio particularly contributed to the dissemination of the knowledge of the Greek language in Italy. E. G. Parodi, 'L'Odissea nella poesia medievale', in *Poeti antichi e moderni* (Florence: Sansoni, 1923), discussed and disagreed with the possibility that Homer could have

that the *Entrée*'s environment was one which still considered Benoît and the Latin summaries of the *Iliad* and *Odyssey* as reliable and sufficient sources. Moreover, the Trojan cycle in the Middle Ages retained an exotic quality that made it appealing to a larger public. The *Roman de Troie* is so successful in capturing that adventurous quality that it should be considered the source, until the first half of the fourteenth century, for the majority of what a medieval poet could gather about Homer's works.

Most of the *Entrée* material that is derived from the *Ovide moralisé* refers to the accounts of the Trojan cycle in books VII, XI

---

been known as early as the eleventh century. A discussion of how the author of the *Liber miraculorum sanctae Fidis* (attributed to Bernard of Anger) could have known the *Odyssey* is found in C. Fauriel, *Histoire de la poésie provençale* (Paris: J. Labitte, 1846; repr. Geneva: Slatkine, 1969), pp. 435 ff. See *Liber miraculorum sanctae Fidis*, ed. by L. Robertini (Spoleto: Centro italiano di studi sull'alto medioevo, 1994). Fauriel's conclusion was that the imitation of Homer in the *Liber miraculorum* was nothing but traditional memory stemming from the times when the *Iliad* and the *Odyssey* were taught in schools of Greek – schools that in Gaul lasted until the fourth or even fifth century. F. Settegast, 'Die Odyssee oder die Sage vom heimkehrenden Gatten als Quelle mittelalterlicher Dichtung', *Zeitschrift für romanische Philologie*, 39 (1918), 267–329, researched the traces left by Ulysses in medieval poems and romances in *langue d'oïl*. Parodi did not agree with the conclusions of Settegast and preferred to quote evidence from Hugo von Trimberg, *Registrum multorum auctorum* (c. 1280), who maintained that 'apud Graecos remanens nondum est translatus'. As Parodi points out, all knowledge of Homer in the Middle Ages can be reduced to the following works: one episode in Virgil (*Aeneid* 3: Polifemus), one episode in Ovid (*Metamorphoses* 14: Macareus), the *Ilias latina* or *Pindarus thebanus* by Baebus Italicus (a summary of the *Iliad* in 1070 hexameters), and the *Periochae Homeri Iliadis et Odyssiae* attributed to Ausonius which is a brief book-by-book summary of the poems. According to Parodi, medieval poets also knew Hyginus' *Fabulae* in which numbers CXXV and CXXVI (namely *Odyssea* and *Ulixis cognitio*) are brief but faithful summaries of the *Odyssey*, at times preserving even episodes omitted in the *Periochae* (pp. 70–71). The *Histoire ancienne* needs to be added to all the works that Parodi refers to, being the most important of all sources. Furthermore, Dante maintains that 'Omero non si mutò di greco in latino, come l'altre scritture che avemo da loro' (*Convivio*, I, VII, 15).

LITERARY INFLUENCES 85

and XII. Deserving of a separate mention are two passages which testify to Ovid's direct influence upon the author.[111]

One contains a reference to Laomedon in line 5686:

> Non fu plus rice de tresors de Laumedon
> Come tu is de noble cousençon.

In *Metamorphoses* 7, Ovid remembers that the Argonauts, returning from their expedition, sacked Troy and killed Laomedon, a reference which could be derived from Ovid. Laomedon in the Latin source is notorious for his meanness, and Ovid refers to the Trojan king as 'perfidiae cumulum', one who 'addit falsis periuria verbis' (*Metamorphoses* 11.205–6).[112] The allusion to Laomedon's wealth could be derived from the verse 'opesque | abstulit agricolis et fluctibus obruit agros' (11.209–10).

In another part of the poem, Charlemagne accuses Roland of treachery when left alone to face a Saracen siege while Roland has independently started a fresh enterprise. He compares Roland with Peleus who sent his nephew Jason to die in Colchis (ll. 9291–93):

> 'Jameis tiel traïsuns, plus orible ni fiere
> Ne fist rois Peleüs, q'envoia por la mere
> Ses niés Jason a mort an l'isle Qalcantiere'.

These lines can only be derived from Ovid. In fact, one must exclude the possibility that this infomation could be derived directly from Apollonius Rhodius. The episode is found in *Metamorphoses* 7.1–397 and in *Heroides* 6.12, and recounts Jason's expedition to Colchis. It could also be derived from Ovid via Guido delle Colonne, as Guido reports the episode referring directly to Metamorphoses 7.[113] It is an interesting choice for a reference, possibly made unconsciously, as the role reversal between the uncle

---

[111] For the knowledge of Ovid in medieval Italy see Everson, *The Italian Romance Epic*, pp. 75–79.
[112] Guido delle Colonne (who admittedly follows Ovid in the account of Jason's expedition) refers to Laomedon as 'ruler of his kingdom and king of the Trojans', but not to his wealth (Guido delle Colonne, *Historia*, ed. Meek, 2.57; 2.67; 2.79).
[113] Guido delle Colonne, *Historia*, ed. Meek, 1.16–18; 1.98–105.

and nephew might suggest criticism of the former: while the nephew would seem to be the traitor, facts will show that the uncle is the one to blame. The Peleus/Jason comparison may be seen as an anticipation of the forthcoming events.

Along with the previous quotation discussed above, this reference shows an interest in the story of the Argonauts which was disseminated in Ovid's version in the Latin language. It proves how the poet's knowledge of classical mythology is comprehensive since it includes all its aspects, from the matters of Rome and of Troy to the Argonauts. In a separate episode the story of Dedalus and Icarus is also mentioned ('Ensi cun fist Dedailus et Ychaire', l. 13465). This further broadens the scope of the poet's classical interests. An account of the story of Dedalus and Icarus is found in *Metamorphoses* 8.183–235; this again reinforces the idea that not only was the poet interested in the entire classical heritage but that he also drew a great deal of information from Ovid and possibly directly from the Latin.

The tradition of Alexander

Limentani suggested, and it is now widely accepted, that the *Entrée* is to a large extent inspired by the *Alexandre*. This is significant when trying to identify how the matter of medieval French epic became hybridised with motifs belonging to romance, giving birth to the diversified phenomenon of the *poema epico-cavalleresco*.

Although the *Aeneid* remained a poetic model throughout the Middle Ages and the supremacy of Virgil was never overturned,[114] the *epos* inspired by the life of Alexander the Great was also immensely popular. It never acquired the *Aeneid*'s authority but it became a point of reference for those poets, such as the *Entrée* author, attempting to depict an epic character. In fact, the *Alexandre* in its many versions was one of the most widely read and inspiring romances in the Middle Ages.[115] As extensively discussed by George

---

[114] D. Comparetti, *Vergil in the Middle Ages*, transl. by E. F. M. Benecke (London; New York: S. Sonnenschein & Co.; Macmillan & Co., 1895; repr. Princeton: Princeton University Press, 1997), p. 182.

[115] The tradition of the story of Alexander is extensive. The life of Alexander the Great circulated during the Middle Ages in the Latin

Cary, the persistence of the Alexander tradition throughout the Middle Ages had left traces in different literary genres, especially in the works of moralists in which Alexander's image was tightly connected to that of his mentor and friend Aristotle. With the version of Alexandre de Paris,[116] the legend of Alexander reached its greatest perfection. It includes four long sections of which the third

---

versions of the *Epitome Julii Valerii*, a shortened version of the *Julii Valerii Alexandri polemi*, written around AD 330 (this is the text associated with the Greek version A of the Pseudo-Callisthenes); the *Historia de Proeliis* (tenth century) by the archpriest Leone who found a *Roman d'Alexandre* in Byzantium; the *Res gestae Alexandri Magni*, by Quintus Curtius Rufus, different from the Pseudo-Callisthenes and closer to Plutarch in the correctness of its historical information. Very successful in the Middle Ages, in the second half of the twelfth century it inspired the *Alexandreis* by Walter of Châtillon in ten books, of which more than 200 manuscripts survive, produced especially in the thirteenth to fifteenth centuries. The text was included in a standard list of school textbooks by Hugo von Trimberg, *Registrum multorum auctorum* and Eberard, *Labyrintus*. Galtieri de Castellione, *Alexandreis*, ed. by M. L. Colker (Padua: Antenore, 1978). In the French language, Alberic de Besançon is the first author who composed a poem about Alexander the Great in the vernacular. He was also the first to introduce feudal societal thinking into the legend of Alexander: A. Roncaglia, 'L'*Alexandre* d'Alberic et la séparation entre chanson de geste et roman', in *Chanson de geste und höfischer Roman. Heidelberger Kolloquium (30. Januar 1961)* (Heidelberg: Winter, 1963), pp. 37–60. In Italy in the fourteenth century, Domenico Scolari composed a *Historia Alexandri regis* in octosyllabic verse in Tuscan dialect based on Quilichinus of Spoleto's *Alexandreis*; see G. Cary, *The Medieval Alexander* (Cambridge: Cambridge University Press, 1956), pp. 53–54.

[116] Alexandre de Bernay or de Paris (d. ca. 1185) is one of the principal authors of poem collection called *Roman d'Alexandre*, comprising 20,000 verses of twelve syllables, named alexandrines after the title of the poem. Having gathered the work done by his predecessors and integrated it into his own, Alexandre re-thought and re-wrote a great part of what was found in it, giving it a conformity, unity and richness it never had before. He gave the *Roman d'Alexandre* its definitive form and set the four branches in the order they occur in the majority of manuscripts. Of this version, two editions have been made: *Li Romans d'Alixandre par Lambert li tors and Alexandre de Bernay*, ed. by H. Michelant (Stuttgart: Lit. Verein, 1846); and *Le Roman d'Alexandre, Version of Alexandre de Paris*, ed. by M. La Du, in *The Medieval French 'Roman d'Alexandre'*, ed. by E. C. Armstrong, 6 vols (Princeton: Princeton University Press, 1976), I.

is the most important and contains all the major episodes.[117] The romance of Alexandre de Paris should be seen as situated halfway between romance and epic; the account of the hero's life and the many hazards he encounters in the great adventure of world conquest affords a deeper insight into the character, while the background and description of warfare still brings it close to an epic. In the version of Alexandre de Paris, too, Aristotle is portrayed as a moralist wanting to save Athens from the violence of his disciple. Aristotle suggests to Alexander that he should be generous, moderate and faithful, and underlines that Darius will be defeated because he is guilty before God. While most anecdotes circulating in the works of moralists up to the fourteenth century tended to cast the Greek hero in a negative light, stressing his weakness and inclination to vice, on the positive side were his liberality and (more rarely) wisdom. The negative portrait of Alexander did not seemingly influence the author of the *Entrée*. Rather he appears focused on one aspect of the tradition: Alexander's historical importance for his political achievements and territorial conquests. Cary makes a distinction between the different approaches to the figure of Alexander: philosophical, theological, exemplary and secular. As he points out, 'the secular writer writes of Alexander as a conqueror for comparison with other conquerors of the past or of his own age, or with patrons who would like to be conquerors. Admiration for so great a man inspires his work and provides the basis for the whole secular portrait of Alexander'.[118]

The *Entrée* author falls into the category of secular writers, referring to Alexander as the most eminent political leader of all ages and the only one worth comparing to Roland. At the same time, according to Cary 'a reference to Alexander the conqueror merely as

---

[117] Although the enormous circulation of Walter of Châtillon's *Alexandreis* might suggest that the Latin text was the one known and read by the *Entrée* author, this may be deceptive. The French text was also in fact circulating in Italy during the twelfth century, the only extant manuscript being preserved in Venice; see *Le Roman d'Alexandre. Riproduzione del ms. Venezia, Biblioteca Museo Correr, Correr 1493*, ed. by R. Benedetti (Udine: Vattori, 1998). The characteristics and provenance of this manuscript leave room for speculation about possible access to the text in the version contained in this manuscript.

[118] Cary, *The Medieval Alexander*, p. 195.

Alexander the conqueror tells us nothing, since it does not reveal the author's opinion of his conquest'.[119] This statement is applicable to the *Entrée*, in which Roland spends most of his time among the Saracens introducing them to the ethics of chivalry, and fully displaying qualities such as moderation and wisdom in his behaviour towards Dionés. He cannot be called *desmesuré* given his wise attitude in the poem's most crucial moments. The poet avoids expressing an opinion about Alexander, which would have been in the tradition of the moralists, and instead concentrates on his valorous side. this makes it easier for the poet to draw a parallel with Roland since it allows him to avoid contradiction. He refers very often to Alexander in relation to Darius (ll. 8481–82, 13294–95):

> Pis de cestor feromes, par le cor sant Elaire,
> Que la gient Alexandre ne fist de cele Daire.
> Ja descunfis Alexandre une fie
> Le grant host Daires a pou de cunpaignie.

Since Darius is said to be the ancestor of the Saracens, the parallel between Alexander and Roland is reinforced by the fact that they both fought the same enemy: 'Se je do voir, Daire l'a tesmoigné, | Vos ancesor, qi en fu mont reté' (ll. 12300–01).

One episode has a direct source in the part of the *Alexandre*[120] dedicated to the siege of Tyre, where the account of this historical event is greatly developed (ll. 9988–90):

> Qe de quatres parties rendirent tiel hestor
> Qe la maigne Alexandre, a cui parla l'aubor,
> A la cité de Tir nel dona mais greignor.

A celebration of Alexander's glory occurs towards the end of the poem when Roland travels in different countries subject to the rule of the Sultan of Persia. In the land of Gog and Magog he finds a monument erected by Alexander after his victory over Darius: 'Et li dos tronpeor de coubre a or brusti | Que Alexandre fist faire chant Dairons desconfi' (ll. 13850–51). It is composed of two mechanical statues of copper and gold. The monument's mention is very brief,

---

[119] Cary, *The Medieval Alexander*, p. 195.
[120] Alexandre de Paris, *Li Romans d'Alixandre*, ed. Michelant, pp. 74–92.

covering only four lines. However, it is noteworthy for being in a section of the poem where Roland/Alexander has defeated Pélias/Darius, and is intended as an explicit homage to the victory of the great emperor with whom he is able to identify.

In the *Alexandre*, battles are portrayed as a succession of duels, such as the encounter with Nicholas (laisses XXVI–LXXII),[121] an episode that the poet mentions three times. In one case, Alexander's rage over Nicholas provides a comparison with that of the French when they attacked Pamplona (ll. 5559–61):

> Non le Maçodonois sor le gient Nicolais
> Furent al desconfir e a l'enchaucer melais
> Com as Pampelonois furent les Frans irais.

The Nicholas episode in the *Alexandre* is one of the most effective descriptions of how Alexander could give full vent to his rage with all restraint vanished, but only in particular contexts, an attitude which parallels his scope for magnanimity. Alexander is a hot-blooded character offering many opportunities for comparison, especially in descriptions of excessive or exuberant behaviour. The second mention of the Nicholas episode is in an illustration of the Greek leader's power as a fighter. By comparing his vigour with that of Pélias, whom Roland wants to challenge for having insulted Dionés, Dionés' brother Sansonet tries to put Roland off (ll. 12259–63):

> 'Pués que Alexandre oucis roi Nicolais
> E qu'il moruit le Maquebeu Judais,
> Non nasqi home qu'il n'aqist da son brais.
> Non le niés Karles croi qe tel fust jamais'.

The closing line states that not even Roland, Charlemagne's nephew, is superior to the Greek king. Roland listens to him disguised as a Saracen and will not surrender to the impulse of revealing his real identity even when implicitly challenged to do so.

---

[121] Alexandre de Paris, *Alexandre*, ed. La Du, I: 14–36. For a commentary upon this episode in the decasyllabic *Alexander* and the *Roman*, see P. Meyer, *Alexandre le Grand dans la littérature française du Moyen Âge*, 2 vols (Paris: Vieweg, 1886).

A third reference to the Nicholas episode is in the description of a panel of a great fresco decorating the walls of a room in the castle of Noble (laisse CCCCLII). After the siege of Noble and with the city taken, the wounded count Gerard de Roussillion is carried to a room of the palace and tended by the doctors. It is there that Roland sees the fresco depicting the story of Alexander the Great. This description matches the information offered by the Michelant edition of the *Alexandre* (ll. 10408–25):

> La sunt toz les batailes d'Alixandre en fin:
> E comant il oncist li suen meistre endivin
> (Naptanabus oit non, sajes d'art e d'engin),
> E comant il tua o buen brant açerin
> Nicolas de Cesaire, qel i estoit mal voisin,
> Pués conquist tote Perse qe Daires oit aclin,
> E desconfist Porus, qe pués le prist dan Clin,
> E parla as deus arbres qe lui distrent sa fin
> Com il devoit morir a poisons de vinin,
> E com lui envoia Candaz de ses terin
> Les muls cargez de pailes e de vair et d'ermin
> [...]
> Quant oncist l'amiral et conquist son demin,
> E com il corona les .XII. palatin.

As in the episode of the monument erected by Alexandre, this ekphrasis offers Roland the opportunity to identify himself with Alexander. In the face of such greatness in battle and magnanimity in life, he is so filled with admiration that he adopts the mighty Greek king's example: 'Qi volt honor conquere sor son felons vesin | Apraigne d'Alixandre la voie et le traïn' (ll. 10433–34).

The boundaries of the world in the *Entrée* are still classical, marked in the west by the Roman Empire and in the east by Alexander – a perspective with the classical world at the very centre and whatever surrounds it defined accordingly. The farthest place on earth is therefore the extreme limits of the territory made subject to Alexander ('Ni a meilor chevaler trosqu'al flum d'Alexendre', l. 4948). Another mention of the breadth of Alexander's dominion, with specific reference to his expedition to India, is found in the *Entrée*'s second section: 'Chant plus avés cunquis en un jor de semaine | Que non fist Alexandre sor la gient Indiaine' (11817–18). This important episode in Alexander's career is extensively reported in the medieval versions of the *Roman d'Alexandre*, for instance the laisses 139–42 of Branch III of the version by Alexandre de Paris. However, the same reference is found within the *Roman de Troie* (ll. 805–10). This shows that Benoît himself was aware of the matter of Alexander of which there were variants in the Middle Ages. The story of Alexander was circulating as a work wrongly attributed to Callisthenes (the version now referred to as the Pseudo-Callisthenes), long before it was canonised as we know it today and became a hybrid of epic and erudition through the different elaborations in various European languages. The poet was also familiar with those versions as Bancourt showed when he identified the source of one episode in the *Entrée*, where Marsile makes a divination before the start of the war (ll. 405–10). This is an episode of the Pseudo-Callisthenes version, translated into many languages including Latin and then summarised by Julius Valerius in his epitome.[122]

An intriguing reference to the story of Dido and Aeneas in the *Alexandre* could have suggested the rhyme in two lines of a significant passage of the *Entrée*, describing Roland's mood as he sets out for the unknown after the rupture with Charlemagne:

(*Alexandre*)
La reïne Dido la perdi per follage
per l'amor Eneas, ont ot mis son corage.[123]

(*Entrée*, ll. 11815–16)
Mais tant vos di qe plus contre corage
Non s'an parti Eneas de Cartaige,

The tragedy of Dido's death after the departure of Aeneas offers a strong point of comparison in that Roland's loyalty to his emperor compares only with that of a lover. In the case of Dido and Aeneas, moreover, departure implies rupture and death, in similar fashion to

---

[122] P. Bancourt, *Les Musulmans dans les chansons de geste du cycle du roi* (Aix-en-Provence: Université de Provence, 1982), p. 466.

[123] Alexandre de Paris, *Alexandre*, ed. La Du, I, laisse 539.

the *Entrée* in which death symbolises the end of the feudal pact. However, the brief development of the motif of Dionés' unrequited love for Roland suggests the possible alternative, that the *Alexandre* rather than the *Enéas* influenced the *Entrée* author. Unlike the *Alexandre*, the *Enéas*' monologues and the dwelling upon the feelings of Dido and Lavinia make it more open to a psychological reading. Of the three great twelfth-century classical romances only the *Alexandre* does not truly follow the major novelty of the *Enéas* and the *Troie*: the expression of feelings and psychological insight. This is bizarre if we consider that the *Alexandre* dates to a period with a *terminus post quem* of 1180, at least twenty years after the *Enéas* and twenty-five after Benoît's romance. For chronological reasons the stylistic distance between the *Alexandre* and the *Entrée* should be wider than it in fact is. However, this particular feature brings them very close together and proves that the *Entrée* poet drew much inspiration from this poem for his characterisation of Roland. Of all the classical romances it is moreover the *Alexandre* whose plot is comparable with of that the *Entrée*, since Roland/Alexander acquires a new identity above all through the conquest and exploration of the world.

It is impossible to compare the characterisation of the pagans in the *Alexandre* and the *Entrée*; the former is set in the atmosphere of the crusades and the pagans are thus Alexander's adversaries, while this is not the case for the *Entrée* except when Roland engages in battle to defend his host. In the early *chansons de geste* it is assumed that Arabs and Christians are natural enemies, so no further investigation of Saracen customs seems necessary. In the *Chanson de Roland* there is only one instance of valid knowledge of the Muslim world: the description of a book holder for the Qur'ān (laisse XLVII). This realistic insert perhaps shows effort to reproduce the enemies' environment. Yet despite this attempt the *Chanson* falls among those texts that labelled the Saracens merely as rivals of Christians. Regarding the *Alexandre*, on the one hand, there is an attempt to present a historically faithful picture of the Muslim world, and a strange mixture of accuracy and invention originates from this endeavour.

On the other, twelve peers are given to Alexander (l. 10425), according with the medieval respect for the canonical numbers of the Christian religion, with a leader always accompanied by twelve people (whether apostles for Jesus, knights for Arthur, or peers for Charlemagne). The *Alexandre* follows the same rule and it could not be otherwise since Alexander is a figure as dignified as the other two heroes of Christendom, Roland and Arthur. Alexander is the hero who exported western civilisation to the eastern borders of the world fighting against the Persians, paving the way for the Roman Empire to take over. The three figures have the same powerful role, and by the end of the Middle Ages this aspect prevailed over more literary ones. The boundaries between genres blurred, resulting in a trade of traits that also made the three figures almost interchangeable, making one single multifaceted emperor/conqueror who interacts with the enemy in a variety of ways. In the *Alexandre*, for example, the author depicts an exchange between the Saracens and the Western world. The emir of Babylon needs an interpreter to communicate with Alexander. Marcabrins, king of the Barbarians, 'parle Sarasinois, n'entend d'autre latin' (speaks only Arabic and does not understand other languages). Suddenly, the poet feels the need to specify the language skills of the Persian/Muslim authorities: this is a very early attempt to provide a non-Eurocentric vision of the world in the *chanson de geste*. The same urge is expressed in the *Entrée* in which a *latiner* (i.e. a translator) is employed to ensure that the two hostile armies can communicate.[124]

---

[124] 'Por ce vos pri que prodome soiois: le maitinet un latiner prendrois' (ll. 5980–81); 'Le latiner s'an veit, qui mont fu sage' (l. 6027); 'Latiner frer, ne le poés scondir' (l. 6189); 'Le latiner dou palés devala' (l. 6212); 'Le latiner che bien soit de renart' (l. 7620).

THE MAIN CHARACTERS

Elements of characterisation

According to the rules of characterisation set by B. Tomaševskij,[1] a complete portrait of Roland can be established by assembling the many motifs relating to his role, and the aspects of his personality/appearance. All these motifs and aspects can be gathered from different sources using two types of approach. A direct characterisation emerges from what Roland confesses or reveals of himself, and from what the author says of his protagonist. An indirect characterisation results from his environment and the characters with which he interacts, and thus from the combination of different outside perspectives. Major characters in the *Entrée* who offer an 'external' view on Roland are Estout, Ferragu, Charlemagne, Dionés, and Pélias. Sansonet's role in this matter is not central in that his view of Roland merely confirms, uncritically, the image that the hero provides of himself. Sansonet can thus be considered as the recipient rather than maker of an image.

Sometimes, indirect characterisation is intertwined with the point of view of the author, or with elements of objective description added to that of a character, so that it is very difficult to separate direct and indirect approaches. As far as Roland's own voice is concerned, his attitude changes between the first and the second section. The speech he delivers in lines 132–75, where he insists on the intervention in Spain, gives a first impression of Roland still quite similar to that of the *Chanson*. His hot-blooded temper remains very much part of his character, which will change dramatically through the events leading to the second section. In

---

[1] B. Tomaševskij, 'La costruzione dell'intreccio', in *I formalisti russi*, ed. by T. Todorov (Turin: Einaudi, 1968), pp. 305–50. See also G. Lukács, *The Theory of the Novel. A Historico-philosophical Essay on the Forms of Great Epic Literature*, transl. by A. Bostock (London: Merlin Press, 1978), pp. 56–69.

line 2245 Roland apostrophises his horse; he talks to the animal as to a friend, reprising the same relation with his horse in the *Chanson*: '"Destrer chrenus, envoiez de luntan, | Cum ambesdos somes de mort proçan!"' (ll. 2245–46). These lines occur at an early stage of the narration, but Roland believes he is close to death as he is apparently losing a duel against Ferragu. The moment of dismay in the face of Ferragu's strength recalls the mood of the Roland at Rencesvals in the *Chanson de Roland* and anticipates the disastrous end (although this is not the subject of this poem).

When Estout escapes from Ferragu, Roland tries to convince him to return to prison. The register used in this direct speech is colloquial (ll. 1459–63):

> 'Por quoi diables vos alés maneçant?
> Non conoisés, ne vos avenoit tant
> De trepaser d'un tel roi le comant
> E pués fuïr par feir altrui spoant:
> Nus hom ne doit prometre ce dunt il n'est pusant'.

This is one of Roland's direct references to the ethics of chivalry, anticipating his imminent and sweeping transformation. Lines 2130–32 are particularly interesting since Roland asks Charlemagne to prevent anybody from intervening in his duel with Ferragu. Further on, he asks that nobody help him should he find himself in trouble, and explicitly demands that the king leave the final judgement to God (ll. 2125–33).

> 'Por l'amor Dieux e moi, vos soit en don requis
> Che me lasez combatre cors a cors l'Arabis,
> Car ambesdeus l'avomes fiances e promis
> Ch'il n'i avra que nos o mortel capleïs.
> Il le feit por Machon e je por Jesu Cris.
> Por ce vos veul proier ch'il soie contradis
> Che je n'aie secors d'ome do segle vis.
> Laserez a Diex faire ses bon et ses delis,
> Car anch ni i servi home qe n'en fust bien miris'.

This request recalls the Germanic custom of an ordeal, survival of which was taken as divine proof of innocence. The duel of Ferragu and Roland is therefore to be understood as the representation of a trial by ordeal.

The confrontation of the two heroes of the opposing armies, and of their contrasting values, positioned at the poem's start and encompassing a large section, creates an anticipation of the second part in which Roland will again encounter the Saracens, albeit under different circumstances. Although Roland is the survivor of the ordeal, which may lead one to read it as a divine judgement, the poet thinks otherwise. Roland himself deems Ferragu a worthy warrior and honourable man. Furthermore, the poet puts in Roland's mouth such words as: 'Il le fait por Machon e je por Jesu Cris' (l. 2129), letting the reader know of Roland's awareness that the pagans' belief is just as strong as that of Christians. Roland's open-mindedness emerges here quietly but with some firmness.

Still, the idea that all is in the hands of God returns in the lines below, where Roland declares that he considers this enterprise (*ceste hovre*, l. 2197) as a penance for his sins (ll. 2196–99):

'Glorios piere, de qui toz bien comançe
Je prant ceste hovre en nom de penetançe
De mes pechiés, e tu sais la fiançe
Que je ai senpre en divine pusançe'.

Roland faces his enemy with the same spirit as that of kings who had undertaken a crusade or pilgrimage. The poem's first part still presents a literary atmosphere very similar to that of a *Chanson*. Yet in the second section the narrative reveals a different poetic intention. During his journey in the East, Roland describes himself as a wandering knight who travels the world to make justice triumph over evil (ll. 12756–58):

'Cant por droiture mantenir et ses non
Vais travalant por estranges rouyon
E prant bataille et trai a fenysson'.

Several times, the author acts as an intermediary between his text and audience, addressing his reader/hearer with observations that help clarify Roland's figure and role in the *Entrée*.² From these remarks I have chosen one which occurs quite late in the narrative: 'Seignor, Rollant estoit apris de maint latin | Car il savoit Greçois, Suriën et Ermin' (ll. 11522–23).

These lines represent a form of climax in the *Entrée* to Roland's characterisation and the intention of the poet; on the one hand, they mark the culmination of Roland's gradual transformation into the perfect traveller and man of the world; on the other, they establish exactly what a fourteenth-century traveller (whether an adventurous knight, a pilgrim or a merchant) is expected to know. They occur so late in the text because Roland's new identity seems to take shape little by little. It also appears that the author was not wholly clear as to his own goals. In the first section, there are three instances of the epithet *filz Millon* establishing a continuity with the tradition: 'Je moi profier primer davant li filz Millon' (l. 281); 'Q'il a trovez le filz Milons d'Anglant' (l. 1678); 'Che moi rendisse al filz Millon d'Anglent' (l. 3968). Again in the first section, on another occasion the poet calls him *lo senator roman* (l. 2250), referring to the fact that for the war in Spain Roland leads a garrison which had been given to him directly by the Pope. This has been interpreted as an attempt to capture Roland in the Italian environment.³ Epithets such as *l'ardiz* (l. 1669) refer to his worldly valour, whereas later the accent will be put on the perfection of his celestial virtues.

On the eve of the Eastern episode the poet's intention seems to have clearly changed direction, as he abandons the tradition for something completely new. Identification with three classical figures contributes to the making of the novel and versatile Roland: the Roland/Aeneas link serves to introduce and clarify the motif of the journey; implied in the Roland/Hector connection is the opposition between the Greeks and the Trojans, and absolute support to the

---

[2] Zarker-Morgan, 'The Narrator in Italian Epic', maintains that '[i]n the *Entrée*, as Limentani points out, most direct interventions of the author (except for the second protasi, 10939–44) are in the first part; anticipatory comments are primarily the second' (pp. 483–84). See also Limentani, 'Epica e racconto. Osservazioni di alcune strutture e sull'incompiutezza dell'*Entrée d'Espagne*', *AIV*, 133 (1974–5), 393–428 (p. 421).

[3] See Limentani, *L'Entrée d'Espagne e i signori d'Italia*, p. 28, who also notices in this epithet an 'apostolic' configuration of the character.

French/Trojans; generosity and magnanimity result from the Roland/Alexander association, which also establishes a parallel with the greatest conqueror of the East.

There are various passages in which the Paduan describes Roland wearing his armour and weapons or taking them off. Of all these the most significant two follow. The first description reports details of his outfit (ll. 706–12, 1954–59, 2087–92):

> De son neveu Rollant a feit son mareschal.
> Le jor seoit li quens el noir de Portegal,
> Armez de totes armes qe se feit a vasal.
> Son hiaume et son escus et son espliez pugnal
> Par derier li aporte son escuer loial.
> En mans tient un bastons a loi de senescal,
> E insir feit le barons por engal.
> Teri desarme, entre lui et Ugon,
> Rollant son sire devant le roi Carlon.
> En un gambaus camosez environ
> Remist le duc, pués aporte l'on
> Un mantel riche que li baile Naymon
> Et autres vestes de mout riche facon.
> A l'endemain, com conte la scriture,
> Leva Rollant, le vasal sanz lusure
> Sor le ganbaus a mis sa vestiure,
> Le blans obers qe ne dote punture;
> Pués çaint l'espee trancant a desmesure:
> Arme dou segle contre cele no dure.

No mention is made here of ornamental elements belonging to the helmet, shield and spear, but the poet states that worldly arms (*Arme dou segle*, 2092) could never withstand the strength of Roland's. If his enemies' arms are worldly then his must by necessity belong to a different category, the only possible one being the arms of the celestial knight. Roland is said to be wearing a cloak and clothing of fine, expensive material (1958–59); a few verses later, however, the poet calls him *le vasal sanz lusure* (2088) and says that he wears a *blans obers* (2090), two details that unmistakingly convey integrity and purity of soul.

The second description of Roland's weapons occurs when Dionés presents him with a surcoat, horse, shield and spear before he sets off to defeat Pélias. The surcoat is embroidered with snakes' heads, the work of a skilled master; the horse is covered with a lavishly decorated cloth displaying golden eagles on the right side and griffins on the left; the spurs of the saddle are made of elephant bone, and the reins of golden thread (12578–83, 12587–92):

> Une pulcelle touche de sa man destre;
> Cele i aporte une riche sorveste :
> Coverte estoit de serpentine teste,
> Et ert cescune ovree si par bon mestre
> Qant vent i fiert, l'une vers l'autre breste.
> Le bon destrer qi mout fu de grant estre,
> Covert de paile d'un chier color celestre :
> A aigles d'or estoit portreit destre
> E a grifons parfilei a senestre.
> Les aubes furent d'une olifante beste
> E frans e estriers d'un chier or de Tolestre.

The shield is made of bronze and decorated with sapphires, covered with elephant skin and that of an old stag captured in a hunt. However, its most interesting detail is the central crystal buckle on which is engraved the figure of Mohammed (12616–25):

> Dionés, la belle plus qe rose ne lis,
> Li apresante un fort eschu bronis :
> Tut anviron fu alistei d'orfris,
> De buons safirs luisans com fou apris ;
> Le son leucher fu d'olifant treitis ;
> Le cuer fu fort, non mie de berbis,
> Mais d'un viel cers qi in chace fu pris
> Grant oit la borcle d'un cristal esclaris :
> Mahon i avoit, sor un trecel asis,
> Con il prediche le pueple a son escris.

Roland quietly laughs at this detail, thinking of what Estout and Oliver would say if only they could see him (12628–32). The spear has a sharp point, ivory handle and plume of silk: 'Sa belle file li an bail un pointis, | Hante d'aiol e penuns de samis' (12634–35). A diptych results from the juxtaposition of the two presentations. Its first panel portrays Roland as *miles Christi* bearing celestial weapons. The colour of his armour and the absence of luxury create a hero corresponding in type to a celestial knight. This characteristic is enforced by epithets such as *le campions do roi celestial* (2209), emphasizing the idea that Roland has been chosen for a higher mission. The second panel shows him wearing weapons of oriental fashion which he will wear during the combat against Pélias, and signifies that he has been accepted as an official member of the court and is now visually recognisable as a Saracen knight.

After the count is fully dressed in the arms donated by Dionés, she can no longer hide her attraction for him: 'Quant fu armei Rolant, li qens honeste, | Dionés le garde; a mervoile li pleste' (12578–79). She declares her love openly, thus causing the portrait of Roland to become subjective. The hero is said to be the most handsome man ever born (*Plus beaus fils enjendrés anc de meres non fu*, 13665) even though a full physical portrait is provided later in which he does not appear as a straightforwardly handsome knight (ll. 13650–61):

> Char le duc estoit loing et quarés et menbru;
> La janbe ot loinge et grose, li pié chanbrés agu,
> Le chuises plates, et dougiés por le bu,
> Anples le spaules, et por le piz gros fu;
> Le main longues et blance, le bras gros e nervu,
> Le cols et loing et gros bien demi pié et plu;
> La bouce avoit polie, les dens blans et menu;
> Le nés ot loing a droit, et non mie bosu;
> Vair oil ot et riant, s'il n'estoit ureschu,
> Le front anples et aut et de zufet tot nu,
> Char il estoit ja chauf, ce avons entendu;
> Blons furent ses zavoil come fin or batu

Roland in this description is *chauf* (bald, in Italian *calvo*, l. 13660), a realistic detail that does not signify inner beauty but that might be a metaphor for the wisdom he has finally acquired.[4] It

---

[4] Limentani, *L'Entrée d'Espagne e i signori d'Italia*, pp. 126–27, pointed out that through one single physical detail the poet aims at a

could also recall St. Bernard's advice on the necessity, in waging *pugna spiritualis*, of turning one's attention from physical attractiveness to moral ability.[5] However, other details hint at physical strength such as of his legs, arms and shoulders.

Roland's new identity is also signified by a change in name and social status (to Lionés/son of a merchant). Dionés' hand is offered to Roland as a reward for his valorous conduct in the war. He refuses but accepts the fief of Persia (l. 13522), thereby actively participating in the administration of the province and from every point of view becoming a Saracen. The combination of all these elements shapes a character that no longer has any connections with the *Chanson* tradition.

While Estout is kept prisoner at the Saracen camp, Ferragu asks him to talk about Roland. Estout's praise of Roland as the *campions de la Cristienté* (l. 1556) irritates Ferragu who accuses him of being a *fablaor prové* (l. 1571) – that is, an expert liar or more accurately an excellent storyteller, adding a touch of sarcasm to his accusation. One part of his speech offers an example of a cinematic technique which gives broad scope to the narrative and of which we will find another occurrence later: via an 'aerial' shot over Charles' field, from the place where Estout and Ferragu are talking the poet's gaze 'zooms' in on Roland (ll. 1545–52):

> 'Esgardez la o il sunt amassé
> Si grant bernaje entor cil sol armé;
> S'un pué fust plus envers nos adrecé,
> Veoir pouses en l'eschu scharteré,
> D'or e d'arçant departiz e sevré,
> Qe cil seroit Rollant, mon avohé,

---

psychological characterisation. Thus, Roland is bald which signifies the opposition *puer* /*senex*, and Sansonet stutters, two realistic elements that do not suggest a comic style but in one detail capture the psychology of the character.

[5] St. Bernard says that *milites templi* shave their heads, for it is a shame for a man to care about his hair (IV, 7, 26–29). In fact, this feature could also recall a monk's tonsure although the text refers specifically to natural boldness: 'estoit ja chauf', l. 13660.

Par chui sperance e par cui segurté
Sui en preson retorné de mon gré'.

The assembled baronage of France is first seen from afar, but the figure of Roland can be recognised by his glittering shield: *scharteré* (l. 1548, *scartellato* in Italian), divided into squares of gold and silver. His shield is thus both a weapon and an element of characterisation which symbolises his high position in Charlemagne's army, representing both his civil and military status.[6]

During the first pause in the duel, Ferragu returns to the city and as he dismounts, starts to praise Roland (ll. 2020–26):

Dist Feragu: 'Ne devez tant pleider:
Vos n'estes daignes d'un tiel home nomenr.
Por Machomet, je ne vi mais son per.
Pro est Rollant et engignos e fier,
Tant q'il se quide tote Espaigne aquiter.
Demain me vient cors a cors encontrer,
Si che porois le meldre al doi monstrer'.

Ferragu is impressed by Roland's valour. He asks for the prisoners (the eleven peers of France whom he had taken hostage) to be released from prison and brought to him, and asks to speak with Oliver, knowing that he is Roland's closest kin and friend. In fact, Oliver had loved Roland more than anyone alive except his uncle ('Fors que son oncle plus d'ome vis l'amoit', l. 4334) and speaks about him in these terms (ll. 2058–67):

'En remembrance do melor chevaler
Che soit o siegles, bien le pués tesmogner.
Tot est garniz de quant ch'i a mester,
Bien le poüt Hector tenir por frer;
E molt mervoil quant il vos veult digner

---

[6] This is also true of classical heroes, who were recognised by their weapons: for example, Achilles' immortal armour, a wedding gift from the god Hephaestus and his spear, made by Cheiron from a tree in Mount Pelion and fought for by Ajax and Odysseus after Achilles' death; or the large shield described in detail by Homer which was shaped as a figure-of-eight, made of seven layers of bull hide, and plated with bronze.

> Por compagnons, mais l'om le puet schuser,
> Car por mesais de gient por home arcer
> Se feit honor au cheitis soldoier.
> 'Vos dites voir' – ce respont Berenger –
> 'Il est le mestre, nos somes li escoler'.

Oliver's praise of Roland as the best knight, corroborated by Berengair's closing line, accentuates Ferragu's desire to fight against him. In fact, he states just a few lines later that he would not give a penny to kill anybody else but would rather either die or vanquish Roland's pride. Ferragu's statement 'O de morir o son orguel mater' (l. 2957) again foregrounds Roland's pride as his main characteristic, to the extent that Ferragu identifies Roland's strength and valour merely as its attributes.[7] Roland does not believe the same about himself, and indeed the following events prove that he does appear an excessively proud character. In two instances Ferragu is defined as a lion as opposed to Roland who is a lamb ('cist lions che con averte brance', l. 2202; 'Hoi ert vencus le lion par l'agnel', l. 2492), a dual symbolism originating from Isaiah 65.25 which is common throughout medieval literature. All this suggests that in the context of this allegory the lion symbolizes Antichrist. However, both animals can have a positive connotation; Jesus is both a lion and a lamb, for example, depending on whether he is confronting his enemies or caring for Christians. While the lion implies strength and power in battle, the lamb suggests physical weakness concealing spiritual force. In fact, Roland is said to be a lion before he sets off to battle against Pélias: 'plus estoit fiers de lion qi porcace' (l. 12599), meaning that Roland is going to war against the Saracen as a lion goes to the hunt. In the *Entrée*, the allegory of the hunt as a symbol for war is developed yet further: when Roland defeats Ferragu the lamb has defeated the lion. Ferragu's epithet may therefore indicate either a negative or a positive quality; it may refer to the fact that *miles Christi* (or Roland as *figura Christi*) has defeated the Antichrist, but it may also refer to the type of strength Ferragu possesses rather than to his role as an enemy.

---

[7] What is meant by *orguel* would deserve separate treatment as in this case it does not seem equivalent to the concept of *desmesure*.

An antinomy between physical and moral power is implied in the two different words used to distinguish them, *force* and *vertuz*. Although the two words are synonyms (for they both mean strength) their shades of meaning are quite different. *Force* (from the Latin *fortis*: strong, powerful, robust, but also violent, tumultuous) is divine. *Fortis* is also used for the power of the sun, signifying moral strength:[8] intense, energetic and courageous. Applied to an army it means heroic.[9] *Fortitudo* means courage: the perfect knight is the one considered able to associate *fortitudo* and *sapientia*.[10] *Vertuz*, by contrast, is a human attribute; deriving from *vir*, it implies superlative physical and moral qualities. It can also mean military prowess if referring to the single fighter and not the whole army. *Virtus* is a concept linked to the physical strength of the individual, corroborated in the text by the use of *vertus* to refer to the power of the wind: *vertus dou vant* (l. 1257). When Ogier attacks Ferragu, the giant simply proves too powerful no matter how much strength he puts into the fight. In this context *vertus* is purely physical (ll. 1155–58):

> Mervellos coup lui done le Donoi por haïr,
> Mais ainc n'i puet l'escu enpirer ni partir,
> Anz convent son espié pecoier e crossir
> Par si tre grant vertuz qe fait le cans tintir.

Roland is 'L'ardiç, le *fort*, le bien endotriné' (l. 1557). When Roland speaking to Charlemagne refers to his duel with Ferragu, he says that 'vers la divine *force vertuz* n'avra' (l. 1615). When the French hero fights against Ferragu, 'En doble *force* le duc Rollant s'argüe | Vers Feragu se dreze et sa *vertue*' (ll. 1793–94). Ferragu says to Roland that he fought death through cleverness and force: 'Che par engins e *force* avez la mort aquise' (l. 1848). In most cases the author associates *force* with Roland's strength and *virtus* with that of

---

[8] Cfr. 'Fortis' in F. Calonghi, ed., *Dizionario della lingua latina* (Turin: Rosenberg & Sellier, 1960), I: 1150.
[9] Cfr. 'Fortis' in Calonghi, ed., *Dizionario della lingua latina*.
[10] Bernard of Clairvaux, *Liber ad milites templi*, IV, 8.

Ferragu; he thereby implies that all of Roland's strength comes from God, while Ferragu's is a purely physical and human attribute.[11]

The theological dispute between Roland and Ferragu, while defining Roland's personality, also bestows philosophical authority upon his role in the *chanson de geste*. From this point on the virtues of reasoning supersede those of coercion in the task of spreading Christian faith and ethics. Roland's character becomes more clearly oriented towards the ethics of chivalry. Towards the end of the duel, Ferragu realises how courteous Roland is when the French paladin puts a stone under the head of the sleeping giant. He considers that if only he could convert the French hero to his religion ('my four gods'), there would be no one left in the world to argue with him (ll. 3575–78):

> 'Plus vault cestui d'onor et de bien faire
> Que tot les homes deci Julis Cesaire;
> Si je le pués a mes quatre Diex traire,
> N'avroit ou munde nus hom qe me contraire'.

Before the poem's climax when Charlemagne slaps Roland's face with a heavy glove (laisse CCCCLXXXV), Richard the Norman and Salomon advise Roland not to present himself before the king, because he is upset (*corocez*, l. 11086). Roland reacts stubbornly, however, as underlined by the adverb *ireemant*. What follows in laisse CCCCLXXXV is possibly the most refined example of the author's style; no other scene in his artistic creation is as significant in showing his ability to create tension by shifting his glance from one detail to another.

The laisse numbers forty-seven verses (ll. 11090 to 11137). The first three lines reprise the dialogue of the preceding laisse. From line 11095 to 11099 (6 lines) Roland is described as a warrior who goes back to his king after a victory. The motif of the warrior's return is

---

[11] For the sake of accuracy, it must be pointed out that a few instances show the haziness of the distinction between the two terms. *Force* is actually intended to mean a physical attribute in the proverb 'Maestrise confont force' (l. 1831), which is to say: mastery (*maestrezza* in Italian) weakens strength where this type of strength is meant to be physical, for moral strength cannot be defeated by any mastery whatsoever. Another instance is the out-of-place use of the word *virtuz*, when Roland maintains that 'La vertu some contre la desfaee' (l. 2003).

rendered with a detailed description of Roland's gestures while he descends from his horse without the help of a servant. He sticks his sword in the ground, his shield still hanging from his horse's flank. He takes off his green and gleaming helmet (ll. 11094–98):

> Au trief le rois s'an vient isnellemant,
> Desist a tere, anc ne requist sarçant,
> En tere afice son roit esplié pongant,
> L'escuz li pent el flans de l'auferant,
> Deslace soi le verd elme luisant.

He then enters the king's tent and looks at the barons sitting around him, who all remain silent. It is a moment of great suspense increased by the assonance, with *maintenant* (closing line 11099, as Roland enters the tent with a certain anxiety to meet the king) in opposition to *taisant*, describing the king's attitude towards Roland. The rest of this scene is as theatrical as the beginning: a sequence of gazes and silences followed by Charlemagne's sudden burst of rage against his nephew (ll. 11099–107):

> El paveilons s'en entre maintenant,
> Voit les barons entor le roi taisant;
> E l'emperere de grant ire esprant,
> Dos guainz de maille veit forment manoiant.
> Li quens le garde, si feit chiere riant,
> Devant ses piez en jenoillons s'estant,
> Salüez l'a dou Piere roiamant,
> De sa vitorie le voloit feir presant;
> Mais l'emperere n'i leit dir plus avant…

The poet's gaze focuses first on the circle of barons, then on the king, then on the gloves that become the centre of attention as if everyone present were expecting Charlemagne to use them as a weapon to humiliate Roland. It is difficult to distinguish between the different points of view of Roland, the author, and the audience.

The king's burst of rage against Roland covers lines 11109 to 11114. From line 11115 begins the most dramatic moment in the poem when Roland is publicly punished for what Charlemagne had considered an act of negligence towards the French army, namely of setting off to fight together with a small force while leaving the others behind. Charlemagne accuses Roland of an excessive pride which could have caused the death of all (ll. 11108–20):

> [...] 'Dan culvers mescreant,
> Avez nos vos encor trovez vivant,
> Qe v'en fuïstes de l'estor solement
> Por quoi morisent e moi el remanant.
> Par vestre orguel, qe demenez si grant,
> N'a estez manchise qe moi e ceste gente
> Ne somes mors, j'en sui bien conoissant.
> Mais segond l'euvre en avroiz loemant:
> A cestui mot a levez le un guant;
> Ferir en veult li quens par mié le dant,
> Quant por le nés le consuet tot avant:
> Le sang en raie, q'en rogist l'açerant.

This accusation against Roland is the result of Charlemagne's frustration at the gradual loss of authority over his nephew, rather than an element of characterisation. In fact, as already mentioned in relation to Ferragu's words (l. 2957), throughout the poem Roland reins in his pride, exchanging it for a wiser universal perspective both of himself and the epic action of which he is the protagonist. For this reason he is bewildered to hear that he is accused of acting irrationally when his intention was primarily to defend the royal army. The poet declares the impossibility of describing Roland's reaction (ll. 11123–26):

> Se Rollant fu irez je ne demand;
> En piez saili e mist la man au brant,
> Le roi ferist, quant il fui remembrant
> Qe il l'avoit noriz petit enfant.

About to put Charlemagne to the sword, Roland suddenly remembers that the king looked after him when he was a child. Then five lines follow that can be compared to the opening verses:

> Au trief le rois s'an vient isnellemant,
>
> *Del trief s'en ist honteus et sospirant*
>
> Desist a tere, anc ne requist sarçant,
>
> *El destrer monte, l'escu et l'aste prant,*

En tere afice son roit esplié pongant,

> Les laces ferme de son heume luisant,

L'escuz li pent el flans de l'auferant,

> Ensi des host belement galopant.

Deslace soi le verd elme luisant

> Quant fu defors, si s'en veit speronant:

(11095–99)   (11127–31)

In the closing lines, the action is developed in a way diametrically opposed to the opening ones: Roland repeats the same actions backwards. He now exits the tent, *honteus* and *sospirant* (sorrowful and sighing), where at the beginning he had entered it *isnellemant* (in haste and anticipation). He mounts the horse, clasps his shield and spear, ties the laces of his glittering helmet, and leaves the camp at a gallop. On solely poetical grounds and against reason, Roland is made to take the shield and spear before fastening his helmet, and in the first passage he in fact first frees his hands from the weapons and then removes his helmet. The scene's whole movement from verses 11095 to 11131 has a strong theatrical flavour, representing the arrival and departure of the hero whose mood is now dramatically reversed by the circumstances – an inversion which might be said to reflect that of the action. The whole episode is very humbling for Roland. It is also a climax in his questioning of the king's authority and recollection of his self-worth; it eventually brings the hero to detach himself from the king's authoritarian figure so as to undertake a process of growth, and acquire status and identity as a literary figure, as he had not done in the *Chanson de Roland*.

In this dramatic clash with the emperor, Roland displays a great deal of maturity and attachment to his king and kin. He does not react to the accusations but keeps his anger to himself and leaves the king's tent without a word. It is now evident that the author's intention is to rewrite Roland's destiny, no longer characterising him as an immature and temperamental bachelor but as a man whose loyalty to his emperor is deeper than the outrage to his own self-esteem.

Thus, Roland sets out on horse without any goal and formulates his unusual revenge. His shame is great, his rage making him forget friends and family. He decides that before he returns he will be missed as a warrior and as a friend, and begged to do so (ll. 11131–37):

> Quant fu defors, si s'an veit speronant:
> En strange guise veult fer son vengemant.
> Honte le maine et hiror si tres grant
> Ne lui remambre d'ami ne de parant;
> Anz q'il retort, par le mien esciant,
> De lui veoir seront plus desirant
> François et Carles qe mer de son enfant.

This scene closes both the laisse and first part of the poem, although the second part is usually considered to start from the second protasis, that is from line 10945.

Roland in *L'Entrée d'Espagne* and in the *Chanson de Roland*: a portrait of the hero

It has been pointed out that the hero of an epic is never an individual: his goal is not personal destiny but that of a whole community.[12] This statement is certainly useful. However, if we consider that Roland's differing fates in the *Chanson* and in the *Entrée* is what distinguishes the two poems, then in the *Chanson*, on the one hand, Roland's death is both the result of a personal attitude (pride) and the extreme sacrifice, comparable to martyrdom for faith, which determines Charlemagne's revenge and final victory; on the other hand, there is something radically new in the chivalric poem in that the element of wonder intervenes to temper the tragic element. In this way, while the chivalric hero is allowed an entire dimension of experience (in the form of adventure) for negotiating his own identity and his own goals, the epic Roland is not given the necessary space to display other facets of his character. A useful insight into the *Entrée* can be gained from a comparison between the original Roland of the *Chanson* and the later Roland of the Franco-

---

[12] M. Bakhtin, *The Dialogic Imagination*, p. 28.

Venetian poem. Differences in adjectives and attitudes produce two types of heroes, of which the epic Roland is the closest to the ideal warrior. It is his pride – his *desmesure,* that is insistence on heroism which hinders more than it helps in winning the cause – which makes him characteristically epic. Roland in the *Entrée,* by contrast, is a multifaceted character who displays more features of the ideal knight than of the standard epic hero. Thus the epic hero undergoes modifications from the earliest days of the *Chanson* to the latest developments of the *Entrée,* so much so that either the Rolands of the *Chanson* and *Entrée* can no longer be regarded as the same character, or two different types of epic hero can be identified. In fact, later developments of *chansons* feature mature heroes – warriors with additional responsibilities[13] – the identity of an epic hero altering according to environment or contingency.

Before proceeding to study Roland's characterisation in the *Entrée,* it is useful to recall a few of its motifs in the *Chanson de Roland* that have consigned to posterity the epic portrait of the hero as a young man. In the *Chanson* Roland is portrayed as a passionate adolescent whose fervour in battle and ardour in serving his uncle's cause lead him to blindly accept any burden, sometimes illogically and against his own interest. His emotional reactions, due to excessive pride, are the most dominant of his features: 'Rollant est proz e Oliver est sage | Ambedui unt me[r]veillus vasselage' (ll. 1093–94).[14] The two aspects of knighthood are here separated and united at the same time in the Roland-Oliver couple.[15] The perfect

---

[13] For example, the Cid. See R. H. Webber, 'Towards the Morphology', p. 7, and above, p. 15.

[14] A comprehensive study of Roland's *desmesure* and the opposition between *sage* and *proz* is J. Misrahi and W. L. Hendrickson, 'Roland and Oliver: Prowess and wisdom, the ideal of the epic hero', *Romance Philology* 33 (1979–80), 357–72. See also C. Lelong, 'Olivier peut-il se passer de Roland? Remarques sur le devenir de l'éternel second dans le récits de la Materia di Spagna', in M. Possamaï-Perez and J.-R. Valette, eds, *Chanter de geste. L'art épique et son rayonnement. Hommage à Jean-Claude Vallecalle* (Paris: Champion, 2013), pp. 241–57.

[15] The image impressed on the seal of the Templars represents two knights on one horse: this is the meaning of knighthood up to the beginning of the fourteenth century (that is until the order of Templars

knight results from a fusion of *prouesse* (valour) and *sagesse* (wisdom or prudence); the result of the mixture of these two qualities is *mesure*[16] of which Turpin is the ultimate example: 'l'arcevesque, ki fut sages e proz' (l. 3691). However, a number of times Oliver is said to be *proz* as well as kind and courteous, thus fusing these qualities together into the portrait of the perfect knight: 'Mult par est proz sis cumpainz Oliver' (l. 546); and again later: 'Mult par est proz Oliver, sis cumpainz' (l. 559); 'E Oliver, sun nobilie cumpaignun' (l. 3690); 'E Oliver, li proz e li gentilz' (l. 176); 'E Oliver, li proz e li curteis' (ll. 575–76); 'E Oliver, li proz e li vaillanz' (ll. 3185–86); 'E Oliver, li proz e li curteis' (l. 3755). In the *Chanson*, therefore, it is Oliver and not Roland who takes up the role of the perfect knight, while Roland's role is the paradigm of martyrdom for faith, and thus his characteristic must be the quintessential *prouesse* without any sign of wisdom (*Rollant li proz*, l. 986).

The motif of *desmesure* is very much present also in the *Entrée*, although it is no longer regarded as a feature characterising Roland at a young age but as a generally dishonourable behaviour affecting the image of the perfect knight.[17] Examples of the word's negative use related to Roland's behaviour occur when Oliver addresses Roland as 'cist hom desmesuré' (l. 1403) or when he refers to his *desmesurançe* (l. 1530) and to 'l'ovre che samble altrui desmesuree' (l. 2005). Another example is again found in Oliver's words, when he says: 'Par ce qu'il soit de tiel desmesurance' (l. 2193). However, this aspect of Roland's personality will soon disappear, starting with the episode of the duel and particularly during the dispute in which Roland, on the one hand, proves to be *sage* and *mesuré*, and on the other is irritated by his interlocutor's lack of reason. In line 1814, Roland's literal counterpart, Ferragu, is *plain d'orgoil*.

---

was extinguished by Clement V, in 1312). On this point see F. Cardini, 'Il guerriero e il cavaliere', pp. 91–93.

[16] F. Cardini, 'Il guerriero e il cavaliere', p. 91.

[17] In the Breton novel, *desmesure* is shameful to the perfect knight. This idea is found in *Perceval*, for example: 'Quar desmesure ne outrage | n'est pas honor ne vasselage' (MS Montp. f. 77d).

THE MAIN CHARACTERS

A part of this study dedicated to the theological dispute contains a reference, among other influences, to the work of Raymond Lull, who may have played a part in the shaping of the character Roland in the *Entrée*. Along with the possibility of converting Saracens using such theological disputes, Lull also speculated on the mystical meaning of chivalry in the *Libre de l'orde de cavayleria*,[18] elaborating the idea (as already expressed by St. Bernard) that war is only an allegory for *pugna spiritualis*.[19] As late as the beginning of the fourteenth century, therefore, the idea of perfect knighthood was understood as merging *prouesse* and *sagesse*. For this reason the Roland in the *Chanson* is perceived as an incomplete character in need of updating.

The episode of the siege of Najera in the *Entrée* shows a Roland who still reflects his early model. Shortly before the siege, Charlemagne and the barons defend themselves from the pagan accusation that they have invaded Spain without having been challenged (ll. 1052–55):

> Rollant respunt: 'J'an fui prime areisné,
> Combatrai lui en l'enor Damedé
> E de l'apostre qe il nos teint serré'.
> 'Neis' – dist le roi – 'par mon chief, non firé.
> Mesajer frere, car vos an retorné'.

---

[18] Written in Catalan and translated into every major European vernacular, this text was circulating so widely that a copy could be found in virtually every nobleman's library throughout the fourteenth and fifteenth centuries. A famous copy belonged to Miguel de Cervantes. R. Lullo, *Il Libro dell'Ordine della Cavalleria*, transl. by G. Allegra (Vicenza: L.I.E.F., 1972).

[19] St. Bernard draws the ideal profile of a new knighthood composed of monk-warriors. This monastic-chivalric order is in sharp opposition to *militia saeculi*, the secular knights, who devote themselves to foolhardy fratricidal wars between Christians. St. Bernard condemns their customs, habits and lack of genuine virility, and contrasts them with *miles Christi*, the Templar, who exclusively practises *pugna spiritualis*.

Roland declares that he will fight in the name of God. A few lines later, Roland is portrayed as the champion of the Christian world by Estout, who provokes Ferragu's irritated reaction (ll. 1553–59):

> 'Crois tu, Paiens, qe tant fus esoté
> Se ne m'avoie Rollant sentis daré,
> Le campions de la Cristienté,
> L'ardiç, le fort, le bien endotriné?
> Car bien savomes qe vos, Paiens, tremblé
> Tot par lui sol, quant il vos vient nomé'.

Later, when Charlemagne proposes that Roland leave Spain and return to France to avoid the duel with Ferragu, Roland replies that he could not bear the shame, for Aude and Girard would think him a coward, and Ogier together with the other peers would be disappointed since they all came to Spain to see him fight. If he did not fight against Ferragu, furthermore, nobody else would be able to defeat the giant who would eventually hang all the French. Roland still feels the burden of being Christendom's champion (ll. 1603–10):

> Le duc Roland vers le roi s'adreça,
> A ses paroles bien responduz i a:
> 'Mon sir' – fet il – 'bel Audan que dira?
> E dam Gerard, que si niés m'ancharja?
> Les autres piers et Ogiers qe fera,
> Che sol par moi sont venus jusque ça?
> Se je les lés, Feragu n'en prandra
> Reançon nulle, mais qe tuit les pendra'.

At the end of the duel's first day, Roland departs from Ferragu to return to Charlemagne's camp where he finds the king awaiting him. Charlemagne again suggests that they immediately leave Spain but again Roland refuses. He will carry on the duel (ll. 1940–48):

> Respont le duc: 'Biau sir, e je l'otri.
> A celui pont tornerois a Pari
> Che je avrai delovrez li cheiti
> Che tantes fois vos ont en camp servi.
> O je serai ensamble lor basti,
> Ch'il ne diront que les aie traï

THE MAIN CHARACTERS

> O je les en trarai o brant d'acer forbi.
> S'a cors a cors Feragu nen onci,
> Je vivrai certes o siegle a grant envi'.

While, on this occasion, Roland's desire to fight against Ferragu may seem dictated by his *desmeasure* and contradict Charles' rationality, the case is rather the reverse because Roland's sense of responsibility is no longer influenced by *desmesure* but by a rational understanding of what can harm or favour the French.

Roland's grasp of the need to outgrow his *desmesure* gradually becomes evident as events unfold. After Charlemagne offers Roland the crown of Spain, Roland refuses using a very down-to-earth argument, as a good servant would address his master, or rather as a good merchant would a bourgeois audience (ll. 4446–60):

> 'Grand merci, syre' – ce dist le pugneor –
> 'Quand de la enprise c'avons feite des hor
> Serons a chief, celui meïsme jor
> Prenderai corone e recevrai ma uxor.
> Se je non sui avant tiel servior
> A ceste graçe qe ele, por sa douçor,
> Moi di: 'Prende – n'avoir nule paor –
> Ce c'as meris de ta juste sudor',
> Ja ne prendroie d'Espaigne un cheitis bor,
> Car le bon serf qe n'aime desenor
> Ne quiert merit se il n'a feit son labor;
> E hom orgoilos, syre, feit gran follor
> Q'en l'altrui ort plant fruit ni aubor,
> Car aul collir ça en ont li pluisor
> Englotis fruit de trop agre sapor'.

Here Roland is no longer a legitimate heir expecting what he considers his by birth, a *conditio* of the nobility. He is a wise young man who wants to deserve whatever he is given and is unafraid to take possession of what he has gained by his own sweat (*n'avoir nule paor*: don't be afraid to take what you have gained, 4452), according to a bourgeois mode of thinking. A colourful metaphor is used to express the idea that nothing is to be accepted before one has fully gained it: the proud man makes a great mistake planting trees in someone else's orchard, for he will gather bitter fruits. This sounds like a proverb, many examples of which can be found in the *Entrée*, or a sentence from Scripture. Regardless of the author's source what is important is that the style is humble and perfectly comprehensible to a wider audience, including wealthy merchants and their offspring.

The poet introduces the section dedicated to Roland's adventure in the East with his appreciation of the young noble's independent personality (9407–09):

> Or lesomes de Carles, si feruns menteüre
> Dou jentil cont Rollant, qe ne garde a mesure:
> Comant il en port bleisme, segir veult sa nature.

In fact, during his journey Roland will have many opportunities to show that he can look after himself regardless of his remoteness from his own environment, and also that he can become popular and necessary to his hosts. Even though Roland carries the blame for his *desmesure*, he acts according to his nature and reacts haughtily to situations only where necessary. For example, in the Spanish port where he landed after so much wandering, two Saracens accuse him of being a robber. Roland replies furiously but while also arguing for the need to defend the weak and poor against the arrogance of the wealthy.[20] Roland accuses the two Saracens above all of *vilanie*, in conformity with the ethics of knighthood (ll. 11543–50):

> De mautalant vient Rollant pali e van;
> Dit au Paiens: 'Tu pués estre vilan,
> Quand vilenie me dis sens nul certan;
> Mais se fuses armé o engual man,
> Dir te savroie, licer, fils a puitan,
> C'anc ne robai tant qe valsist un pan.
> Por que is d'avor e de richeçe plan,
> Altrui desprises com orgoilos e van'.

Roland's argument is just: because they are wealthy, they assume they can insult and despise other people. This is a single occurrence

---

[20] On this episode see also S. Sturm Maddox, '"Non par orgoil, mais por senefiance". Roland Redefined in the *Entrée d'Espagne*', *Olifant* 21: 1–2 (1996–97), 31–45.

in the poem of an insult directed at Roland, which triggers a violent reaction inspired not by *desmesure* but by his sense of justice. Of course, Roland easily slaughters the two nasty Saracens. The scene ends with a motto of the author: 'Por ce dit voir dan Caton li Roman: | Gran vertus est a metre la lengue le fran' (11562–63). The accusation of *vilanie* (as opposite to *chevalerie*) and the author's half-serious closing motto make the whole episode a very lively sketch, which could certainly belong with Breton romances.

Roland and the Saracens

In the East, Roland acquires a new identity and disguised as a Saracen he enters the court of the king of Persia. His new identity is made up of multiple aspects: a new name (Lionés), lineage (the son of a merchant), and religion (a Muslim). Differing from preceding cases of an epic hero undertaking adventures in the East,[21] Roland in the *Entrée* in fact gains legitimisation and approval from the Saracens, having offered some decisive guidance in a domestic affair of great importance. His presence amidst the pagans is therefore completely accepted when he assumes the governance of Persia.

Before Roland goes on a mission to Syria on behalf of the Sultan, Dionés forecasts his victory against Malquidant, and her mother the queen insists that Dionés marry Lionés. The Sultan promises to discuss the matter of the marriage between Dionés and Roland after the war is finished. It is at this point that Roland is caught in the temple of Mohammed, pretending to worship the god of the Saracens but in his heart praying to God (ll. 13631–43):

> Tres en mi leu dou tenple s'est Rolant jenoilé;
> En sun cuer reclama le Rois de maïsté.
> 'Precios Sir' – dist il – 'vos souiés mercïé
> De si grant honor chun vos m'avez apresté,
> Que il non m'avint pas de la moie bonté,
> Mais, Sir, de votre grace, glorios sire Dé.
> Senpre vos soit mon oncle le roi recomandé,

---

[21] As in *Huon de Bordeaux*, for example, where the hero still has a degree of detachment from the new environment; the pagans maintain their role as the hero's antagonists.

> Oliver et Estous et le noble berné
> Que sunt par mon amor in Espaigne lojé:
> Non soufrés qu'il soint de Païn domajé.
> Et, se il est honors de vostres Deïté,
> Ancor et sans et saus entr'els me ramené:
> Tant que je le revoie jamés n'iert mon cors lé'.

His prayer shows how Roland preserves his own identity and religion despite having been integrated into Muslim society, by pretending to pray like other Saracens but in fact worshipping his own God in the pagan temple. This episode is set at a stage of the narrative where the reader has become almost accustomed to identifying Roland as a Saracen; it works as a reminder that Roland is expected to return to Spain at some point and that he still retains his Christian identity, though temporarily disguised as a Saracen. It is also a thought-provoking narrative device in that identity is not made to coincide with disguise – and quite groundbreaking considering that in the poem's literary milieu characterisation depended mostly on external traits. Of course, examples of disguise abound in medieval works. This instance, however, seems to invite reflections on the authenticity of a hero rather than work as a mere complication for the sake of the plot.

Although catapulted into a new world, disguised as a Saracen and deprived of his noble birth, Roland's consistent exhibitions of loyalty and chivalry prevent him from entirely deluding his new friends. Even Pélias, the utmost enemy of Lionés/Roland and though unaware of Roland's real lineage, recognises a hero beneath his disguise as a merchant's son (ll. 12925–36) and changes his feelings towards him, indeed deeming his enemy a great fighter. This also happens when Dionés gives Roland new arms for the battle against Pélias. While she ties the helmet on his head, she comments on his social status: 'Dist la roïne, com dame aperceüe: | "Lionés, bien sambles home de grant nascue"' (ll. 12565–66). Roland comes across as a nobleman despite his change of identity.

However, Roland seems to be at ease with his new persona as his identification with both merchant and wandering knight results from the osmosis of two different ethics: that of the urbanised knight detached from the feudal context, and of the adventurous merchant dealing with the practical risks of trade. He displays the first in the defence of the lady, one of the main motifs of chivalric literature. Although scholars have often recognised behind the stereotype the sexual impetus of chivalric literature, this is not the case here. Roland does not offer to champion Dionés in hope of a sexual reward, which comes to him anyway as an offer of marriage. His offer follows closely the standard behaviour and is formulated with the words of the *chevalier parfait*.

As already discussed, Roland's predominant practice in the second section is to circulate the ethics of chivalry among his Saracen fellows. The first episode occurs before the war when he explains the cult of chivalry to Sansonet and the young Saracens (ll. 13702–15):

> Le uns non velt sens l'autre manjüer ni dormir,
> A l'uns riens n'adelite que l'autres s'en aïr.
> Rolant aprant sovant le valet d'eschrimir,
> Et legier et sailant le ha fait devenir.
> Aprant li chun il doit honorer et servir
> Li pobres civaler[22] et voluntiers oïr,
> Et largement doner sens grant proiere dir.
> 'Amis' – ce dit Rolant – 'se tu veus esanplir
> Chun is plus gentils home, garde toi de mentir,
> Et non impromet zouse qe tu non vois balir,
> Char ce est une teche qe molt fait repantir
> Les bons de si fait home honorer ne seguir.
> Se tu soz mes peroles te savras bien covrir,
> A ton preus m'as veüz en ces regne venir'.

He has another opportunity to introduce courtly manners to the Saracens upon returning to court from the journey through Syria, during a feast (ll. 13968–91). Bancourt's view is that the purpose of the Eastern episode is to depict the civilising role of the French in

---

[22] *Li pobres civaler* (l. 13707) reminds us of the *fraternitas* of *pauperes milites Christi* led by Hugues de Payns, a chivalric monastic order composed of ex-crusaders and pilgrims to the Holy Land which became the order of the Templars. Their duty was to protect the weak and defend the pilgrims in the newly conquered territories. This is the second occurrence of a reference to St. Bernard's *Liber ad milites templi*.

the East.[23] Read in the light of the distinction between secular and celestial knighthood, however, the meaning of Roland's teaching of the art of chivalry to Sansonet expands beyond that of performing a *rôle civilisateur* in the East. It completes the hero's characterisation, introducing a modification in the structure and meaning of Carolingian epic. Roland's relationship with the Arab world seems to be functional to this modification in meaning, eventually leading to the inclusion of the figure of Roland in the Italian environment.

Charlemagne in the *Chanson de Roland*

Since characterisation is a result of both objective description and the character's interaction with the other figures of the narrative, as discussed in the previous section, Charlemagne in the *Chanson de Roland* could hardly be defined as a character. In every circumstance the emperor appears hieratic and as immobile as a statue. He is detached from ordinary human emotions apart from a constant sorrow that seemingly prevents him from making any independent decisions. He comes to accept the risk of losing his nephew, the person dearest and closest to him, to preserve his dignity in the face of Ganelon's arrogance and evidently cruel intent. As for Charlemagne's physical portrait, his main attribute is his long white beard which is to be looked upon as a symbol of authority rather than a physical trait.

When members of his army fail to display affection towards him (which is almost everyone) or persist in behaviours that might affect the prosecution of the war, the king is never blinded with rage nor becomes vindictive. Verses 259, 262, 271 and 273 of the *Chanson de Roland* are the only exceptions, when he quite brutally silences Roland, Oliver and Turpin during a dispute over who should go to Saragossa (ll. 259–62, 271–73):

> Respunt li reis: 'Ambdui vos en taisez!
> Ne vos në il n'i porterez les piez
> Par ceste barbe que veez bla[n]che<ie>r,
> Li duze per mar i serunt jugez!'
> Li empereres respunt par maltalant:

[23] See Bancourt, *Les Musulmans*.

alez sedeir desur cel palie blanc!
N'en parlez mais, se jo nel vos cumant!

Another exception in the *Chanson*, though milder, is when Charlemagne realises that the assembly gathered to decide on Ganelon's treachery favours mercy for the traitor. He reacts by calling the whole assembly felons (ll. 3814–17):

Ço dist li reis: 'Vos estes mi felun'.
Quant Carles veit que tuz li sunt faillid
Mult l'embrunchit e la chere e le vis.
Al doel qu'il ad si se cleimet caitifs

Charlemagne does nothing except scratch his head, lower his eyes, and call himself a prisoner and miserable man, but he takes no action. It is left to Thierry to intervene and form a second party to resist showing mercy to Ganelon. It seems that the emperor is enslaved by his vassals. A similar situation is found at the poem's climax, in laisses CXXXII to CXXXVI: Ganelon's treachery becomes evident and his imprisonment scene is farcical – except that the retaliation against Ganelon is not meant to be comical (an effect perhaps suggested by the realism of the cooks featuring in the scene)[24] but rather to emphasise the tragedy underpinning the plot. In these crucial laisses of the *Chanson de Roland* it is not Charlemagne who accuses Ganelon. While Roland blows the horn Charlemagne limits himself to stating what is happening: 'Karles l'oït e ses Franceis l'entendent | Ço dist li li reis: "Cel corn ad lunge aleine!"' (ll. 1788–89). Again, it is the intervention of wise Naime that leads the emperor to have Ganelon imprisoned (ll. 1790–92):

Respont dux Neimes: 'Baron i fait la peinte!
Bataille i ad, par le men escïentre.
Cil l'at traït ki vos en roevet feindre'.

Only after Naime's recognition of the baron's falsehood does Charlemagne give the order to leave the traitor to the rage of the

---

[24] As discussed by E. Auerbach, *Mimesis. The Representation of Reality in Western Europe*, transl. by W. R. Trask (Princeton: Princeton University Press, 1974).

cooks, who will torture and chain him as though a captive beast (ll. 1825–28):

> Bien le batiren a fuz e a bastuns;
> E si li metent el col un caeignun,
> Si l'encaeinent altresi cum un urs;
> Sur un sumer l'unt mis a deshonor.

Meanwhile the emperor, mounted on horseback, is full of disdain.

Every laisse witnesses the tragic air which pervades the poem. There are two postures typical of Charlemagne in the *Chanson* which emphasise this overwhelmingly tragic spirit and underline the impossibility of the emperor intervening personally to redirect events. As above, one is of Charlemagne riding upon his horse when perturbed by events or in his distinctive hieratic fashion, depending on what is happening.[25] In context, this seems to be the only possible attitude which allows him to endure an acutely painful situation. The idea is repeated three times in the course of four laisses (l. 1812, where he rides *par irur* which again does not signify 'raging' but 'in disdain', that is simultaneously disgusted and upset by the betrayal of one of his best men; ll. 1834, 1842). The moments when the king is captured in this attitude create suspense and usually anticipate the onset of tragic action.

Charlemagne's other typical gesture is pulling his beard as a sign of pained or angry hesitation. The verb occurring in all these situations is *irer*, conveying the idea of a painful emotional state that he tries to control (ll. 2414, 2930, 2982, 3711–12):

> Tiret sa barbe cum hom ki est irét
> Sa barbe blanche cumencet a detraire
> Carles li reis en ad prise sa barbe,
> Si li rimembret del doel e <del> damage
> Carles en ad e dulor e pesance,
> Pluret dez oilz, tiret sa barbe blance

He also lowers his head and remains pensive when circumstances would require him to be decisive. He is said to be in no haste to

---

[25] Ll. 739, 1812, 1834, 1842, 2444, 3117, 3121, 3695. Besides riding, he very often mounts and dismounts the horse: ll. 2448, 2457, 2479, 3096, 3112, 3679.

speak and when delivering a speech, does so as a person of great authority. His face is proud when he raises his head (ll. 139–42):

> Li empereres en tint sun chef enclin,
> De sa parole ne fut mie hastifs:
> Sa costume est qu'il parolet a leisir.
> Quant se redrecet, mult par out fier lu vis.

Sometimes the two gestures merge. After Roland had fiercely contradicted him on the matter of waging war against Marsile, the king maintains a serious gaze, strokes his beard and has no answer for his nephew (ll. 214–16):

> Li emper<er>e en tint sun chef enbrunc,
> si duist sa barbe, afaitad sun gernun,
> Ne ben ne mal ne respunt sun nevuld.

The same attitude is shown when Roland is forced to agree to lead the rearguard. Furthermore, it is frequently repeated that the emperor cannot keep himself from crying (ll. 771–73, 825, 841, 1404, 2855–56):

> Li empereres en tint sun chef enbrunc,
> Si duist sa barbe e detoerst sun gernun.
> Ne poet müer que de s<es> oilz ne plurt.
> Pitét l'en prent, ne poet müer n'en plurt
> Carles li magnes ne poet müer n'en plurt.
> Karles li magnes en pluret, si's demente
> En Rencesvals en est Carles [entrez];
> Des morz qu'il troevet cumencet a plorer.

At the very end of the poem, when the martyrs of Rencesvals are vindicated and Christendom is victorious over the pagans, Charlemagne welcomes St. Gabriel who comes to call him to a new mission in the land of Bire. The king shows no enthusiasm and in fact does not at all long to undertake another task (ll. 3999–4001):

> Li emperere n'i volsist aler mie:
> 'Deus!' – dist li reis – 'si penuse est ma vie!'
> Pluret des oilz, sa barbe blanche tiret.

This hardly seems like exemplary behaviour from the supposed champion of Christianity. Throughout the text the impression that one gets is that the king is trapped and cannot move a step without the approval of all the assembly and the twelve peers of France.

Such a character may reflect the political situation of early medieval France; the king had very little independence and every act, military and domestic, required an agreement with the many vassals who held a fief and small army, and could fight for themselves:

> The Emperor's entire position is unclear; and despite all the authoritative definiteness which he manifests from time to time, it seems as if he were somnambulistically paralyzed. The important and symbolic position – almost that of a prince of God – in which he appears as the head of all Christendom and as the paragon of knightly perfection, is in strange contrast to his impotence. [...] It is possible to find various explanations for all this: for example, the weakness of the central power in the feudal order of society, a weakness which, though it had hardly developed by Charlemagne's time, was certainly prevalent later, at the time when the *Chanson de Roland* originated.[26]

Charlemagne in *L'Entrée d'Espagne*

The sense of the tragic Christian role of Charlemagne in the *Chanson* is no longer conceivable at the time of the *Entrée*'s writing. The latter's major modifications to Charlemagne's characterisation can be read in the light of a different social and political context in which the handling of foreign and domestic affairs took on more complex forms – to this one should add the lessened urgency to construct a national myth for the area where the poet very possibly lived and composed, namely Lombardy.

The *Entrée*'s author no longer represents the emperor as hieratic, remote and statuary but as *desmesuré*, unutterably furious, incapable of profiting from Roland's achievements because they stem from autonomous decisions. By creating a character who functions as a despot, the poet queries the precept that supreme power is not to be

---

[26] Auerbach, *Mimesis*, pp. 100–101.

contradicted, allowing a reassessment of Roland's importance as an independent figure.

Charlemagne in the *Entrée* is still defined as the emperor but this title alternates with the more frequent one of king. In a number of laisses (for example CLXXXII; CLXXXIII; CLXXXVII; CCXXXIV) the two words occur in proximity to each other and always refer to Charlemagne. In one interesting case in the *Entrée* the French monarch is said to be (ll. 459–61):

> [...] gentis rois Carlemaigne
> Sire de France et d'Alemagne,
> Enpereor de Rome e roi

It is intriguing to investigate how the characterisation of the emperor/king as a despot on the defensive might relate to the debate, taking place in Italy at that time, about the necessity of self-government and the opportunity for opening Italian territory to imperial influence.

In the *Entrée*, there is a gradual change in the king's feelings towards his kin. It appears increasingly evident that Charlemagne cannot suffer Roland's intellectual independence. In the *Chanson* tradition, whenever a problem arose every member of the baronial court could express his own opinion and suggestions; here it seems that the king is not very willing to accept his nephew's point of view, given that Roland does not fully agree with his uncle in most cases and is undiplomatic in displaying his aversion to decisions by the council of peers. Charlemagne's hostility to Roland's initiative gradually increases from subtle irritation to open rage, to such an extent that he eventually decides to have Roland murdered.

One of the first situations in which Charlemagne appears is while dealing with the pagans at Najera when he is accused of invading Spain without having been challenged. In this passage he appears proud but diplomatic, in contrast to the offence of the invasion (ll. 997–1009):

> 'Amis' – dist l'amperer – 'tu pués dir ton coraje,
> Qe par nus hom n'avras engombre ne doumaje.
> Proz puet ton seignor estre, mais mout petit fu saje,
> Quant il sor un tés per encarga son mesaje.

> Di lui de nostre part et dou nostre barnaje
> Qe retraions Marsille hom decahu d'omaje.
> Par ploisors anz nos a tenuz le treüsaje:
> Or domandons Espaigne par nos droit heritaje.
> Ja n'avons revestuz le filz de mon soraje
> Et par lui coroner somes en cist viaje.
> Se ton sir en veult contradir le pasaje,
> Repantir se poroit dou grant fais q'el encarje,
> Car bone gent avons et de grant avantaje'.

On two occasions Charlemagne begs Roland to return to France with him, openly admitting that he considers the conquest of Spain unworthy of the enormous effort. When Roland wants to fight against Ferragu, Charlemagne cries, expressing his disapproval of and sadness over Roland's decision (ll. 1586–602):

> Atant ech vos l'enperer corajos
> Al frains le prist dou rice destrer ros,
> E, larmoiant de ses oilz anbedos,
> Li dist: 'Biaus niés, et ou aleroiz vos?
> Vorez morir vers cil Turc diablos
> Che non resoigne, biaus niés, ne nos ne vos?
> Li .XI. piers a pris e Ogier le pros.
> Par vos sui jé, biaus ami, fortunos
> Et obeïz et honorez de tos:
> Se je vos pert, ensi remanrai sos
> Cum pobre dame quant a perdu l'espos.
> Tornomes, frere, ou regne glorios,
> Car cist païs commance estre anoios.
> Ja n'ai plus fils. Pres ma mort, ami dos,
> Rois vos feront Franços et Herupos,
> Et le Romans vos clameront a vos
> Lor emperere, dont il sont desiros'.

We can notice several points in this long speech. The king here appears much closer to the character in the *Chanson*, especially in the closing lines where he seems reluctant to take responsibility for Christendom's defence. Charlemagne proposes a much more reasonable plan to Roland: to return to their glorious country where the Francs and Europeans will crown Roland king, and the Romans acclaim him their emperor.

The terminology here is very interesting. Why should both French and Europeans call him king? Who does the author refer to with the word 'Europeans', and does he mean Germany, Spain and Flanders? Why should the Romans (perhaps signifying the Italians?) want him as an emperor? From the time of Frederick I, the emperor was German. It is necessary to investigate what significance the poet might have attached to the word 'emperor'. There is a great difference between the idea of empire in feudal society as represented in the *Chanson* (that dates back to the eleventh century), and at the end of the thirteenth and start of the fourteenth century in Italy as represented in the *Entrée*. The idea of universality, which belonged with that of emperor in the feudal system, did not apply to the era of Philip IV, considered an emperor in his own kingdom without implying his absolute power over an extended territory.[27]

The efforts of Philip IV to consolidate his rule over a larger territory lasted throughout his reign. In the political and cultural environment of Italy these efforts were received in various ways. Petrarch, for example (in *Rime Sparse*, XXVII and XXVIII) considers Philip, king of France, to be a new Charlemagne, referring to the common identity that France had found under the great king. What is important to Petrarch is the idea of national identity that accompanies subjection to the French monarch.

While it is clear that the mention of the French and Europeans may reflect Philip's efforts to expand his dominions, that of the Romans is more obscure. On the one hand, the poet makes a distinction between Europe and 'Romans'. On the other, he combines the expansion of the French kingdom with the possibility that an emperor (presumably German) can bring peace to Italy.

As the poem goes on the king becomes more aggressive as he senses the peril to his authority. When Charlemagne thinks Roland has been killed by Ferragu, he experiences a moment of genuine

---

[27] A classic treatment of the idea of the empire and its distinction from kingdom is in R. Folz, *L'Idée d'empire en occident du Ve au XIVe siècle* (Paris: Aubier, 1953), especially pp. 135–67.

desperation: he pulls his beard and cries, and recalls the *Chanson*'s Charlemagne (ll. 1757–61, 1767):

> Le roi revien e se garde anviron
> Sa barbe sache e tire son grignon,
> Pués bat ses paumes e escrie a fiers ton:
> 'Rollant amis, Rollant mon compaignon,
> Biaus niés, biaus frere, n'ai parent si vos non'.
> Lor cheit pasmez;

The same situation reoccurs a few laisses later when Roland and Ferragu decide to separate for a while and continue their duel later. Charlemagne welcomes Roland very warmly and again repeats the idea that there is no need to remain in Spain. He sounds highly protective towards Roland and talks to him like a father (ll. 1923–39):

> Ne demandez, seignors, je vos en pri,
> Se l'enperere dou baron s'esjoï.
> Qui donc veïst quant il le recoli
> En ses dos braces e le dist: 'Biaus ami,
> Par pué ne m'ais encué le cors parti
> Quant al Paiens aporter vos en vi!
> Lors quidai bien, par viritiez vos di,
> Che Nostre Sir m'aüst mis en obli.
> Pués que vos estes par divine merci
> E sans e saus retornez jusque ci,
> Alons en France, por amor vos en pri.
> Soz fier planez en fer punt sui parti;
> Trop ai trové felons cist enemi,
> Trop a Marsile son païs bien garni
> D'un seul diable che m'a plus esmari
> Ne fist Braibant le jor chel conbati.
> Ne tornerois plus ci, jel vos afi'.

Starting a few lines later, however, Charlemagne's attitude changes. During the temporary ceasefire after the French defeat of Najera, the king is caught looking at his young nephew from a window of his palace. He had just offered him the crown of Spain but Roland had refused it on the grounds that he will consider himself worthy to become a king only when the entire campaign is finished. After the baptism of Najera's citizens there follow a few days of rest and feasting, and then Charlemagne decides to talk to Roland and remind him that capturing one city does not mean the war is finished. Charlemagne displays no trust that Roland will ever bring the war against Marsile to a conclusion (ll. 4481–93):

> Mais li emperere, plein d'aut entendiment,
> Avoit son cor mis sor autre talent.
> As fenestre ert a un evesprement
> E voit Rollant chevaucher bellement,
> Li doçes per avec lui solement,
> Gardand les dames qe as baucons estoient.
> A l'emperere en est pris mal talent;
> Croule le cief e dist: 'Trop malement
> Feisons scemblant d'ostoier longement.
> Se devrons guere mener sifa itement,
> Ja roys Marsille, a cui Espaigne apend,
> Non perdra mais de sa tere un arpent;
> Mais, por san Jaches, il ira autrement'.

He announces to Roland that it is necessary to besiege Pamplona, where Malgeris lives. He condemns the long rest after the conquest of Najera, and Roland declares he is ready for the battle and will leave immediately. The king commands him to take only half of his 10,000 men and to leave the rest guarding the *oriflamme*. He gives him instructions not to start the battle until the king has joined him with the rest of the army, an order which Roland will not obey, causing the king's rage and initial desire to retaliate. Naime intervenes, saying that there are not enough men, but Charlemagne allows nobody to contradict him (ll. 4551–54):

> Respond li emperere: 'Ne vos en redoté.
> Bien sai ce qe puet fere Malçeris l'amiré;
> S'il eüst plus de gent qe il non a asé,
> Ja n'enseroit des portes; trop le croi ensené'.

It is evident that Charlemagne gives questionable orders despite the intervention of Naime who is always shown to be wise and trustworthy in his advice. Roland displays no reactions, merely accepting the orders and leaving. In this delicate situation there is no sign whatsoever of Roland's desmeasure.

Another episode in which Charlemagne displays a despotic attitude is found in and following laisse CCXXXIX. Roland is in a bad mood, having lost most of his men during the battle, and Estout has been captured by the pagans. Roland had previously captured Isoré, Malgeris' son, and sent him to the French camp. He reports the result of the expedition and tells the king that his garrison was much inferior to the number of the fighting pagans, and that he would like to know what has happened to his cousin. Charlemagne wants to retaliate against Isoré for the death of Estout but Roland does not agree (ll. 5667–70):

> 'De Hestou' – dist Carles – 'se perdus le avon,
> Est grant domaje de prous e jantils hon;
> Mais sor le fil Maugeris le fellon
> Prendrai vengiançe de mon gentil baron'.

Roland replies in a kindly manner ('con benigne façon', l. 5674) to Charlemagne's proposition (ll. 5682–84):

> 'S'est mort Hestous, Deu li face perdon,
> Que ja en teil gise n'en ferai vengeison,
> S'il fust celui qui ja m'oncist Million'.

At this point all those present express their appreciation for Roland's noble heart: '"Non fu plus rice de tresors Laumedon | Come tu is de noble cousençon"' (ll. 5686–87). But the king displays the same kind of irritation as a man who does not want to be contradicted in his own house (ll. 5688–702):

> Le roi oi ce, ne lui fu trop de bon,
> Si com le home qu'en sa propre maison
> Ne veult de rien avoir contrediçon.

Charlemagne quotes the proverb:

> 'Home qui taise e sofre orguel sa hoisor,
> Si li mete hos sor le chief le raisor,
> Car il subjete liberté et honor'.

Then he reproaches Roland:

'Je l'ai ja dit, si le dirai ancor,
Tant com je vive n'avrai teran seignor:
Por qoi le die, jel tais por le meilor.
Si niés Roland, grant est vostre valor,
Mais ne voudroie qe fil de ma seror
A qui je fais honor de jor en jor…
Se bien fait ai, non veul estre pejor'.

He orders Roland to bring him Isoré. Roland's answer is again very cautious and circumspect. In his speech, Charlemagne all but suggests that Roland is arrogant and puts him in his place; he is the son of his sister, whom he does not need to honour. To such an extent will accusations of arrogance will be repeated later that Roland will take them as a grave affront. In this situation, though, he prefers to control his emotions and appeal to Charlemagne's chivalry: 'Le duc Roland s'aïra durement, | Mais ne le veult demonstrer autement' (ll. 5716–17). As usual when friction occurs between Roland and Charlemagne, the intervention of Naime, Oliver and Ogier lead the two to find agreement. In this case, although the French all agree with Roland that the king is being despotic, they will convince Roland to come to terms with his uncle. Oliver's words are the most significant: 'Dist Oliver: "Le roi feit vilanie: | Qui l'en conseile feit ancor plu folie"' (ll. 5764–65). Two things are implied here: first, it is a *vilanie*, the contrary of *chevallerie*, to retaliate against an innocent man. The idea is that every episode is treated as an adventure in which the knights and king should behave according to the dictates of chivalry. Secondly, the king does not make his own decisions: he has someone counselling him. This is in evident contradiction to the king's constant endeavour to stress his independence of action and thought, as witnessed a few lines before.

Predictably it is during a banquet that they find a solution after Naime and Ogier have persuaded Charlemagne to restrain his rage: 'Tant i dist Naymes et Oger d'Alemagne | Que l'emeperere sa grant ire refragne' (ll. 5816–17). The king proposes to Isoré that he should go back to his father[28] and convince him to convert and yield

---

[28] Charlemagne sends Bernard, an educated knight of Roland's garrison who speaks Spanish, as a *latinier* (a translator) together with Isoré: 'Qi

Pamplona. If Estout is still alive, alternatively, they will bargain to exchange the prisoners. If neither of these two options applies then he will take his revenge on Isoré.

He remarks that his nephew will have no reason to complain: '"Rolant, mes niés, tot si com el immagne; | N'avras por moi cosse dont il se plagne"' (ll. 5829–30). He finally agrees to delegate the matter to Roland. The prisoners are returned although Malgeris refuses to convert and surrender. Even if being contradicted in his own court and by his own men thoroughly irritates Charlemagne, this can be considered as a temporary upset and a first sign of pent-up frustration that will come to a head only later, when the king faces increasing criticism from his own men, including Roland.

Later when Roland decides to besiege Noble without consulting the king, Charlemagne's authority is more seriously threatened. During a feast following Estout's return to Charlemagne's camp, the king is informed that the French vanguard has been defeated at Noble, and that the major part of the food supplies has been stolen and the camp destroyed. The king is said to sweat from rancour while the barons stand in silence: 'Le roi l'entent, de maltalant trasue; | Sa baronie en sun taisant e mue' (ll. 6690–91).

On another occasion Charlemagne is said to be sweating from anguish. Referring to the episode when the king slapped Roland in the face and caused the hero's departure, Estout declares in front of all the barony of France that if he had suffered the same from the king it would not have helped the latter's claim to kingship because, in spite of all consequences, Estout would have wounded him with his sword ('Lors moille Karles d'angose e de sudor', l. 11206).

Even Roland admits to sweating when Charlemagne declares that he wants Roland to bring his prisoner to him: '"Sir – dist Roland – je n'ai trop grant sudor | Por celes paroles, car il seroit floor"' (ll.

---

bien savoit de Espaigne le latin' (l. 5843); 'Le latiner s'en veit, qui mout fu sage' (l. 6021); 'Por droit parler l'Espagnois, bien vos di, | Cun de enfançe iluec il fust nori' (l. 7171). The poet is concerned with the problem of different languages and makes his audience aware that the Spanish cannot communicate with French people, except through a translator, unless one of the parties speaks the other's language. Although this is not openly said in the text, Roland seems to be fluent in Arabic when he goes to Persia.

5711–12). This realistic detail contrasts with the dignity of the two figures in the *Chanson*. There, the eponymous protagonist is often caught unleashing his youthful power, the most characteristic of his features. Since he is expected to be *desmesuré*, the reader is not tempted to consider this a simply human reaction. It is in fact the hero's characterising trait, and as an attribute it contributes to the forming of his portrait. Similarly, the king is often oppressed by the burden of his stature or, when driven by circumstances to disdain, is full of pride and never lets go of himself. Even Charlemagne's tears in the *Chanson* still belonged to the stylised portrayal of an icon, so often do they occur and in precise and invariable situations. The realism of this new portrait in the *Entrée* reveals that neither Charlemagne nor Roland are treated any longer as icons or representations of noble characters superior to all human experience – eating, drinking, sweating and bursting out in a very credible and human rage as they do when events force them.

Charlemagne decides to send an expedition to Noble but beforehand he gives instructions to prepare reinforcements outside Pamplona, to avoid any surprises while most of the army is away. He orders the Tiois (a Germanic people) to carry the wood to the camp which the king's *maître des œuvres* needs to build the defences and which has already been cut by the French. The king expresses his appreciation of the Germans by saying that they are hard workers, thus displaying a noticeable regard for those who earn their living. He does not realise that he is reducing the Germans to the humiliating rank of hewers of wood and drawers of water (ll. 6780–88):

> 'Quant il avront copé les grant arbor,
> une partie des Alemans de sor
> (Che nel tienent a mal ne a desonor,
> Mais tote voie furent bon servior),
> Cestor serunt des aubres condutor,
> Car il sont grant e ne dotent labor,
> Mais de travail vivent e de suor;
> Decique a l'ost serunt mi portaor:
> Ne lor en faut merit e grant honor'.

Everyone seems happy with the task they are given, except for the Tiois who go around the camp complaining that the king is treating them like fools (ll. 6820–25):

> Ne li fu gent che lor clamast sordois,
> For solemant les montanier Tiois
> Chi vunt par l'ost disant a dos e a trois:
> 'Cist roi entant de fraper nos le dois?
> Chi nos comande, por feir de nos gabois,
> A porter ce che coupent ses Franzois'.

They plan to leave Charlemagne's camp during the night, when everyone is sleeping, and go back to their countries. However, one of them decides to betray the plot to the emperor. At first the king is surprised ('Dunt l'emperere s'en mervoile forment', l. 6848). Thus, *merveille* is his first reaction.

The next laisse opens with an image of the worried king. The interruption between one laisse and the next seems to give the king's shock just enough time to ripen into a state of worry ('De ces novelles nostre roi mult s'esfroi', l. 6849). His behaviour is bizarre: he calls Salomon and makes him believe that Marsile is sending a part of his army to Navarra. He wants Salomon to await and attack the supposed pagan garrison, and expresses his urge for vengeance to the baron: 'Vos savés bien omei che je voldroie: | Se moi venjés, mout joiant en seroi' (ll. 6865–66). What is impressive is the amount of energy that Charlemagne employs in retaliating over one marginal episode of insubordination. From his supreme position of command he could easily have ordered the Germans to complete their task or have just sent them home, since their rank in his army was practically insignificant. Had Charlemagne wanted to be openly despotic, in fact, he could have had them slaughtered without further explanation or the need to weave secret plots to catch them. Instead, he prefers to conceal his plan and deceive Salomon into believing they are pagans, so that he will attack them as they flee. What emerges in this episode is the emperor's rancour towards anyone who dares to contest his authority. Two full laisses pass before it is clearly stated that the king is aiming to fulfil his desire for revenge upon the traitors ('Mout fu de soi vanger nostre roi desirans', l. 6900). In the next laisse it is said that: 'Sor son lit se couga pensis et irascu' (l. 6926).

The Tiois hear the noise of the French army led by Salomon, who is convinced he is approaching the pagans. When Salomon sees the garrison he rejoices, thinking he has found his target, and the battle starts, bitter and harsh. But when the French start chasing the Germans in the woods, Salomon suddenly recognises the colour of the flag and realises that they are Christians. He blames himself, thinking he has made a mistake and killed half of the allied army. Charlemagne sees the traitors coming back still alive and tells the baron about the deadly treachery which had spawned his rage. Seized with fury he asks the barons to vindicate him and not to allow themselves any pity (ll. 7016–22):

> A ses barons plu maistre les mostre, e conte a lor
> La mortel traïson dunt il out grant iror.
> Nostre roi Çarlemaine si mue sa color
> E dist irieemant: 'Por Deu, le roi de sor,
> Proier vos voil tratot, les grant e li menor,
> Che de cil moi venjés, ne vos pragne tendror,
> Car je plu lour ahei che la jent l'Aumansor'.

As in any difficult circumstances, it is Naime's intervention that makes the king rethink his position. Naime here is particularly harsh towards the king, accusing him of foolish behaviour, and fully supporting his cousin Herbert who led the Germans' retreat (ll. 7023–29):

> 'Par Deu, sire' – dit Naimes – 'ci oit mauvés labor;
> Une si grant folie ne feïstes anchor,
> Quant si leiseç oncir de vos jent le milor.
> Mon queisin est Erber, neç somes de seror,
> E quant ne mel disistes, mout m'en tein a peior.
> Bien mostre Salemon ch'el nen i oit gaire amor;
> Repantir se poroit biet tost de son furor'.

The king does not of course take these words lightly but because he appreciates Naime he does not want to contradict him: 'De ces paroles l'enperer mout s'aïre; | Tant ama Naimes nel volt pais contradire' (ll. 7030–31). Naime then goes to his cousin Herbert who still believes it was the pagan army that charged them, and lets him know that they were in fact attacked by the French whose aim was to prevent them from deserting Charlemagne's camp. He asks Herbert to beg for the king's mercy, for they all deserve to be hanged or burnt and so they have no other choice. Herbert bends his knee before the king, who has him guarded as a prisoner and then brought to his tent where he will eventually take his revenge.

The situation then becomes very confused and even, to an extent, comical: Naime goes to Salomon to blame him for the slaughter of the Germans. Being a German, Naime declares that as soon as the war is over he will challenge Salomon to prove whether the Germans or the French are superior. Quite shocked, Salomon replies that the emperor sent him to stop the pagan garrison heading towards Navarra, and shows no suspicion that he might have been fooled by the king himself. Naime at this stage does not know how to reply. No sooner is the conversation over than the king arrives on horse, accusing Salomon of spoiling his plan (ll. 7091–96):

> 'Por foi' – feit il – 'mort m'avez deservie
> Quant les traïtes, cui Damedeus maudie,
> Esparagnastes, chi ma host hoit gerpie.
> Confunduç soit chi plu en vos s'en fie!
> Serviç m'avez hui jor de trecarie;
> Nel fist hanc home de vestre ancesorie'.

Yet how was Salomon supposed to know about the German's treachery if the king did not tell him, and how can the king now insult him and claim to be disappointed when all this confusion was nobody's fault but his? In fact, in the following lines Salomon turns to Naime and blames the king for his misleading conduct (ll. 7106–08):

> 'Mal fist mon sire quant il bien ne m'aprist,
> Car tot celor che pont deshobeïst
> A tort son sire, Deable ert ses minist'.

A long dialogue follows where Naime begs for mercy on behalf of the Germans. Roland and Estout intervene and fully support Naime. Not surprisingly, Estout's intervention is the most amusing, for he compares the situation with his experience as a student when his teacher used to beat and then forgive him. The whole scene is highly entertaining; the reader becomes completely absorbed by the different voices and opinions surrounding this complicated matter (a complete muddle in fact). In the end they find a reasonable and merchant-like solution: the Germans will be charged a fine consisting of four measures of gold and silver. As we can see, the penalty finally imposed is rather mild compared with all the fuss the king made about the episode of treachery. He could certainly have solved the matter in a less complicated way, if only he had not been blinded with rage and hatred when he saw his authority questioned by ordinary soldiers.

Nevertheless, when Charlemagne hears that the war-engines built to assault Pamplona have been moved beneath the city walls and subsequently burnt by the pagans, he is seized with gloom. Even though the responsibility lies with a part of his own army (which decided to move the engines without consulting him), this time he exhibits no rage. Indeed, the adjective used to describe the king's mood is no longer *irez* but *mautalentis*, sorrowful in the face of the disaster ('Por mal talant oit le roi sospiré', l. 7406). In the *Entrée*, the words most frequently used by the poet to characterise Charlemagne are undoubtedly the adjective *irez* and variants, and adverbs derived from the verb *irer*. In the *Chanson*, too, it is often the meaning conveyed by *irez* that characterises Charlemagne – but this is not wholly translated by 'rage', for the idea of the emperor suddenly unleashing his anger does not tally with the character described in the twelfth-century poem, and on the very few occasions when he loses his temper the words used are *par maltalant* (l. 271). The two words, although apparently synonymous, need to be translated in different ways in the two poems, conveying different degrees of rage and distinctive modes of its expression.

The situation is critical. Malgeris hears that Marsile has sent reinforcements led by Turquis de Tortolose; a spy informs Charlemagne about the new threat while he is sitting at his table in deep gloom: 'Noncer le vait au roi poesteïs | Che sist a table forment mautalentis' (ll. 7509–10). He decides that Roland shall go first and stop the additional pagan troops while Charlemagne with the rest of the army will join him later and together they will fight against the pagans. Roland therefore rides to Pamplona with his army and once there finds that Malgeris' and Torquis' military contingents have come together. He decides to join battle, but the pagans are successful and the city is lost. Not long after the defeat, Roland, now 'plain de grand desplaisir' (l. 7906), sees Salomon and Richard joining together with Charlemagne's army. He starts blaming them for being late (ll. 7913–19):

> 'Signor' – feit il – 'mout saveç bien dormir:
> Dormant quidés vos nemis desconfir?
> Ja ne verois li quatre jor complir
> Che de repois n'avrois trop grant desir
> E cils che voi environ moi sorir
> Gardant l'un l'autre, si cum por escrignir,
> Ferunt lor rois cum mout aguç sopir'.

Hearing these harsh words addressed to his barons, Charlemagne replies severely. He accuses Roland of being arrogant and acting proudly (ll. 7920–36):

> Çarles respunt, che ne se poit teisir:
> 'Orguel fist ja mant pros homes morir,
> Sire Rolant; je vos voil descovrir
> Une raisons che vos doit abelir
> (Ja le dist Naimes por Estous garentir,
> Quant le rescuis por Ysorés garpir):
> Une sol home ne poit le must conquir,
> Soit beus quant veult, fort e de grant haïr,
> Che s'il pur veult a l'orgueil consentir,
> La ou doit pros estre, orgueil li feit fuïr.
> Por vos le di, ne vos en sai blandir:
> Quant vos veïstes de Païn tiel enpir
> E jent n'avoies par celor sostenir,
> Cortoisemant v'en deviés partir,
> Si poviés la mort a mant homes guencir.
> La vostre fam, chi tot cuide anglotir,
> Aprés mangier vos fera mal geisir'.

The allegation is particularly bitter. Charlemagne is saying that Roland is responsible for many Frenchmen being killed on the battlefield. He should have withdrawn the army rather than assault the city. It is the fault of Roland, not of those who 'were sleeping', as Roland puts it: he should not have exposed his men to such a danger in the first place.

In Charlemagne's speech two things are particularly striking apart from his allegation against Roland. First, he uses the adverb *cortoisement* as if the battle were a courtly matter; likewise, he had called the siege of Noble an *aventure* (l. 7211); suddenly, Charlemagne seems to be quite concerned about courtesy. Secondly, he associates Roland's pride with the sin of gluttony, and compares his appetite for glory with physical hunger when after a few generous servings at dinner one cannot rest properly because of indigestion. These words sound fairly coarse in the king's mouth: they would have been more appropriate if spoken by Estout whose frequent down-to-earth remarks at this stage of the poem are familiar to the reader. Moreover, the reader wonders how Charlemagne can be so shameless as to blame Roland for being too proud when he himself, a few laisses before, had through his irrationality caused a situation as fraught as that of the German treachery. This is not to mention line 5764 where it was Oliver who accused the king of *vilanie* (which is to be understood as the contrary of *chevalerie*) when he wanted to hang Isoré, an innocent man and of high rank, in retaliation for the loss of Estout. At this stage, the reader would no longer expect Charlemagne to be particularly full of wisdom and courtesy. In fact, as emphasised above, his words sound very much out of tune with his character.

One wonders whether the poet was completely aware of the inconsistent portrait of the king that he was offering. Many reasons may have caused him to alternate moments of excessive passion with others of sudden regret and a return to rationality. It may be that the poet was inspired by edifying literature in use at the time, in which moralising lessons against sinful behaviour could be derived from *exempla*. More likely his attempt to remain faithful to the traditional image of Charlemagne faltered in the face of the historical context in which he was writing. The composition of a poem of such length must have stretched over many years, during which the poet's point of view may have changed from time to time according to the political circumstances. Northern Italy in the fourteenth century was undergoing a transition from government by the commune to that of the lordship, the latter's political structure imitating, on a minor scale, the model offered by the kingdom of France. The increased influence of the French monarch on Italian territory may have affected the poet's approach to French epic.

One event particularly disconcerted intellectuals in the first years of the fourteenth century: Philip's aggression against the authority of the Pope, who was attacked at Anagni by William of Nogaret on the orders of the French monarch. The transfer of the papal court from Rome to Avignon was a memorable *débâcle* for papal authority. The complete subsequent subjugation of ecclesiastical to monarchical power culminated in the election of Clement V, a French pope who was manipulated by Philip and refused to be consecrated in Rome, instead holding the ceremony in Lyon. The events of Anagni and Avignon changed the image of the king of France forever in Italian eyes. These events contributed to ignite the debate over authority in Italy, and particularly over whether the Pope's authority should be replaced by that of the emperor, conceding to the clergy only moderate scope for political interference.[29]

The question of authority

The episode of the siege of Pamplona creates a divide between Roland's spontaneous behaviour and his awareness of there being no

---

[29] The thought of Marsilius of Padua is particularly enlightening in this context. It is nowadays possible to examine the *Defensor pacis* and other works by Marsilius as documents of a precise historical situation, expressing a gradual transformation and annihilation of the feudal structure of European society at that time. While Marsilius was not an idealist but promoted a realism grounded in contemporary developments, aiming to adjust it to the reality of the communes, Dante was the strongest supporter of the myth of a unified Empire; he specified that subjection to the emperor was bound to solve the Italian issue. Like Dante, Marsilius did favour an Imperial intervention in Italy but was mainly interested in depriving the clergy of its power over the people. Marsilio da Padova, *Il difensore della pace*, ed. by C. Vasoli (Turin: UTET, 1960); Marsiglio of Padua, *Writings on the Empire. Defensor minor and De translatione imperii*, ed. by C. J. Nederman (Cambridge: Cambridge University Press, 1993). Folz, *L'idée d'empire*; F. Adorno, T. Gregory, and V. Verra, *Storia della Filosofia* (Rome/Bari, Laterza, 1984), pp. 530–31.

possibility for him to act autonomously. From now on in the poem, this awareness grows gradually until it reaches a climax in the scene of Charlemagne's blow with the gauntlet.

After Charlemagne's words (ll. 7920–36), Roland becomes pale and his blood boils. He attempts a reply but Hugue steps in and (relieving the situation with a *boutade*) then carries Roland away. Roland is thereby virtually prevented from expressing an opinion about his autonomy. Even though all the barons are bewildered by Roland's words to the emperor, in the next scene where they are gathered all together, Roland emerges as the only character in the whole poem who has become genuinely intolerant of Charlemagne's despotism. Roland, Girard, Estout, Oliver, Eçeler de Bordelois and Hugue de Blois discuss Charlemagne's conduct. Estout opines that Roland has no rights over the king and must respect the hierarchy, as the king had already pointed out (ll. 5996–6702). He suggests that Roland not display his annoyance since there is no possibility of winning over the emperor. It is made clear, and generally accepted, that the king owes no explanation whatever to his barons, who are certainly to be considered as subjects (ll. 7962–64):

'Sir' – dit Estous – 'ver lui n'avrés ja drois.
Por les paroles ne vos mostreç irois,
Car il poit dir se feir tote fois'.

Estout and Oliver then convince Roland to join the king's banquet in his tent. However, Roland is utterly disheartened by his uncle's words. He decides to restrain his temper and stay quiet but the frustration he feels is about to manifest itself: 'Mais de parole fu Roland si grevois | Qu'il le mostra avant compli li mois' (ll. 7975–76). Meanwhile, Charlemagne attempts to lighten his reproach by showing him that submission is a good cure for pride. His words remind the reader of ll. 7920–36: 'A soi li appelle, e mostra e descovri | Che hobedïence senpre orgueil venqui', (ll. 7981–82). Roland's endeavour to defend his autonomy, however, causes him to clash once more with the king in the following episode. Having decided to launch the attack against Pamplona, Charlemagne arranges the details of the expedition. He offers Roland the marshal's baton which would put him in control of the entire army. The king's words are kind and affectionate (or might be understood as patronising), and he speaks to Roland as he would to his own son (ll. 8301–33):

> Rolant apelle dousemant por amor
> 'Prenés, biaus niés, cist baston frasenor,
> Sevrés les renges des grans e des menor'.

The relationship between the two characters at this stage is completely directed by Roland's frustration and resentment. Charlemagne's attitude is lenient since he has established for Roland his unquestionable supremacy. The king is therefore willing to move on and again treat his nephew as he has always done in the past. It is Roland who now no longer disguises his disapproval of Charlemagne's despotic attitude (ll. 8304–07):

> Respont li duch: 'Non ferai, mon signor.
> Ne m'entremet de jent alienor,
> Fors de la moe, dunt je sui senator,
> De qui m'a feit lo pape condutor'.

Once more Roland manages to annoy Charlemagne who again blames his excessive pride and confines him to the rear guard as punishment for his insubordination (ll. 8314–21):

> De ces parole oit li roi grant iror.
> 'Roland – feit il – trop estes plain d'ardor,
> Tiel cum vos fustes senpre vos trov ancor
> Mais, por la foi che doi au Salvator,
> De la bataile anchoi n'avrés l'onor.
> Je vos comant e tuit vos seguior
> Qu'aprés ma ensagne soie vestre demor
> En la bataile derere, qui ch'en plor'.

This excerpt recalls the most famous episode of the *Chanson* in which Ganelon proposes Roland as the leader of the rearguard (laisses LVIII to LXII), albeit in reverse: while in the *Chanson* Charlemagne was saddened by this decision, in fact, in the *Entrée* it is he who punishes Roland by confining the young hero to the rearguard. One finds the same situation as in the *Chanson*: the council is gathered to assign ranks in the army before the start of the military expedition. However, the two passages are different in register and motivation. Roland's *desmesure* in the *Chanson* is a self-defence mechanism, since he understands that he is being betrayed by his stepfather and reacts impulsively. In general, his reaction is amply justified by the king's inability to change Roland's destiny; while he still depends upon the barons' judgement, none of those present, except (as usual) for Naime, says a word in his support. The impossibility of finding another solution and the resultant frustration make this passage intensely dramatic in register. In the *Entrée*, conversely, Roland is pushed to oppose Charlemagne by his resentment towards him. As Charlemagne in the *Entrée* assigns the ranks in the army at his own discretion, Roland can blame him directly for assigning him to the rearguard. There is no sign of tragedy: the king gives the insolent youth the lesson he deserves and carries on allocating tasks. Once again his authority is not a matter for discussion; there is no pulling of beards, tears shed or commotion as the emperor confronts and punishes insubordination from his position of unquestionable authority.

While Roland is guarding the oriflame during the siege of Pamplona, Bernard (the spy sent to Noble, laisse CCCVI) returns to tell him that the city has no garrison and can easily be taken if he leaves immediately. But the king is in battle and there is no time to wait for his return and decision. Roland therefore decides to set forth for Noble, taking the entire garrison except for five hundred knights left with Ogier to guard the oriflame. No sooner has he left the battlefield than a German cries out that Roland is deserting his uncle's army to return to France. Charlemagne witnesses the sudden withdrawal of his army and, full of ire, asks Hugue what is happening (ll. 9206–208):

> L'enperer, quant les voit, a pué d'ire ne fent.
> Il a gardez a destre, a suen arestemant,
> Le cont Hue percuet, par mié l'escuz le prent.
> 'Par qoi – feit l'emperere – s'an veit arier ma gient?'

Hugue tells him that Roland has abandoned them. The author again opts for the device of dividing the two stages of Charlemagne's reaction between the end and the beginning of two succeeding laisses, as in ll. 6848–49. The three closing lines of the first laisse are descriptive and their purpose is to create suspense. The king is caught by surprise which he expresses with a rhetorical question. He turns back towards the oriflame where Roland's troop was supposed to be but he does not see anybody and is about to faint. The first action describes a state of mind (surprise), the second a physical movement, the third action is this movement's product (*garde-voit*), and the fourth returns to a moral condition – pain (ll. 9218–20):

> 'Est ce voir?' – feit le rois – 'Oïl, par san Climent'.
> Le rois si garde ariere, o l'orieflor resplent;
> Ne voit la gient ses niés; a pué le cors n'i fent.

The action is repeated in the following laisse, in which the king's anger is fully developed. Charlemagne declares that he had many other occasions in the past to prove himself vindictive, and this time he has no intention of being lenient with Roland: he will chase him over hill and vale, and will deem himself less than a slain wild animal if he does not have him hanged (ll. 9221–34, 9239–40, 9242–43, 9301–02, 9399–406):

> Irez fu l'enperere e dist: 'Par saint Silvestre,
> De ploisors grant outraje et ovres desoneste
> Me su je ja vangez: si fera ge de ceste.
> Cest feluns traïtor a feit une moveste
> Por voloir qe je moire: ce sa je manifeste.
> Mout m'a renduz bon cange qe sui en sa conqeste
> E par lui honorer su je an peril d'estre
> Perdanz, moi e mes homes, ou de membre ou de teste.
> Par cil Dieux q'en la cros sofri paine et moleste,
> N'ala si Galaaz por le Graal en queste
> Con je ferai par lui en plains et en foreste;
> En lui vaudra mie de suen brant la poueste,
> Que bien pis me tenroie d'une scorchie beste
> Si pandre ne le faiz; si an soit q'en puet estre'.

> 'De ce prendrai venjance, se unqe mais port veste,
> E non lairai en vie un tot sol de sa jeste'.

> Irez fu l'enperere, coroçous et despers;
> Ses homes voit fuïr, s'an devient paile e pers.

> L'enperere en son tref fu forment d'ire caus;
> Anz ne l'osent garder François ni Provençaus:
>
> Dedanz la rice tende, dun d'or fu l'orleüre,
> Comant asalirent Paiens trosqu'en la mure
> E de la maistre porte ont rumpue la penture.
> Li roi respont irez et saint Donis en jure
> Qe de Rollant prendra une venjance dure,
> Car por son departir et sol por sa fature
> A hoi de Pampelonie perdue la droiture.

Roland returns to Charlemagne's camp after the conquest of Noble, and Charlemagne renews his intention to take revenge on him for having escaped the battle (ll. 11049–50, 11060–62):

> Le roi oi dir qe retornoit Rollant:
> Le cor li enfle d'ire et de mautalant;
> 'Je en prenderai encué tiel venjament
> Dont il se garderont cescuns de ci avant
> De non partir nde moi si fetemant'.

When the barons hear that Charlemagne persists in wanting to retaliate against Roland (after all the misery the French army has suffered since the paladin's departure), they refuse to conform to Charlemagne's foolish behaviour. Not only do they all thoroughly dissent but they also address the king as a fool and declare they will not obey his insane rancour. They all agree that Roland, not the king, is the only reason they are there (ll. 11067–71):

> 'Qi a soi meïsme feit onte et mespeison,
> L'en le dovroit pandre come leron.
> E donc n'est Rollant li canpion
> Qe nos mantient en peis et en reison?
> Par cui somes nos ci se par lui non?'

At this stage Roland's autonomy seems to be openly acknowledged by the entire court; it is a collective opposition that Charlemagne must face to such an extent that it becomes impersonal and expresses a view of social injustice. One unidentified speaker (*uns*, l. 11072) laments that his son suffered a punishment when he dared to say a bad word against Roland, but that the king can speak at his discretion without facing any sort of consequences (ll. 11072–76).

> Respondi uns: 'Par li cors saint Simon,
> Je ai lessé un fils a ma maison:
> Anç le ferroie sor le chief d'un bastun
> Qe je disis Rollant un mal sermon;
> Le rois puet dir ses talant et ses bon'.

This anonymous voice, speaking amidst an audience of barons, is that of the people. The fact that it is impersonal is a device aimed at allowing a representative fourteenth-century bourgeois, fully aware of his significant contribution to the contemporary economy, to speak up for his class in this highly important political assembly where the matters of autonomy and authority are definitively discussed. This is an isolated case in the *Entrée*. Nonetheless, it is important to acknowledge it as a reflection of the spirit of the time. It may also suggest that the onlookers participated in the assembly, opening the possibility that elements of storytelling helped shape the *Entrée* so as to allow a collective voice to be heard. Philip IV had summoned the Estates-General in 1302 to receive aid and counsel from the three estates, thereby including the participation of commoners in the event of a major crisis; therefore, it is not surprising that in an early fourteenth-century poem the atmosphere of a general assembly is recalled.

Meanwhile Roland is prepared to present himself before the king, unconcerned by the advice of Richard and Salomon to keep away for a while, and on the contrary seemingly annoyed by their insistence. Roland trusts the king and does not want to believe that he can be so mean (*bricon*) as to harm him (ll. 11084–91):

> Qe lui distrent: 'Par algune equeisun
> Devant li rois non alez a cist pon:
> Corocez est, anc si nel vit nus hom'.
> Le cont respont: 'Je nel sant si bricon
> Q'il moi fesist ni disist se bien non
> Ne domajast por consoil de fellon'.
> 'N'i aler, frere' – dist Riçars li Normant.
> 'Si ferai certes' – dist il ireement.

THE MAIN CHARACTERS

He enters Charlemagne's tent and finds all the barons gathered quietly around the angry king. Two mail gauntlets are lying on the table right in front of him as a weapon ready to be used, in anticipation of what is about to happen (ll. 11101–02):

> E l'enperere de grant ire esprant,
> Dos guainz de maille veit forment manoiant.

Roland bends his knee, but the king does not allow him to talk and at once attacks him verbally (ll. 11107–16):

> Mais l'enperere n'i leit dir plus avant,
> Ançois li dist: 'Dan culvers mescreant,
> Avez nos vos encor trovez vivant,
> Qe v'en fuïstes de l'estor solemant
> Por quoi morisent e moi el remanant.
> Par vestre orguel, qe demenez si grant,
> N'a estez manchise qe moi e ceste gent
> Ne somes mors, j'en sui bien conoissant.
> Mais segond l'euvre en avroiz loemant:
> Ferai vos pandre, par le cor sant Amant'.

Charlemagne relentlessly accuses Roland of excessive pride. In the *Chanson* the emperor never reproached Roland, while Charlemagne in the *Entrée* speaks his mind and is no longer portrayed as a paralysed puppet. In order to develop Roland's characterisation, it was perhaps necessary to create a character who would express his views and interact with the other characters in the court. The author's intention is to create a hostile environment in which, on the one hand, the character of Roland becomes fully rounded, and on the other, his escape is justified.

In the following scene, besides his vehement reproach, the king punishes Roland with the highest offence a knight can ever receive: he is slapped in the face with a gauntlet (ll. 11117–20).

> A cestui mot a levez le un guant;
> Ferir en veult li quens par mié le dant,
> Quant por le nés le consuet tot avant:
> Le sang en raie, q'en rogist l'açerant.

Roland decides not to react and instead departs. The king is left in his tent, regretting what he has just done. Estout, Girard and another hundred men arrive at the king's tent. Estout is the first to speak. His speech is worth quoting in full for it proves again that the French solely rely on Roland and that the king is excessively confident of his own authority; in fact, Estout is not afraid to question it (ll. 11184–207):

> Le roy trovent dolant e plein d'iror,
> Car repentis estoit de cil folor.
> Primer parole Hestos le pugneor:
> 'Dam roy' – dist il – 'qe fais scemblant de plor?
> Quele part ais mandé li mon signor?
> Qe l'ais feru, ce disent li pluisor.
> Est cist le bien e le gré e li honor
> Qe tu nos portes, qe estais en sejor
> E nos te conquirons le cités e li bor?
> As gran peril de bataile e d'estor
> Somes devant li primer feridor;
> A mort alomes por esamplir ta honor.
> Trop bien nos ais meris en cestui jor,
> Quand cil por cui avons force e valor
> S'en veit irés, Diex sait de son retor.
> Mout l'ais trové ancui plain de douçor.
> Por celui Sire c'un clame Redemptor,
> A moi Rolland ne val pas un tambor:
> Se tu m'aüses ferus por tiel labor,
> Bien qe sor moi en tornast la peior,
> Poi te valsist dir qe eis emperor
> Qe je ne te ferise de mon brand de color'.
> Lors moille Karles d'angose e de sudor,
> N'ouse parler por ceus qe sunt d'entor.

Estout's speech against the emperor is harsh, blaming him for his injustice and especially reminding Charles that they are all there fighting to the death to defend his honour ('A mort alomes por esamplir ta honor', l. 11195), and so he has no right to mistreat them. The emperor sweats with anguish. Following Estout, Girard de Roussillon accuses the king of being short-sighted and proud.

Although his register is more diplomatic than Estout's, he declares there is no reason for him to stay when Roland has left, and so he will return to Roussillon (ll. 11210–15):

> 'Syre emperer, por li temp qi depart
> Vos tenoient plus saje e plus manard
> Q'encor fust roy ni François ni Lombard;
> Mais an present petit fu vostre esgard,
> Car por orguel, qe sovant trop vos ard,
> S'an veit celui qe meis revira tard'.

Oliver expresses his opinion that the emperor is to blame since he should be wiser than anyone else (ll. 11233–37):

> 'Droit emeperere – ce a dit Oliver –
> Si m'aït Diex, mout feites a blasmer.
> Nuls sajes hom ni devroit mais errer
> E plus doit estre sajes li justxer
> Qe cil qe vient a lui droit demander'.

Like Girard de Roussillon, he asks the king to be released from service. Since his lord and brother Roland is no longer with him, he will first go to Vienne to communicate the painful news to Girard and Aude, and then disguised as a pilgrim he will go in search of Roland. He will cross the sea and will either find him or die.

As usual, his speech is the most moving: as soon as he stops speaking, in fact, he starts to shed tears, thereby moving more than two hundred hearts: 'Lor comença si fort a larmoier | Q'il en a feit plus de dou cent plorer' (ll. 11281–82). This is an important sign of how public opinion changes at this point. As Oliver is one of the most beloved of all the peers of France, the fact that he makes public display of his desperation convinces all those still needing to be convinced that Roland is right and the king wrong.

The only one who is not so harsh to Charlemagne is Salomon, his devoted assistant, and in fact the only one who always appears entirely subject and faithful to the king. He suggests that they all keep their distance from the emperor's family troubles and follow him regardless. According to Salomon, the barons do not have the right to criticise. It is thanks to his intervention that the king and the French eventually reach an agreement (ll. 11313–14, 11317–18, 11335–36):

> Karles est nostre syr e fa droit e raixon.
> Se il a feru son niés, de qoi s'entremeton?
> Se li roys a mesfeit, repentis le veon,
> Si n'est mie droit q'il en qere pardon.
> Al roy s'acordent, tuit i quirent perdon;
> Kales lui perdona, n'a convint reançon.

However, at the end the king admits he has repented and sends the knights in search of Roland (ll. 11352–53, 11319):

> Neporquant se je ai fet ver mon niés nul desrois
> E j'en sui repanti, sor mon cheit li sordois.
> Mais alez mon niés qerre, se trover le porois

Thus, Charlemagne does not necessarily emerge as a negative character, although in the *Entrée* he tends to act according to his impulsive temper. The situation in the *Entrée* is thereby unexpectedly reversed; while Roland is no longer a temperamental youth but a sensible knight, aware of what can harm or favour the French, Charlemagne cannot control his temper. It is only when the friction has reached a climax that Charlemagne understands how important Roland's presence is in his army, and how much the barons trust and love him - so much so that he must finally accept his own failure.

Roland cannot be found and the king is overwhelmed with grief ('"Ce poise moi", dist Karles, plorand des oil del front', l. 11377). His sorrow presumably endures throughout the time Roland spends in the East – which covers a section of around four thousand lines, but ought to be half the length of the entire poem, considering that a large lacuna (of an estimated 5000 verses) unfortunately disrupts the narrative. Roland's Eastern adventure focuses only on him. Charlemagne's court, the Spanish war and all the problems Roland left behind are no longer mentioned until the hero returns to Spain at the very end of the poem.

Roland returns to Spain

When eventually Roland returns to Spain, Rainier de Nantes, who had gone out hunting hawks, recognises him from afar and rushes to Charlemagne to report. The king is found drowning in despair and pain since, as Roland has not been found, the barons have finally decided to leave Spain.

The king cannot decide whether or not he ought to dismiss them. He deeply regrets having caused Roland's departure (ll. 15344–45, 15380–86):

> Por le roi conforter, qi mout estoit dolant,
> L'enperer ne le seit ne doner ne tolir;
> Lor reclama Roland cun un agu sospir:
> 'Dous fiuz, se tu is mort, car me vien a oncir,
> E se tu is vivant, vin ma plage garir,
> Que tantes fois me feit et jor e nuet morir.
> Rolant, or conois jé qe je feri le sir
> De mon guant par le vis, qi me fesoit servir;
> Ne puis més dolant estre, ne sai fors de taisir'.

The king finally admits his unfairness towards his nephew. Yet despite his sorrow, Charlemagne displays a sudden spark of self-esteem when Oliver promises that he will not abandon him. The king does not allow anybody to feel any pity for him. He declares that anyone can go who so wishes, but that he will die in Spain rather than be responsible for the defeat of the empire: '"Qui veult, aler s'en puet, qe ci vuel definir | Ains que por moi s'en fue le signal de l'anpir"' (ll. 15406–07).

The episode of the final encounter is emotional and through a gradual increase of theatrical *vis*, the use of such devices as dramatic retardation, and by lingering over narrative details, it provides fully rounded characters for Roland and Charlemagne. As Roland embraces the king's right leg and foot, Charlemagne is overwhelmed by pity and joy ('De pietié e joie', l. 15754), and cannot speak (ll. 15750–56):

> Roland encontre son oncle s'en venoit,
> Tost che le roi descendre luy voloit,
> Le duc l'enbrace la janbe et le piez droit.

> Le roi desend del cival o seoit;
> De pietié e joie le cor oit si destroit,
> Qu'en celu pont, par tot l'or che ce soit,
> Non poust mie ver lui parler un moit.

The king kneels in front of his nephew and pleads for mercy but Roland, who is the living example of humility and pity, kneels and pleads for mercy too (ll. 15757–62):

> Davant son niés engenolé seroit
> Mercé crïer de ce che feit li oit,
> Més cil, che tot de bonté sormontoit,
> S'engenola, si con fere devoit,
> Davant celu che plus de cor amoit
> D'ome del secle, e merci le crioit.

Now that he has repented Charles is called 'the good king', and still cannot speak for emotion (ll. 15782–85):

> De la grand joie c'oit Karles le bon rois
> A poi non pasme por desus le caumois;
> Plus d'un arpaint de terre alerisois
> Anz che parler poüst a clere vois;

Finally he finds his voice, and declares that Roland has resurrected him from death. Great praise of Roland follows in which all the attributes that in the text hinted at his role as the perfect knight are repeated and gathered together – along with epithets that underline his closeness to the king (Roland is his hope, his comfort and his rest, blood of his own blood – 'Cuer de mon vantre', l. 15797, and the light of his eyes), and others referring to his personal virtues (he is the most humble, without pride and arrogance). The king also finally admits that he is nothing without Roland (ll. 15792–805):

> 'Douz fil' – dit il – 'resuresi m'avois
> Da mort a vie; vesqui n'aüse un mois.
> Douz ma sperançe, mon confort, mon repois,
> Brais de justiice envers les orgolois,
> Plen d'unbleté, sanz orgoil e bufois,
> Cuer de mon vantre, clere lus de mes ois,
> Se je vos fi oltraje e sordois,

THE MAIN CHARACTERS

Car pur des ore, biaus duz niés, je conois
Que senz vos bras non valdroie un pois,
E si pri Diex l'altisime gloriois,
Che mort moi soit in compagnie tot fois
Che mas je voie cil pont, quand finirois'.
De la pieté del roi des Romanois
En plurent environ tuit François.

Amidst a crowd of tear-shedding barons, a happy ending concludes the poem. Although the question of this ending is treated further in this study, in concluding this chapter two things must be pointed out generally about the *Entrée*. First, Charlemagne admits that the enterprise of the conquest of Spain depends entirely on Roland, thus elevating his nephew's role. Secondly, at the ending the poet tends to call Charlemagne 'king' rather than 'emperor' (only six times emperor[30] and twelve times 'king';[31] but once he also calls Charlemagne *fil Pepin*, l. 15679; and three times 'Charles': *Karlon*, l. 15511 and 15634, *Karles*, l. 15520, *Çarlemaine*, l. 15507). It looks as if the poet is making great efforts to avoid the use of the word 'emperor'. While in the beginning the author called him *Enpereor de Rome e roi* (l. 461), in the final duplet he is only the king of the Romans (*roi des Romanois*, l. 15804), while in l. 15558 his role is that of *enperer de France*, limiting the area of his jurisdiction and confining his authority to the territory of France. While on the one hand this title connects him to the historical Charlemagne, on the other it diminishes the real role of Holy Roman emperor that he had received upon his crowning in Rome. One may wonder whether these different word choices imply a political stance by the author or whether is it perhaps accidental. In all cases except the last (l.

---

[30] Emperor: *anpereor*, l. 15351; *enpereor*, l. 15356; *enperer*, l. 15379; *enperer*, ll. 15558, 15766; *enperaor*, l. 15740. It is now possible to apply this type of linguistic research to the entire *Entrée* thanks to the invaluable FIOLA (Franco-Italian On-Line Archive), project directors L. Zarker-Morgan and D. Bénétau, at http://www.loyolanotredamelib.org/fiola/ [accessed December 2017].

[31] *Roi*: ll. 15344, 15358, 15743, 15751, 15753, 15791, 15804; *rois*: ll. 15404, 15408, 15483, 15741, 15782.

15740), the words occur within the verses and therefore their choice does not depend on matters of metre and rhyme.

It is possible to conclude that in the course of the *Entrée*, Charlemagne's authority is not simply contested but definitely overcome. Roland meanwhile takes a direction of his own and finally becomes an independent character in the Italian tradition, in that the poem merges the epic genre with the romance to create a unique hybrid, the ancestor of the Italian poem in *ottava rima*.

REPRESENTATIONS OF ISLAM

Islam, Europe and the *chanson de geste*

The two great episodes of the *Entrée* in which Roland interacts directly with the Saracens are the duel between Ferragu and Roland set in the first section of the poem, and the journey to Syria which occupies a large part of the second. These two episodes are rich in elements that suggest an approach to the Muslim world influenced either by the author's personal readings or, more simply, by a different spirit permeating the age in which the poem was written. While a socio-historical treatment of the *esprit du temps* of the fourteenth century would not be wholly appropriate in this context (and partially repeat what has already been convincingly said),[1] a survey of the readings that may have interfered with representation of Islam in the *Entrée* is useful, especially to make progress in the systematic study of the poet's personality and culture.

A number of impressive studies have appeared over the last four decades on the question of knowledge of Islamic sources in Western Europe during the Middle Ages.[2] On the one hand the complex and

---

[1] See, for example, J. Huizinga, *The Waning of the Middle Ages. A Study of the Forms of Life, Thought and Art in France and the Netherlands in the XIVth and XVth Centuries*, trans. by F. Hopman (London: Edward Arnold, 1924; repr. 1976).

[2] N. Daniel, *Islam and the West. The Making of an Image* (Edinburgh: Edinburgh University Press, 1960); N. Daniel, *Heroes and Saracens. An Interpretation of the 'Chanson de Geste'* (Edinburgh: Edinburgh University Press, 1984); R. W. Southern, *Western Views of Islam in the Middle Ages* (Cambridge, MA: Harvard University Press, 1962); Bancourt, *Les Musulmans*; M.-T. d'Alverny, 'Conaissance de l'Islam dans l'Occident médiévale', in *L'occidente e l'Islam nell'alto medioevo*, 2 vols (Spoleto: Centro italiano di studi sull'alto medioevo, 1965), II: 577–602; D. R. Blanks and M. Frasetto, eds, *Western Views of Islam in Medieval and Early Modern Europe. Perception of Other* (New York: St. Martin's Press, 1999). John Tolan's research provides extensive treatment of primary sources: J. V. Tolan, *Medieval Christian Perceptions of Islam. A Book of Essays* (New York: Garland, 1996); J. V.

ambivalent ideas, conceptions and reactions to the Muslim world of the Latin Middle Ages, as analysed for example by T. E. Burman,[3] led medieval writers to portray the Saracens as belligerent and blasphemous, devoted to an obscure cult in their polemical treaties against Islam; and on the other hand to passionate desire for knowledge both of Greek texts transmitted via Arabic versions and commentaries, and Arabic texts on natural philosophy.[4] A similar

---

Tolan, *Saracens. Islam in the Medieval European Imagination* (New York: Columbia University Press, 2002).

[3] T. Burman, *Reading the Qur'ān in Latin Christendom, 1140–1560* (Philadelphia: University of Pennsylvania Press, 2009), who uses manuscripts of the Qur'ān circulating in Europe in Arabic and Latin in the later Middle Ages. Burman's study is a genuine breakthrough in analysis of medieval European reception of Islamic culture, offering original insight into the question.

[4] Dante is a good example of this ambivalent reaction; while providing perhaps the most brutal description of Mohammed ever seen in the Western world, he drew his knowledge of Aristotle from the translations of the great School of Toledo. The academy of translation in Toledo was very active and working on the transmission of the Arabic heritage of Spain. G. Menéndez Pidal, 'Còmo trabajaron las escuelas alfonsìes', *Nueva rivista de filologìa hispánica*, 5 (1951), 363–80; E. S. Procter, *Alfonso X of Castile. Patron of Literature and Learning* (Oxford: Oxford University Press, 1951). The transmission of Arabic culture to Italy officially started when some of the translators working in the school of Toledo moved to the court of Frederick II of Sicily. Later, the exodus of Sicilian minds caused the Arabic heritage to circulate throughout the south and centre of Italy, mainly Tuscany. Michael Scotus, translator of Averroes' large commentaries on Aristotle's *On the Heavens, On the Soul,* and *Physics and Metaphysics*, moved from Toledo to Frederick II's court before 1236. His translation is likely to have circulated in Florence thanks to the Sicilians who moved there. Dante at least knew Aristotle's *Metaphysics* and *Physics* through Averroes' great commentaries, as *Inferno* IV, 144 testifies, and he refers specifically to Michael Scotus' translation. In Toledo, Hermannus Alemannus prepared a Latin translation of the Arabic version of Aristotle's *Poetics* (1253), and shortly after of Averroes' *Middle Commentary on the Poetics* and of Aristotle's *Nicomachean Ethics*. This particular version came from Toledo to Tuscany via the court of Frederick II, where Hermannus moved and was identified as a *translator Manfredi* by Roger Bacon in *Opus tertium*, 25. Furthermore, it was very likely that Dante had before his eyes the Latin or a Romance version (e.g. *Le livre de l'eschielle de Mahomet*, 1264) of the *mi'raj*, and

attitude can be found in the *Entrée* in which the Muslim world is at the same time antagonist and protagonist, offering a great deal of material for a new interpretation of the interaction between the European West and Saracen East. The *Entrée* conveys the flavour of a broader understanding of the Muslim world, as depicted by fourteenth-century writers on Muslim matters and as received by their contemporary readers. A great deal of literature might have influenced the author's depiction of the Saracens and his view on the Muslim world. In this section, I will provide a general picture of some of the most interesting representations of Islam between the thirteenth and fourteenth centuries which will be of use for the analysis of our text.

A crucial episode in the history of European contact with Islam is that of the Franciscan missions to the East, started by St. Francis himself who in 1219 travelled to Syria and Egypt from where he returned in 1221. He joined the forces of the crusaders engaged in the siege of Damietta. His purpose, becoming more evident as his mission went on, was not to convert the Muslims but to win the crown of martyrdom, a goal he pursued through his entire life. This purpose led him to confront Islam openly and courageously, reaching a climax in his encounter with the Sultan. According to Thomas of Celano's version, despite being beaten by the Sultan's soldiers Francis was welcomed very kindly by the Sultan, who listened to his defence of Christianity and was apparently filled with admiration for him.[5] The Sultan welcomed him into his tent and

---

that individual elements of this book were integrated into *Comedy*'s broad architecture. In 1260, Brunetto Latini was for several months ambassador in Spain at the court of Alphonse X who promoted the study and transmission of Arabic culture. Brunetto therefore certainly came into contact with philosophy and legends of the Arabic world. M. Asín Palacios, *La escatología musulmana de la Divina Comedia, seguida de Historia y crítica de una polémica*, 4th edn (Madrid: Hiperión, 1984) considers this the strongest argument for the transmission of the legend of Mohammed's *mi'raj* to the West and in particular to Dante, who had Brunetto as a teacher. Maria Corti also agrees with this view: M. Corti, *Dante a un nuovo crocevia* (Florence: Sansoni, 1981).

[5] His meeting with the Sultan is narrated in Franciscan sources that differ slightly from one another but that are confirmed by an Arabic source. The different medieval accounts of this story are collected by G.

treated him as a *Sufi* – one of the holy men of Islam who are covered with a *suf*, a white woollen cloth with a hood similar to that of the Franciscan robe of poverty. St. Francis' *Regula non bullata*, issued in 1221, expresses the awareness that Islam is a part of the providential design and the plan of revelation. Like that of Peter the Venerable, Francis' attitude towards Islam was one of interest and curiosity. Yet this curiosity was always aimed at easing the task of conversion.

Franciscan endeavours to convert the whole of the East did not end with the mostly unsuccessful journey of St. Francis. Probably the most interesting of all Franciscan travellers was William of Rubruck, who started a different approach to mission by using scholastic theology to prove the superiority of Christianity to the infidels.[6] His journey to Karakorum in 1253–55 is documented in his *Itinerarium*,[7] where he describes his main purpose which was to convert the Mongols by engaging in debate with them. In the account of his journey he tells how he was granted the unique opportunity to participate in a religious debate with Nestorians, Muslims and Buddhists before the Möngke Khan himself. 'The stereotype that emerges from William's description of the debate is that of an Oriental other, Nestorian, Muslim, or Buddhist, who is uninterested in and impervious to the clear, rational thinking of a Western Christian'.[8]

The contemporary Dominican missionary strategy was quite different and resulted in a number of outstandingly important works as far as comprehension of Islam in the West is concerned. Ramon Martí, who was extremely well educated in Arabic and Hebrew, composed his *Pugio fidei adversus Mauros et Judaeos* in 1278, a handbook for future debates between Dominican missionaries,

---

Golubovich, *Biblioteca bio-bibliografica della terra santa e dell'oriente francescano*, 5 vols (Florence, 1906–13), qtd in Tolan, *Saracens*, p. 336 n. 5. See also J.V. Tolan, *Saint Francis and the Sultan. The Curious History of a Christian-Muslim Encounter* (Oxford: Oxford University Press, 2009).

[6] Tolan, *Saracens*, pp. 221 ff.
[7] P. Jackson, *The Mission of Friar William of Rubruck. His Journey to the Court of the Gran Khan Möngke, 1253–55* (London: Hakluyt Society, 1990).
[8] Tolan, *Saracens*, p. 225.

Muslims and Jews. There is in fact very little anti-Islamic argumentation in this book, which is directed especially against the Jews. Rather, it is directed against the Latin Averroists in Paris whose position on faith differed from both the Dominican and Franciscan approaches, maintaining a solid attachment to Aristotelian logic through the interpretation of Averroes.[9]

The clash between Dominicans and Latin Averroists is the basis of many philosophical developments in the fourteenth century of which the *Entrée* reflects some outstanding aspects. The theological dispute is one exceptional example of how this debate took on such proportions as to influence the least philosophical of all medieval genres, the *chanson de geste*.

Another famous case of enthusiastic study of Islam is that of Riccoldo da Montecroce, a Florentine Dominican who set out for the Levant in 1288. His voyage is described in his *Liber peregrinationis*[10] which he wrote around the year 1300 when he had returned from his long journey. In this work he combines a description of his pilgrimage with ethnographical information of the different people he encountered. Similar to the Franciscans, Riccoldo's interest in the Qur'ān was only aimed at fostering the

---

[9] Translations from Averroes were sent by Frederick II to Bologna around 1230–32 and from there reached Paris, influencing the course of thinking in the Parisian school so far that in 1270 Stephen Tempier bishop of Paris banned a number of theses of Averroist nature. The Dominican masters attempted to eliminate the influence of Averroes' interpretation from Aristotelian doctrine. The main purpose of Ramon Martí's *Pugio fidei* was to contribute to the debate rather than attack the Muslims or Jews (although parts II and III are anti-Jewish chapters, touching on hypotheses traditionally not accepted by Jews such as the coming of the Messiah and the Trinitarian argument). Both Ramon Martí and Thomas Aquinas had studied together with Albertus Magnus and it was apparently Ramon who transmitted the request from Ramon de Penyafort that Thomas should compose another treatise to serve as a weapon for the dispute against Islam. In Thomas' *Summa contra gentiles* there is very little specific mention of Islam. Thomas' knowledge of Islam is inadequate and there is no evidence that he had ever seen a Latin translation of the Qur'ān. See Tolan, *Saracens*, pp. 242–45.

[10] The text is found in Berlin: Staatsbibliothek Preußischer Kulturbesitz, MS lat. qu. 446, ff. 1r–24r. Vernacular translations were made of Riccoldo's account, the most famous being a Tuscan version from Pisa, now in Florence: Biblioteca Nazionale, MS Magl. II. IV. 53, ff. 1r–26r.

ability to convince the learned Muslim that Christianity was better than Islam. The account of Riccoldo's journey in the East became very popular: he sailed to Acre, travelled inland and reached the Jordan. He walked through Armenia, reached Syria and sailed down the river Tigris. In Baghdad, he studied Arabic and read the Qur'ān. Having returned to Florence around 1300 he lived in the monastery of Santa Maria Novella – and there probably met another famous Dominican friar, Ptolemy of Lucca, who from 1300 to 1302 was the prior of the monastery, and is nowadays regarded as one of the great ecclesiastical historians of the early fourteenth century. Ptolemy's description of the Orient in his *Exameron* was probably influenced by Riccoldo's stories which provided him with first-hand information about the geography of Syria.

Riccoldo is an invaluable source of information about the Muslim world. What troubled him the most was that God should permit the blasphemies of the Muslims. In a famous passage of his *Five Letters on the Fall of Acre*,[11] he expresses his frustration with God who seemed to accept and even condone the dissemination of the Qur'ān:

> "As You know, frequently as I read the Koran in Arabic, with great grief and impatience in my heart, I would place this book on Your altar, before the image of You and your holy mother and say: 'Read! Read what Muhammad says!' And it seemed to me that You did not want to read."[12]

These are by and large the same ideas that shocked the anonymous annotator of the Parisian manuscript of the Qur'ān translated by Robert of Ketton.[13] It is worth noticing that the command to read (*Iqra* in Arabic) stands at the beginning of countless Qur'ānic passages. Thus, while Riccoldo wants to invite God to read the Qur'ān and take measures against its dissemination, he is doing so by using the same dialectic method as the Qur'ān

---

[11] Riccoldo da Montecroce, *Epistolae V de perditione Acconis 1291*, ed. by R. Röhricht, in *Archives de l'orient latin*, 2 vols (Paris: Leroux, 1881–84), II: 258–96.

[12] Riccoldo da Montecroce, *Epistolae V*, II, p. 286, transl. by Tolan, *Saracens*, p. 247.

[13] Tolan, *Saracens*, p. 247.

itself. Furthermore Riccoldo insists on reading directly from the Arabic, as he states in the passage above, even though two Latin translations were available at that time. When Riccoldo specifies he is reading the Qur'ān in Arabic, we can now understand that the Latin versions were not considered reliable and suitable for serious discussion by a reader who was fluent in Arabic and grasped the weakness of the translation.

What emerges from Riccoldo's experience is the idea that the Saracens are irrational because they do not allow missionaries to convert them by means of logical arguments. The image of the Saracens he circulated was that of 'violent and irrational zealots who are impervious to reason and can only be countered by force'.[14] This idea will become a stereotype prevalent throughout the fourteenth and fifteenth centuries, so much so that humanists will simply dismiss the Saracens as being too unsophisticated for serious dialogue.[15] Riccoldo's work became one of the most widely read anti-Islamic treatises from the fourteenth to the sixteenth centuries.

While the Tartars and Muslims were pressing on the borders of Christendom, another figure engaged with Arabic culture for the purpose of conversion was Raymond Lull (1232–1316), a Franciscan from Mallorca who was expert in Arabic and a great esteemer of the Qur'ān's poetic beauty. Despite his appreciation of Arabic culture Lull always remained very firm in his belief in the necessity of missions among the unbelievers, and that Franciscan missionaries should learn Arabic to communicate with the infidels and convert them through peaceful preaching and discussion. In 1312 Lull promoted an edict at the Church Council of Vienne calling for chairs in Arabic to be set up at four universities and the Papal curia, which was never put into effect but demonstrates intellectuals' interest in the university teaching of Arabic. All Lull's works have in common a deep dislike of Parisian Latin Averroists. His strategy was very different from all approaches used by his predecessors. The goal of his work, as he explained it, was to argue with infidels not against but through the Faith ('Et ideo ego, qui

---

[14] Tolan, *Saracens*, p. 254.
[15] On this point see N. Bisaha, '"New Barbarian" or Worthy Adversary? Humanist Constructs of the Ottoman Turks in Fifteenth-Century Italy', in Blanks and Frasetto, eds, *Western Views of Islam*, pp. 185–205.

sum verus Catholicus, non intendo probare Articulos contra Fidem, sed mediante Fide').[16] Lull developed a system which soon became very famous, placing a great emphasis on Divine Attributes or Dignities which came to him from Christian sources. One can find the Divine Attributes in Psalms, Augustine and the medieval Augustinian tradition, and in the Pseudo-Dionysus, and they ultimately derive from Platonic ideas as interpreted by Plotinus.[17] The most important of Lull's works, as regards this analysis, is the *Libre del gentil e los tres savis* which he wrote in Mallorca between 1271 and 1276.[18] This work's setting and atmosphere belong entirely to the fourteenth century, its allegorical structure anticipating and influencing many other allegorical works of its age. There are similarities between the gentile philosophers of Lull and Peter Abelard,[19] both being neutral, intelligent observers belonging to none of the three major monotheistic religions. The *Libre del gentil* is an exceptional work, in which four wise men calmly discuss religion in a verdant grove. There are no attacks on Mohammed and no charges of blasphemy or of Jewish deicide. Generally, medieval texts of religious disputation end in conversion: the only two not to do so are Peter Abelard's *Dialogus* and Raymond Lull's *Libre del gentil*. As discussed further in this chapter, it is to these two texts that one must look when analysing the structure and sources of the theological dispute between Ferragu and Roland in the *Entrée*.

The majority of intellectuals in the Middle Ages would have formed their knowledge of Islam based on the sources that Daniel analysed in his early book on Islam, such as apologetic writings, or

---

[16] Ramon Lull, *Liber de convenientia fidei et intellectus in objecto*, qtd in T. E. Burman, 'The Influence of the Apology of al-Kindî and *Contrarietas alfolica* on Ramon Llull's Late Religious Polemics, 1305–1313', *Medieval Studies*, 53 (1991), 197–228.

[17] J. N. Hillgarth, *Ramon Lull and Lullism in Fourteenth Century France* (Oxford: Clarendon Press, 1971), p. 15.

[18] *Doctor Illuminatus. A Ramon Llull Reader*, ed. and transl. by A. Bonner (Princeton: Princeton University Press, 1993).

[19] Peter Abelard, *Dialogus inter philosophum, Iudaeum et Christianum*, ed. by R. Thomas (Stuttgart - Bad Cannstatt: Frommann, 1970); *Dialogo tra un filosofo, un giudeo e un cristiano*, ed. and transl. by C. Trovo (Milan: Rizzoli, 1992).

enthusiastic writings in support of the so called 'thirteenth-century dream of conversion'.[20]

Yet as Daniel himself admits, an analysis of apologetic writings and their influence on the poets of the *chanson de geste* is not of much use given that the purpose of the two types of writers was very different. Daniel in his 1984 study on heroes and Saracens rectifies his theory that the *chansons de geste* are crusade propaganda.[21] Daniel's book together with that of P. Bancourt represent the best studies published so far on the representation of Islam in the *chanson de geste*. In Daniel's words

> there is no question but that the theologians sincerely sought authenticity, although their move was only to refute Islam the better for knowing more about it; [...] They wanted to persuade where the poets wanted only to entertain.[22]

This seems to agree with the view of Limentani who did not trust the orientalist thesis of a possible penetration of Muslim culture into Italy:

> Sembra venga formulata qui una tesi ardita, quella di una coesistenza pacifica cristiano-musulmana, terzi esclusi, naturalmente, gli Ebrei. Questa tesi deve essere interpretata come un tentativo di parafrasi di tesi musulmane o come un loro adattamento forzato?[23]

The subtle irony of this comment indicates that Limentani regarded the *Entrée* as a product merely of an early pre-humanistic environment, overlooking the link between Spain, Sicily and Tuscany, and the influence of Brunetto's teaching on Dante. Also, Limentani considers the whole dispute over Arabic influence a sterile

---

[20] John of Damascus, the *Risâlat al-Kindî*, Alan of Lille, and Petrus Alfonsi in the earlier centuries; Raymond Lull, Ramon Martì, and Riccoldo da Montecroce in the thirteenth and fourteenth centuries. See Daniel, *Islam and the West*.

[21] He himself admits his change of mind in 1984, p. 267. He also admits his ignorance of Bancourt, *Les Musulmans*, until his own book was in press: p. 281.

[22] Daniel, *Heroes and Saracens*, p. 270.

[23] Limentani, *L'Entrée d'Espagne e i signori d'Italia*, p. 305.

attempt to assign more responsibility for cultural developments in Southern Europe to the Arabs than in fact (in his opinion) they had.

It is more likely that the poets of the *chansons* took their information about Muslims from chronicles than from theologians, as Daniel stressed, for chronicles found themselves closer to the purpose of the *chanson* which was to entertain. The writing of the chronicles is fictitious, descriptions are fantastic, and their wider circulation versus that of apologetic writings would easily explain the persistence of the stereotype, depicted in chronicles, of the Saracens as pagans. A controversy against Islam, consisting of a point-by-point disputation of the major issues, results in a literature offering very little entertainment. By contrast the fantastic account of the enterprises of the lords of France in the Holy Land, full of lurid details about the local Muslims, corresponds in genre to present-day fantasy novels. It would therefore seem reasonable to identify chronicles as the sources for any distorted information the poets might have used to portray the Islamic world.

The approaches of both Daniel and Limentani have the limitation of only considering the purpose of entertainment; and despite Limentani being the first scholar to study in depth the versatility of the *Entrée* poet, he seemingly overlooks the enormous scope of the traditional Saracen presence in the *chanson de geste* genre to represent a changing society. It is somewhat difficult to imagine that such a poet, who wrote a poem of fifteen thousand verses on the events preceding the battle of Rencesvals in an era when the crusades were definitely over,[24] could still depend on the idea of violent Saracen opposition to the supremacy of Christianity. Since the fourth crusade, the Italian (or, rather, the Venetian) attitude had always been one of collaboration with both parties.

---

[24] The crusading movement finished amid little glory in 1308 with the great trial of the Templars charged with heresy by Pope Clement V. See S. Runciman, *A History of the Crusades*, 3 vols (Cambridge: Cambridge University Press, 1954), III: 437. The idea of crusade was re-examined from the viewpoint of historical significance in *X Congresso internazionale di scienze storiche, Roma, 4–11 settembre 1955 – Relazioni*, III: *Storia del medioevo* (Florence: Sansoni, 1955). A treatment of the subject is found in P. Alphandery and A. Dupront, *La Chrétienté et l'idée de Croisade* (Paris: Albin Michel, 1959).

> The Italian maritime cities, whose merchants were the shrewdest money-makers of the time, had at first been alarmed by a movement that might well ruin the trading relations that had been built up with the Moslem of the Levant. It was only when the Crusade was successful and Frankish settlements were founded in Syria that the Italians offered their help, realising that they could use new colonies to their own advantage.[25]

Although the *Entrée* shows an understanding of the Saracens unique at that point in the *chanson de geste* genre, some textual elements demonstrate the full inaccuracy of the sources used by the *Entrée* author. Saracen institutions are described in a rather imaginative way, not based on historical reality but on the application of western customs. For example, the caliph is said to be the vicar of God, as the Pope is the vicar of Jesus Christ in Christianity ('Nostre calif, qi est de Dieux vicaire', l. 12223). At the date of the *Entrée*'s composition, in fact, the city of Baghdad had been conquered by the Mongols and the caliph was no longer an authority, although certain Muslim authors had referred to their caliphs as such.[26] The mention of *Le Viel de la Montagne* shows that the author had little knowledge of the subjects of the Sultan of Persia (*le Viel de la Montagne le sert por convenant*, 11976). It was by this name that the French used to call the chief of the Ismailis of Syria, the sheikh al-Djabal du Djabal Nusairi in the south of the principate of Antioch.[27] By the time the *Entrée* was written, however, this figure had been weakened by the influence of the Sultan of Egypt.[28] The mention of this name may be the result of the author's reading of Marco Polo's account of his journey which contains the story of the *Veglio de la montagna*. In Marco's book, the story is told without precise reference to chronology so that it sounds as if the figure was still alive.[29] Furthermore, this may hint at

---

[25] Runciman, *A History of the Crusades*, III: 351.
[26] R. Grousset, *Histoire universelle*, 3 vols (Paris: Gallimard, 1958–62), II: 571–73.
[27] Grousset, *Histoire universelle*, p. 22.
[28] Bancourt, *Les Musulmans*, p. 461.
[29] Marco Polo, *Milione. Le divisament dou monde*, ed. by G. Ronchi (Milan: Mondadori, 1988), ch. 40.

the influence of Polo's book on the *Entrée* although there is no other evidence in the poem.

The Saracen Pantheon

In the *chanson de geste* genre the Saracens were either depicted as pagans or as heretics. This distinction draws a line between what can be considered pure fiction, and an analysis of Islam as the religion of the enemy. The identification of the Saracens with a pagan tribe entails the creation of an easily recognisable literary Other, identifiable with the idols they worship, and also allows for more frightening aspects in their depiction. It also has a number of interesting implications such as the identification of the Muslims with the Romans who had also persecuted the Christians, justifying the warlike attitude towards them. The case of the *Chanson d'Antioche*, for example, a twelfth-century epic describing the first crusade through to the conquest of Antioch, is quite revealing on this point. In this *chanson* the Saracens' paganism justifies the crusade since the pagans killed Jesus and the Christians should seek revenge. The Saracens must be portrayed as pagans in order to be appropriate objects of vengeance.[30] Generally speaking, in the *chanson de geste* the Muslims are often defined as traitors.[31] This term has a very close connection with 'infidel' and 'heretic'. In the Christian West, the *Apocalypse de Bahira*[32] portrays Islam as heresy. The idea that Islam is nothing but a Christian heresy is repeated by all Christian polemicists in the East and West.[33] Their depiction as heretics by polemicists in apologetic writings implies an attitude which is, surprisingly enough, more positive than negative in that it confirms a certain curiosity about Islam because of desire to know

---

[30] *Chanson d'Antioche*, ed. by S. Duparc-Quioc (Paris: Geuthner, 1977), ll. 205–11, qtd in Tolan, *Saracens*, p. 121 n. 67.

[31] 'Or renoié': *Chevalerie Ogier*, l. 2191; *Gaydon*, ll. 218, 1140; *Macaire*, ll. 346, 601, 671, 1812; *Aiol*: ll. 2829, 4813. See Bancourt, *Les Musulmans*, p. 343.

[32] See *Le Roman de Mahomet d'Alexandre du Pont*, ed. by Y. G. Lepage (Paris: Klincksieck, 1977).

[33] Bancourt, *Les Musulmans*, p. 344; A. D'Ancona, 'La leggenda di Maometto in Occidente', *Giornale storico della letteratura italiana*, 13 (1889), 202 ff.

more about its origins and laws, a desire generated by the necessity to fight Islam like any other type of heresy.

How much medieval epic poets really knew about Islam remains very much a live debate. This contribution to the dispute focuses on the case of the *Entrée*, which presents a variation from all other *chansons de geste* in that the poet seems be involved in portraying a no-longer-hostile East while simultaneously keeping the traditional view of the Saracens. Although not possible to say how far the author was informed about Muslim religion and customs, it is possible to register the discrepancy between his agreement with, and diversion from, the traditional view. Although the stereotype persists in the *Entrée*, entire parts hint at his reading of works other than chronicles.

In the *Entrée* the Saracens are defined from the very beginning as *la gent Paganie*. The concepts of paganism and Islam are therefore understood as identical. Islam is not yet recognised as a monotheistic religion with its own dignity but as a form of polytheistic religion. In fact, the Saracens are said to be devoted to Mohammed as well as Apollo. According to the tradition Mohammed himself, as with the other Arabs, originally worshipped Venus. Since the poet defines the Saracens as pagans, all the pagan barbarians are Saracens.[34] Historically speaking, nothing is more incorrect than the definition of a Saracen as a pagan since Mohammed had broken the relationship with paganism through the affirmation of a monotheistic religion, against the resistance of the polytheist Meccans who worshipped the black stone Ka'ba.[35]

The confusion of Muslims with pagans derives from the Latin chroniclers (like Guibert de Nogent), who in defining the Muslims

---

[34] Bancourt, *Les Musulmans*, p. 341. Tolan, *Saracens*, maintains that '"Saracen" and "pagan" are such intertwined terms that when Peter Abelard (in the twelfth century) composes his *Dialogue of a philosopher with a Jew and a Christian*, he portrays the "pagan" philosopher as a sort of cross between an ancient Roman and a contemporary Muslim, as one who is circumcised yet cites Ovid' (p. 127).

[35] Bancourt, *Les Musulmans*, p. 342; R. Blachère, *Le Problème de Mahomet. Essai de biographie critique du fondateur de l'Islam* (Paris: PUF, 1952), pp. 46–59.

used both the terms *pagani* and *gentili*.[36] It is true that up until the sixth century Arabia was populated by pagan tribes who held in common the cult of the black stone. The same territory was inhabited by Nestorians, Monophysites and Jews. However, after the diplomatic treaty of 628 and Islam's eventually peaceful widespread adoption, polytheism was over.[37] Moreover, the massive Muslim presence in Spain and southern Italy should have made authors of *chansons de geste* aware that Islam was not by any means a polytheistic religion.

The characterisation of Arabs as cruel and demonic pagans (*la gient tafure*, ll. 2072, 9395) derives from the long tradition of the *chanson de geste* which aimed, along with the entertainment factor (the enemy was made recognisable through vivid details of character and religion), to circulate propaganda against Christendom's enemies in the age of the crusades. However, the vocabulary available at the time defines all enemies of western Christendom as pagan, as Bancourt points out,[38] regardless of whether they were Muslims, Eastern Christians or Jews. The definition of pagan replaced that of barbarian as the empire became Christian.[39] Pagans and infidels exist only as opposed to Christians; all enemies of Christendom fall into the same non-Christian category.

---

[36] Guibert de Nogent, *Dei gesta per Francos*, ed. by R. B. C. Huygens, CCCM 127A (1996). Transl. into English by R. Levine, *The Deeds of God through the Franks* (Woodbridge: Boydell Press, 1997).

[37] See P. M. Holt, A. K. S. Lambton and B. Lewis, eds, *The Cambridge History of Islam* (Cambridge: Cambridge University Press, 1970). Mohammed had insisted on the idea of divine unity against the resistance of the polytheist Meccans: Bancourt, *Les Musulmans*, p. 357. The first of the five theses of the Muʿtazila school of theology, founded at Baṣra (south-east Iraq) in the first half of the eighth century, maintained the radical defence of the unity of God. The five theses were based on Aristotelian thought and became the official doctrine of Islam under the caliphs al-Maʾmūn and al-Muʿtaṣim: G. Filoramo, *Islam*, in *Manuale di storia delle religioni* (Rome/Bari: Laterza, 1999), pp. 239–40.

[38] Bancourt, *Les Musulmans*, p. 342.

[39] Bancourt, *Les Musulmans*, p. 342; M. Villey, *La Croisade. Essai sur la formation d'une théorie juridique* (Paris: Vrin, 1942), p. 27.

The Saracens in the *chansons de geste* are often described as the people of the Antichrist.[40] Mohammed is depicted as the Antichrist for the first time by Eulogius of Cordova. His *Liber apologeticus martyrum* refers to Mohammed as *praecursor Antichristi* because he rejects Christ's divinity.[41] Possibly the most famous identification of Mohammed with the Antichrist was made for a rhetorical reason by Pope Innocent III between 1198 and 1216, when the Pope found grounds in the Gospels to provide theories to underpin the fourth crusade.[42]

In the *Entrée*, one occurrence identifies Ferragu directly with the Antichrist himself ('Sor son escuz ferir veit l'Antecris', l. 1362). In the *chansons de geste* the Saracens are treated as devils. In the *Entrée* they are said to be enemies of God and offspring of Satan ('Chi dunt veïst li Deus nemis ensir', l. 7376; 'Je croi q'il dort, cist fil de Satanais', l. 3539). The Saracens in the *Entrée* are also called *orgueillous* (ll. 1814, 8087), and they reproach the Christians for being proud (*bofoi*, l. 934; *orguoil*, ll. 970, 5121). A need is therefore felt to keep the traditional friction between the two parties. Nevertheless this attitude only appears in the first part of the poem, the so-to-speak traditionally epic part in which the French are depicted as usual while they try to throw the Saracens out of Spain, and the Saracens are the typical enemies of Christendom.

All medieval western poets who engaged in writing *chansons de geste* seem to ignore the fact that the Muslims actually worshipped one god, who was neither Mohammed nor any the other divinities of the fantasised Saracen pantheon. In all *chansons de geste* Islam is not considered as a real religion but solely either a corruption (on a par with other heresies) of Christanity, the one possible monotheistic religion, or its antithesis.

---

[40] Bancourt's analysis has shown how the definition the Saracens as devils, offspring of Satan, and heretics is to be considered rather as 'exagération epique' than the expression of a serious opinion: Bancourt, *Les Musulmans*, p. 354. Daniel, *Heroes and Saracens*, is of the same opinion.

[41] Eulogius, *Liber apologeticus martyrum* 12, in *Corpus scriptorum Muzarabicorum*, ed. by J. Gil, 2 vols (Madrid: Consejo Superior de Investigaciones Cientificas, 1973), II: 481, qtd in Tolan, *Saracens*, p. 90 n. 80.

[42] Alphandery and Dupront, *La Chrétienté et l'idée de Croisade*, p. 44.

In the *chansons de geste* in general all Muslim divinities are interchangeable and their various names are chosen to match the rhyme. This epic *topos* of Islam as a polytheistic religion is kept in the *Entrée*, in which the Saracen Pantheon consists above all of four Gods ('Vos quatre Diex sunt feit par vos traïr', l. 3620). These are Mohammed (also called *Machon*, ll. 2149, 2242, 2950, 4324, 4411, 11855, 12790, 12845, etc.), *Tervagant* (in the *Entrée* known by the variant of *Trivigant*, l. 8237, and *Trevegant*, l. 10593) and two pagan gods in the more traditional sense, borrowed from the Roman pantheon: *Apolin* (or *Apollins*, l. 12783; *Apolin* is father to *Machon* in l. 3223) and *Jopin* (l. 8236) (or *Jupinel*, l. 10903, or *Jovis*, l. 12784). These last two are mentioned together towards the end of the poem: 'Le Turs l'oï, a pué non raige vis; | Il en juroit ses Dex, Apollins et Jovis' (ll. 12783–84). The name *Apolin* is explained either as a highly common translation into French of the name of the Greek god Apollo,[43] or by derivation from the Arab *al-la'in* (the cursed, or Satan).[44] As for *Trivigant* (ll. 1914, 2233) a number of scholars have discussed its etymology. It has been variously suggested that the word derives from Hermes Trismegistus or from Trivia (Diana)[45], or is a poetic creation *ex nihilo*.[46] Other authors explain it as derived from an Arabic name.[47] However, none of these theories

---

[43] Simon de Fraisne, author of a *Vie de St. George*; *Vies de St. Eustache*; cfr. Bancourt, *Les Musulmans*, p. 377.

[44] C. Pellat, 'Mahom, Tervagant, Apollin', in *Actas del Primer Congreso de Estudios Árabes e Islámico, Córdoba 1962* (Madrid: Maestre, 1964), p. 268.

[45] H. Grégoire, 'L'Etymologie de Tervagant (Trivigant)', in *Mélanges d'histoire du théâtre du Moyen Âge et de la Renaissance offerts à Gustave Cohen* (Paris: Nizet, 1950), pp. 67–74.

[46] L. Spitzer, 'Tervagant', *Romania*, 70 (1948–49), 397–409.

[47] C. Virolleaud, 'Khadir', *Bulletin des études arabes*, 49 (1950), 151–55 (p. 153); A. Dauzat, 'Tervagan', *Revue internationale d'onomastique*, 4 (1950), 273–74: both Virolleaud and Dauzat support the view that Tervagan is derived via the Arab name *Kadhir*, a Muslim saint. F. Viré, 'A propos de Tervagan idole Sarrasins', *Cahier de Tunisie*, 2 (1953), 141–52. Viré bases his hypothesis on the idea that the Christians misunderstood and misspelled the name Koran from which corruption would derive the name Tervagan. Pellat acknowledges that it would be better to explore the milieu of the Christians of Spain for evidence of

seems to have acquired such credibility that it can be regarded as true, and the origin of the word Tervagan still remains a mystery.[48]

To the main gods are added others, in particular *Margoit* (l. 4324), *Chaü* (probably derived from χάος: ll. 7709, 14506), and *Baraton* (l. 1173). In Noble there is a temple dedicated to Venus (l. 9841) and in Baghdad one to Mars (l. 13267). *Sante Nefise* is Machon's mother (l. 1707). *Machomerie* (l. 2148) is the disparaging definition of the totality of gods worshipped by the Saracens.

Surprisingly, in the *Entrée* Mohammed takes up a role very close to that of Jesus. During the long theological discussion Ferragu wants to prove to Roland that Mohammed was sent by God to save mankind through his teaching (ll. 2441–43):

> [...] Damediex manda
> Machon en terre, et quant qu'il nos mostra
> Fu garisons de cescuns qu'il crea.

At the end of the discussion, after Roland has given up trying to convince Ferragu (who proves to be rather stubborn) and just before the duel begins, Ferragu again says to Roland (ll. 4040–42):

> Feragu dist: 'Rollant, je sui ci por prover
> Que Machomet fu de Diex mesajer:
> Qui en lui croit puet sa arme salver'.

The mission of Mohammed therefore approximates to that of Jesus to whom he is placed second in the *Entrée*: "'Depué ce, Sire, invouyaste Machon: | Aprés Yesus fu in segunde eslizion'" (ll. 12845–46). *Segunde eslizion* may be intended as 'second choice' (which is the interpretation accepted by Bancourt, putting Mohammed in the second position of importance) but it could also be read chronologically, as a second opportunity given to mankind after the earthly defeat of Jesus who died on the cross before he could rescue mankind.

The *Entrée* offers two definitions of Mohammed: either he is the main pagan god in the Saracens' pantheon,[49] or the protagonist of

---

what they actually knew about the Arabs dominating their territory at that time.

[48] Bancourt, *Les Musulmans*, p. 383.

the late version of the legend according to which he was a Christian preacher, frustrated in his ambition, who betrayed his religion. Mohammed went to convert the Saracens but he aimed to become Pope (ll. 2446–56):

> Cristiens fu e predicer ala
> La sancte foi que nulle per nen a;
> Maint Saracins converti et lava,
> Car en bien fer le glot mout se pena,
> Car le mantel papel avoir quida.
> […]
> Quant l'apostoile de Rome devia
> Les cardenaus de Machomet pensa
> Par le meilor qu'il remanist dela,
> Car plus de gient a Dieux convertira
> E le batisme melz en esanplera:
> Un apostoile ferent que Diex ama.

Disappointed by this news Mohammed started preaching a new religion to his followers (ll. 2459–62):

> Par cist desdaing al poeple designa
> La prime loi, dist qu'il les salvera,
> La sant batisme e la loi Diex blasma,
> Sa predicance et ses dit trestorna.

This *topos* is repeated towards the end when Roland returns to Mecca after his journey through Syria: '[…] dou faus pradizeor, | Par quoi li gardinals non le firent pastor' (ll. 13894–95). The legend of Mohammed as a Cardinal of the Roman Curia had a certain success in Italy during the thirteenth and fourteenth centuries, and can also be found in Latini's *Trésor* and the early commentators on Dante.[50] The *Entrée* gives us the ultimate stage of the legend of the monk Sergius who by then was identified with Mohammed himself.

---

[49] Ll. 591, 812, 907, 1034, 1679, 1707, 2184, 2233, 2439, 2442, 2457, 2491.

[50] Bancourt, *Les Musulmans*, pp. 375–76. Cfr. A. D'Ancona, 'La leggenda di Maometto', pp. 199–201, 245–47, 254–55. See also E. Doutté, *Mahomet Cardinal* (Chalons-sur-Marne: Martin Frères, 1899), pp. 5–6.

Although the poet was certainly aware that Mohammed was the prophet of Islam,[51] the persistent legend of Mohammed as a Roman Cardinal who founded a new religion, traceable to the work of French grammarians in the eleventh and twelfth centuries,[52] proves to be very much alive as late as the fourteenth.[53]

According to Bancourt the *Entrée* deserves a special place in the history of this genre because, among the traditional gods worshipped by the Saracens other particular divinities are mentioned such as 'the great Kibir', whom Ferragu worships before Machon ('Le grant Kibir promer e Machon prie', l. 2149). The same god is mentioned again as 'l'atisme Kibir' (l. 3141), and in the course of his discussion with Roland Ferragu maintains that he believes in Alabahir: 'Dist

---

[51] The thirteenth-century Franciscan friar Servasanto da Faenza explains that the Muslims believe Mohammed not to be God but prophet of God, qtd in Tolan, *Saracens*, p. 221.

[52] See D'Ancona, 'La leggenda di Maometto', p. 245; A. Mancini, 'Per lo studio della leggenda di Maometto in Occidente', *Rendiconti della Reale Accademia dei Lincei*, 10 (1934), 325–49 (327).

[53] The image of Mohammed as false prophet is found in much of the literature of the Middle Ages, and through the Crusading period from the Risâlat al-Kindî to Petrus Alfonsi's *Dialogi contra Iudaeos*, in which the author debates with a Jew who presents him with a summary of Muslim belief and asks Petrus why he did not choose to convert to Islam: J. V. Tolan, *Petrus Alfonsi and his Medieval Readers* (Gainesville: University Press of Florida, 1993). One of the aims of Alexandre du Pont's *Roman de Mahomet* (1258) was to dismiss the Muslim faith despite the great losses of Louis X, who had just retreated from his disastrous crusade to Egypt, and despite the fables of Arabic magnificence circulated by the crusaders. Mohammed is portrayed as a Christian heretic who preached his faith among the pagan Arabs: see Bancourt, *Les Musulmans*, p. 345. In Vincent of Beauvais' *Speculum historiale* 24.51, the Qur'ān is a corruption of the Old and New Testament. Vincent of Beauvais, *Speculum historiale*, ed. by C. Bauer, L. Boehm and M. Müller (Freiburg: Alber, 1965). The most important source for the idea of Mohammed as a Christian heretic is found in Jacobus de Voragine, *Legenda aurea*, in which the monk Sergius is said to have been persecuted for falling into the Nestorian heresy; therefore he fled to Arabia and joined company with Magumeth. According to Jacobus, it was Sergius who taught Magumeth much about the Old and New Testaments: Jacobus de Voragine, *The Golden Legend*, transl. by W. G. Ryan, 2 vols (Princeton: Princeton University Press, 1993), II: 370–73.

Feragu: "Ja cro je Alabahir | Che fist le munde e le puet difinir'" (ll. 3627–28). Another Saracen swears to Alakibir (l. 12415). This is nothing exceptional as it refers to the opening of the Qurʾān, which reads 'Allāhu Akbar' (God Almighty or the Greatest), a common exclamation among Muslims of all times. The idea is expressed here of a superior (*grant, atisme*) entity whose name is by antonomasia *Kibir* (*kabīr* in Arabic means 'great'). As discussed further, the recognition of one god's superiority over the pantheon would attribute to the *Entrée* a very distinct role in the historical development of the *chanson de geste*. In earlier products of this genre there was no space among the many gods for the only real god of Islam, i.e. Allah. Notwithstanding that Islam was well known to have imposed monotheism upon its opponents from the outset, the western world had never accepted the idea of their enemies likewise having a real monotheistic religion, with its God and prophet. This stereotype is repeated throughout the history of the *chanson de geste* from the *Chanson de Roland* to the *Prise de Pampelune*. This conception seems to change slightly in the *Entrée*, despite the presence of a variety of divinities worshipped by the Saracens.

> Avec les chansons tardives que sont l'*Entrée d'Espagne* et la *Prise de Pampelune*, le polythéisme traditionnel cède le pas devant l'idée qui se fait jour du monothéisme des musulmans. Bien que Sarrasins, les personnages qui entrent en scène se réfèrent nommément à Dieu, comme font les chrétiens. Ferragu, désireux de se mesurer à Roland et à Olivier, s'en remet «al Dieux comandement» (024). Roland lui ayant confessé sa croyance en un Dieu éternel, Ferragu répond que c'est aussi la croyance des Sarracins (3639, 3643), lesquels invoquent en effet, «Le Roi Superior» (8167) ou le «Dieux Superior» (12403). Le soudan de Perse prend Dieu à témoin (12330, 12335).[54]

While in the *Entreé* the pantheon of the Saracens is still as present in the description of the Saracen environment and mentality, the identical role of each god progressively undermines the hypothesis of polytheism. The difference between Christianity and Islam is thereby reduced by the continuous interaction of the

---

[54] Bancourt, *Les Musulmans*, p. 386.

two parties, and at times by the confusion of the two rites. P. Bancourt talks of religion in the *Entrée* in these terms:

> Les différences de religion ne comptent plus. Les chrétiens et les Sarrasins ne sont plus séparés verticalement, pourrait-on dire, par les hostilités. La ligne de clivage est horizontale, distinguant dans les deux camps l'élite et la masse des autres. Dans l'affrontement, le Sarrasin et le chrétien se découvrent frères par l'éthique chevaleresque.[55]

Bancourt speaks of religious syncretism: 'La prière de la jeune Sarrasine Dionès pour son champion chrétien Roland, dans l'*Entrée d'Espagne*, est le couronnement de ce curieux syncrétisme'.[56] Dionés in her prayer considers God as the creator of the world ('Glorios Dei qui mers, teres et mon | Trestot faisistes par voustre devison', ll. 12817–18). She calls Jesus a prophet ('Le voir proufete que on appeloit Jeson', l. 12835) and even puts Mohammed in second position to Jesus ('Depué ce, Sire, invouyastes Machon | Après Jesus fu in segunde eslizion', ll. 12845–46). She says that Mohammed and Jesus will be the judges ('Car au novisme jornal que atendon | Mahomet et Jesus nos justisier seron', ll. 12849–50). Those who sinned, both Christians and Saracens, will go to hell, while those who were good will go to heaven ('Cel que vers eus avront fait mes prison | Serunt danez en l'ouschure maison', ll. 12852–53; 'Les cristians et les saracins bon | En Paraïs avec eus s'an iron', ll. 12856–57).

Pélias admires Roland so much that he is indifferent to his being Saracen, Christian or Jewish (ll. 13086–92):

> 'Cevallers frere' – ce a dit Pelliais –
> 'Si Sarracins, Crestians o Judais
> Is, nel sai; mes par la loi que tu ais.
> Et par cel ordre dont civaler te fais
> [...]
> Chuntente moi de voir dir, non de gais,
> De quel lignaze es tu nez et estrais'.

---

[55] Bancourt, *Les Musulmans*, p. 324.
[56] Bancourt, *Les Musulmans*, p. 564.

Although I have drawn inspiration from Bancourt's invaluable work on the Muslims in the *chanson de geste*, I found most surprising his statement that the *Entrée* author was inspired by the *Chanson d'Aspremont* concerning the paradox of Christian civilisation's superiority to that of Islam.[57] This is how he puts it:

> L'auteur padouan de l'*Entreé d'Espagne* doit sans doute à la *Chanson d'Aspremont* qui a joui d'une grande vogue en Italie, l'ideé paradoxale de la supériorité de la civilisation chrétienne sur la civilisation musulmane. Cette idée trouve dans cette chanson un prolongement et un développement curieux. Roland, passé sous un déguisement au service du soudan de Perse, exerce dans ce pays lointain sous le pseudonyme de Lioné un rôle civilisateur. Il affine les usages: au lieu de manger à 6 ou 7 le même plat comme le "Tiois" le font encore, les convives auront chacun leur assiette (13975–80)! Il importe en Perse la pratique et l'éthique de la chevalerie: devenu l'ami de Sanson, fils du Soudan, au point que tous deux portent les mêmes vêtements (13647), mangent et dorment ensemble (13702), Lioné entraîne le jeune prince aux sports chevaleresques: escrime (13704), quintaine (13718), tournoi (13720); et lui enseigne les devoirs du chevalier: largesse (13706–8), haine du mensonge (13710), respect de la parole donnée (13711).[58]

Bancourt's point is interesting[59] although in order to see Roland in a 'rôle civilisateur', arguably, one must accept that he conceived

---

[57] It is noteworthy that the date for the *Entrée* proposed by Thomas and Limentani remains the most widely accepted, while the *Aspremont* is normally considered to have been composed during the decade of 1358–68, i.e. at least thirty years after the accepted date of the *Entrée*. Nevertheless, Thomas himself claims that both the *Aspremont* and its continuation were familiar to the poet: Thomas, *L'Entrée d'Espagne*, I: XLVII.

[58] Bancourt, *Les Musulmans*, p. 221.

[59] See also S. Sturm-Maddox, '"E fer en cortoisie retorner li villan": Roland in Persia in the *Entrée d'Espagne*', in B. K. Altmann and C. W. Carroll, eds, *The Court Reconvenes. Courtly Literature Across the Disciplines. Selected Papers from the Ninth Triennial Congress of the International Courtly Literature Society, University of British Columbia, Vancouver, 25–31 July 1998* (Cambridge: Boydell & Brewer, 2003), pp. 297–308.

his journey to Persia as a kind of non-violent mission to convert the Saracens, appearing to the reader as a momentary pause in his war activity. Unfortunately, as the reader knows, this is not Roland's real aim: his journey to the East starts when he only half consciously boards the boat which will take him to Persia. He then ends up in a foreign land where he must literally improvise a way to survive.

This is how the author describes Roland's intent and embarkation, happening almost by accident. In fact, the ship's *estormant* (helmsman) offers to transport Roland to repay the great favour Roland has just done him, of killing the two brigands threatening the merchant (ll. 11589–63):

> En son langaje dist: 'Ci t'a envoié,
> Vertuos home, la divine bonté:
> De dous dyables m'ais encui delivré.
> [...]
> Garis m'avés, qe estoie perilé:
> Bien en devés estre geardoné.
> Se vos d'avoir eüsés volunté,
> Tot cil dormons en est plain e rasé.
> E se volrés venire en mon reigné,
> Moi e cestors vos ferons fiauté:
> En pluisor leu gran besoign nos avré'.

By a fortunate coincidence, the helmsman's offer tallies with an intuition Roland had just had before he met the two brigands (ll. 11506–98):

> De retorner al roi a poi ne forsena,
> Quand un autre penser sorvient, qe revela
> E dist qe ens en la mer ancois s'anoiera.

Roland's journey thus happens through happy circumstance; it was certainly not a plan to bring civilisation to the East and Saracens. Roland is furthermore presented as a somewhat cosmopolitan character, educated in many languages and cultures, highly open-minded and a free spirit (ll. 11522–23).

Saracens in *L'Entrée d'Espagne*

Baudor, Isoré and Sansonet

These three Saracens can be grouped together on the basis of all being entirely positive characters. Isoré is the young prince kept as a hostage in Charlemagne's palace, while Baudor appears as an isolated character. Sansonet is the prince of Syria who becomes Roland's companion throughout the Eastern section and eventually follows him through Spain. Therefore, they differ only in the quality and extent of their interaction with other figures. As their characterisation is derived from elements that often originate in comparisons, they all appear as one-dimensional characters. Their personalities are not delineated, either psychologically or symbolically. They are invested with roles that are functional to the unfolding of the plot, act as interlocutors, and counterbalance Roland's role, causing new aspects of his personality to emerge. Nevertheless, it is difficult to maintain that they are simply portrayed as stock characters. These figures are very different from each other and although they display traits that are stereotypical of the Saracens, their social condition eclipses their image as Saracens.

Isoré is presented to the audience as an exceedingly beautiful prince ('A grant mervoile il stoit de beus senblant', l. 6284), his physical beauty mirroring that of his delicate soul. He is a young knight who does not agree at all with the violence of the war between French and Spanish Saracens. His perplexity over the role he is given is great, and it is exposed through a monologue in which he summarises, in few but poignant words, his *Weltanschauung* (ll. 5464–72):

> 'Quant moi, je sui un chevaler novel
> Ch'entrepris sui defendant mon ostel.
> Enbatus sui as mains de ces chael;
> Mengier me qident come lous li porcel.
> Si n'est mon pere garçons ni bedonel,
> Mais roi clamé, e tient sot son seiel
> Cil bel paleis, le mur e le burçel.
> Non sai por qoi me voie a cist flaiel,
> Car non sui Jude ne cil c'oncist Abel'.

He appears at a strategic point in the plot, with Charlemagne and Roland's relationship at a dangerous crossroads. Isoré is captured at Pamplona and dispatched to Charles under Roland's instructions to treat him as a royal prisoner. The newly knighted son of Malgeris ('chevaler novel', l. 5464) is icily received by Charlemagne, however, who promises to hang the youth and later justifies his decision as retaliation for Estout's imprisonment and possible death. The young knight is the first to express his trust that Charlemagne, for the love of his nephew, will not reject Roland's request (ll. 5546–50). Upon Roland's return the matter causes a harsh dispute over Isoré's life. Roland refuses to accept that the prisoner should be harmed, especially in retaliation which he considers as infamy (ll. 5682–84). Charlemagne delivers a speech in which he articulates his hierarchical vision. The two figures take opposing sides, and thus it can be said that the episode and indeed the figure of Isoré effectively introduce new elements characterising both protagonists and contributing to their divergence of views.

The young Saracen does gain much out of the situation in terms of characterisation. On the one hand, his presence exalts the patronising attitude of the French king, while on the other it creates a situation whereby Roland's compassion and loyalty can emerge. In the last verse of his monologue, Isoré quite clearly expresses his point of view: he is neither a traitor nor fratricide and thus does not understand why this punishment is imposed over him. He appears as a completely innocent figure whose naivety is moving and whose presence creates a dispute over the legitimacy of Charlemagne's authority, which becomes generally questioned as a result. There is no mention of Isoré's religion; he simply seems a prisoner of war and his role triggers discussions about loyalty.

What happens next, in fact, becomes in its turn an opportunity for a confrontation between two generations of Saracens: of Isoré and of his parents. In the end Roland frees Isoré, trusting in his promise to free Estout. When the young Saracen arrives at Malgeris' camp he reports the pledge made to Roland and wants Estout freed at once, but his father refuses. This creates a conflict between Isoré and his parents, as Isoré threatens otherwise to return to the French camp and fight against his father. His mother Geophanais is a dramatic figure in this context; she loves her son above all else but believes at first that she cannot support him on this occasion, while in the end taking her son's part; both threaten to convert if the French knight is not freed. There is a flavour of tragedy in this episode entirely played out in the Saracen camp (ll. 6390–466). The three characters are portrayed in a moment of extreme tension during which they deal with their emotions as Christians would. As in many other places of the *Entrée*, it is not religion that defines who is good and bad but the issue of right and wrong dividing two generations of fighters. This is a conflict in which the youth is set against his own parents out of loyalty and friendship to another youth. The situation at the Saracen court resembles the friction between Roland and Charlemagne; and just as in that case the poet again sides with the young against the old, which may reflect his own views (and those in Italy) of chivalry and feudalism.

The mutual affection and admiration of the two young knights anticipates the relationship that the reader will later find in the Eastern section, when Roland befriends Sansonet and their loyalty overcomes any obstacle, including religion. Estout is freed at last and Isoré sends him back to the French camp with a horse that the young Saracen donates to Roland. This knightly exchange of gifts concludes the negotiations successfully and under the sign of chivalry. It is the two young knights who win over their old-fashioned parents (Charlemagne is uncle to Roland but their relationship can be considered that of father and son, Roland being the French king's only heir), who do not take matters of courtesy and chivalry into account in their negotiations with the enemy.

On his way to the East Roland meets Baudor, a ship-owner and captain (*estormant*), who offers to take him to Syria. Baudor does not suspect Roland's identity, and takes him on board simply due to Roland's bravery and not his rank. As in the case of Ferragu, Baudor's nationality is confused: he is called *l'Endien* (the Indian, l. 11852) and the *Açopard* (the Ethiopian, l. 11894),[60] and is said to be at the service of the king of Albania (l. 11810). When they get to Syria, he explains that: "'Le saint Mahon que nos vient predicer; | Soudans de Perse en est le justisier'" (ll. 11855–56). Having

---

[60] Another occurrence of this term is *les Accopard* (l. 13270). For the origin of *Açopart* see E. C. Armstrong, 'Old French *açopart*, "Ethiopian"', *Modern Philology*, 38/3 (1941), 243–50.

considered Roland a Muslim since their first encounter, Baudor should not have deemed it necessary to specify that the god of the Muslims is Macon and the defender of Islam is the sultan of Persia. Yet however superfluous that piece of information may be for another Saracen, it is not for the reader of the *Entrée*.

Baudor appears as a very positive character. The author displays sympathy for him, as the portrait emerging from his interaction with Roland is that of any ship owner and captain one might meet in Venice. His expertise in handling the ship is described in detail as is his willingness to comfort Roland whom he thinks is seasick (when in reality Roland is mortified at having abandoned Charles' camp, ll. 11765–73). Overall, Baudor's role as the helmsman taking Roland to the East is quite straightforward and does not present any incongruities. Yet he does provide us with insights into the utilitarian relationship of Christians and Muslims in the fourteenth century, especially regarding trade between the *Serenissima* and the East. In that century, trade was widespread all over Europe and the East, and involved risks and adventures, often borne by the merchant in person travelling with his merchandise (a figure represented very well in the poem by the Saracen Baudor).[61] Baudor has no suspicions about Roland's identity and does not question it. He accepts him not only as a very improbable Saracen (Bacharuf is the false name Roland gives) but above all as a merchant. This creates common ground between the two, uniting them in a kind of brotherhood in the face of peril and the vagaries of fortune. Particularly for merchants, a strong sense of class identity created the conditions for the sharing of views and experiences.[62] For this reason especially, and not only out of gratitude, Baudor treats Roland throughout the journey like a friend. Furthermore, if the journey between Spain and Syria can be read as a quest then Baudor is the traditional figure of the *nocchiero* – the one who transports the dead from one shore to another. Baudor's part in the narrative is very short and is undoubtedly that of a guide, offering kindness, friendship and, more practically, knowledge of the waters and lands where the hero needs to travel.

[61] Such figures can also be found in the *Decameron* (for example II, 5) and *Novellino* (907).
[62] This theme is also represented in the *Decameron* (for example X, 9).

Sansonet first appears in the *Entrée* when Roland joins the court of the king of Persia. During the scene of the dispute over Dionés' marriage to Malcuidant, Sansonet is the first character to notice the presence of Lionés/Roland at court. His approach to Lionés is from the outset friendly. When Sansonet explains to Roland that nobody in the court of the Persian king would be able to defend Dionés in defiance of Malcuidant, Roland immediately offers to do so. In this way Sansonet is impressed by the generosity of Roland/Lionés before he knows that he is a Christian.

When the first part of the war is won, with Pélias dead and Dionés vindicated, Sansonet declares eternal friendship for Lionés (ll. 13202–04):

> Sanson l'acoulle et baise stroitement:
> Iluec i fist de sun amor pressent
> Que pué dura trusque sun finiment.

The two friends are inseparable now and Roland dedicates his time to teaching him the art of chivalry (ll. 13702–15). In this context, Sansonet appears as a young boy who worships Roland and wants to learn the secrets of his valour. All the rules of chivalry that Roland teaches make a strong impression on him. Elements of realism in his characterisation accentuate his young age and shy nature. The tone of his conversation with his father is honest and loyal, but also somewhat shy: '"Peres" – ce dit Sanson, qe un petit baubetoit – | "Qui ce vos desloast, petit vos ameroit"' (ll. 13769–70). Whereas Sansonet is said to stutter a little, Roland is bald on his temples, two elements suggesting that Roland is the more mature and self-confident; and so Sansonet is bound to be influenced by the Christian hero to the extent that he spontaneously chooses to convert.

While in the beginning Sansonet appeared to be a substitute for Roland's companion Oliver, it becomes clearer as the plot unfolds that this relationship is not on the same level. Oliver is Roland's *sage* friend whose companionship completes Roland's *prodesse*, in the sense that it was only the combination of the two valorous fighters, Roland *proz* and Oliver *sage*, that created a completely perfect knight. In the East, conversely, Roland is the perfect knight already and only in this capacity can he impart as he does lessons on perfect knighthood. He no longer needs a wise companion to soothe his temper when his *desmesure* surfaces. Thus Sansonet learns from Roland rather than contributes to his personality.

Sansonet's conversion must have happened in the section of the poem now missing, and this prevents the reader from following the events as originally narrated by the poet. Fortunately we have a reconstruction of the events originally represented in the lacuna, patiently assembled by Léon Gautier[63] by analysing a few re-elaborations of the matter of the *Entrée* and other Franco-Venetian works, of which Thomas' introduction to his edition of the *Entrée* gives a brief but sufficient summary. After Malcuidant is defeated and Jerusalem freed, all the inhabitants of the Holy City are converted. It must have been on that occasion that Sansonet converted too. Before the lacuna, in fact, up until line 13991, Roland is still busy teaching the art of chivalry to the Persian youths, and between lines 13633 and 13643 he is taken to a Muslim temple where he prays to the Lord in his Muslim disguise.

While it is possible to a degree to speak of the Muslims of the *Entrée* as being religious syncretists, it is clear that Roland does not adapt his faith by embracing elements of Islam to please or comply with the practice of his Muslim friends. Although he is in a Muslim temple, Roland still worships the Christian God and prays for Charlemagne not to be defeated by the pagans (ll. 13637–40):

> 'Senpre vos soit mon oncle le roi remandé,
> Oliver et Estous e le noubles berné
> Que sunt par mon amor in Espagne lojé:
> Non soufrés qu'il soient de Païn domajé'.

Sansonet's conversion comes as a natural consequence of his interest in chivalry, initially as a way of displaying friendship and loyalty towards Roland, having understood that the very concept of loyalty underpins chivalry. By the time he converts Sansonet has comprehended that there is no genuine chivalry without the Christian faith, as the two practices are intertwined. He is the only character allowed to follow Roland to Spain. His journey is a process

---

[63] L. Gautier, *Les Epopées françaises*.

of growth; he becomes an entirely Christian character and remains close to Roland for the rest of the narrative.

Dionés

> Non avoit que .XV. ains, et son per la voloit
> Marïer a uns rois qi ele riens amoit. (ll. 11949–50)

Dionés is introduced to the reader as a young woman with a strong personality who raises a case in the court of her father, the king of Persia. The court must gather to make a decision since she refuses to take Malcuidant as her husband or to accept an imposition by her father ('Dit que mari ne veut, dont cil grant onte en oit', l. 11955). It is also said that the young bachelors at the court take Dionés' part (ll. 11957–60):

> E disoint entr'aus: 'Par Mahon, elle a droit,
> car plus belle pulcele ne menjue ni boit,
> E tort a cist veiars; que soit maleoit
> Qui cesti li donast q'en amor vient e croit!'

The king of Persia has made a promise and is resolved to keep it, even against his daughter's will. Pélias, Malcuidant's nephew, asks for her to be burnt if she does not accept the marriage: 'Les diz que ele a fait a mervoile me ploit: | Je l'an ferai ardoir ains ch'un mois compli soit' (ll. 11966–67).

A detailed description of Dionés' physical attributes follows the typical sequence of romances[64] and occurs in a highly sensual

---

[64] The heroine in Breton romances is always described from the head downwards, starting with the hair. One example is the way that Erec, looking at Enide, admires her fair hair, laughing eyes, radiant forehead, nose, face, and mouth. He gazes upon her down to the waist, at her chin and snowy neck, her bosom and sides, her arms and hands (*Erec et Enide*, ll. 1479–85). Another example is the description of Blanchefleur whose features also correspond to the canonical ideal of beauty: 'Les chaveus tiex, s'estre poïst | Que il fuissent tot de fin or, | Tant estoient luisant et sor | Le front ot haut et blanc et plain | Comme s'il fust ovrez a main, | Et que de main d'ome ovrez fust | De pierre ou d'yvoire ou de fust. | Sorciex bien fais et large entrueil, | En la teste furent li oeil | Vair et rïant, cler et fendu ; | Le nez ot droit et estendu | Et miex avenoit en son vis | Li vermeus sor le blanc assis | Que li sinoples sor l'argent' (*Perceval*, ll. 1811–25).

context, as she comes in front of Roland to remove his helmet. Just as she is irresistibly attracted to the hero, so he finds her beauty overwhelming (ll. 12550–59):

> La file ou roi est devant venue,
> L'eume i alach
> e, duremant s'en argüe:
> Anch teil sargient ne fu por hom veüe;
> Angle resanble qi desande de nue.
> Vis oit bien feit e gardeüre agüe,
> La char oit blanche com nif desendue,
> Color vermoil come graine vendue,
> Boche petite, danteüre menue,
> Oil oit riant, qant ert plus ireschue;
> Sa blonde crine ne vos ai manteüe;

The standard beauty of the Christian maiden applies to the Saracen princess, her skin being pale ('Dionés al frois collor', l. 10954) and her hair blonde. As with the portrait of the Saracen knight, what counts is not ethnic origin but social status: 'Car une file le roi de Perse avoit, | Belle e cortoise e molt de bon endroit;' (ll. 11947–48). The emphasis is on her western features and courtly education, which make her the perfect feminine model for the fourteenth-century reader. Courtly manners are still a point of reference as far as attractiveness is concerned. The portrait of a lady, just like that of a knight, must conform to a precise model in order to be fully recognised by the reader/audience.

The theme of love in the *Entrée*, if not irrelevant (which is unprovable given the great lacuna exactly where the topic may have been developed), is certainly marginal to other highly prominent elements that persuasively argue the influence of the romances. The idea that a Muslim princess should fall in love with the Christian hero is not new to the French epic.[65] Nonetheless, the case of the *Entrée* is different in that Roland introduces himself to the Sultan's court as a Saracen. The question of Roland's concealed identity eliminates any possibility that the episode might conform to the

---

[65] See F. M. Warren, 'The enamoured Moslem princess in Orderic Vital and the French epic', *PMLA*, 19 (1914), 341–58.

stereotype of the enamoured Saracen princess in love with a Christian man. Technically, in the *Entrée* Dionés falls for a Saracen. Furthermore, the motif of the enamoured Saracen princess implies a type of interaction normally leading to marriage. This kind of alliance results in the conversion of the princess to Christianity: it is a subtle and milder form of victory of good over evil than the defeat of a Saracen fighter by a Christian hero (a metaphor for Christianity's ultimate victory over Islam through violent imposition).[66] Again, the lacuna in the text prevents any assumptions as to the narrative development of this matter, leaving the reader without an explanation why she ends up being married to Anseïs. The fact that Roland is betrothed to Aude explains neither his refusal to marry the Saracen princess nor the details of the following events. In the prologue to the second section, the poet summarises in a couple of lines what it is that Roland accomplishes in the East (ll. 10945-51):

> Se vos vorois entendre, je vos dirai ancor
> Cum Rollant pasa mer en tere alïenor
> E com dou roi de Perse fu loial servior,
> Quant il fist la bataile en la loi Paienor
> Por la fille a Soudans, Dionés al frois collor,
> Vers le Turc qe de force estoit superior
> (Pelias oit a nom, mout avoit de valor)

---

[66] The striving for harmony typical of the medieval concept of order in all disciplines could have resulted in the harmony of the two dissonant cultures whose opposition had for many centuries caused war, destruction and hatred. One case of harmony in Italian literature contemporary to the *Entrée* is the *Cantare di Florio e Biancifiore*. The Marriage of Flore the Saracen and Blanchefleur the Christian harmonises two different cultures, aspires to the highest human ideal of perfect love and disregards the experience of mundane reality: see D. Metlitzki, *The Matter of Araby in Medieval England* (New Haven and London: Yale University Press, 1977), p. 250. For a treatment of world harmony see L. Spitzer, *Classical and Christian Ideas of World Harmony. Prolegomena to an Interpretation of the Word 'Stimmung'*, ed. by A. Granville Hatcher (Baltimore: Johns Hopkins Press, 1963).

The prologue says that Roland waged war against the pagans *for* the daughter of the Sultan ('por la fille a Soudans'), which does not explain much. It could indicate that Dionés is the cause or the object of this war, and that Roland underwent battle because of her, in her defence, or to win her over. While she falls in love with him because he is strong, he does not display any interest at all. Although there is no grown man who would not wish to have her naked in his arms ('Soz ciel n'a home, tant ait chiere barbue | Ne la qerist avoir en si braz nue', ll. 12560–61), Roland simply accomplishes his knightly duty according to the rules of chivalry, which impose upon him protection of the weak, including women in danger. That does not imply that there will be consequences of any sort, although it is interesting to observe how Dionés looks at Roland and how she prays for his victory, and especially to understand why she prays.

Roland is not a suitable candidate for marriage to Dionés for a variety of reasons. First, there is the tradition: as he is meant to die in Rencesvals, he must return to Spain. Secondly, he already has a fiancée whom at this stage he is not yet ready to forget (as he will in the *Innamorato* and *Furioso*). Aude stands as a constant reminder of Roland's mission and is thus more of a symbolic figure than a real character. She does not play an active role in the *Chanson* but is only mentioned once by her brother Oliver (l. 1720). She appears for the space of two laisses (CCLXVII; CCLXVIII) at the end of the poem, where she is introduced as 'une bele dam[e]' (l. 3708) asking for Roland at Charlemagne's court. When Charlemagne tells her that Roland died in battle, she too dies in a single laisse (CCLXVIII). What is at the same time tragic and surreal about the figure of Aude is that nobody bothers to tell her of her fiancé's death, although her brother was Roland's closest friend and she had been awaiting his return for years. This absolute absence of realism transforms the figure of Aude into a symbol, signifying in the *Chanson* (and through her mention, in the *Entrée*) the highest of Roland's goals. Once the hero is dead she has no reason to be alive either, existing only as a function of Roland's heroism.

Dionés is the antithesis of Aude. Her beauty leaves Roland breathless because she reminds him of Aude, but that is where the comparison ends. It seems that the figure of Dionés has a double function in this text: as a reminder of Aude/the mission, and of creating an opportunity for Roland to set the example of the perfect knight. Furthermore, when Pélias asks for Dionés to be burnt alive ('l'an ferai ardoir', l. 11967) if she does not accept the marriage, the question arises whether that is not a typical punishment of the Christian West rather than of the East. The promise to burn Dionés as a witch produces an immediate effect of cruelty and terror. While Dionés is said to be an expert in magic and astrology, a practice belonging with witchcraft, she is also said to be very young and beautiful, and is characterised as a lady. This double aspect of her personality creates a complexity suggesting that she does not represent a typical case of an enamoured princess but rather anticipates figures of the Renaissance epic.[67]

The Roland/Dionés interaction therefore gives rise to a double consequence: on the one hand, the Aude-reminder limits the action in the East; on the other, Roland is given the opportunity to perform a gesture of *chevalier parfait*. Furthermore, Roland is presented through the eyes of the princess, adding further facets to his well-rounded character.

As already suggested in this study, the Dionés/Dido association leads to a more general consideration about the type of love inspired by Roland's manly valour, which is antithetical to the aesthetics of secular knighthood. In Breton romances, moral attributes are never sufficient for maidens to fall in love with a knight. As well as being the strongest and most chivalrous knight, he must be the most handsome. Maidens in Breton romances all fall for knights bearing the same physical attributes, with admiration for valour, signified by the knight's beauty, coming next in importance. However, even though a long description of Roland has just been provided (ll. 13650–61), including of his baldness, Dionés still thinks him the most handsome man ever born (ll. 13665–68):

> 'Hai Mahomet' – 'dit elle, et que a je veü!
> Plus beaus fils enjendrés anc de meres non fu.
> Celui me fait sentir ce que ancor n'ait feit plu,
> Ce est Amor, que m'a mis en sun amoros fu'.

---

[67] For example, Angelica in the *Furioso*. See above, p. 63.

This is perfectly in agreement with her characterisation as wise, and with the love story's epilogue: her marriage with Anseïs (another Christian and a more suitable candidate), which is unlikely to be the product of passion.

Roland's characterisation as a celestial knight represents a landmark in the hybridisation of the matter of Charlemagne. Although we cannot ever know, there are elements in the plot's unfolding events to suggest that Roland's positive action in the East must have produced some agreement or alliance, resulting in Anseïs' acceptance among the Saracens as a representative of Christianity. The happy ending of the Eastern section, along with a general atmosphere of victory of good over evil, results in a mass conversion to Christianity – or perhaps in a type of religious syncretism that makes everybody happy. The *Entrée* thus represents a very distinctive case of intertextuality in which the aims of the *chanson de geste* fuse miraculously with the priorities of romance. The treatment of the Saracen *Others* is exemplary of this blend of genres.

Malcuidant and Pélias

Malcuidant only appears briefly and his role is confined to that of the evil enemy *par excellence*. Indeed, a clear-cut characterisation is provided by his very name. It is also said that Malcuidant, the menacing king of Persia, was an extremely powerful ruler and for this reason very much feared (ll. 11968–72):

> Le roi qi menechoit mout par estoit pusant:
> Les Turs e les Roseus e des Greçois auquant
> E celor de Baudaqe i erent apendant,
> Estier les Esclavons e Blach e Nobiant.
> Sis rois apendoit a lui, senz li parant;

Roland is welcomed to the court of Persia disguised as a Saracen. However, no sooner does Lionés/Roland start displaying his chivalric nature than the surrounding Saracens understand him to be of a noble and mysterious lineage. In particular, Pélias acknowledges that Lionés' chivalric behaviour betrays a noble origin, and asks the hero to disclose his identity and the reason why he is helping a Saracen (ll. 13086–98):

'Cevallers frere' – ce a dit Pelliais –
'Si Sarracins, Crestians o Judais
Is, nel sai; més par la loi que tu ais
Et par cil ordre dont civaler te fais,
Par tot l'amor de l'ami plus verais
Ch'ais en ces mont, se tu le voies mais,
Chuntente moi de voir dir, non de gais,
De quel lignaze es tu nez et estrais,
De roi, de quens, de duch ou de plus bais?
Non te creroie, se tu le moi jurais.
Quele oqueisun, qel penser, quel forfais
Te cunduit ci servir une Satenais
De qui merit dou servis non avrais?'

Friction between Roland and the Saracens in the *Entrée* is always caused by a specific behaviour that is despicable to Roland's knightly mentality. One very clear example of this is when Roland approaches the two Saracens in the Spanish port from where he starts his sea journey. In this episode, the focus is not on the *identity* but on the *attitude* of the two enemies. In the same way, Roland perceives the dispute over Dionés' hand as a case of anti-chivalric conduct. Pélias' threat of retaliation causes the grief of the Persian king, who thus acquires a human dimension when confronted with possibly losing both the love of and authority over his daughter. In this way, as Roland meets the good and the bad Arabs, a sharp division is made between the two parties. As with Ferragu and Isoré, what matters in the *Entrée* is not necessarily that the antagonist believes in a different religion but where they stand in terms of loyalty and friendship, and their capacity to embrace the chivalric values of the Christian world. The matter in the *Entrée* is therefore more elaborated than elsewhere in the *chanson de geste* genre; there are no longer Christians and Saracens, understood as categories of good and evil, but rather good and evil existing beyond any pre-established category. The whole idea of the Other understood as the enemy in the *Entrée* receives an unprecedentedly multifaceted treatment.[68] This extends what is happening in the French camp to

---

[68] Bancourt noted that the originality of the *Entrée* author lies primarily in his position on the Saracens: 'Au terme d'une évolution dont l'*Entrée*

the Saracen one: it is Ganelon and not a Saracen who causes the death of Roland. The real enemy lurks among Roland's own kin.

When Pélias is finally killed in battle by Roland, the poet makes it clear that 'Mort est le Turc por sa desmesurance' (l. 13172). Roland has no pity for his enemy not because of politics or religion, or *par orguel*, but because his enemy was *desmesure* and acted against the law (*contre droit*). In this case it is the celestial law, since the terminology the author employs here is clearly inspired by the language of the *Queste* in which, after every *aventure* (the *semblance*), a *senefiance* is provided. We are in the realm of chivalry and not of a holy war. Had Pélias been a Christian his uncivilised behaviour would have caused precisely the same reaction. Conversely, Sansonet instinctively recognises in Liones/Roland a friend, thanks not to a cultural affinity but rather to a spiritual proximity and Roland's valorous behaviour in offering to defend his sister.

Ferragu

Clearer nowadays are the purpose of the poets of the *chanson de geste*, their target audience, influences, and the motives that led them to make certain choices in the characterisation and behaviours of their Saracen protagonists. From the earliest motto *Paien unt tort e chrestiëns unt dreit*[69] to the theological dispute in the *Entrée* and beyond, a wide variety of Saracen characters populate the *chansons*. It is difficult to determine whether Saracen traits were represented in order to conform to a stereotype, or to entertain. In actuality, it is risky to generalise as to the purpose of the *chanson de geste*'s portrayal of the Saracens and their religion, as John Tolan pointed out.[70]

The *chanson de geste* has sometimes been described as a variation of the Wild Western plot – and it has been stressed that, just as the Indians in Westerns were not real natives at all but only served the purpose of creating a goodies-versus-baddies antagonism, so the

---

d'Espagne constitue le témoignage le plus marquant, chevaliers chrétiens et sarrasins se découvrent moralement, socialement, naturellement frères dans la chevalerie'. Bancourt, *Les Musulmans*, p. 325 (see also p. 324).

69 *Chanson de Roland*, ed. Finoli, l. 1015.
70 Tolan, *Saracens*, p. 129.

Saracens are not real Saracens: the *chansons* authors found the right enemy for the stories they wanted to tell.[71] The portrayal of quintessential bad guys allows the reader 'to enjoy the violence, to revel in the blood and killing, without remorse. Only by dehumanising the adversary, making him sufficiently "other", is this possible'.[72] However, this analysis does not seem applicable to the *Entrée*, in which the Other is represented according to a different ethic and following a different inspiration.

Many of the events which take place in the Eastern section define a new relationship between Roland and the Saracens. It gradually becomes clearer that friendship and friction are prompted by proximity and distance in ethical matters. Ideology has no part in Roland's fondness or dislike of the Saracens, a distinctive trait of the *Entrée*.

Roland's interaction with the Saracens in the *Entrée* only partially follows the stereotypes established in the *chanson de geste* tradition. The poet claims to be the original author of the part set in the East ('Tot ce vos savrai dir, ch'en sui estez houtor', l. 10960), and while the old hostility between the two cultures is still present to an extent, different reasons justify aversion to the Muslims, and alliances with them are influenced by new perspectives on the question of the Other. What is excluded *tout court* is ideological opposition and religious hatred: the old rule 'Paien unt tort e chrestïens unt dreit' is out of the question in the *Entrée*. While matters of ideology have already been extensively treated, this chapter will identify positive and negative images of Saracens, and explain what underlies them. I will take into account aspects of the narrative that influence the characterisation of the Saracens. The purpose is to establish a general rule to clarify rivalry and alliance according to the new societal thinking emerging in the poem.

In the poem's first section, the Saracens are still the enemies of the French because of the question of dominion over Spain, to which is added a more general religious antagonism. In the second section the picture changes completely, since the friction between the two parties is represented by the opposition between Roland and

---

[71] Daniel, *Heroes and Saracens*, p. 263–66.
[72] Tolan, *Saracens*, p. 126.

Pélias, and is only caused by Roland's wish to protect his host, the Saracen king. Roland being disguised as a Saracen, this friction cannot be understood as an opposition between two worlds and faiths but rather as a rivalry between enemies belonging more broadly to the same side.

Ferragu is Roland's great enemy in section one. The character of Ferragu is modelled on the prototype of the Saracen giant Ferracutus in chapter XVII of the Pseudo-Turpin chronicle (the source of the *Entrée* and of every epic on Charlemagne, often referred to as 'the book'). There the characterisation of Ferragu as a giant is explicitly based on Goliath:

> [...] gygas quidam Ferracutus nomine de genere Goliath advenerat de horis Syrie, quem cum .c.xx. milibus Turcorum Babylonis ammiraldus ad bellum contra Karolum regem miserat.[73]

Ferragu, who perishes by Roland's sword, can also be found in *Otinel*, the *Enfances Vivien*, *Floovant*, *Florent et Octavien* and (under the name of Ferragu) in *Valentine et Orson*.[74] He is the first major Saracen character that we encounter in the *Entrée*, his initial portrait given through the words of Ogier. From the very beginning he is characterised using his enormous size, and Ogier, following Pseudo-Turpin, compares him to Goliath (ll. 758–61):

> 'Au segle n'a Paiens si fort ni grant.
> A mout grant poine li porte un auferant:
> Dou legnaz fu, bien pert a son semblant,
> De cil Gollie qe fu mort por l'enfant'.

Several other times Ferragu is said to be an offspring of Goliath, for example in the following passages (ll. 1630–31, 3548–50):

---

[73] *The Pseudo-Turpin. Bibliothèque Nationale fonds Latin Ms. 17656*, ed. by H. M. Smyser (Cambridge, MA: The Mediaeval Academy of America, 1937), ll. 18–20, p. 75.

[74] *Les Enfances Vivien*, ed. by M. Rouguier (Geneva: Droz, 1997); *Les Enfances Vivien*, ed. by C. Wahlund and H. von Feilitzen (Uppsala: Librairie de l'Université – Paris: Bouillon, 1895); *Floovant, chanson de geste du XIIe siècle*, ed. by S. Andolf (Uppsala: Almquist Wiksells, 1941); *Florent et Octavien*, ed. by N. Laborderie (Paris: Champion, 1991); D. Arthur, *Valentine et Orson. A Study in Late Medieval Romance* (New York: Columbia University Press, 1929).

> Vers Feragu, le parant Golias,
> Mist son cheval Rollant a petit pas;
> Or vo je bien e croi de cors verais
> Ch'is de lignaje al jaiant Goliais
> C'oncist Davit de son sant...

The reference to Goliath is useful for conveying a physical characterisation, and its function is to provide a ready visual reference. While in the case of the Greek heroes we can only imagine their size and valour, we have a description of David and Goliath's confrontation. Ferragu's size has remained in the later tradition as his main characteristic. In the same period when the *Entrée* was written, this portrait of Ferragu is also found in the English tradition, where he appears in the early fourteenth-century *Rouland and Vernagu*.[75] He seems double the size of Charlemagne and his features are described with great precision.[76] In the *Entrée*, when the French prisoners are taken to Ferragu because the Saracen wants to speak to them about Roland, they look at him and are impressed by his scale: 'Les host de France prist formant a garder | De si grant gient se puet mereveiller' (ll. 2034–35). While the reference to Goliath provides a biblical argument supporting a possible allegorical reading of the figure of Ferragu, gigantism is also a synonym for the demonic or satanic (as present in Dante's treatment of the giants in *Inferno* XXXI). This size may therefore be intended as a demonic feature rather than a sign of physical strength.[77]

However, Ferragu's strength is characterised in opposition to Roland's. Ferragu is described twice as a lion ('cist lions che con averte brance', l. 2202; 'Hoi ert vencus le lion par l'agnel', l. 2492). The lion is not a negative symbol but implies power in a situation of battle (i.e. physical). In the context of the *Entrée*, Ferragu is said to be a lion both in isolation and in opposition to Roland's description as 'lamb", which is to say that the Saracen is virtuous, i.e. physically

---

[75] Metlitzki, *The Matter of Araby*, p. 192.
[76] Metlitzki, *The Matter of Araby*, p. 193.
[77] See also for comparison Dante's treatment of Lucifer in *Inferno*: 'e più che con un gigante io mi convegno | che i giganti non fan con le sue braccia' (XXXIV, 30–31).

strong.[78] In a different situation Ferragu is *le grand, le fort, le fiers, le plans d'orgoi* (l. 1814). The co-existence of *fort* and *plans d'orgoi* here is theoretically wrong since the type of strength implied is a moral one, entailing the overcoming of pride (*desmesure*). Ferragu comes across as *desmesuré*, taking over Roland's original lack of measure (his sword is also called *desmesuree*, l. 2528). Verse 1814 should be divided in two sections, therefore, with the two attributes in the first section implying positive qualities which are combined with the two negative attributes of the second hemistich. Another possible reading could refer to Ferragu's strength being in fact a divine attribute, although given to him by Macon rather than God. Thus it is rather the case that the author is consistent in that he gives a fully rounded characterisation of a Saracen, who is simultaneously positive and negative. Ferragu's hybrid nature will be made manifest during the plot as he shows potential for conversion which he himself chooses not to exploit. An interesting aspect of Ferragu's personality connected with these four attributes is that he comes across as proud. The giant is therefore doomed not because he belongs to the wrong party and is the embodiment of evil, but because pride is the sin that leads to death. The theological dispute, discussed further in this study, shows that religion and traditional antagonism have little to do with Ferragu's defeat.

The *Entrée* represents a unique case in which the giant receives a full moral and physical characterisation. A long passage in which the Saracen is described both physically and morally can be quite sharply divided into two sections: the first covering lines 830 to 843, and the second lines 844 to 873. In the former, lines 834 to 836 and especially lines 840 and 841 provide a complete moral portrait of a knight (ll. 830–43):

> Feragu s'arme en la sale voutie.
> N'oit plus biax home en tote Paienie,
> Ne mielz cortois ni plus sans villanie.
> Largeçe fu por lui mantenue e sanplie,
> Avarice destruite e de son cor bandie;
> Jameis de son nemi non dist outrequidie,
> Mais envers tote gient grant bien e cortesie;

---

[78] See discussion of the *force / vertuz* antinomy at p. 109.

> E quant les oit devant a bataille rengie,
> Vers aus non oit amor ne nulle compaignie.
> Jameis ne sofri tort an trestote sa vie;
> Cent fois s'acombati o l'espee forbie
> Por orfres e por veves, por gient a tort blesmie.
> Sajes fu ens escriz de la Mahomarie;
> Rices fu a mervoille et pobre mante fie;

All the moral qualities belonging to Ferragu are the standard virtues of the perfect knight: he is *cortois* (l. 832), generous (*largeçe*, l. 833), an enemy of avarice (834), never speaking a mean word against his enemy (l. 835) and defending orphans and widows (l. 841). Ferragu thus becomes a perfect antagonist for Roland; no longer the very embodiment of evil whom Roland must annihilate, he is the most valorous and courteous knight on the opposing side. However, Ferragu is also said to be a fiery character, although his 'fiery figure' relates to a physical rather than moral force: *Feragu a la fiere figure* (l. 2074). He may be seen as a secular as opposed to celestial knight, according to a popular distinction belonging to the later Grail tradition.

The second section provides a great number of details about his physical appearance, age, height, hair colour, and finally the essential one of the single weak point in his invincibility, his navel (ll. 844–55).

> Vint anz avoit a point, l'estorie le nos crie;
> .XII. coubes fu long, ce est voir sans boisdie;
> La ganbe oit longe e grosse, la forqueüre lie;
> Anples fu en espales; bu ne li desdist mie;
> Le braz oit long e gros, la mans blance e pollie,
> Le doi long de troi paumes, cil q'a plus seignorie;
> Entre l'uns oilz et l'autre une paume et dimie;
> Ceveleüre blonde et longe e trecelie;
> Gros fu e colloriez, n'a nulle or n'en rie;
> Gracios a tot homes. Ne sai qe plus vos die:
> Se pur deignast acroire el filz sante Marie,
> Au segle n'eüst pier de tote baronie.

The moral and physical characterisation of Ferragu is ample. Looking closely at the text, the most interesting of his features are his white and polished hands (l. 848) and his blonde hair gathered in tresses (l. 851). The lack of virility in worldly knights (*militia saeculi*) that so irritated St. Bernard is testified to by their excessive attention to physical appearance. The object of the saint's harsh and satirical criticism was the handsome lay knight: his soft white hands, beautiful hair and luxurious clothes covering his armour. He compared such secular knights unfavourably to the Templars, being hard men by contrast who shaved their hair and paid no attention to their skin and beard, and who were focused on their task of protecting all the Christian brothers in the East.[79] The model imposed by St. Bernard influenced the development of courtly culture and poetry to the extent that it established the distinction between secular and celestial knighthood. This distinction was brought to its highest development in the *Queste*.[80] If Ferragu is characterised as *miles saeculi*, this means that his opposite, Roland, is presumably *miles Christi*, the perfect knight whose superior goal (above any display of vain mundane chivalry) was celebrated by St. Bernard. The mention of white polished hands and blonde hair is not a simple characterisation based on common medieval ideas of beauty but predicts Ferragu's future in that it denotes the profile of a character soon to perish, for he belongs to the past. His characterisation anticipates the outcome of the theological dispute: in every aspect of his personality, appearance and thought, Ferragu embodies all that the poet considered incompatible with the world he intended to celebrate. Many adjectives reserve the same ignominious treatment for Ferragu as for any other Saracen in the *chanson de geste*: he is a *mescreant* (ll. 1165, 1660, 1692), a criminal (l. 2214) and swears against his own gods (*leideçer, laider*: l. 2233). He is a *Satanas* (ll. 1298, 1660), *Antecris* (ll. 1362, 2122, 2418), and *Paiens* (ll. 1820, 2019, 2527, 3324). However, all these heavily dismissive attributes are rather stereotyped and add nothing truly

---

[79] Cardini, 'Il guerriero e il cavaliere', p. 98.
[80] The figures of Galaad and Boort in the *Queste* represent the quintessential celestial knights, while Lancelot and (ultimately) Perceval maintain their attachment to the things of the world and are thus excluded from the vision of the Grail.

distinctive to his character. For a classification of the giant as Roland's perfect enemy, one should look not there but to the symbolic value of his physical traits and the allegorical potential of his behaviour.

As far as his nationality is concerned, he is called *Feragu l'Espanoi* (l. 1813), *le Paiens de Galise* (l. 1843), *Amoraïs* (l. 1371), *Esclé* (the Slavonic: the land of the Muslims is also called *Sclavonie* by the Venetians; ll. 1383, 1538), *Aragon* (l. 1434), *Africant* (l. 1677), *Aufricant* (ll. 1886, 3075); *Aufaje* (l. 2108).[81] He is also called *Turs* (l. 1696), *Turch* (l. 2217), *Arabi* (ll. 1816, 1824, 1918), *Arabis* (l. 2126), *Saracins* (ll. 1861, 1878), though the poet could have found an ethnic distinction between Turks, Arabs and Saracens in the *Gesta Francorum*:

> As soon as our knights arrived, the Turks, Arabs, Saracens, Angulans, and all the barbarian tribes speedily took flight through the byways of the mountains and plains. The Turks, Persians, Paulicians, Saracens, Angulans, and other pagans numbered 360,000, besides the Arabs, whose numbers are known only to God.[82]

Ferragu is at the same time a Spaniard, Aragonese, Slav, African, and of course a Turk.[83] This suggests a general reference to the area

---

[81] Old French *aufage, aufaige, auffage, alfage*, a word that seemed to have indicated noble and powerful people; also *aufaine, allfaigne, aufaingne, aufeigne, aufainie, aufarain, aufart*.

[82] *Gesta Francorum*, transl. by James Brundage, *The Crusades. A Documentary Survey* (Milwaukee, WI: Marquette University Press, 1962), 49-51. See *Gesta Francorum*, ed. by R. Hill (Oxford: Oxford University Press, 1998), p. 20: 'Statim autem uenientibus militibus nostris, Turci et Arabes, et Saraceni et Agulani omnesque barbarae nationes dederunt uelociter fugam, per compendia montium et per plana loca. Erat autem numerus Turcorum, Persarum, Publicanorum, Saracenorum, Agulanorum aliorumque paganorum trecenta sexaginta milia extra Arabes, quorum numerum nemo scit nisi solus Deus.'

[83] As Limentani showed, the epithet *Turc* in the *Entrée* means specifically Turkish as the poet was perfectly aware of who the Turks were. He was able to localise them in a particular geographical area, for they represented such a concrete threat to the Venetians that the whole people of the *terraferma* would have been able to tell where they were from: Limentani, 'Venezia e il pericolo Turco nell'*Entrée d'Espagne*', in *L'Entrée d'Espagne e i signori d'Italia*, pp. 358 ff. All the other names

occupied by the Muslims at the beginning of the fourteenth century. It was a very wide area: at the time of the *Entrée*'s composition, Islam had spread over half of Asia, northern Africa, and, in Europe, southern Spain and Sicily (which still hosted a large number of Muslims), and these last were historically the Muslim strongholds of the West. Marsile's dominion is said to be *le regne Asian* (l. 1515), embracing the whole of the Asian region (from Anatolia, to Egypt, to Syria). The poet is inclined to keep a generic definition of the Saracens, which constitutes one of the *Entrée*'s most archaic and traditional aspects. Apart from this very few textual elements suggest continuity with the tradition.

Ferragu proves a quite eclectic character when he makes an open display of generosity and chivalry in the episode of Girard de Roussillon; when the French champion falls from his horse and loses his helmet in this lively little sketch, Ferragu could easily have decapitated him, but instead he spares his life (ll. 1301–08):

> Le ber Gerarz lors chiet en mie l'erboi;
> Le chief oit nuz, dont il forment s'esfroie.
> Cil treit l'espee, sor le duc la paumoie.
> 'Rend toi' – dist il – 'c'oncir ne te voldroie;
> Prodom me senbles; trop repris en seroie.
> S'ensi non fais, a noiant m'en teroie
> S'a uns seul colp – se je ma main t'envoie –
> Ne t'oncesis, se fus Hector de Troie'.

Ferragu can be identified with Achilles as the closing line suggests. He would not kill Girard even if he were Hector of Troy, Achilles' worst enemy. Roland himself is often compared to Hector and, since the two characters mirror each other, this supports the Ferragu/Achilles connection. The question of Ferragu's navel further corroborates this connection (ll. 868–73):

---

must be generally understood as synonyms for Saracen, i.e. Muslim. In the *chanson de geste*, the Muslims are generally called Saracens since there existed no other name to define them; the word Muslim enters the French language only in the fourteenth century. For this point see the chapter on 'Musulmans, sarrasins et sarrasins epiques', in Bancourt, *Les Musulmans*, pp. 1 ff. See also Daniel, *Islam and the West*, p. 14.

> Cist Feragus, de qui nos ramenton,
> Estot faez par itel devison
> Qe de sa cars detrencer ne puet hon,
> Fors endroit l'anbellil: tel fu sa nasion.
> Iloc avoit tel armes qe ne feit a garçon,
> Et toz les autres porte par retrair a baron.

The Ferragu/Achilles identification adds a new element to the gradual construction of a negative totem, as a symbol of all that needs revision. Achilles is the great adversary of those Trojans who founded Padua and the Roman Empire, and started the fortunate lineage that brought reason and peace to the Western world.

The antagonism between Roland and Ferragu is introduced as a necessary element in the plot. One of the aspects of this antagonism is suspense, created by a number of stratagems such as retardation of their encounter, and previous encounters with mediators whose function is to anticipate information while delaying the unfolding of the plot. By the time the two really meet a great deal of expectation has been created. Epic retardation is a device common to the *chanson de geste*, so that 'a listener arriving in the course of recitation receives a coherent impression'.[84] In the case of the *Entrée*, epic retardation is not employed according to the medieval model of the *chanson de geste* but is more akin to the classical type of retardation. For example, Homer deliberately describes the weapons so as to delay an impending event. In the duel between the two protagonists there is an incessant alternation between Roland's and Ferragu's thoughts and gestures so that, along with creating the retardation, the reader can form a clear idea of the opinion each holds of the other.

The evolution of Ferragu's feelings towards Roland is slow. At first, he despises the Christian. When Estout is kept prisoner in the Saracen camp Ferragu asks him to talk about Roland, and Estout describes his friend as the champion of Christianity, provoking Ferragu's irritation: '"Tei toi" – dist il – "qe trop le m'ais loé; | Je croi qe soies un fablaors prove"' (ll. 1570–71). He will soon show a change of mind: after the first day of the duel, he openly praises

---

[84] Auerbach, *Mimesis*, p. 105.

Roland and admits in front of the other Saracens that he respects him for his valour (ll. 2020–24):

> Dist Feragu: 'Ne devez pleider:
> Vos n'estes daignes d'un tiel home nomer.
> Por Machomet, je ni vi mais son per.
> Pro est Rollant et engignos e fier,
> Tant q'il se quide tote Espaigne aquiter'.

Although the concluding line expresses a certain sarcasm about Roland's arrogant attempt to conquer Spain, and implies scepticism of his valour, Roland's loyal attitude becomes evident to him when the French knight regrets having killed Feragu's horse and offers his own in return (ll. 2841–45):

> Respont Rollant: 'Si bien m'ait la Diex mere
> Com bien me poise se serois peonere;
> Prendez le mien, s'il est par vostre afere.
> S'il fust meilor, foi qe je doi sant Piere
> Jel vos donas asés plus volantere'.

Ferragu refuses Roland's gift despite showing appreciation. The Saracen is very hard-hearted. At the end of day one, he makes a full display of his pride and arrogance when the Saracens try to convince him to cancel the next day's confrontation. In front of Estout and Oliver, who remain prisoners in the Saracen's camp, he declares that Roland's valour infuriates him to the extent that he only desires to kill him. He can no longer conceal his admiration for his enemy's unbelievable strength, which he expresses in the form of utter irritation (ll. 2950–57):

> 'Machon' – dist il – 'vos dont grant engonbrer,
> Ch'en tiel mainiere me volez aonter!
> Com peüs je greignor honor trover
> Com de Rollant, se le pués aquiter?
> De tot les autres che sunt neschus de mer,
> S'oncir le pués, non doroie un diner.
> Afermez sui dou tot sor un penser:
> O de morir o son orguel mater'.

These lines are central to the plot in that they create a double repercussion. On the one hand, they anticipate Ferragu's admiration for his enemy, which will finally lead him to propose staging a diatribe to complete the duel. On the other, the last line expresses the giant's ultimate design, which seems to fade away for a while during the dispute through an illusionary agreement on some questions, but is fiercely reiterated at its end. The next day, when Ferragu returns to the duel without a horse, Roland descends from his own out of loyalty. Ferragu is later deeply impressed by Roland's kindness and extreme trustworthiness when the French knight puts a stone under the sleeping giant's head (ll. 3545–47):

> Li chef li leve sens mal e sens forfais
> E par itant cil ne s'erveille pais.
> Mist li la piere, pués a dit el testais

The highly vivid sketch is impregnated with realism. Roland stands in front of the snoring Ferragu, respectful of his enemy's sleep. Of course, Ferragu is enthusiastic about his antagonist's trustworthiness, and wishes to show his appreciation of Roland's valour so far as to offer him his sister's hand (ll. 3585–603):

> 'Je voul un poué ensamble o toi parler,
> Plus ne te pués mon coraje celer.
> Quant de ton estre me vient bien a penser,
> Soz ciel n'a home, tant sache deviser,
> Que te poüst de bontez amender'.
> [...]
> 'Al roi Marsille te ferai pardoner
> E ma seror, qe de bontez n'a per
> E ne plus belle ne se poroit trover,
> Cangeona te donrai a moiler:
> Filie est de roi e de raïne mer;
> Soz ciel n'a home ne s'an post contener.
> Anz q'il soient pasez li .V. fevrer
> Cro je cist segle tot a moi conquister:
> De la moitez te farai coroner,
> De l'autre part me farai honorer'.

Ferragu offers Roland all the honour and half of the conquered land of Spain, even as he fails quite to grasp that the French champion stands before him. There is something humiliating about his offer, especially when he mentions a deadline for completely annihilating the French army ('Anz q'il soient pasez li .V. fevrer' etc., l. 3600 ff.). These lines convey the standard offer of a gift in exchange for surrender, a *topos* of *chansons de geste*. While Roland laughs at his proposal, Ferragu's enthusiasm creates a good opportunity for starting a theological dispute.

Apart from the discussion of more subtle theological questions, Ferragu's characterisation becomes increasingly realistic from a literary point of view during the dispute. The Arab loses his gigantic, fabulous dimension and acquires a human stature. Rather than anticipating an eventual enlightened acceptance that Saracens are human beings after all, this modification may be viewed as an attempt to dismiss the Arab by reducing him to a human being.[85] At the theological dispute's conclusion, the end of Ferragu's literary life is marked by a rather tense finale as the giant signs his own death sentence, by accidentally and naively revealing his unique vulnerability. In every way, Ferragu is dismissed as an unworthy adversary: as an unbeatable enemy (the secret of the navel, revealed, reduces him to a mortal); an interlocutor (he takes up the role of a Latin Averroist); and as one incapable of compromise and thus unreasonable (he returns to his original *desmesuré* proposition to either kill or die).

In this way a parallel can be drawn between Ferragu and another famous pagan, Dante's Ulysses. As Maria Corti pointed out in her analysis of the figure of Ulysses, 'l'interpretazione figurale, il ruolo di simbolo richiede che le qualità di Ulisse *stiano al posto di qualcosa d'altro* a cui Dante vuole riferirsi'.[86] The idea of a *senso figurale*, which belongs to Christian exegesis and blossoms in the literature of

---

[85] During the Renaissance, the old stereotypes of barbaric invaders were used by humanist literature in such a way as to suggest the impossibility of viewing Islam as a serious intellectual adversary. See Tolan, *Saracens*, p. 276; Bisaha, '"New Barbarian" or Worthy Adversary'.

[86] Corti, *Scritti su Cavalcanti e Dante*, pp. 255–83. See also in the same collection of essays, 'Parigi e Bologna: novità filosofiche e linguistiche', pp. 312–26 (p. 336).

the thirteenth century (the most exemplary case of all being the *Queste*), can be applied to Ferragu who becomes a *figura* for something else. As a general rule (doubtless applicable to a number of texts), the negative character who by tradition dies is the one who embodies the wrong, in this case the method of radical Aristotelians. Ulysses' philosophical drowning is thus described by Corti:

> Un complesso culturale che consentiva a Dante di fare di Ulisse un contemporaneo, imparentato sia ai coraggiosi navigatori del proprio tempo sia a quegli intellettuali del XIII secolo che avevano aspirato a divenire *sapientes mundi* ed erano finiti, con metafora risalente lontano, a sant'Agostino, in un naufragio filosofico.[87]

What the unconscious suicides of Ulysses and Ferragu have in common is that they both originate in a hubristic, unreasonable defiance of the undefiable. While the sea swallows the first, the iron of a sword penetrates the second. It is amusingly notable that during his fight with Turpin (laisses LIX–LX), Ferragu is likened to a sailing ship pushed by the force of the wind ('Nef resemble qi cort par la vertus dou vant', l. 1257), which reinforces the symbolic comparison with Ulysses.[88]

---

[87] Corti, *Scritti su Cavalcanti de Dante*, p. 268.

[88] The bottom of the sea to which Ulysses is confined presents us with a grand allegory of his defeat. Just as in the original Latin version of the voyage of St. Brendan, Ulysses travels westwards, or away from God and daylight, towards the sunset, sin, and death. What version of Brendan's voyage Dante might have read cannot be proven, but the journey's direction suggests that it was the Latin version in which Brendan travels towards the West just like Ulysses. I would like to thank Mark Davie for his suggestion that no evidence proves that any of the *volgarizzamenti* were widely diffused, as they all survive in only one manuscript apart from the Venetian version, whereas the Latin text was widely copied. Nonetheless, a saint as popular as St. Brendan cannot possibly travel towards error. In the Venetian version, the journey is in fact turned towards the East, corroborating the idea that as late as the fourteenth century the West was strongly symbolic of defeat and death; the story is thereby rendered intelligible to an audience relying entirely on that fixed allegorical system, and the saint preserved from his literary death. However, while St. Brendan not only finds his *terra repromissionis* but in the Venetian version has his journey redirected, Ulysses sinks at the beginning of his last journey: he pursues the wrong quest and does not deserve to survive. Most importantly, just

The treatment of the Saracen in this fourteenth-century masterpiece detours from tradition and deploys a stereotypical figure to convey through symbols what words cannot. Ferragu's navel, the centre of his otherwise invulnerable body, may appear as a grotesque or ironic parody of Achilles' heel, while as a symbol it in fact lends itself to deeper insight. As a centre, it symbolises the origin of all things; in Ferragu's case, this is a negative centre, the origin of all errors. In Christian terms, it is the Antichrist. Theologically, it is radical Aristotelianism leading to the extreme consequences of dismissing theology as a non-philosophical discipline. To accomplish the great allegory of Ferragu, he must be pierced right in the centre by Roland's sword.

Thus, Roland's sword is a *figura* of the sword of the Spirit which is the word of God, *Verbum*, found in St. Paul, *Ephesians*, VI, 17. In this famous passage the Apostle describes the armour of God, which the Christian must put on so that he can take his stand against the devil's schemes (VI, 10). It is composed of the belt of truth, the breastplate of righteousness, the shield of faith, the helmet of salvation and the sword of the Spirit. An association between *Verbum* and the sword is also found in Matthew 10. 34,[89] where it is said that Jesus came not to bring peace but the sword. In Christian allegorical literature, the sword becomes the symbol of the spirit following the model of St. Paul. This allegorical interpretation of the knightly weapons can be found, for example, in Lull's *Libre de l'orde de cavayleria*, which became a reference textbook for European nobility.[90] The sword that kills Ferragu is also a *figura* of the symbolic double-edged sword of the Apocalypse (1. 16; 19. 15), representing the *Verbum*'s double power, that creates and destroys.

---

as in the *Navigatio sancti Brendani*, the sea is the place of doubt and error, the ideal setting for a quest. St. Brendan travels the seas for years in search of the *terra repromissionis*, that is wisdom. It is a symbol of the door to the Otherworld, or wisdom. The idea that the sea of wisdom would swallow Ulysses conveys a very powerful image of failure. A treatment of the symbol of the sea is found, for example, in Guénon, *Simboli della scienza sacra* (pp. 297–99).

[89] See Guénon, *Simboli della scienza sacra*, p. 165.
[90] Cardini, 'Il guerriero e il cavaliere', p. 101. Lull's text has already been shown to have influenced the *Entrée*, see p. 113.

These two aspects of the sword are apparently contradictory but in fact they complement each other[91] since from the destruction of evil and wrong a new order can emerge. The sword that penetrates Ferragu's centre acquires a positive value when compared to the sword that cut his umbilical cord at birth ('En totes part ert plus fort qu'esmeri | fors en cel leu o il fust celui di | trenciez de *fers*', ll. 4012–14): while one sword contributed to the making of his magic/devilish nature, Roland's sword destroys it.

The death of Ferragu by means of Roland's symbolic sword can also be seen as a form of *contrappasso* (like Ulysses' sinking), since given his role in the dispute the giant could easily belong in the eighth of the *Malebolge*, together with the fraudulent counsellors. This reading of the figure of Ferragu would add to Limentani's hypothesis that the Paduan knew the *Commedia* (perhaps only the *Inferno*), and may contribute to the discussion on the early circulation of Dante's poem. It may not be at all excluded that the giant's defeat can be interpreted in the light of Dante's *contrappasso* in *Inferno* XXVI.

Roland in Syria

After Roland's violent altercation with Charlemagne, he embarks disguised as a Saracen merchant on a ship headed for the Holy Land. There he comes into contact with the Saracens among whom he lives for a long period. To fulfil his obligations to the Persian king, he travels in search of men to enlarge the army and thus experiences the East. Although the description of the lands Roland visits is brief, this section confirms that the poet certainly did not know the East through personal experience and that he had a quite fictitious idea of it, probably acquired through reading a variety of indirect sources. What were these sources and how does the author treat them?

Roland's journey to the East has antecedents in the French tradition in *Huon de Bordeaux* and in *Renaut de Montauban*. However, the *Entrée*'s treatment of this episode is entirely original and cannot be reduced to a re-reading of these two poems. Neither

---

[91] Guénon, *Simboli della scienza sacra*, p. 167.

can it be reduced to the knowledge of Marco Polo's *Milione*, the circulation of which is still much debated. I will proceed first by examining the episode and then by identifying possible sources.

The ship-owner, Baudor, is a Muslim variously identified as an Egyptian or Albanian. He is grateful to Roland for helping him against some bandits. As a gift, he gives him a green velvet robe lined with grey fur in the fashion of the pagans, as the author says (ll. 11777–79):

> Neporchant li aporte Baudor, le viel floris,
> Une robe d'un vert velus, fouree de gris,
> A la gisse entaillie des Païns de Tortis.

The word *Tortis* seems obscure but might well be a corruption of Torquis, the Turks. Thus the disguise of Roland as a Turk starts almost accidentally, soon to become a temporary shift of identity which proves highly convenient during his attempt to explore the East. While he still regrets the friction that has caused him to leave Charles (Roland looks so sad and worried that Baudor mistakes his mood for sea-sickness and tries to comfort him, ll. 11800–12), he seems almost passively to accept the direction his life has taken, not having the strength to decide for himself. This is the spirit in which he first approaches Syria. The author makes Roland's first change of costume seem like a detail, whereas the reader will shortly come to know that it is exactly his non-foreign appearance that will make his fortune at the court of the Sultan.

They enter Syria across the Jordan River, which ends in a lake. On the shores of that lake, towards the south, a marvellous city can be seen from afar. In a fairy-tale atmosphere there appears the city of Mecca where the Muslims worship their God (*Dex*) who is Machon, the Sultan of Persia being his defender. It is peculiar that the poet should still confuse Mohammed with a god, after the articulated theological dispute which is placed much earlier in the text. Roland asks Baudor the name of the city (ll. 11854–56):

> 'Ce est La Mech, o allons Dex orer,
> Le saint Mahon que nos vient predicer;
> Soudans de Perse en est le justisier'.

Epic poets very often allude to Mecca; they know it is the sacred city of Islam. In the *Entrée*, it is said that Muslims worship their god, Machon, in Mecca (also in 'Soz la cité, la o la giant Paiaine | orent Mahon', ll. 12789–90). The poet shows himself to be aware that Mecca is the goal of many pilgrims. While approaching the holy city of Islam, Roland sees the valley in front of it covered with pilgrims' tents, so many that it looks like a siege: 'S'en vient as tendes dont la plaigne est remplie, | Qe il sembla que fust une ost bandie' (ll. 11916–17). Mecca's geographical position is rather vague, as are most geographical references in medieval literature. In this sense, the *Entrée* is no exception. Having reached Persia without leaving the boat he embarked upon from Spain, Roland asks the merchant to let him land at *Port Vellant* (ll. 11865, 11913). According to the *Entrée* author, Mecca is a city set in a valley on the seashore: '[...] Mech, en la praierie | Lez la marine, par sillong la rivière' (ll. 12677–78). It borders a lake on the plain of Persia (ll. 11855, 11914), although from there it is possible to access deserts (l. 13859). This geographical description suggests the reading of sources of a fictitious kind and certainly the author had a rather vague idea of how the place looked in reality.

Roland's heart starts beating fast when he hears where he has arrived (ll. 11861–63). He suddenly feels the urge to leave the disappointed Baudor and meet the Sultan. In doing so, for the first time he tells Baudor his name and accomplishes his first gesture of genuine chivalry in the East. From this point onwards, Roland becomes an example of chivalry; Baudor had proposed sharing the goods on the ship in exchange for Roland's help, but Roland tells the pagan to give them all to a poor knight (ll. 11876–85):

> Dist Roland: 'Sire, avoir ne m'a mester:
> tot soie votre, senz autre parchoner.
> Mes bien vos voil par mon amor rover,
> Chant vos serés la o deveis aler
> E vos trouveis nuls poubre cevaler,
> Par mon amor l'en doveç visiter.
> Par moi le di, que sui uns estranger:
> Ensi poroit d'un autre home incontrer.
> Se de mon nom voulisez domainder,
> C'est Bacharuf: ensi moi faiz nomer'.

Roland points out that he is a foreigner (l. 11882) and he makes himself known as Bacharuf. These two elements contribute to the dissemination of hints that he is not a Muslim but rather a Christian in disguise. Baudor, though, does not take any notice and salutes his friend sadly, wishing him good luck.

Roland sets off on a horse with his Durindal and helmet. Presumably these two elements should be enough to make him recognisable to a keen observer as a Christian. However, Baudor pays no attention and just prays to Mohammed to protect him (l. 11908). Nonetheless, a character identified as a spy (*une spie*, l. 11922) recognises him as a Frenchman or Lombard ('François me sanble ou de vers Lombardie', l. 11923). Welcomed by the members of the court, Roland lies when a damsel asks him where he is from (ll. 11935–37):

> Il dist: 'De Ispagne, d'une tere asalie
> Por Carlemaine, qe ensi la mestrie
> Qe roi Marsile a grant mester d'aïe'.

He pretends to be from Spain and to have come to Syria as an ambassador of Marsile, who needs help against Charlemagne. The damsel, daughter of the king of *Orquenie* (l. 11931), takes him to the Sultan's tent where Roland is immediately introduced to the troubles of the court: the king of Persia wants to marry his fifteen-year old daughter to the horrible but powerful king Malquidant, and the barons in his court display sympathy for the poor young girl who is too beautiful to be sacrificed for political reasons. Malquidant, whose very name (meaning misbeliever or heretic) conveys a distinctive negative trait, has many supporters and the help of the *Viel de la Montagne* (l. 11976) – historically a sheikh of the principate of Antioch, but perhaps just a figure borrowed from popular literature. It is clear from the beginning of Roland's adventure in the East that names of people and places are unreal, and convey a feeling of fairy tale and distance from reality. The author remains in the realm of fantasy, providing a picture of the East very much his own invention. Malquidant is the real misbeliever among the Saracens, replacing Ferragu in the second part of the poem. As for all the other pagans, including the Sultan of Persia, the general impression is that of a non-hostile environment characterised by the kindness of its inhabitants. Roland does not feel estranged but on the contrary throws himself into the matters of the court as he would in the courts of any Arthurian romance.

Roland witnesses a dispute between Malquidant and the king of Persia in which the former threatens the king, demanding his daughter if he does not want to exacerbate the conflict between them. What follows are harsh exchanges between both parties, from which it is clear that the Sultan is in great peril. Roland feels immediate sympathy for the king and his participation in the affair comes naturally, as a knight would offer to help a king in danger. The portrait of Roland as the *chevalier parfait* starts to take a distinct shape from this very first scene. Pélias, Malquidant's nephew, speaks after the king and aims to demonstrate in his speech the bad nature of all women, providing examples from the Bible: Adam was expelled from paradise because of Eve, while Lot and Samson let themselves be fooled by a woman, and David and Solomon depended on women. If Dionés will not do what her father commands and marry Malquidant, she should be burnt alive for she is the cause of a conflict and, as Seneca says, anyone who causes murder must be murdered ('Qi comuet omicide, mort soit, dit Seneca', l. 12039). Pélias is thus introduced to the reader as an evil, fierce and merciless character. As a typical Saracen he is scarcely credible for his whole speech is shaped according to Western rhetoric, employing examples from the Bible and the classics.[92]

Amidst all this turmoil Roland explains to the king that he has just arrived from Spain, carrying news about Maisile who needs help. Roland tells the story of Charlemagne's campaign from the point of view of the Saracens of Noble, who had been invaded by the Franks. He talks about the death of Ferragu and about Roland whom he reports to be the great champion of Charlemagne's army. Roland then says of himself that he escaped Noble; he had no armour and killed a French soldier whom he found asleep and then set off on an Egyptian's boat. The Sultan asks him his name, and for no reason Roland changes his false identity from Bacharuf to Lionés, a name that to him seems more appropriate for introducing himself

---

[92] Laisse DXIX. Other examples from the Bible are Adam and Eve, Lot, Samson, and David.

to the splendid court.[93] When requested to provide his lineage he defines himself as a knight, the son of a merchant and indeed the richest in Spain. His wealth has now turned to poverty, as he laments in lines 12145–48, but nonetheless his poverty led him towards the Sultan. With this well-orchestrated example of *captatio benevolentiae* Roland succeeds in gaining the attention of the Sultan who invites him to stay. He recommends him to his son Samson while the damsels all fall for him. The author's intention is that Roland can interact in a peaceful manner with the Persian court so that he can teach the Saracens how to be civilised and abide by the rules of chivalry. The latter were already in fashion in the newly established courts of northern Italy; it is therefore likely that the author wanted to use this opportunity to introduce chivalry's importance to a genuinely civilised society. However, the *rôle civilisateur* that Bancourt bestows on Roland in the *Entrée* can only be regarded as acceptable if one looks exclusively at the episodes where he teaches the art of chivalry to the Saracens, as there is no other justifying evidence.

On behalf of the Sultan, he undertakes a journey around Syria to find out how many men the Sultan can count on in his war against Malquidant. Despite the variety of sources upon which the poet could have drawn to describe the East, this journey through Muslim territory proves rather disappointing. In fact, apart from mentioning a few fictitious places derived mostly from common knowledge (Momir, ll. 13785–839; Carsidony, ll. 13843–47; Gog and Magog, ll. 13848–51; the city of Sidogne, ll. 13860–67, where the inhabitants are so lascivious that they offer guests their women) the poet does not employ more than a few laisses to paint a rather uninteresting East. What is instead interesting is that only two references are made to Islam as a false religion, and Roland stays mostly focused on his goal, to find a large number of valiant men to win the war against Malquidant. The first reference concerns Roland's visit to the temple of Mohammed (ll. 13633–43) where he prays to his Christian God. The other is when Roland and Samson

---

[93] Perhaps because the name Lionés recalls Arthurian romances (Lionel the knight, the realm of Lyonesse).

return to Mecca, which the poet reports as *la cité dou faus pradizeor* (l. 13894).[94]

Although Roland is apparently not there to convert anyone and there is no trace of arrogance in his behaviour, he shines even amongst the best Muslim warriors, and his virtue is so greatly appreciated that he gathers a few proselytes who will then convert to Christianity in order to follow his example. The lacuna does not allow us to understand how the conversion happens.[95] What we know is that at the end of his sojourn at the court of Syria, not only has he converted a few people merely through his camaraderie, but he has also gathered three companions for his return to France who are willing to help Charlemagne win the battle against the Muslims.

The peaceful manner whereby Roland advertises true Christian/chivalric behaviour reminds us of the equivalence between the concepts of chivalry and Christianity in the *Queste*. Corroborating this idea, the final scene before the lacuna contains two occurrences of the word *graaus/grahaus* (ll. 13971, 13991), which could be seen as mere coincidence and is not at all intended to mean Graal, but leads the reader in just one direction: the romances of the Round Table.

The correspondence between chivalry and Christianity establishes yet another point of contact between Roland and thirteenth-century Franciscan missionaries. Roland's peaceful approach recalls the message of Raymond Lull and his Franciscan antecedents who attempted to bring the two worlds together in peace under the word of the one God. Roland's almost Franciscan attitude can be compared to that of St. Francis himself who met the Sultan al-Kâmil during his journey to Egypt in 1219. The Sultan treated Francis kindly and tried to win him over with gifts, as the Persian king tries to win over Roland with the promise of land and Dionés' hand. However, both Francis and Roland refuse. The

---

[94] This is in accordance with the popular legend of Mohammed as a Cardinal of the Roman Curia, discussed above (pp. 172-73).

[95] Some information on Roland at the court of Syria is given in R. Specht, 'Cavalleria francese alla corte di Persia. L'episodio dell'*Entrée d'Espagne* ritrovato nel frammento reggiano', *AIV*, 135 (1976–77), 486–506.

Sultan is filled with admiration for Francis, just as the Persian king is for Roland.[96]

All that Roland wants to achieve in the East is that the Saracens learn the art of chivalry through his own preaching and by witnessing his own heroic behaviour, in similar fashion to the Franciscans who were seeking to preach the word of God and convert the Saracens to Christianity by example and not violence.[97]

---

[96] See Thomas of Celano, *Vita prima*, in *Analecta Franciscana 10* (Florence: Quaracchi, 1926–41), pp. 1–117; transl. by P. Hermann, *St. Francis of Assisi* (Chicago: Franciscan Herald Press, 1963). Bonaventura da Bagnoregio also reported the episode of al-Kâmil, expanding the story of Thomas of Celano: see *Legenda maior s. Francisci Assisiensis*, transl. by R. Paciocco, in *Opere di San Bonaventura*, Vol. XIV/1, *Opuscoli Francescani* (Rome: Città Nuova, 1993), pp. 193–407.

[97] William of Rubruck was a Franciscan missionary in the East. His *Itinerarium* documents his mission to Karakorum in 1253–55. See C. Dawson, *Mission to Asia* (New York: Harper & Row, 1965), pp. 89–220. There he describes his purpose of converting the Mongols by engaging in debate with them. He recounts how he was granted the unique opportunity to participate in a religious debate with Nestorians, Muslims and Buddhists before the Möngke Khan himself. Bartholomew of Cremona travelled to Karakorum with William. They are probably the most interesting of all Franciscan travellers. William's approach to the mission is analysed in Tolan, *Saracens*, pp. 221 ff.

5. HISTORICAL CONTEXT AND TEXTUAL MATTERS

Current hypotheses

The *Entrée* presents several problems that are still unresolved, the most challenging of which is the work's attribution to a single author and its affiliation with one specific environment. Since the author conceals his identity, all we know about him has been deduced from eight lines, part of one of the two laisses forming the prologue of the poem's second section (ll. 10972–79):

> [...] Oiez hom soveran!
> Je qe sui mis a dir del neveu Carlaman
> Mon nom vos non dirai, mai sui Patavian
> De la citez qe fist Antenor le Trojan
> En la joiose Marche del cortois Trivixan,
> Pres la mer a .X. lieues, o il est plus proçan.
> En croniqe lettree, qe escrist da sa man
> L'arcivesque Trepins, atrovai en Millan.

A substantial amount of information can be drawn from this passage. First, we understand that it is the author's choice to remain anonymous ('I shall not tell you my name', l. 10974), that he is from Padua, and that in Milan he found the Turpin prose chronicle which, as he says further down, he used as his source for the events narrated in the *Entrée*. He quotes the chronicle, following a habit of all *chansons de geste* poets of the Charlemagne cycle and in this way claiming for his poem the lustre traditionally reserved to the French tradition.

On the question of the poet's location while writing the *Entrée*, the fact that he mentions Padua as his native city led scholarship to assume that he spent his life entirely within the general vicinity of his birthplace. For example, Limentani located the poem's writing within the courts of the Gonzaga or perhaps even the Carraresi. He hinted at the possibility that the author may have been living far from Veneto. However, he maintained that the literary inspiration permeating the *Entrée* reflects the pre-humanistic atmosphere predominant in the Gonzaga and Carraresi courts, suggesting that the author's personality combined the type of the pre-humanist learned poet with various other cultural interests.[1] Yet while the literary inspiration of the author to which Limentani refers is reminiscent of his education in Padua, it is not necessarily a sign of his location when writing his masterpiece.

Inspired by Limentani's hypothesis that the author was located at the Carraresi court in Padua, Mandach attempted to attribute the poem to an existing author whom he identified as the Paduan judge Giovanni da Nono,[2] the compiler of a Latin topographical description of Padua.[3] This attribution is based on an analysis of the cultural background emerging from the poem which suggests that the poet was perhaps a judge or notary,[4] and also on the shared citizenship (Paduan) of the author and the judge. Giovanni da Nono never left Padua, however, whereas the *Entrée*'s anonymous author may have possibly moved away to work in a capacity at the service of a *signore*. This, I think, is sufficient to re-open the question of attribution. The author's location in the period of composition thus becomes a central point when deciding where to look for another eligible name.

Basing himself on the allusion to Milan, Dionisotti maintained that the *Entrée* is an original work of art composed by an anonymous Paduan author in Milan at the court of the Visconti.[5]

---

[1] Limentani, *L'Entrée d'Espagne e i signori d'Italia*, p. 313.
[2] A. de Mandach, 'Sur les traces de la cheville ouvrière'.
[3] *Visio Egidii regis Patavie*, ed. by G. Fabris, 'La cronaca di Giovanni da Nono', *Bollettino del Museo civico di Padova* 8 (1932), 1–33; 9 (1933), 167–200.
[4] An interesting suggestion about the identity and cultural background of the author was put forward by Zarker-Morgan, 'The Narrator in Italian Epic', who stated that 'the Narrator steps in and explains, as to a child, what is going on [...] This might support Francesco Torraca's suggestion that the *Entrée* author is a schoolteacher' (p. 486 and n. 12); See F. Torraca, '*L'Entrée d'Espagne*', in *Studi di storia letteraria* (Florence: Sansoni, 1917), pp. 164–241 (p. 177).
[5] Dionisotti, '*Entrée d'Espagne, Spagna, Rotta di Roncisvalle*', p. 213.

Dionisotti's intuition has been favourably received by Lorenzo Renzi who spoke of the *Entrée* as 'un'opera originale composta probabilmente alla corte dei Visconti',[6] and by Corrado Bologna who wrote that

> la lingua dell'*Entrée*, così come la sua esattezza metrica [...] nonché la straordinaria profondità del suo spessore culturale, parlano a favore d'una origine colta del testo, la cui origine è con tutta probabilità legata a committenza signorile. Il poema, pur essendo conservato solo nella biblioteca gonzaghesca, secondo una suggestiva e bella congettura di Dionisotti, non a Mantova andrebbe ricondotto, né a Padova, bensì alla Milano dei Visconti.[7]

By contrast, Limentani did not see any connection with the Milanese court: 'la correlazione del poema con l'ambiente visconteo è ipotesi (dubbia) che spetta al Dionisotti'.[8] Nonetheless, as Bologna points out, Limentani himself suggested the possibility that the anonymous author lived and worked at the Gonzaga's court: 'e "per l'appunto sono ben compresi ancora nell'orbita viscontea i Gonzaga del primo e medio Trecento"'.[9] Paradoxically, Limentani's idea of a connection with Mantua would be reinforced if it referred to an earlier situation, thus accepting Roncaglia's earlier date of 1320s for the poem, because the Bonacolsi were in fact active supporters of the Visconti.[10]

However, Limentani's cautious approach has eventually prevailed over Dionisotti's. Bradley-Cromey also preferred the generic

---

[6] Renzi, 'Il francese come lingua letteraria', p. 570, and n. 35. See also Dionisotti, '*Entrée d'Espagne, Spagna, Rotta di Roncisvalle*', p. 213.

[7] Bologna, 'La letteratura dell'Italia settentrionale nel Trecento', pp. 511–600 (p. 539); Dionisotti, '*Entrée d'Espagne, Spagna, Rotta di Roncisvalle*', p. 213.

[8] Limentani, *L'Entrée d'Espagne e i signori d'Italia*, p. 81.

[9] Bologna, 'La letteratura dell'Italia settentrionale nel Trecento', p. 539, quoting Dionisotti, '*Entrée d'Espagne, Spagna, Rotta di Roncisvalle*', p. 213.

[10] For the literary and social history of Mantua in the 1320s see Bologna, 'La letteratura dell'Italia settentrionale nel Trecento', p. 521, and C. Vivanti, 'La storia politica e sociale. Dall'avvento delle signorie all'Italia spagnola', in *Storia d'Italia*, ed. by R. Romano and C. Vivanti, 6 vols (Turin: Einaudi, 1974), II: 275–427.

suggestion that the reference to a sovereign (*hom soveran*, l. 10972) recalls a lord possibly in the region of Lombardy.[11] Thus Dionisotti's intuition was neither refuted nor corroborated by further analysis. However, I believe that it is possible to return to Dionisotti's proposal that the poet was resident at the Visconti court, and while accepting Roncaglia's hypothetical date in the 1320s rather than Dionisotti's in the 1340s, this idea can be supported with more data drawn from the text.

One piece of interesting information is the repeated mention of Alexander's lieutenant Eumenidus. The points of contact between the *Entrée* and the *Roman d'Alexandre* have already been extensively investigated.[12] Broadly speaking, the presence of elements in the *Entrée* from the *Alexandre* tradition testify to the *Alexandre*'s wide circulation in the area of Veneto. Specifically, Eumenidus features five times in the *Entrée* in different contexts and with various versions of his name, at least two occurrences of which (*Euminiadus*, l. 5195 and *Eumenidu*, l. 5425) suggest closeness to the *Alexandre* of the Museo Correr.[13] The Greek noble fighter is addressed with the epithet of duke of Achaia in l. 14925 towards the end of the poem. Commenting on the prowess of the hermit who killed many Saracens in the woods to defend his hermitage, Roland says: 'Or cro gie bien d'Ector e dou bon duch d'Archaje: Jamais non mescrerai nul antis vasalaje'. This is just one of the myriad historical and mythical references in the *Entrée* which contribute to a general impression of the author's highly learned background. Here, Hector and Eumenidus are mentioned together to complete the portrayal of the hermit-soldier who prophesies the death of Roland on his way

---

[11] Bradley-Cromey, *Authority and Autonomy*, p. 13; Limentani, *L'Entrée d'Espagne e i signori d'Italia*, p. 173.

[12] Limentani, *L'Entrée d'Espagne e i signori d'Italia*, especially pp. 183–84; M. Infurna, '*Roman d'Alexandre* e *Entrée d'Espagne*', in *La cultura dell'Italia padana e la presenza francese nei secoli XIII–XV* (Alessandria: Edizioni dell'Orso, 2001), pp. 185–99; A. Marchesan, *Treviso medievale* (Treviso: Tipografia funzionari comunali, 1923), pp. 287–93.

[13] Benedetti, *Codice, allocuzione e volti di un mito*, in *Le Roman d'Alexandre*, ed. Benedetti, pp. 29–53. The other versions of the name are *Heumenedu* (l. 8366) and *Heumenidum* (l. 8536); finally, the author calls him *Emenadus* (l. 10076).

back to Charlemagne's campaign in Spain. Once again, the text seems to hide an allusion to the political circumstances of early fourteenth-century Milan. Philip of Savoy, the real duke of Achaia and a key figure in the series of disgraceful events that created much difficulty for Matteo Visconti and his family around 1320, could be the intended recipient of the author's flattery. In fact, the treaty of Lambriasco (1318) guaranteed mutual support between Matteo Visconti and Philip of Savoy-Achaia against Robert of Anjou, who was expanding his power in Piedmont at the time. Philip enjoyed a good reputation in the Visconti's household for acting in their mutual interest. Thus, recalling the fourteenth-century habit of creating genealogies for outstanding families (a habit lasting well into the Renaissance and part of the process of legitimising the power of the early Po Valley *signori*), Philip features in the *Entrée* in the guise of Alexander's heroic lieutenant. The Visconti were reasonably satisfied with their treaty with the Savoy, at least until 1320 when the duke of Achaia breached it by allowing Philip of Valois (coming from France supported by Pope John XXII)[14] to pass through his territory to reach Lombardy.[15] From then on a number of actions were taken against the Visconti by both the Pope and the Valois, including a heresy trial begun in 1321 and based on a number of false testimonies, which were then disclaimed.[16] If the poet was writing the final verses of his poem while in the service of the Visconti and before 1320, he would have had good reasons to look for an opportunity to mention the good (*bon*) duke of Achaia, *socius et amicus* of the lords of Milan. However, the duke of Achaia could no longer be regarded as 'good' after 1320, since he was responsible for creating much trouble for the Visconti by letting the Valois traverse his territory. If so, this mention could help to

---

[14] F. Cognasso, 'L'Unificazione della Lombardia sotto Milano', in *Storia di Milano*, 16 vols (Milan: Treccani, 1955), V: pp. 122–25.

[15] F. Cognasso, 'L'Unificazione della Lombardia', pp. 132–33. Philip of Savoy-Achaia's indecisiveness and instability led him to continuously breach and reform his alliances. See P. Brezzi, 'Barbari, feudatari, comuni e signorie', in D. Gribaudi, ed., *Storia del Piemonte*, 2 vols (Turin: Casanova, 1966), I: 144–49.

[16] F. Cognasso, 'L'Unificazione', pp. 142–54.

strengthen the affiliation of the poem with Matteo Visconti's entourage and date it to around 1320 as Roncaglia suggested.

Bologna observed that 'né l'Anonimo Padovano, né Nicolò da Verona che ne continuò l'opera, sarebbero stati in grado di lavorare senza avere alle spalle un lungo, approfondito magistero assorbito alle fonti della cultura cortigiana',[17] which emerges clearly from the poem's style and content. Among the courts of Northern Italy in the early Trecento, the cultural milieu of the Visconti in the 1320s looks like the ideal environment to have hosted the *Entrée*'s anonymous author.[18] Although it was Azzone in the 1330s who started a revival of the Aristotelian theory of magnificence so as to cultivate a new image of himself and his state,[19] this was in some continuity with what Castruccio Castracane had done in Lucca during the previous decade – and especially with what had been started by Matteo Visconti, who first invited eminent philosophers and scholars to Milan to form an exceptionally versatile intellectual environment;[20] 'What Azzone did was to develop an earlier tendency, taking it to a new stage'.[21]

Dionisotti's intuition that the *Entrée* was created at the court of the Visconti can be supported by some considerations concerning the area of the *Entrée*'s circulation, one subjected to the strong political and cultural influence of Milan. The only extant manuscript of the *Entrée* at the Biblioteca Nazionale Marciana originally belonged to the Gonzaga collection, while at its early stage it can be located on the Milan-Bologna axis; the earliest part of its illumination follows the iconographic model created in Bologna, the rest of the decoration is close to the 'maniera lombarda' except for

---

[17] Bologna, 'La letteratura dell'Italia settentrionale nel Trecento', p. 539.

[18] This environment is described, for example, in Viscardi, 'La cultura milanese nel secolo XIV', in *Storia di Milano*, V: 569–634.

[19] L. Green, 'Galvano Fiamma, Azzone Visconti and the Revival of the Classical Theory of Magnificence', *Journal of the Warburg and Courtauld Institutes*, 53 (1990), 98–113 (p. 109).

[20] Galvano Fiamma, Marsilius of Padua, Niccolò da Casola, Brunetto Latini, and Petrarch all found themselves sharing the same hospitality at different times. Brunetto Latini's *Tresor* is dedicated to Galeazzo Visconti and written in an Italian variety of French, thus representing a similar case to the *Entrée*.

[21] Green, 'Galvano Fiamma', p. 109.

one hand comparable to the style used in Veneto in the 1350s.[22] Bologna fell under the dominion of the Visconti in the early Trecento[23] which guarantees some degree of cultural interference from the dominant city. The presence of the *Entrée* on this axis is also documented by one fragment from Reggio Emilia.[24] Under these premises it can be said that the *Entrée* belongs to an area 'lontano dunque dalla Milano viscontea cui pensava Dionisotti, però sull'asse che lega la capitale lombarda a Bologna'.[25] The idea that the *Entrée* circulated in a geographical zone connected with Milan is also strengthened by the finding of another fragment belonging to the Hector Passerin d'Entrèves ex Challant collection, from Châtillon,[26] Piedmont, which relied very much on Visconti support.[27]

---

[22] The model generated in Bologna is the dominant style in Emilia Romagna at the beginning of the fourteenth century. This part of the miniatures includes ff. 1r–29v and the two great miniatures on ff. 160v and 161r. See P. Toesca, 'Le miniature dell'*Entrée d'Espagne* della Biblioteca Marciana', in *Scritti di varia erudizione e di critica in onore di Rodolfo Renier* (Turin: Bocca, 1912), pp. 747–53; P. Toesca, *La pittura e la miniatura nella Lombardia, Dai più antichi monumenti alla metà del Quattrocento* (Milan: Hoepli, 1912).

[23] Luchino Visconti (1292–1349) and his brother Giovanni (1290–1354) took control of Bologna. For the Visconti dominion of Bologna see Bologna, 'La letteratura dell'Italia settentrionale nel Trecento', p. 520; G. Chittolini, 'Infeudazioni e politica feudale nel ducato visconteo-sforzesco', *Quaderni storici*, 7 (1972), 57–130; Tabacco, *Egemonie sociali*.

[24] Reggio Emilia: Biblioteca Municipale 'A. Panizzi', MSS vari E. 181. A. Monteverdi, 'Un fragment manuscrit de l'*Entrée d'Espagne*', *Cahiers de Civilisation Médiévale*, 3 (1960), 75–78 (p. 75); Specht, 'Cavalleria francese alla corte di Persia', pp. 486–506; Specht, 'Il frammento reggiano dell'*Entrée d'Espagne*', pp. 407–24.

[25] Bologna, 'La letteratura dell'Italia settentrionale nel Trecento', p. 548.

[26] P. Aebischer, 'Ce qui reste d'un manuscrit perdu de l'*Entrée d'Espagne*', *Archivum romanicum*, 12 (1928), 233–64; Specht, 'La tradition manuscrite de l'*Entrée d'Espagne*', pp. 749–58.

[27] Piedmont is situated outside the Milan-Bologna axis; however, it was allied with the Visconti. For the relationship between Piedmont and the Visconti see Vivanti, 'La storia politica e sociale', pp. 275–427.

My suggestion is that the author was writing for Matteo Visconti between 1311 and 1322,[28] and that the text was then copied several times from a lost original generated in Milan. The Venetian manuscript is its most luxurious copy and the only one surviving almost entirely intact (except for the large lacuna in the poem's second part), probably thanks to its lavish decoration rather than the text. It may have been commissioned as a gift from the Milanese lord to a Ghibelline friend although one cannot really say anything for sure about its path to Mantua. We do not have any letters or documents testifying to its movements – such as the letter dating to 1371 which shows how Bernabò Visconti's son Ambrogio, being in Reggio to help Feltrino Gonzaga under siege by the marquis of Este, requested from his father a copy of the *Aspremont*,[29] this manuscript never being returned to its original location of Milan.[30] The story of Ambrogio and his *Aspremont* exemplifies the exchange of manuscripts as one of the most fascinating forms of traffic of the Middle Ages. However, it also suggests that it is probably more useful to sift the text for the elements of a secure theory than to insist on obsolete views based on the provenance of the Venetian manuscript and the author's mention of his birthplace.

The second prologue

The excerpt from the second prologue quoted above proves very useful for its content but also its exact position in the text. It opens the second part of the poem, anticipating the narrative's vivid, striking detour from a conception of epic which is fundamentally that of the French *chanson de geste*, to a hybrid idea of the genre which mixes epic and romance. The friction between Charlemagne and Roland, created by the young hero's excessively independent behaviour and by their disagreements over how to conduct the war

---

[28] Matteo died in Crescentago on 24 June 1322 having abdicated in favour of Galeazzo. Cognasso, 'L'Unificazione', p. 163.
[29] This copy of *Aspremont* is identified with Venice: Biblioteca Nazionale Marciana, MS fr. Z. 6 (=226). See Viscardi, 'La cultura milanese nel secolo XIV', p. 574.
[30] F. Novati, 'I codici francesi del Gonzaga', in *Attraverso il Medioevo* (Bari: Laterza, 1905), p. 272.

in Spain, culminates with Roland's open challenge to the emperor's authority and with the final breach of the feudal pact between king and nephew, at the end of the poem's first section. This is represented using the episode when Charlemagne slaps his nephew with a gauntlet.[31] In contrast, the second part develops the theme of Roland's voyage to the East and diverges from the *chanson de geste*'s typical narrative modes of representing power and the hero. The poet catches Roland on his own, wandering as a *chevalier errant* and eventually reaching Syria, where he experiences adventures of a Breton-romance type. The introduction to the second section provides elements that can help clarify the question of patronage and the place of composition.

Hom soveran (l. 10972).[32] The author addresses one particular sovereign. Although we do not know this lord's identity, we can assume that there was perhaps no need for the author to pronounce it because in the reader/audience's mind it was quite clear. Unfortunately this is not equally clear to us. Therefore, the real question one should ask about these two words is not who this lord might be, but to what the generic Franco-Italian formula *hom soveran* corresponds in the geo-political landscape of Northern Italy at the start of the thirteenth century. The use of *soveran* (Old French *souverain/susserain*; Lat. *superānus*: one who has supremacy, rank or authority over others) instead of *syre/seignor* suggests that the addressee is not a king, but one man (*hom*) whose position is equivalent to that of a monarch or its substitute. The only monarchical government in the Po valley in the early Trecento was that of imperial vicars.[33] This title was conferred by the German

---

[31] 'A cestui mot a levez le un guant; | Ferir en veult li quens par mié le dant, | Quant por le nés le consuet tot avant: | Le sang en raie, q'en rogist l'açerant' (ll. 11117–20). Bradley-Cromey, *Authority and Autonomy*, analyses this dynamic in depth throughout her study.

[32] Marco Infurna translated this line into Italian quite differently: 'Sentite che uomo superiore!' ('see, what a superior [i.e. better] man!', my translation), understanding *hom soveran* as referring to Roland teaching courtly manners to the Pagans. See Infurna, *L'Entrée d'Espagne*, p. 111.

[33] The case of the Duke of Venice can be excluded *a priori* as this office was in essence not at all monarchic but on the contrary characterised by typically Venetian democratic traits. Regarding imperial vicars,

emperor since the empire's political circumstances in the Trecento prevented him from intervening directly in domestic Italian affairs. The title was requested by individual lords to strengthen their power in case of political instability. The title of imperial vicar is thus an 'imperfetta condizione raggiunta dal signore nella città sul piano giuridico locale'.[34] This situation is typical of the institutional uncertainty that characterised the early *signorie* in northern Italy. Matteo Visconti, *signore* of Milan since the late thirteenth century (by which time he had established his superiority over the Della Torre), was nominated imperial vicar for the first time by king Adolph in 1294.[35] Visconti was reconfirmed in July 1311 in Brescia by Henry VII.[36] When John XXII started openly showing aversion to the political and military achievements of the three imperial vicars of the time (Visconti, with Cangrande and Bonacolsi), he renounced the title in 1317 to become *Signore Generale*, a turning point in how he conceived of his own authority over the territories subjected to Milan.[37] It is of note how vehemently the poet requests the monarch's attention when he addresses him; *Oiez* (l. 10972) in Thomas' edition is followed by an exclamation mark.

Mon nom vos non dirai (l. 10794). The cause of the poet's refusal to disclose his identity may be that he was hiding from a figure of authority in the Church, perhaps the Pope himself.[38] However, it is not the authority of the Church that is questioned in the *Entrée* but a lay form such as that of a monarch. The author's desire to conceal himself may also stem from fear of exile, as in the famous case of the

---

Tabacco, *Egemonie sociali*, p. 357, offers a useful insight: 'Si consideri come sotto l'aspetto formale il "vicario" si distinguesse nettamente da un vassallo investito di poteri pubblici in feudo, poiché il "vicariato" non esprimeva l'idea di un possesso patrimoniale e autonomo, bensì di una delegazione non trasmissibile, o – per gran parte ancora nel XIV secolo – di una delegazione trasmissibile nella famiglia soltanto col beneplacito via via manifestato in modo esplicito dall'imperatore'.

[34] Tabacco, *Egemonie sociali*, p. 358.
[35] Tabacco, *Egemonie sociali*, p. 357–95.
[36] Cognasso, 'L'Unificazione', p. 65.
[37] Cognasso, 'L'Unificazione', pp. 111–12.
[38] Bradley-Cromey, *Authority and Autonomy*, pp. 94–99.

notary Niccolò Da Casola.[39] In line 10973[40] the author reminded the addressee that he had committed himself to 'dir del neveu Carlaman', and not of Charlemagne himself. Any encomiastic purpose is even further discounted if we consider that Roland is not characterised as the representative offspring of a great lineage but as his uncle's challenger. In other words, Roland is a *baron révolté*.[41] This choice of subject suggests that the poet is applying the motif of the rupture of feudalism to the quest for autonomy by individual Italian lords. The *hom soveran* addressed by the poet is a lord whose authority he does not fully recognise, and having depicted Charlemagne as a despotic monarch he prefers to conceal his identity. In the *Entrée*, Roland's mutiny and defection from Charlemagne's army creates grief and repentance in the emperor ('"Ce poise moi", dist Karles, plorand des oil del front', l. 11377). The poet's subtle challenge sounds like a warning at a historical moment when what had happened to Charlemagne could befall any lord careless in dealing with allies. Matteo Visconti's circumstances in that period show how, while waging war against the Guelph

[39] Everson, *The Italian Romance Epic*, p. 115. Niccolò, chased from the court of the Visconti, found in the Este the ideal patrons to whom he could dedicate his *Guerra d'Attila* between 1358 and 1368. See M. Villoresi, *La letteratura cavalleresca. Dai cicli medievali all'Ariosto* (Rome: Carocci, 2002), pp. 57–61; Limentani, *L'Entrée d'Espagne e i signori d'Italia*, p. 158. His residence at the Visconti court therefore dates to about a decade later than the *Entrée*.

[40] The poem lacks a considerable number of laisses, calculated to be of about 5000 verses, which set these lines of the prologue half way through the narrative. On the lacuna see Thomas, *L'Entrée d'Espagne*, I: XVIII–XIX and n. I.

[41] This is a subset of the French *chanson de geste* found in the so-called *chansons de revolte*, namely *Renauld de Montauban*. In Italy the figure of Renaut de Montalban follows an independent tradition (Rinaldo da Montalbano). See Villoresi, *La letteratura cavalleresca*, pp. 86–89. The figure of Roland in the *Entrée* is strongly influenced by the type of the *baron révolté*. See Bradley-Cromey, *Authority and Autonomy*, pp. 47–49. Incidentally, it is noteworthy that the challenge to authority in Roland's characterisation as a *baron révolté* goes hand in hand with the author's open challenge to the genre representing authority, namely the *chanson de geste* of the cycle of Charlemagne, which the poet crosses with the genre of Breton romance.

families of Lombardy to enlarge his dominion, he was exposing himself to attack by the Pope and his allies (as in fact occurred).

Sui Patavian (l. 10974). Though withholding his identity, the poet introduces himself as a citizen of Padua and also displays a need to specify the geographical position of his birthplace. To this he dedicates three lines which state that 1) the city was founded by Antenor (l. 10975), a reference highlighting his city's noble origin and representing a point of honour for the poet; 2) it is located in the *gioiosa marca* of a courteous Trevisian (l. 10976);[42] 3) the city is ten leagues away from the sea at its closest point (some thirty or forty kilometres, Padua's current distance from the seaside, l. 10977). All this information should sound redundant to an audience at the Paduan court of the Carraresi as such a readership/audience was surely familiar with their city's topography and illustrious origin. It is hard to explain why the author should mention these facts at all unless the monarch he addresses is a foreigner. It may be useful to recall that Matteo's son Galeazzo was *Podestà* of Treviso in 1310, before becoming *Capitano del popolo* and *signore* of Milan in 1322. Could it be that, returning to Milan, Galeazzo offered a position at his court to a Paduan based in

---

[42] Behind the epithet of *cortois* it is possible to recognise Gherardo da Camino, the 'buon Gherardo' of *Purgatorio* XVI, 124, 133–35, who according to Dante was one of the last examples of chivalric nobility. Gherardo governed Treviso by popular consensus between 1283 and 1312. See B. J. Khol, *Padua under the Carrara (1318–1405)* (Baltimore: Johns Hopkins University Press, 1998), pp. 35–38. During his *signoria*, the culture of the troubadours was protected and even worshipped. See G. Folena, 'Tradizione e cultura trobadorica nelle corti e nelle città venete', in *Culture e lingue nel Veneto medievale* (Padua: Editoriale Programma, 1990), pp. 1–137 (pp. 78 ff.); M. Pastore Stocchi, 'Le fortune della letteratura cavalleresca e cortese nella Treviso medievale e una testimonianza di Lovato Lovati', in A. Mazzarolli and E. Castelnuovo, eds, *Tomaso da Modena e il suo tempo. Atti del convegno di Treviso, 28 agosto – 1 settembre 1979* (Treviso: Stamperia di Venezia, 1980), pp. 201–17; L. Lazzarini, 'La cultura delle signorie venete del Trecento e i poeti di corte', in Folena, ed., *Storia della Cultura Veneta*, II: 477–516; G. Peron, 'Cultura provenzale e francese a Treviso nel medioevo', in E. Brunetta et al., eds, *Storia di Treviso*, 3 vols (Venice: Marsilio, 1991), II: 487–544; S. Collodo, *Una società in trasformazione. Padova tra XI e XV secolo* (Padua: Antenore, 1990), p. 164.

Treviso? The exchange of intellectuals between Padua and Treviso in the early Trecento is a known fact.[43] Furthermore, the Châtillon and Panizzi fragments mentioned above show a wider circulation for the *Entrée* than the area of Padua and Treviso, and also make a strong case for the poem in fact being written in a quite different environment to Padua.

The poet may be reminding his patron that the imposition of authority can be challenged, and that this can cause unending conflicts.[44] 'It is within the chronological parameters of two tyrannies (i.e., 1256–1320), a reality in Padua and throughout the Marca Trevigiana, that the *Entrée*'s ideological orientation should be sought'.[45] While Albertino Mussato in 1315 was writing his *Eccerinis*,[46] great attention was devoted to the question of tyranny and imposed lordship.[47] In the republican and anti-tyrannical environment in which the author of the *Entrée* was educated, the dangers of tyranny were seen as possibly also arising from within the state. A 'sizeable corpus on the theory and practice of government from the mid-thirteenth to mid-fourteenth centuries expresses a strong aversion to external imposition of authority such as the Lombard League was intended to prevent'.[48] In this framework, the author of the *Entrée* takes his first steps as a young poet participating actively in the cultural and perhaps public life of the commune.

The poet's refusal to disclose his name can be read as a statement of autonomy as an intellectual, strengthened by a reference to his region of birth where the idea of authority was under debate. Nonetheless, to serve and live at the court of an overlord could be

---

[43] The literature on this is vast. A good starting point is Brunetta et al., eds, *Storia di Treviso,* particularly G. M. Varanini, 'Istituzioni società a Treviso tra comune, signoria e poteri regionali', II: 135–211.

[44] For Padua's independence in the post-Ezzelinian age see J. K. Hyde, *Padua in the Age of Dante* (Manchester: Manchester University Press, 1966).

[45] Bradley-Cromey, *Authority and Autonomy*, p. 102.

[46] 'The tragedy that traced "the infamous career of the regional tyrant Ezzelino da Romano" and stressed the "lessons to be learned from a twenty-year reign of terror"': Bradley-Cromey, *Authority and Autonomy*, p. 11; A. Mussato, *Ecerinide*, ed. by L. Padrin (Bologna: Forni, 1969).

[47] See the works of Marsilius of Padua.

[48] Bradley-Cromey, *Authority and Autonomy*, p. 102.

done without necessarily agreeing completely with his foreign policies. As Corrado Bologna has also illustrated, from the start of the fourteenth century onwards Milan was becoming the most powerful Italian court, 'in grado di coordinare con munificienza e limpidezza un'idea di civiltà, un progetto globale di cultura'.[49] Milan is the centre of a 'fittissimo va-e-vieni'[50] of men of letters and scientists who, around the mid-century, were also spurred by the opportunity of access to its rich libraries and whose passage through Milan enriched its splendid collections.[51]

En croniqe lettree (l. 10978). These arguments obliterate the thesis that the poet was based in Padua while he was composing the *Entrée*. At this point, the Patavian says that he found a prose chronicle in Milan written by Turpin's own hand. He is probably blowing his own horn but there is no real reason to mistrust him when he says that (perhaps when working in the Visconti household) he came across one of the many versions of the twelfth-century fake. On the contrary, this throws some light onto where he may physically have been and from where he took his inspiration while on the verge of starting his own poem.

---

[49] C. Bologna, 'La letteratura dell'Italia settentrionale nel Trecento', pp. 521–22.

[50] Bologna, 'La letteratura dell'Italia settentrionale', p. 522.

[51] See for example the library of the castle of Pavia, which was founded by Galeazzo II and then dismantled by Louis XII who brought the manuscripts to Paris. This is the most extraordinary collection about which we have information: G. D'Adda, *Indagini storiche, artistiche e bibliografiche sulla libreria visconteo-sforzesca del castello di Pavia compilate per cura di un bibliofilo* (Milan: Tip. Brignola, 1875); G. D'Adda, *Appendice alla parte prima* (Milan: Tip. Brignola, 1879; G. Mazzatinti, *Inventario dei codici della Biblioteca Visconteo-Sforzesca del castello di Pavia* (Milan: Brigola, 1875); L. Delisle, *Le Cabinet des manuscrits de la Bibliothèque Nationale*, 3 vols (Paris: Imprimerie impériale, 1881); A. Thomas, 'Les Manuscripts françaises et provençaux des Ducs de Milan au Château de Pavie', *Romania*, 40 (1911), 571–609; E. Pellegrin, *La Bibliothèque des Visconti et des Sforza ducs de Milan au XVe siècle* (Paris: Service des publications du C.N.R.S., 1955); Viscardi, 'La cultura milanese nel secolo XIV', pp. 571–84; M. G. Albertini Ottolenghi, 'Codici miniati francesi e di ispirazione francese nella biblioteca dei Visconti e degli Sforza nel castello di Pavia', in *La cultura dell'Italia padana*, pp. 281–94.

Ferragu's birth

In my opinion, another passage of the *Entrée* can now be considered in support of a possible identification of the patron. This excerpt belongs to the section dedicated to the episode of the duel between Roland and the Saracen giant Ferragu, and occurs at a much earlier stage in the narrative than the passage I analysed above.

Both contenders having failed to establish superiority through force, on the duel's third day they decide to rely on reason, and start a theological dispute to explain the difference between the Saracen faith and Christianity. It is Ferragu who initially proposes that he and Roland discuss theology, but Roland accepts willingly. The attempt to find a peaceful alternative to the duel proves unsuccessful in that Roland eventually accuses Ferragu of being a devil for refusing to convert. Ferragu replies to this accusation, explaining his magical birth so as to justify his devilish nature. This point in the narrative can be separated from the context of the dispute and looked at individually, isolating particularly the astrological component of the passage (ll. 4002–14):

'Non sui Diable, home m'engenuï.
Volez oïr qi moi faa ensi?
Soz un planez, Chavachabas, naqui:
Si li noment li Saracins anti.
Chavachabas est planet si basti,
Ne feit son cors en .XX. ans n'en .XXVI.;
Cil a vertu que celui o cili
Che soz lui naist quant il ombre Çeli
– Un'autre estoile c'est, el cercle Jovi –,
La car de cil qe naistra desoz li
En totes part ert plus fort qu'esmeri,
Fors en cel leu o il fust celui di
Trenciez de fers: cil leu ne l'afi...'

The Saracen points out that he is not a devil but born of human lineage, although the conditions of his birth emphasise his body's noble and magical features. Moreover, he was born under the positive influence of the planet *Chavachabas* (l. 4004). We read in line 4007 that this planet's nature is such that it does not complete its course in twenty or even twenty-six years, and from line 4008 that it has such power that the flesh of the one born when it overshadows the star *Çeli* is stronger than emerald. This is expressed more clearly a few lines later in the poem: 'Cil planez est si fer | Chi soz lui naist ni puet arme doter' (ll. 4020–21).

My purpose is to relate this astronomical information to lines 10972–79, to create a much fuller picture of the political and cultural environment in which the poem can be inscribed.[52] It is possible to read behind the name of the planet *Chavachabas* a French transcription of the name of the rebellious Cavalcabò family – and behind both passages a reference to the traditional Lombard Guelph families, struggling against the Ghibelline Visconti for their right to local rule and to escape the unifying force of the newly born *signoria*.

The Visconti were the dominant protagonists of the political scene in the years when the *Entrée* was presumably composed. Thanks to the support of Henry VII, by the 1320s the Visconti had succeeded in expanding their power over the whole of Lombardy. However, they included in their politics anti-imperial objectives.[53] In their efforts to take control over the region, they therefore stipulated favourable political agreements with the Lombard Guelph families.[54] Among the communes they aimed at including in their territory (for example Como, Lodi, Bergamo, and Piacenza),[55]

---

[52] As discussed by Monica Azzolini, genitures were often received by political leaders as gifts from court astrologers and had an important political function: '[A] leader's horoscope possessed considerable political value, and its interpretation could be regarded as a confidential matter. In cases in which the horoscope was particularly positive, however, it could be used to one's advantage, often in the form of political propaganda'. M. Azzolini, *The Duke and the Stars. Astrology and Politics in Renaissance Milan* (Cambridge, MA / London: Harvard University Press, 2013), p. 17.

[53] Bologna, 'La letteratura dell'Italia settentrionale nel Trecento', p. 520; Tabacco, *Egemonie sociali*; G. Chittolini, 'Infeudazioni e politica feudale', pp. 19, 57–130.

[54] Bologna, 'La letteratura dell'Italia settentrionale nel Trecento', speaks of an 'oculata gestione dei rapporti con le antiche signorie locali' (p. 521), and refers to Vivanti, 'La storia politica e sociale', especially p. 300. Cognasso, 'L'Unificazione', pp. 1–567 (especially pp. 65–179).

[55] Chittolini, 'Infeudazioni e politica feudale', and Bologna, 'La letteratura dell'Italia settentrionale nel Trecento', p. 520.

Cremona was a noteworthy case. Differing from other ancient Lombard Guelph families who managed to negotiate with the ambivalent Visconti, the Cavalcabò consistently tried to oppose them despite sporadic collaboration. Particularly interesting are the events of 1312 when Guglielmo Cavalcabò, lord of Cremona since 1306, defeated and expelled Galeazzo and the Ghibellines from his city. In the battle of Soncino on 16 March 1312, Guglielmo Cavalcabò opted to delay the offensive, believing in astrology and scared by a negative astral conjunction.[56] Thus, the Ghibelline forces had the time to organise and there followed a massive slaughter of Guelphs in which Guglielmo himself died. In Piacenza, however, his brother Giacomo negotiated the city's capitulation to the Guelphs. The Visconti needed to stop the ruling families of the countryside from undermining their attempts to strengthen their position in Lombardy. A document by Bernabò Visconti dating to 1316 grants the regions surrounding the Po River 'fino alla bocca dell'Oglio nel luogo di Viadana' to the family Cavalcabò, marquises of Viadana.[57] In the same year, Giacomo Cavalcabò was nominated *signore* of the city of Cremona. Albeit temporarily, the relationship between Bernabò Visconti and the Cavalcabò family was thus repaired.[58] Then came the years of the consolidation of Visconti lordship by Luchino and Galeazzo, Matteo's sons, who headed all military action decided by their father. In January 1322, Galeazzo attacked Cremona with a large army of more than 3000 troops (drawn from Milan, Pavia, Lodi and Como) while Giacomo Cavalcabò's sons had

---

[56] G. Andenna, 'Cavalcabó', in *Dizionario Biografico degli Italiani* (Rome: Treccani, 1979), XXII: 593–99 (pp. 598–99). The role of the court astrologer has been studied by Azzolini, *The Duke and the Stars*, who writes: 'Astrology's relationship with political power, especially in a courtly context, however, has yet to receive organic treatment, and the role of the court astrologer still awaits a major study', p. X.

[57] P. Ugolini, 'Sistema territoriale e urbano della valle padana', in C. de Seta, ed., *Storia d'Italia - Annali*, 11 vols (Turin: Einaudi, 1985), VIII: 159–240 (p. 231).

[58] C. Manaresi, 'Le origini della famiglia Cavalcabò', in *Miscellanea di studi lombardi in onore di Ettore Verga* (Milan: Castello Sforzesco, 1931), pp. 198–99.

only sixty knights from Bologna to support their defence. Cremona was taken and the Cavalcabò defeated.[59]

It is said in line 4005 that the planet protecting Ferragu is called *Chavachabas* by the ancient Saracens, presumably the authors of astronomical treatises circulating at the author's time in both Latin and vernacular, translated directly or indirectly from the Arabic. Limentani noted how the expression *wa-l-'arab tusammi* used by Sufi to introduce his arguments on the forty-eight Ptolemaic constellations is similar in meaning to *Saracins anti* (l. 4005).[60] These ancient Arabic treatises explain that *kawkab* is the word for planet. They also explain that planets are divided into inferior and superior (*al-kawakib al sufliyah*: Venus, Mercury and the Moon; *al-kawakib al sayyarah*: all other planets as opposed to stars).[61] The combination in Arabic phonetics of the article al- and the first consonant s- of the words *sufliyah* and *sayyarah* produces a double -ss- sound (a-ss-ufliyah; a-ss-ayyarah), so that in both cases this combination would produce an —ss— sound at the end of al-kawakab (al-kawakab-ass).[62] It is possible that the poet or his source were not able to isolate the article and instead considered it part of *kawkab*. In this way, the combination of *kawkab* and the article of the following word would produce the sound Ka-waw-kab-as. Thus, the name *Chavachabas* would be the result of a misreading from Arabic (or a bad transliteration into Latin), meaning simply 'planet'.

Line 4007 says that this planet 'ne feit son cors en XX ans n'en XXVI', a negative property that sounds irrelevant and unintelligible to the modern reader. However, it may possess more significance for the meaning of the whole passage than seems the case at first sight. The most viable way to explain numbers appearing in unusual contexts is to rely on the Qabala which identifies Kawkab as

---

[59] Cognasso, 'L'Unificazione', p. 157.
[60] Limentani, *L'Entrée d'Espagne e i signori d'Italia*, pp. 300–301 and nn. 11–12.
[61] R. Rashed, ed., *Encyclopedia of the History of Arabic Science*, 3 vols (London: Routledge, 1996), I: 1.
[62] See D. Cowan, *Modern Literary Arabic* (Cambridge: Cambridge University Press, 1958; repr. 2000), pp. 9–10.

Mercury.[63] Breaking the name into kay-waw-kaf (-bayt), its meaning can be interpreted as action towards action (leading into consciousness).[64] Action as force/energy in isolation corresponds to the first letter of *Kawkab* (Kaf), and direction towards another action corresponds to the second part of the word (waw-kaf). Translated into numbers according to the Qabala, the result is 20+6+20 (+2).[65] Interpreted according to the meaning of numbers of the Qabala one obtains in this way the two numbers 20 and 26, which mean two different concepts: 20 means energy, and 26 energy put into action (akin to the Aristotelian concepts of potentiality and actuality, the former being static, the latter dynamic). This explains line 4007 where Mercury/*Chavachabas* appears constituted so as to accomplish its course neither in a static or dynamic mode, meaning neither potentially nor actually; in other words, it needs an exterior impulse to succeed (again recalling the Aristotelian idea of the Prime Mover). Furthermore, the association between the colour green and the planet Mercury is found in many treatises on alchemy and astrology, and in lapidaries where green minerals, stones and plants are subjected to the influence of this planet, the principal stone under this influence being the emerald.[66] This leaves very little doubt over which planet the name *Chavachabas* refers to, according to the medieval astronomical and astrological tradition.

In astrology the ruling planet of a sign, house or chart is called the Lord.[67] The idea of a planet ruling one's life is repeated in the

---

[63] C. Suarès, *The Sepher Yetsira. Including the Original Astrology according to the Cabala and its Zodiac* (Boulder: Shambhala Publications, 1976), pp. 131 and 159.

[64] Suarès, *The Sepher Yetsira*, p. 133.

[65] Suarès, *The Sepher Yetsira*, p. 170. See also C. Suarès, *The Cipher of Genesis. The Original Code of the Qabala as Applied to the Scriptures* (London: Stuart & Watkins, 1970), pp. 47–53; G. Scholem, *Alchimia e Kabbalah* (Turin: Einaudi, 1995); G. Scholem, *Zohar. The Book of Splendour* (New York: Schoken Books, 1995).

[66] The association between emerald and Mercury is discussed at great length in Albertus Magnus' *Lapidarium* (c. 1280), where he associated properties of stones with astrological phenomena. However, this can be considered common knowledge in the Middle Ages and has no single authoritative source.

[67] S. J. Tester, *A History of Western Astrology* (Woodbridge: Boydell & Brewer, 1987), p. 120.

Entrée: 'Soz fier planez en fer punt sui parti | Trop ai trové felons cist enemi' (l. 1935). The planet ruling Ferragu's sign is Mercury or, in other words, Ferragu's lord is *Chavachabas*, which is equivalent to saying that Ferragu is at the service of the Cavalcabò. If the giant is the enemy, he must also be at the service of the enemy.

Çeli (l. 4009) could be easily related to the Latin word *caeli*. However, line 4010 says that this is a star (a satellite) belonging to the orbit of Jupiter. This name could be read in the light of other similar words from the lexicon of astronomy or astrology. The first that comes to mind is the Zenith (from Old French and medieval Latin *cenit*, derived from the Arabic *samt*). If *Çeli* does refers to the zenith, but which the author mistook for a planet, then the sentence would mean 'that planet has such virtue that anyone born when it reaches the zenith has flesh stronger than emerald, save for that part where, on the day of his birth, he was cut with an iron blade'. Unfortunately, the zenith is not a planet but the part of the celestial sphere above the observer, and neither overshadows nor is overshadowed by anything. It is very unlikely that the author could be ignorant of this as the information provided in this passage proves that his sources are not fictitious, nor is he inserting astrological data merely to reinforce the exoticism of Ferragu, already sufficiently exotic being a giant Saracen and invulnerable apart from his navel. However, Saturn in Arabic is variously called Zuhal/Zuhil/Zahil. While difficult to prove, depending on the poet's source it might have been known as Zahil, in which case an old French transcription as *Çeli* is possible: Z > Ç + a > e + hil > li (inter-vocalic -h- disappears; -i- is palatalised before -l-; ending -i- is a supporting vowel). One must also bear in mind that Zahil is itself a transcription into the Latin alphabet and in actuality written Arabic does not use vowels (which explains the three versions of the name depending on regional pronunciations); thus the word would originally be written as ZHL with a strong pharyngeal 'h', and vowels would appear as easily confusable signs under or above the consonants. The two strong consonants Z and L also dominate the French word.[68]

---

[68] I would like to thank Antoine Lonnet at the French National Centre for Scientific Research (C.N.R.S.) for his helpful advice on Arabic planets and phonetics.

Corroborating the idea that the name *Çeli* refers to the planet Saturn, the text offers another piece of information: *Çeli* is described as a star in the orbit of Jupiter ('Un'autre estoile c'est, el cercle Jovi', l. 4010). Jupiter is called by its Latin name instead of the Arabic, and this is understandable since a degree of linguistic syncretism can be accepted in matters of this kind. However, why should Saturn, discovered thousands of years before this text and whose position was quite clear in the sky, belong to the orbit of Jupiter? This question is intriguing. One possible answer is that Saturn precedes Jupiter in the astral planes. While Jupiter is a more powerful planet, Saturn is called 'the predecessor';[69] thus 'el cercle Jovi' (l. 4010) would mean that it circles Jupiter and so is exterior to it, which Saturn in fact is. Thus the reference to *Çeli*'s preceding Jupiter can substantiate the *Çeli*/Saturn identity.

To summarise: he who was born under the influence of Mercury when it overshadows (in astrological terms this can be understood as 'conjuncts') Saturn has flesh stronger than emerald. We could interpret this passage as an indication of a Mercury-Saturn conjunction, which may suggest a precise chronological reference or more likely a specific astral situation relevant to Ferragu's circumstances. We know from medieval astrologers that Saturn is considered a static planet while Mercury is dynamic. Alchemists associated Saturn with lead because of the heaviness and slowness of this metal attributed to it because of its weight. Saturn was also known as the planet of gloom and consequently the one ruling melancholic temperaments, while conversely alchemists associated Mercury with lightness, vitality and sprightly natures, and with the liquid metallic element taking its name from this planet. The astral conjunction of Mercury and Saturn, according to both ancient and contemporary astrology, has the power to hinder the mobility of Mercury and inflict slowness on its movement. In relation to individuals, it has the faculty of sapping the vitality and sharpness of those born under signs ruled by Mercury (Gemini and Virgo), and of alleviating the melancholy and sluggishness of those ruled by Saturn. Since it is Mercury that overshadows Saturn, and our giant is ruled by the planet Mercury, the astral conjunctions probably

---

[69] Tester, *A History of Western Astrology*, p. 120.

refer to Saturn's negative effect on the sign ruled by Mercury (for example, Saturn in Virgo). Therefore the giant was born under the influence of a planet identifiable with Mercury, and Mercury is indeed a planet that accomplishes its course neither in 20 nor in 26 years (i.e. neither in static nor in dynamic mode, according to the Qabala). Furthermore, Mercury has such virtue that the one born when it conjuncts Saturn has flesh undoubtedly stronger than emerald, although with the exception of the navel – meaning that it is not a wholesome type of strength but one weakened by an exterior negative influence, which could be that of Saturn.

This leads one to say that the passage alludes to a moment in time characterised by a specific astral conjunction, by which the Cavalcabò (ruled by Mercury) did not succeed in maintaining their territory either in static or in dynamic mode (see the 20/26 question above, l. 4007), meaning either potentially or actually, and were in a phase where they needed external support to succeed. In other words, it refers to a situation of defeat or impasse such as that of the Cavalcabò in 1312, or more generally that of a Guelph lord struggling to keep his territory when this is being conquered by Ghibelline forces supported by the emperor. In short, this passage translates into a complex astrological metaphor the situation of a lord who had no hope of resistance against overwhelming Visconti power. This is no novelty since in Dante's *Commedia* there are several astrological and philosophical digressions, most of them bearing a metaphorical surplus of meaning.

We have seen how various elements in the *Entrée* offer grounds to place its creation within the boundaries of early fourteenth-century Milanese history. The text's astrological data form an appealing picture of the situation in which the Guelph Cavalcabò family (protected by Mercury/*Chavachabas*) figure as very strong, but not enough to resist the conqueror. The poet shows himself aware of the advantages of the Visconti's policy and averse to the conflict with the Guelph families of Lombardy. Another element in support of a Visconti patronage for the poem's anonymous author is the mention of the duke of Achaia as a positive figure. Thus, that the author speaks of himself as a Paduan should not necessarily lead us to conclude that he was still writing there in his maturity. The text corroborates Dionisotti's hypothesis that the author lived and worked at the court of the Visconti, a suitable environment for hosting intellectuals who could produce culture at a high level. My suggestion is that Matteo, at some point between 1311 and 1322, may have been the patron of the *Entrée*'s anonymous author. Combining the problematic ideological issues of autonomy and internal conflict in the commune (issues with which the author was familiar from the years of his Paduan education) later in life he created a hybrid reflecting the cultural-theoretical and political situation in northern Italy at the beginning of the Trecento.[70] On a final note, I would like to recall a sumptuous fresco dating to the 1330s when Azzone Visconti's policy of display was fully in action, as documented by Galvano Fiamma. The fresco is found at Azzone's residence which adjoined the chapel of the Blessed Virgin, now that of San Gottardo in Corte:[71]

> Along the side of the large cage in which the birds are, and opposite, is a most splendid great hall, in which are depicted Vainglory and the illustrious princes of the Gentile world, such as Aeneas, Attila, Hector, Hercules and many others. Among these, there is (besides Azzo Visconti) only one Christian, namely Charlemagne.[72]

Azzone is standing beside Charlemagne and among the greatest figures of antiquity, all of them featuring in the *Entrée* where they lend themselves to distinguished comparisons with the protagonists of the Franco-Italian poem.

---

[70] This agrees with the statement that 'ideologia feudale e *chanson de geste* erano prodotti d'importazione che si dovevano sostituire con concezioni proprie': H. Krauss, *Epica feudale e pubblico borghese. Per la storia poetica di Carlomagno in Italia*, ed. by A. Fassò, transl. by F. Brugnolo, A. Fassò, and M. Mancini (Padua: Liviana, 1980), p. 238.

[71] Green, 'Galvano Fiamma', pp. 102–109.

[72] Galvano Fiamma, *Opusculum de rebus gestis ab Azone, Luchino et Johanne vicecomitibus ab anno MCCCXXVIII usque ad annum MCCCXLII*, ed. by C. Castiglioni (Bologna: Zanichelli, 1938), XVII, pp. 16–17, transl. by Green, 'Galvano Fiamma', p. 102.

The question of authorship

The text is not addressed to a general audience but to one particular sovereign who is called upon to listen. The poet is obviously addressing one lord as he introduces himself as a citizen of Padua in the *gioiosa marca* of Treviso. On the one hand he conceals his identity, while on the other he feels the urge to specify the geographical position of his birthplace. He even refers to a courteous Trevisan; this figure cannot possibly be the tyrant Ezzelino who spread terror and bloodshed in the marquisate under the protection of Fredrick II, although Ezzelino's sympathy for the troubadour culture would justify the poet's use of the epithet *cortois*. Since Ezzelino's defeat in the middle of the thirteenth century, the mission of the marquisate and territory of Padua had been to fight the very idea of tyranny. Thus, the epithet understood as referring to Ezzelino would imply a degree of approval of his conduct which would be inconsistent with the poet's vision of politics. A possibility is that the epithet refers instead to Gherardo da Camino who by popular consensus governed Treviso between 1283 and 1312, in a period when Padua was still under the influence of the marquisate although on its way towards independence.[73]

The most interesting aspect of this passage is that the author only provides these hints to his identity having cleverly constructed, episode by episode, a crescendo of irritation leading to an open challenge to Charlemagne's authority, and to the final rupture of the feudal contract – that is, between the end of the first section and the beginning of the second so-to-speak romance section, which represents a dramatic diversion from the epic matter.

Because of its exact position in anticipating the dramatic fracture in the narrative, this part of the prologue is amenable to a number of readings. The author may be:

hinting at his place of origin to illustrate how imposed authority can be fought, and how this can cause unending conflicts;

warning the addressee that what happened to Charlemagne in the section of the poem he has just finished writing (i.e. hostility

---

[73] See also above, p. 226, fn. 42.

from his own kin) could happen to him. As the warning is a challenging one, he prefers to conceal his identity;

having challenged authority itself, now ready to challenge the very genre that traditionally represents authority, by sympathetically representing the degrees of Roland's impatience towards authority;

claiming his right of independence as an author, stressing that he comes from a place where the issue of authority is debated, and by doing so indirectly rejecting the very idea of patronage.

Bradley-Cromey suggested that the poet might be hiding from an authority in the Church, perhaps the Pope himself.[74] I do not find this suggestion convincing, because it is not the authority of the Church that is questioned in the *Entrée* but a lay form such as that of emperor or overlord. Padua in the fourteenth century was a well-known centre of philosophers and political theorists who focussed on defining the nature of authority, among them Marsilius of Padua. As for the addressee, Mandach proposed Francesco il Vecchio da Carrara.[75] Neither Bradley-Cromey nor Limentani tackled the question, preferring instead to remain on a more general level.[76] At this point it is essential to clarify the question of patronage if one wants to look for the identity of the poet.

Mandach was the first and to date only critic to suggest a name for the author of the *Entrée*, but his thesis is not convincing; Giovanni di Nono never left Padua to work in the service of a *signore* while the poet, as we have seen, might have spent much of his life far from his native land. The question of patronage becomes somewhat intriguing in the light of several passages discussed above which provide different hints: the theological dispute, for example, in which Roland accuses Ferragu of being a devil, with Ferragu finally said to have been born under the influence of the planet *Chavachabas*; later, the author introducing himself proudly to an *hom soveran* as a Paduan but only after the crescendo of Roland's

---

[74] Bradley-Cromey, *Authority and Autonomy*, pp. 94–99.
[75] A. de Mandach, 'Le Destinataire de l'*Entrée d'Espagne* de Venice (Marciana fr. XXI): Francesco il Vecchio da Carrara?', *AIV*, 148 (1989–90).
[76] Bradley-Cromey, *Authority and Autonomy*, p. 13; Limentani, *L'Entrée d'Espagne e i signori d'Italia*, p. 173.

challenge to the authority of Charlemagne.[77] The way the author introduces himself, providing geographical co-ordinates that stretch from the marquisate of Treviso to the sea's closest point, indicates that he is clearly writing in an environment not his own. He is writing for a lord who either does not know this territory, has just acquired it, or has designs to do so: perhaps for a lord whose authority the author does not fully recognise, either because he does not agree with imposing authority itself, or from pride at being the native of a land where the very concept of authority was in question. Acceptance of patronage was often due to a lack of alternatives, however, as the example of Dante illustrates. Living and serving an overlord, without necessarily agreeing with his foreign politics, was a common position for intellectuals throughout the age of the *signorie*. Corrado Bologna has shown how at the beginning of the fourteenth century Milan was powerful, rich and in a position to attract men of letters, mostly coming from the Paduan area.[78]

Regarding authority and autonomy in the *Entrée*, one should refer specifically to the perpetual strife of Northern Italy in which the Visconti were the overlords, much opposed by those traditional Guelph families fighting against that centripetal force for their right to local rule. One can easily envisage the lines of the *Entrée* concealing a polemic against the Visconti, the paramount protagonists in the years when the *Entrée* was presumably composed, and against the efforts of Giacomo Cavalcabò who resisted both the Ghibellines and the Visconti.[79] The Visconti availed themselves of the aid and support of the ancient families ruling the territory of

---

[77] See above, pp. 229, 223.
[78] Bologna, 'La letteratura dell'Italia settentrionale nel Trecento', pp. 520–26.
[79] A famous case of an intellectual exiled because of the Visconti is the notary Niccolò Da Casola, who disguised within the lines of his poem a polemic directed against the powerful family. Originally under the patronage of the Pepoli until 1350, Niccolò found refuge under the protection of the Este. There he composed his *Attila* (1358), glorifying his patron Aldobrandino III d'Este in the character of the hero Foresto. See Everson, *The Italian Romance Epic*, p. 115; Limentani, *L'Entrée d'Espagne e i signori d'Italia*, p. 158; Niccolò da Casola, *La Guerra d'Attila. Poema franco-italiano*, ed. by G. Stendardo, 2 vols (Modena: Società tipografica modenese, 1941).

Lombardy. Guglielmo Cavalcabò was proclaimed lord of Cremona in 1306 following his father's death and dominated the city until 1311. When Henry VII arrived at Cremona he was banished from the city by the emperor who put it in the hands of the imperial vicar, Galeazzo Visconti. On 10 January 1312, the Guelph alliance headed by Guglielmo conquered the city and threw out Galeazzo and the Ghibellines. Subsequently the Cavalcabò entered Piacenza and freed it from the Visconti. The Guelphs of Cremona became the strongest opponents of the imperial forces of Henry VII. Their army was strong, strategically well organised, and succeeded in defeating the Visconti in the whole area of Piacenza (which did not prevent Guglielmo from dying in the battle of Soncino). The Cavalcabò, regardless of momentary phases of collaboration, always opposed this imposition of authority. The events following the withdrawal of the army of Henry VII, who left Lombardy in the hands of the Visconti, tell us of the permanent struggle of the ancient families of the Lombard communes to maintain a degree of autonomy within their own territory. The history of this struggle against the Visconti covers the whole of the fourteenth century, from the events of 1311 to the crowning of Gian Galeazzo as duke of Milan and Lombardy by the emperor Wenceslaus in 1397.

The Visconti imposed their power on the region with the help of Henry VII, who supported the Ghibellines of Italy but at the same time displayed anti-imperial conduct by aiming to enlarge their territory independently of the emperor. The emperor only supported the Ghibelline party, while the Visconti maintained a policy of compromise where they found collaboration, and of suffocation of local rule when harshly opposed. This attitude was not completely in line with imperial foreign politics. One episode of that struggle was the siege of Cremona attempted by Galeazzo Visconti in 1319, which Giacomo managed to break on various occasions. Galeazzo tried again in 1321 when he sent a fleet with four hundred knights along the Po from Piacenza responding to new friction between Giacomo and the Ghibellines of Cremona. Giacomo again resisted but died soon after. In the history of early northern Italian *signorie*, the ten-year rule of Giacomo Cavalcabò remains the most persistent, valiant and long-lived attempt by a local *signore* to resist the powerful Visconti dominion. His four sons

(Cavalcabò, Marsilio, Guglielmo and Guberto) did not manage to retain power over the city and Cremona surrendered to Galeazzo in January 1322. The surviving Cavalcabò moved their seat to Viadana. The family was eventually exiled from Cremona, and the Visconti, despite the occasional alliance, always remained suspicious of them.[80]

The history of Milan from the beginning of the fourteenth century is also one of rivalry with Venice, especially when the *Serenissima* started showing interest in the territory of the *terraferma*. It is both natural and possible that a man of letters born in Padua, awarded a position as a notary or diplomat at a powerful court, would because of his background participate intellectually in this struggle by supporting tendencies to autonomy.

Given the lifelong struggle between the Visconti and the Cavalcabò it is possible to envisage behind the French transcription of the family name a reference to the historical events of those days. Thus Ferragu's protection by the planet *Chavachabas* can be read as the playful attribution of yet another negative trait to the Saracen giant. Not only is Ferragu in this way a pagan, a radical Aristotelian and a Greek, but he also defends and is defended by the eponymous planet of Visconti's most bitter enemy! This does not at all mean that the poet was necessarily sympathetic to his patron's policy. As the data offered by the text suggest, he is not in agreement with imposing any signorial authority.

The playful mention of invented planets suggests an interest in astrology, while the reference to an astrological framework sounds strangely grotesque. If one were to seek a cause for the unexpected parody there would be only two possible causes. On the one hand, that Dante had the habit of suggesting astrological co-ordinates of major events in the *Commedia* might have influenced the Paduan.[81] On the other, the superstition that led Guglielmo Cavalcabò to the

---

[80] Andenna, 'Cavalcabó', p. 597. On this period see also Viscardi, 'La cultura milanese nel secolo XIV'; Chittolini, 'Infeudazioni e politica feudale', and G. Tabacco, *Egemonie sociali*.

[81] For example the spring equinox, at which it was believed that God created the world, is described as the sun rises with Aries: 'l sol montava in su con quelle stele | ch'eran con lui quando l'amor divino | mosse di prima quelle cose belle' (*Inferno* I, 38–40).

disastrous defeat at Soncino must have produced a great deal of sarcasm among both rivals and supporters.

By characterising Roland as a *baron révolté* and describing his gradual assumption of authority over his own troops, resulting in insubordination, the poet transfers the motif of the ruptured feudal pact to the acquisition of autonomy by individual Italian overlords such as the Visconti. The Cavalcabò represented on a smaller scale what the Visconti achieved more successfully by gaining gradual autonomy from the emperor. Thus while the poet is averse to the conflict between the Visconti and surrounding families, and is sympathetic to the cause of the Cavalcabò, he is also aware of the advantages that the Visconti's centripetal policy will produce. This would explain the sarcasm and the parody hidden beneath these lines directed towards the Cavalcabò, regardless of the author's dislike for any sort of tyrannical rule.

Another argument in support of a Milanese origin for the *Entrée* can be provided. The circulation of the *Entrée* is documented by the presence of two fragments, one in Châtillon and another in Reggio Emilia. These testify to the *Entrée*'s area of dissemination, one subjected to the influence of Milan. Both Piedmont and Bologna belonged to the Visconti sphere of influence in the early Trecento, and Mantua always remained faithful to their high lordship until Luigi I Gonzaga became 'capitano generale' in 1328, turning the city into a unique example of complete autonomy. The *Entrée* circulated in an area subjected to the family's strong influence. The date of 1320 suggested by Roncaglia and supported by Renzi was based on the cultural background emerging from the poem. Matters of ideology and precise references to the historical framework of the first two decades of the fourteenth century, as discussed above, now corroborate this date. The process leading to the constitution of the *signorie*, which Krauss defines in his three-period classification of audience and patronage[82] as the third (1330–1350 and beyond) and

---

[82] Until c. 1260 (the death of Ezzelino da Romano), a feudal-aristocratic public was dominant, and adaptations such as *Buovo d'Antona* were made for a more humble public; personal entrepreneurism, social equality, and freedom were praised (implicitly or explicitly) until c. 1300, with the growth of city bourgeoisie; between 1330–1350 and after, with the formation of the *signorie*, the most evolved branch of the

to which he also maintains that the *Entrée* belongs,[83] in reality starts earlier and could include the first three decades of the century.[84] The republican and anti-tyrannical environment in which the *Entrée*'s author was educated as a young man left its traces in the poem. In more than a few cases, including Padua's, the failure of the commune was due to conflict rather than external pressure.[85] Once Frederick II had died the problem was the internal dissension within the communes and their capacity to survive. The subdivision of the people into multiple economic and professional groups, and the establishment of an armed force of the *popolo*, represented a challenge to the traditional oligarchy of the *magnati*.[86] It is in this framework that the poet makes his first steps as a participant in the cultural and perhaps public life of the commune. Milan grew in autonomy between 1235 and 1250, but the relationship of the empire with the Lombard and Venetian communes has been characterised as the most bitter conflict of the Middle Ages between bourgeois and monarchical power.[87]

In conclusion, the question of patronage is of foremost importance when trying to solve the problem of the author's identity. The fact that we know he is a native of Padua should not necessarily lead us to conclude that he was still writing there in his maturity; the cultural environment surrounding the Visconti in the first half of the fourteenth century attracted many intellectuals to join their court. Based on the evidence presented here it is possible to suggest that the anonymous author of the *Entrée* was serving at

---

bourgeoisie aimed at the elitist appropriation of the old feudal aristocracy's ideals and behaviour. On this point see Krauss, *Epica feudale e pubblico borghese*.

[83] Krauss, *Epica feudale e pubblico borghese*, pp. 334–35.
[84] See the suggestion of Bradley-Cromey, *Authority and Autonomy*, p. 102, qtd above, p. 227.
[85] Bradley-Cromey, *Authority and Autonomy*, p. 99.
[86] Bradley-Cromey, *Authority and Autonomy*, p. 100.
[87] H. Appelt, 'La politica imperiale verso i comuni italiani', in C. D. Fonseca, ed., *I problemi della civiltà comunale. Atti del Congresso storico internazionale per l'VIII centenario della prima Lega lombarda (Bergamo 4–8 settembre 1967)* (Bergamo: Cassa di Risparmio delle provincie lombarde, 1968), pp. 23–32.

the court of Matteo and Galeazzo Visconti around 1320, thus profiting from their magnificent libraries (for example at the castle of Pavia). As illustrated in this chapter, there are many valid reasons to move forward from broadly attributing the *Entrée*'s creation to the Paduan environment, which takes into consideration only the mention of the city and the author's cultural background. The culture displayed by the poet during the narrative does attest to a learned upbringing under a great variety of influences which characterises the profile of a lay intellectual, possibly a diplomat; but that does not hinder the thesis that it was specifically his culture and education, and his desire to open up to new and diverse influences, that led him to look for new career perspectives in the fascinating entourage of the Visconti and the splendid environment of their castles.

Limentani suggested that only a cultural analysis of the poem would lead to an identification of the author. This study reinforces the idea that the *Entrée* should be inserted within the framework of Visconti patronage. It is not among the Paduan scholars that further research should look for a name but within the entourage created by the Visconti dream of the first two decades of the Trecento, of gathering northern Italy's intellectual life into Milan.

The question of language

The variety of French language used by the author may indicate the type of literature that the poet encountered at both an earlier and later stage in his life. A central question was raised by Thomas:

> Comment le Padouan à qui nous devons l'*Entrée* s'est-il initié à la connaissance de notre langue? […] le français qu'il avait sous les yeux ne pouvait être qu'une langue composite, car les scribes, a quelque nationalité qu'ils appartiennent, respectent rarement leurs modèles, et y laissent, en les trascrivant, bien des particularités de leur idiome ou de leur graphie propres.[88]

As the only surviving manuscript in the Biblioteca Nazionale Marciana is not an autograph, it is extremely difficult to disentangle

---

[88] Thomas, *L'Entrée d'Espagne*, I: LXXXIV–V.

the matter of the variety of language, and identify the basis of the author's acquisition of written French. Limentani maintained that he was not necessarily a scholar or a *jongleur*[89] although his closeness to Provençal literature is testified to in line 10964 by his words 'me sui mis a trover dou meilor Cristian'. He refers to the art of composing poetry with the technical term of *trover* (*trobar* in *langue d'oc*). This means, on the one hand, that he may have read his *chansons de geste* and Breton romances in French manuscripts; on the other, that Provençal language could have interfered with his learning of written French while he entertained himself with the reading of the various *chansons* written to commemorate that tragedy. He may also have derived some Provençal endings from the same sources. The hybridism of his language is thus not necessarily a by-product of his learning French through Italian manuscripts of the matter of France. It could be derived from the author's interest in both *oc* and *oïl* literatures. The *Entrée* does indeed lack any sign of a theory of love and the general arguments of the *fin'amor*, and where the subject of love is touched upon[90] he lingers on physical attraction rather than inaccessible love as in the love lyric of the troubadours. However, the poet chose to represent one of the typical topics of troubadour lyric – measure and courtesy – inserting it into the typical account of anti-courtesy and anti-moderation, and thus turning the champion of *desmesure* into a perfect example of moderation.

Once the autonomy of the south of France disappeared the culture of the troubadours was imported into Italy by the *jongleurs* and poets of a more intellectual profile, exiled after the tragic events of the Albigensian crusade. In the Venetian region the most important troubadour cultural centre was Treviso.[91] Provençal was

---

[89] See also A. M. Finoli, 'Note sulla personalità e la cultura dell'autore dell'*Entrée d'Espagne*', *Cultura Neolatina*, 21 (1961), 175–81.

[90] As discussed by Limentani, chastity plays a very small role even in the episode where Roland is attracted to Dionés: Limentani, *L'Entrée d'Espagne e i signori d'Italia*, pp. 313–14.

[91] During the lordship of Alberico da Romano, whose entourage was composed of bourgeois tending to isolate themselves as an élite. The institutional assent promoted by him and by Ezzelino converged with that of the South of France's feudal courts, which would justify the *cortois Trivixan* in line 10976.

taught, based on grammars (for example the *Donatz Proensals* by Uc Faidit), and Uc de Saint-Circ found in Treviso a suitable environment where, along with his collection of poetry he composed his *vidas* and *razos*, which can be considered the first critical works on Provençal lyric.[92] Bernard de Ventadour, Bertrand de Born, Guiraut de Bornelh, and Jaufré Rudel lived in Italy too. The feudal lords of the Po valley commissioned collections of Provençal poetry. Troubadour culture found even more fertile ground in environments similar to that of its origin, such as the aristocratic courts of the lords of Monferrato and Lunigiana which were subjected to the domination of the Visconti.

Between 1300 and 1350 the most powerful and culturally mature branch of the bourgeoisie aimed at acquiring the behaviour and ideals of the ancient feudal aristocracy. With the birth of the *signorie*, the urbanised landowners allied with the great trade magnates and high urban bourgeoisie, so that the wealth of the former was adapted to the latter's need for legitimisation and ennoblement. This type of exchange underpinned the enormous fortune of some of the greatest families of the Italian Renaissance, starting with the Visconti and Gonzaga. It is at this early stage of the *signorie* that the *Entrée* was produced. Galeazzo and his successors led the first full-scale project of merging aristocratic and bourgeois values by surrounding themselves with artists and men of letters in the fabulous castle of Pavia. The castle's library was among the richest ever known, although it has not been preserved, containing at least eighty-seven French and five Occitan manuscripts.[93]

A great deal of Occitan literature deals with the matter of the destruction of the Cathar community of Albi. Epic is the genre that best represents the tragic events of the crusade against the

---

[92] Limentani, *L'Entrée d'Espagne e i signori d'Italia*, p. 337; Renzi, 'Il francese come lingua letteraria', p. 565.

[93] See A. Thomas, 'Les manuscrits français et provençaux des Ducs de Milan au château de Pavie'. Limentani, *L'Entrée d'Espagne e i signori d'Italia*, notes that a number of references to Pavia appear in the text: 'pavois' (currency of Pavia, l. 10186); 'liart de Pavie' (l. 11929); 'por l'onor de Pavie' (l. 15147); 'li Lombart de Pavie' (l. 14660); and one reference to 'Disirer de Pavie' (l. 662). Limentani also admits that there may be a reference to the Visconti: 'in periodo visconteo da non perdere di vista' (p. 82).

Albigensians, and it is not to be excluded that the heterogeneous Paduan culture could include epic celebrating the destruction of the peaceful courts where the celebrated troubadour culture had flourished. In the *Entrée*, the author's sympathy for the Cathar tragedy can be easily justified by the troubadour culture's influence.

There is an episode in the *Entrée* in which, having returned to Charlemagne's camp during the first pause in the duel against Ferragu, Roland is given very rich garments to wear. However, he calls a Provençal minstrel ('un jogleors provençal d'Avignon', l. 1961) and presents him with the garments (ll. 1962–69):

> 'Prend les' – feit il – 'ci a mout pobre don.
> Bailez te soient par tiel entencion:
> Sor Cil meïme que vient a pasion,
> Je ne metrai mantel ne caperon
> Fors que la cofie de mon hiaume reon
> Tant que avrai delivrez de prison
> Cel par cui sui en duel et en fricon'.
> Par itant fu mout loé le baron.

These lines testify to Roland's generosity, a side of his character appearing throughout the poem, but they also suggest that the poet may have held respect for the condition of the *jongleurs*. Its cause may be the poet's awareness of historical facts related to the crusade. The environment in which the troubadours lived and produced their lyrics came to a definitive end after the crusade (ll. 1209–29). The introduction of the Inquisition (ll. 1233) and torture as an instrument for its realisation (ll. 1252) led to the annihilation of the spirit of the French *Midi*. The end of the major nobles' autonomy in the south of France after the acquisition of their territories by the king, the major sponsor of the crusade, wrought the end of an entire world. The *Entrée* presents problems related to abuse of power and insubordination which is also a *leitmotiv* of the Albigensian tragedy – except that Roland's temporary breaking of the feudal contract mirrors an Italian actuality which established the vassal's right to autonomy, whereas history shows how the French king never lowered himself to compromise with the fiercely independent lords of the *Midi*.

A genuine admiration for Provençal poetry may also underpin the episode of the gift to the *jongleur*, and one may add the literature of the crusade against the Albigensians to the variety of sources that contributed to the 'origine colta'[94] of the poem.

Is the poem really unfinished?

As a conclusion to this study, one question remains to be discussed: was the poem left unfinished by the author (either intentionally or unintentionally), or is the abrupt ending justified by the poet's aim, to characterise a different Roland and his relationship with Charlemagne?

Having elaborated the character of Roland to such an extent, was it still possible to make him feature as the martyr of Rencesvals? How could the author go on to tell the traditional story after enriching its protagonist, a character traditionally formed in the canon of feudal obedience, with a deeper psychological insight?

The Venetian manuscript of the *Entrée* contains 131 additional verses (five laisses), possibly composed by Niccolò da Verona who wrote a continuation of the *Entrée*[95], and added by a later hand at the poem's end. These verses link the ending as recounted by the *Entrée*'s poet to Niccolò's continuation. The five laisses do not narrate anything exceptionally interesting, only that the king wanted to crown Roland but Roland refuses the crown (ll. 1–18), the French hero recounts his adventure *outre mer* (ll. 36–59) and Sansonet was made a peer of France to replace Sanson from

---

[94] Bologna, 'La letteratura dell'Italia settentrionale nel Trecento', maintains that: 'la mancanza di purismo linguistico non andrà intesa come affioramento dal basso in sede signorile di tratti "popolari", né quale "organismo patologico", alla maniera in cui Mussafia leggeva ad esempio il *Machario*, bensì come prova cosciente, originalmente creativo ricorso a quello che Lorenzo Renzi ha definito "francese di lombardia", caratterizzato soprattutto da tratti fonologici piuttosto arcaici, bloccati all'altezza del Duecento, in opposizione ad un "franco-lombardo" in sostanza dialettale-mescidato'. (pp. 538–39). See also above, p. 217.

[95] *La Prise de Pampelune*, in *Altfranzösische Gedichte aus venezianischen Handschriften*, ed. by A. Mussafia, 2 vols (Vienna: Gerold, 1864); Niccolò da Verona, *Opere. Pharsale, Continuazione dell'Entrée d'Espagne, Passion*, ed. by F. Di Ninni (Venice: Marsilio, 1992).

Guascogne who died in Pamplona (ll. 62–68). At the end, six verses announce that Niccolò now intends to continue the story and explain why it remained very little known (ll. 125–31):

> Ci tourne Nicolais a rimer la complue
> De L'Entree de Spagne, qe tant est stee escondue
> Par ce ch'elle n'estoit par rime componue
> Da cist pont en avant, ond il l'a proveüe
> Por rime, cum celu q'en latin l'a leüe.
> Our contons de l'istoire qe doit etre entendue
> Da cascun q'en bonté ha sa vie disponue.

The scribe (or Niccolò himself) says that the *Entrée* has remained hidden ('est stee escondue', l. 126) because from that point on it was unfinished ('Da cist pont en avant n'estoit par rime componue', ll. 127–26). Niccolò has therefore provided it with an ending ('ond il l'a proveüe por rime', ll. 128–29).

These verses reveal two important things: the *Entrée* seems not to have been very popular, in fact remaining hidden until the time of its continuation (dating to 1344) b); and the reason for its unpopularity is precisely that it is incomplete. This is the opinion of Niccolò/the scribe, however, and when these verses were added to the Venetian manuscript it is likely that la *Prise de Pampelune* had already been composed and was circulating.

All this raises questions about the actual success and circulation of the *Entrée* in the fourteenth century. Yet it does not say whether the *Entrée* was left unfinished either accidentally or intentionally. It is quite possible that what is in fact a happy ending was misunderstood as an abrupt one. The evolution of the character of Roland as surveyed in this study suggests that the poem is concluded, and that what Niccolò or the scribe perceived as the narrative's interruption in fact resolves the matter of the friction between Roland and Charlemagne with the *Entrée*'s final scene: the latter's acceptance of his nephew's autonomy.

It was the poet's initial purpose to tell of the seven years prior to Rencesvals. Yet as we have seen, many elements show that the second part was written under different inspiration from the first. A lack of consistency between the first and second sections emerges in that events announced in the first section remain untold at the end.

The first of these events is the liberation of Compostella from the Moors, announced in the first protasis (ll. 1–12, 26–29):

> En honor et en bien et en gran remembrançe
> Et offerant mercé, honor et celebrançe
> De Celui che par nos fu feruç de la lance
> Par trer nos e nos armes de la enfernal poissançe,
> Et de son saint apostre, qi tant oit penetançe
> Por feir qe cescuns fust en veraie creançe
> Que Per e Filz e Spirt sunt in une sustançe
> – C'est li barons saint Jaqes de qi faç la mentanze –
> Vos voil canter e dir por rime e por sentençe
> Tot ensi come Carles el bernage de France
> Entrerent en Espagne, et por ponte de lançe
> Conquistrent de saint Jaqes la plus mestre habitançe.
>
> Par ces vers qi ci sunt poroiz oïr conter
> Cumant le bons rois Carles, il et li douçe per
> Entrerent en Espagne por Rollant coroner
> E le chemins l'apostre saint Jaqes recovrer.

As it emerges from these lines, the liberation of Compostella was meant to be the subject of the poem. Yet while the poem tells of many sieges, Compostella is the only one it does not report.

The second element anticipated and never narrated is Roland's knowledge of the death of one of his companions, announced by the hermit (ll. 15123–25):

> 'Toi e tes compaignons qu'enz ou val troverais
> E tut ti compagnons, voir c'un perdu en ais:
> Je ne sai qel il soit, mais deman le savrais'.

In the *Entrée* Roland is never told the identity of his lost companion. However, Niccolò da Verona tells how Samson was replaced by Sansonet, which presumably realises the hermit's prophecy as Samson is the one the hermit was referring to. It is very bizarre that the hermit himself is called Samson! This fact is inexplicable, like many others in Niccolò's continuation, and it creates confusion not only in itself but as to Niccolò's intentions.[96]

To these loose ends in the *Entrée* Limentani adds the death of Sansonet.[97] However, the text does not say explicitly that Sansonet will die but that his family will not see him again. This is broadly justified by Sansonet's choice of following Roland and needs no further elaboration (ll. 14177–79, 14290–92):

> C'est la derere cene qe il o lui fera,
> Tot ce qe le bon roi mie ne le quida;
> Ni son enfant ni lui jamais ne revera.
>
> Recomandé fu Sanses en la grace Rolant.
> Plorant remis la mer au partir de l'enfant:
> Jamais nel revera a jor de son vivant.

These missing developments, while resulting in a lack of consistency in the text, fall outside the *Entrée*'s scope[98] along with Gano's treachery (mentioned in the first protasis as the reason why Roland will not be crowned king of Spain in the end, ll. 14–17), and the death of Roland and his peers. For this reason, it does not necessarily surprise.

Elements particular to the Breton romances appear mostly in the second section in which Roland starts to appear a completely different character. Features such as the technique of *entrelacement*, which is typical of the romance, support the idea that the poet was working towards a conversion of the *chanson* into a hybridised form of Breton romance. The lack of consistency of the narrative is quite normal in medieval romance. The unaccountable changes of subject through the technique of *entrelacement* (as for example in the *Tristano Riccardiano*, to mention just one Italian creation contemporary to the *Entrée*) make the book difficult to read as a whole, and its plot inconsistent.[99]

---

[96] On this point, see Limentani, *L'Entrée d'Espagne e i signori d'Italia*, p. 81–82.
[97] Limentani, *L'Entrée d'Espagne e i signori d'Italia*, p. 79.
[98] Limentani, *L'Entrée d'Espagne e i signori d'Italia*, p. 79.
[99] *Tristano Riccardiano*, ed. by M.-J. Heijkant (Parma: Pratiche, 1991).

However, the case of the *Entrée* is different even from this last example. As shown in different parts of this study, it is possible to read the first section as a mounting of tension between the emperor and his nephew, fully justifying Roland's escape. Thus, there is a relationship of cause and effect between the first and the second part. The fact that a few topics anticipated in the protasis are not recounted does not necessarily indicate that the poem is incomplete, and the author might have changed his mind about their place in the narrative.

What Limentani cautiously suggests is that one must examine the author's cultural background more deeply, and look for his doctrinal interests to understand whether the divergence between the first and second part impedes the story's continuity, leaving the poem unfinished, or whether he implemented a rushed conclusion with the sole purpose of not betraying the tradition.[100] If the second hypothesis is accepted the poem should be considered complete, regardless of what has been left untold. Since several threads would thereby remain ungathered, perhaps the author intended to follow a centrifugal movement opposite to that of the epic, which tends to conclude without excessive dispersion.

The problem of the poem's completeness or incompleteness needs situating in the wider discussion about whether it should be divided into three sections or two. Limentani suggested that it is a contradiction to try and structure an incomplete work.[101] However, he argued that it was the author's intention to develop a third section (epic – romance - back to epic), and instead he proposed that the poem aimed at a narrative *continuum* of two parts: I *geste* of Spain, II *geste* of the Orient. On the other hand, he also maintained that 'né l'*Entrée* può assolutamente essere analizzata come un grande dittico',[102] because the uncompleted topics announced in the protasis are many (the attempt to take over the empire, Sansonet's death, and the siege of Pamplona). The question thus remains open.

---

[100] Limentani, *L'Entrée d'Espagne e i signori d'Italia*, p. 78.
[101] Limentani, *L'Entrée d'Espagne e i signori d'Italia*, p. 53.
[102] The division into two sections never completely convinced Limentani. Although thinking it more sensible than Torraca's subdivision of the plot into several parts, he maintained that it needed justification: Limentani, *L'Entrée d'Espagne e i signori d'Italia*, p. 75.

In length, the two parts are quite consistent: the first contains 10938 lines; the second, including the protasis (ll. 10939–96, amounting to 57 lines spread over the end of laisse CCCCLXXVII and up until CCCCLXXX) can be fittingly said to begin from laisse CCCCLXXVIII and would thus contain 4860 verses (from ll. 10945 to 15805), to which about 4000 verses must be added, the calculated length of the lacuna.[103]

The poem's final part, in which Roland returns to Spain and travels with Sansonet and Hugh, would be the ideal beginning of any third section containing the topics anticipated in the protasis and never developed. It has a strong flavour of romance and in fact opens with the episode of the hermit, one typical of a Breton romance. It could thus be perceived as an attempt to build a third part although instead of being a return to epic it would end the poem on a romance note, reprising the romance element of the Eastern section.

While in the epic the figure of the narrator is detached from the events (as the poem treats a traditional subject already known to the public) in this text many interventions by the author are present. The author participates in the plot, for example: 'Que vos doi je plus dire, ne parlonger le plait ?' (l. 1245); 'Si vos di plus avant' (l. 1276); 'Se de la force Feragu dir devroie | a maint de vos non creable parroie' (ll. 1281–2); 'Seignor, oiez cançon de droite loi | Ja de meillor nulle n'orrez, ce croi' (ll. 1810–11); 'Mais tant fu grant le colp, se dir le doi' (l. 1818); 'Chi de Rollant, seignors, omeis disist' (l. 2428). It is a prerogative of romances and not of the epic that the plot is enriched with the addition of new characters playing new roles and interacting with the protagonists, thus contributing to their characterisations. In short, new voices reply to that of the epic hero, so that in its transition between poem and romance the narrative becomes dialogic rather than monologic. The issue of the ending is strictly linked to those of structure and genre. Incompleteness itself demonstrates that the hero is a character in progress; it is a symptom of the latter's evolution.

It would in fact seem impossible to link the Roland as developed in the *Entrée* to the redoubtable hero of the *Chanson de Roland*. The

---

[103] Aebischer, 'Ce qui reste d'un manuscrit'.

Entrée's Roland may die, but not for an episode such as Rencesvals and especially not as a tragic hero. The sense of the tragic, so strong in the *Chanson*, is completely lost in the *Entrée*. The poem's real aim is akin to that of the *exempla* widely circulating and popular at the time of the poem's composition. It offers a case of friction and resolution between two figures symbolic of an overlord and feudal vassal, showing how political discord can be overcome through necessity. Roland is necessary for Charlemagne to win the war in Spain as his absence is cause for discontent and insubordination, and Charlemagne is necessary for Roland to recover his own rightful role in French society. Mutual interest leads the two characters to a compromise. The peaceful solution of a conflict of interest reminds one of Terence and the final recognitions and reconciliations that are so typical of his comedies.[104] Along with elements of realism and a strong accent on ethos,[105] the ending of the *Entrée* reinforces the idea that the intention was to create a hybrid, thus adapting a traditional plot to a new environment which would receive it only when acceptable to its own views.

Representing a tragic hero becomes impossible in the fourteenth century. The literary end of the epic hero in fourteenth-century French and Italian literature entails a discussion of the birth of

---

[104] In the six surviving comedies of P. Terentius Afrus (*Andria, Heautontimoroumenos, Eunuchus, Phormio, Hecyra, Adelphi*), the device of mistaken identity is employed as a normal solution to a complicated plot, as for example in *Andria* where Glycerium is recognised by the rich old man Chremes, making marriage between Pamphilus and Glycerium possible.

[105] A discussion of *ethos* as applied to epic is found in G. Zankler, *Realism in Alexandrian Poetry. A Literature and Its Audience* (London: Croom Helm, 1987): 'Quintilian calls *ethos* more similar to comedy, *pathos* to tragedy (*Institutio Oratoria* 6.2.20). As a consequence of this view, critics came to regard the *Odyssey*, because of its preoccupation with *ethos*, as a comedy. So for example Pseudo-Longinus claims in *On the Sublime* 9.15 that Homer's description of Odysseus' household makes "a sort of comedy of manners." [...] The idea is generalized to refer to the whole poem in the Latin *Prolegomena* by Euanthius who says that Homer composed the *Iliad* "according to the pattern of a tragedy", the *Odyssey* "in the image of a comedy" (XXV 1.25–28 Koster)' (p. 143).

individualism;[106] the questions of identity and the human being's inner condition were connected to the romance from its birth. The re-creation of Roland as an epic hero without a tragic ending is a great innovation of the author of the *Entrée*.

The last lines of the poem clearly indicate the impossibility of progressing further in the account given that the sequel of the matter recounted in the *Entrée*, from Roland's return to Spain until his death, belongs with the tradition. After the friction has reached its climax, Charlemagne understands just how important Roland's presence is in his army and how much the barons trust and love him, and finally accepts his own defeat (ll. 15791–805):

> Quand le roi parle, si dist con unble vois:
> 'Douz fil' – dit il – 'resuresi m'avois
> Da mort a vie; vesqui n'aüse un mois.
> Douz ma sperançe, mon confort, mon repois,
> Brais de justice envers les orgolois,
> Plen d'unbleté, sanz orgoil e bufois,
> Cuer de mon vantre, clere lus de mes ois,
> Se je vos fi oltraje ne sordois,
> Car pur des ore, biaus duz niés, je conois
> Que senz vos bras non valdroie un pois,
> E si pri Diex, l'altisime gloriois,
> Che mort moi soit in conpagnie tot fois
> Che mais je voie cil pont, quand finirois'.
> De la pieté del roi des Romanois
> En plurerent environ tuit François.

Since the portraits of Roland and Charlemagne are complete and no longer resemble the martyr of Rencesvals and the emperor, one may wonder if the poet had any interest at all in merging the story he had just told with the events narrated in the *Chanson*.

All these elements aid the argument that the poem was not left unfinished accidentally, but that the author stopped it where his innovation also finished. Is it therefore still possible to define the *Entrée* as the mere account of Charlemagne's seven years of war in

---

[106] See for example A. Gurevich, *The Origins of Medieval Individualism* (Oxford: Blackwell, 1995).

Spain as Limentani did, taking up Thomas' definition? Does this account not clash rather than merge with the subject of the *Chanson*? As shown throughout this study, the questions of autonomy and imperial authority in fourteenth-century Italy, along with the poet's deep interest in the romance genre that obscured his concern with the epic structure, are central to understanding the *Entrée* as a finished work of art of profound significance for the development of genres at the end of the Middle Ages, and which represents the spirit of its age.

BIBLIOGRAPHY

Manuscripts cited

Histoire ancienne jusq'à César
Venice: Biblioteca Nazionale Marciana, MS fr. Z. 2 (=223)

Armannino Giudice, Fiorita
Florence: Biblioteca Nazionale Centrale, MS II. III. 139 (prov. Strozzi 1261 <e 308>)
Oxford: Bodleian Library, MS Canonici It. 2

Roman de Troie
Venice: Biblioteca Nazionale Marciana, MS fr. Z. 17 (=230)
Venice: Biblioteca Nazionale Marciana, MS fr. Z. 18 (=231)
Milan: Biblioteca Ambrosiana, MS D. 55. sup.
Florence: Biblioteca Riccardiana, MS 2433
Naples: Biblioteca Nazionale Vittorio Emanuele III, MS XIII. C. 38

Cantare d'Hector et Hercule
Paris: Bibliothèque nationale de France, MS fr. 821, fols 1r–12v
Venice: Biblioteca Nazionale Marciana, MS fr. Z. 18 (=231), fols 143r–152v
Florence: Biblioteca Riccardiana, MS 2433, fols 1r–13 v
Oxford: Bodleian Library, MS Canonici Misc. 450, fols 120v–171v

Roman d'Alexandre
Venice: Biblioteca Museo Correr, Correr 1493
Riccoldo da Montecroce, Liber Peregrinationis
Berlin: Staatsbibliothek Preußischer Kulturbesitz, MS lat. qu. 446, fols 1r–24r
Florence: Biblioteca Nazionale, MS Magl. II. IV. 53, fols 1r–26r (Tuscan version)

Aspremont
Venice: Biblioteca Nazionale Marciana, MS fr. Z. 6 (=226), fols 6r–69r

Primary Sources

Abelard [Peter Abelard], *Dialogo tra un filosofo, un giudeo e un cristiano*, ed. and transl. by C. Trovo (Milan: Rizzoli, 1992)

— *Dialogus inter Philosophum, Iudaeum et Christianum*, ed. by R. Thomas (Stuttgart-Bad Cannstatt: Frommann, 1970)

— *Ethical Writings*, transl. by P. V. Spade (Indianapolis: Hackett, 1995)

Alexandre de Paris, *Le Roman d'Alexandre*, ed. by M. La Du, in *The Medieval French 'Roman d'Alexandre'*, ed. by E. C. Armstrong, 6 vols (Princeton: Princeton University Press, 1976), II

— *Le Roman d'Alexandre. Riproduzione del ms. Venezia, Biblioteca Museo Correr, Correr 1493*, ed. by R. Benedetti (Udine: Vattori, 1998)

— *Li Romans d'Alixandre par Lambert li tors et Alexandre de Bernay*, ed. by H. Michelant (Stuttgart: Lit. Verein, 1846)

Alexandre du Pont, *Le Roman de Mahomet*, ed. by Y. G. Lepage (Paris: Klincksieck, 1977)

Albertino da Mussato, *Ecerinide*, ed. by L. Padrin (Bologna: Forni, 1969)

Ariosto [Ludovico Ariosto], *Orlando Furioso*, ed. by P. Gioacchino (Milan: Rizzoli, 1991)

Baebii Italici Ilias latina, ed. by M. Scaffai (Bologna: Pàtron, 1997)

Benedeit, *Il Viaggio di San Brandano*, ed. and transl. by R. Bartoli and F. Cigni (Parma: Pratiche, 1994)

Benoît de Saint-Maure, *Le Roman de Troie*, ed. by L. Constans (Paris: Société des Anciens Textes Françaises, 1904–12)

Bernard of Clairvaux, *Liber ad milites templi de laude novae militiae*, intr. and transl. by C.D. Fonseca, in *Opere*, vol. I, *Trattati* (Milan: Fondazione di studi cistercensi, 1984), pp. 425–83

Boiardo [Matteo Maria Boiardo], *Orlando Innamorato*, ed. by A. Scaglione (Turin: UTET, 1984)

Bonaventura (St.), *Legenda maior s. Francisci Assisiensis*, transl. by R. Paciocco, in *Opere di San Bonaventura*, Vol. XIV/1, *Opuscoli Francescani* (Rome: Città Nuova, 1993)

Brendan (St.), *Navigatio sancti Brendani*, ed. by Carl Selmer (Notre Dame-Indiana: University of Notre Dame Press, 1959)

BIBLIOGRAPHY

— *Navigatio sancti Brendani - La navigazione di San Brandano*, ed. by M. A. Grignani (Milan: Bompiani, 1992)
— *La navigazione di San Brandano*, ed. and transl. by A. Magnani (Palermo: Sellerio, 1992)
— *The Voyage of Saint Brendan*, ed. and transl. by J. J. O'Meara (Dublin: Dolmen Press, 1976)
Chanson d'Antioche, ed. by S. Duparc-Quioc (Paris: Geuthner, 1977)
Chanson de Roland - Canzone di Orlando, ed. by A. M. Finoli, transl. into Italian by F. Pozzoli (Milan: Mursia, 1984)
Chrétien de Troyes, *Le Chevalier au lion ou Yvain*, ed. by D. Hult (Paris: Livre de Poche, 1994)
— *Cligès*, ed. by C. Méla (Paris: Livre de Poche, 1994)
— *Le Roman de Perceval ou Le conte du Graal*, ed. by W. Roach (Geneva: Droz, 1959)
Compilazione della 'Eneide' di Virgilio fatta volgare in sul principio del secolo xiv da Ser Andrea Lancia, ed. by P. Fanfani (Florence: Stamperia sulle logge del Grano, 1851)
Dante Alighieri, *Convivio*, ed. by F. Brambilla Ageno, 3 vols (Florence: Le Lettere, 1995)
— *La Divina Commedia*, ed. by N. Sapegno (Florence: La Nuova Italia, 1955–1960; repr.1968)
— *De vulgari eloquentia*, in *Opere minori*, ed. by P. V. Mengaldo and B. Nardi, 6 vols (Naples: Ricciardi, 1995–96), III/1: 3–237
Daretis Phrygii de excidio Troiae historia, ed. by F. Meister (Leipzig: Teubner, 1873)
Duello tra Rolando e Feragu nell'Entrée d'Espagne, transl. by P. Gresti (Mantua: Arcari, 2012)
Dictis Cretensis ephemeridos belli Troiani libri, ed. by W. Eisenhut (Leipzig: Teubner, 1958)
Enéas. Roman du XIIe siècle, ed. by J.J. Salverda de Grave (Paris: Champion, 1964)
Les Enfances Vivien, ed. by M. Rouguicr (Geneva: Droz, 1997)
Les Enfances Vivien, ed. by C. Wahlund and H. von Feilitzen (Uppsala: Librairie de l'Université – Paris: Bouillon, 1895)
L'Entrée d'Espagne. Chanson de geste franco-italienne publiée d'après le manuscrit unique de Venise, ed. by A. Thomas, 2 vols (Paris: Firmin-Didot, 1913)

L'Entrée d'Espagne. Chanson de geste Franco-italienne. Ristampa anastatica dell'edizione di Antoine Thomas, ed. by M. Infurna (Florence: Olschki, 2007).

L'Entrée d'Espagne. Rolando da Pamplona all'Oriente, ed. and transl. by M. Infurna (Rome: Carocci, 2011).

Eulogius, *Liber apologeticus martyrum*, in *Corpus scriptorum Mozarabicorum*, ed. by J. Gil, 2 vols (Madrid: Consejo Superior de Investigaciones Cientificas, 1973)

I fatti di Cesare, ed. by L. Banchi (Bologna: Collezione di opere indite o rare, 1863)

Floovant. Chanson de geste du XIIe siècle, ed. by S. Andolf (Uppsala: Almquist Wiksells, 1941)

Florent et Octavien, ed. by N. Laborderie (Paris: Champion, 1991)

The Franco-Italian Roland, ed. by G. Robertson-Mellor (Salford: University of Salford Reprographic Unit, 1980)

Galtieri de Castellione, *Alexandreis*, ed. by M. L. Colker (Padua: Antenore, 1978)

Galvano Fiamma, *Opusculum de rebus gestis ab Azone, Luchino et Johanne vicecomitibus ab anno MCCCXXVIII usque ad annum MCCCXLII*, ed. by C. Castiglioni (Bologna: Zanichelli, 1938)

Gesta Francorum, ed. by R. Hill (Oxford: Oxford University Press, 1998)

Girard de Viane, ed. by F. G. Yeandle (New York: Columbia University Press, 1930)

Guibert de Nogent, *The Deeds of God through the Franks*, transl. by R. Levine (Woodbridge: Boydell Press, 1997)

— *Dei gesta per Francos*, ed. by R. B. C. Huygens (Turnhout: Brepols, 1996)

Guido da Pisa, *I fatti di Enea*, ed. by F. Ageno (Florence: Sansoni, 1957)

Guido delle Colonne, *Historia destructionis Troiae*, ed. and transl. by M. E. Meek (Bloomington: Indiana University Press, 1974)

Guittone d'Arezzo, *Rime*, ed. by F. Egidi (Bari: Laterza, 1940)

Jacobus de Voragine, *The Golden Legend*, transl. by W. G. Ryan, 2 vols (Princeton: Princeton University Press, 1993)

John of Damascus, *Die Schriften des Johannes von Damaskos*, ed. by P. B. Kotter, 5 vols (Berlin: Walter de Gruyter & Co, 1969)

Liber miraculorum sanctae Fidis, ed. by L. Robertini (Spoleto: Centro italiano di studi sull'alto medioevo, 1994)

Lull, Raymond, *Il Libro dell'Ordine della Cavalleria*, transl. by G. Allegra (Vicenza: L.I.E.F., 1972)

— *Doctor Illuminatus. A Ramon Llull Reader*, ed. and transl. by A. Bonner (Princeton: Princeton University Press, 1993)

Lucan [Marcus Annaeus Lucanus], *Pharsalia. La guerra civile*, ed. by R. Badalì (Torino: UTET, 1988)

Marco Polo, *Milione. Le divisament dou monde*, ed. by G. Ronchi (Milan: Mondadori, 1988)

Marsilius of Padua [Marsilio da Padova], *Il difensore della pace*, ed. by C. Vasoli (Turin: UTET, 1960)

— *Writings on the Empire. Defensor minor and De translatione Imperii*, ed. and transl. by C. J. Nederman (Cambridge: Cambridge University Press, 1993)

Niccolò da Casola, *La Guerra d'Attila. Poema franco-italiano*, ed. by G. Stendardo, 2 vols (Modena: Società tipografica modenese, 1941)

Niccolò da Verona, *Opere. Pharsale, Continuazione dell'Entrée d'Espagne, Passion*, ed. by F. Di Ninni (Venice: Marsilio, 1992)

Il Novellino. Le ciento novelle antike, ed by G. Manganelli, 4th edn (Milan: Rizzoli, 1999)

Ovid [Publius Ovidius Nasus], *Ibis*, ed. by A. La Penna (Florence: la Nuova Italia, 1957)

— *Metamorphoses*, ed. by W. S. Anderson (Leipzig: Teubner, 1977)

Ovide moralisé. Poème du commencement du quatorzième siècle publié d'après tous les manuscripts connus, ed. by C. De Boer, 5 vols (Amsterdam: Johannes Müller; Uitgave van de N. V. Noord-Hollandsche Uitgeversmaatschappij, 1915–1938; repr. Wiesbaden: Verhandelingen der Koniklijke Academie van Wetenschappen te Amsterdam, 1966)

Petrarch [Francesco Petrarca], *Rime e Trionfi*, ed. by R. Ramat (Milan: Rizzoli, 1971)

La Prise de Pampelune, in *Altfranzösische Gedichte aus venezianischen Handschriften*, ed. by A. Mussafia, 2 vols (Vienna: Gerold, 1864)

The Pseudo-Turpin. Bibliothèque Nationale fonds Latin Ms. 17656, ed. by H. M. Smyser (Cambridge, MA: The Mediaeval Academy of America, 1937)

La Queste del Saint Graal, ed. by A. Pauphilet (Paris: Champion, 1984)

Riccoldo da Montecroce, *Epistolae V de perditione Acconis 1291*, ed. by R. Röhricht, in *Archives de l'orient latin*, 2 vols (Paris: Leroux, 1881–84), II: 258–96

Dal Roman de Palamedés ai cantari di Febus-el-Forte. Testi francesi e italiani del due e trecento, ed. Alberto Limentani (Bologna: Commissione per i testi di lingua, 1962)

Le Roman de Mahomet d'Alexandre du Pont, ed. by Y. G. Lepage (Paris: Klincksieck, 1977)

Servius [Maurus Servius Honoratus], *Commentarius in Vergilii Bucolicon*, ed. by G. Thilo and H. Hagen (Leipzig: B. G. Teubner, 1887; repr. Hildesheim, Zürich, New York: Georg Olms, 1961)

Statius [Publius Papinius Statius], *Thebais*, ed. and transl. by G. Faranda Villa (Milan: Rizzoli, 1998)

Thomas of Celano, *First Life of St. Francis*, transl. by C. Stace (London: Society for Promoting Christian Knowledge, 2000)

— *St. Francis of Assisi*, transl. by P. Hermann (Chicago: Franciscan Herald Press, 1963)

— *Vita Prima*, in *Analecta Franciscana 10* (Florence: Quaracchi, 1926–41), pp. 1–117

Tristano Riccardiano, ed. by M.-J. Heijkant (Parma: Pratiche, 1991)

Vincent of Beauvais, *Speculum historiale*, ed. by C. Bauer, L. Boehm and M. Müller (Freiburg: Alber, 1965)

Virgil [Publius Vergilius Maro], *Aeneid*, in *Opera*, ed. by R. A. B. Mynors (Oxford: Oxford University Press. 1969)

Visio Egidii regis Patavie, ed. by G. Fabris, 'La cronaca di Giovanni da Nono', *Bollettino del Museo civico di Padova* 8 (1932), 1–33; 9 (1933), 167–200

William of Malmesbury, *Gesta regum Anglorum*, ed. and transl. by R. A. B. Mynors, R. M. Thomson and Michael Winterbottom, 2 vols (Oxford: Clarendon Press, 1998–1999)

Secondary Works

Adler, A., 'Didactic Concerns in l'*Entrée d'Espagne*', *L'esprit créateur*, 2 (1962), 107–109

— *Rückzug in epischer Parade* (Frankfurt am Main: Klostermann, 1986)

Adorno, F., T. Gregory and V. Verra, *Storia della Filosofia* (Rome/Bari, Laterza, 1984)

BIBLIOGRAPHY

Aebischer, P., 'Ce qui reste d'un manuscrit perdue de l'*Entrée d'Espagne*', *Archivum romanicum*, 12 (1928), 233–64

Albertini Ottolenghi, M. G, 'Codici miniati francesi e di ispirazione francese nella biblioteca dei Visconti e degli Sforza nel castello di Pavia', in *La cultura dell'Italia padana*, pp. 281–94

Alphandery, P. and A. Dupront, *La Chrétienté et l'idée de Croisade* (Paris: Albin Michel, 1959)

Alvar, C., 'Las inquietudes linguisticas en L'*Entrée d'Espagne*', in P. G. Beltrami, M. G. Capusso et al., eds, *Studi di filologia romanza offerti a Valeria Bertolucci Pizzorusso*, 2 vols (Pisa: Pacini, 2006) I: 1–21

Andenna, G., 'Cavalcabó', in *Dizionario Biografico degli Italiani* (Rome: Treccani, 1979), XXII: 593–9

Appelt, H., 'La politica imperiale verso i comuni italiani', in *I problemi della civiltà comunale. Atti del Congresso storico internazionale per l'VIII centenario della prima Lega lombarda (Bergamo 4–8 settembre 1967)*, ed. by C. D. Fonseca (Bergamo: Cassa di Risparmio delle provincie lombarde, 1968), pp. 23–32

Armstrong, E. C., 'Old French *açopart*, "Ethiopian"', *Modern Philology*, 38/3 (1941), 243–50

Arthur, D., *Valentine et Orson. A Study in Late Medieval Romance* (New York: Columbia University Press, 1929)

Asín Palacios, M., *La escatología musulmana de la Divina Comedia, seguida de Historia y crítica de una polémica*, 4th edn (Madrid: Hiperión, 1984)

Auerbach, E., *Mimesis. The Representation of Reality in Western Literature*, transl. by W. R. Trask (Princeton: Princeton University Press, 1971)

Azzolini, M, *The Duke and the Stars. Astrology and Politics in Renaissance Milan* (Cambridge, MA / London: Harvard University Press, 2013)

Bakhtin, M., *The Dialogic Imagination. Four Essays*, ed. by M. Holquist, transl. by M. Holquist and C. Emerson (Austin: University of Texas Press, 1981)

Bancourt, P., *Les Musulmans dans les chansons de geste du cycle du roi*, 2 vols (Aix-en-Provence: Université de Provence, 1982)

Barbieri, R., *Uomini e tempo medievale* (Milan: Jaca Book, 1986)

Baron, H., *The Crisis of the Early Italian Renaissance*, 2 vols (Princeton: Princeton University Press, 1955)

BIBLIOGRAPHY

Bartoli, R. A., *La Navigatio sancti Brendani e la sua fortuna nella cultura romanza dell'età di mezzo* (Fasano: Schena, 1993)

Baumgartner, E., *L'Arbre et le Pain. Essai sur la Queste del Saint Graal* (Paris: Sedes, 1981)

Bédier, J., *Les Légendes épiques* (Paris: Champion, 1913)

Billanovich, G., 'Il preumanesimo padovano', in Folena, ed., *Storia della Cultura Veneta*, II: 19–110

— *La tradizione del testo di Livio e le origini dell'Umanesimo* (Padua: Antenore, 1986)

Bisaha, N., '"New Barbarian" or Worthy Adversary? Humanist Constructs of the Ottoman Turks in Fifteenth-Century Italy', in Blanks and Frasetto, eds, *Western Views of Islam*, pp. 185–205

Blachère, R., *Le Problème de Mahomet. Essai de biographie critique du fondateur de l'Islam* (Paris: PUF, 1952)

Blanks, D. R. and M. Frasetto, eds, *Western Views of Islam in Medieval and Early Modern Europe. Perception of Other* (New York: St. Martin's Press, 1999)

Boitani, P., *L'ombra di Ulisse. Figure di un mito* (Bologna: Il Mulino, 1992)

Bologna, C., 'La letteratura dell'Italia settentrionale nel Trecento', in A. Asor Rosa, ed., *Letteratura italiana. Storia e geografia*, 3 vols (Turin: Einaudi, 1987), I: 511–600

Bono, B. J., *Literary Transvaluation. From Virgilian Epic to Shakespearean Tragicomedy* (Berkeley: University of California Press, 1984)

Boscolo, C., 'La disputa teologica nell'*Entrée d'Espagne*', in C. Alvar and J. Paredes, eds, *Les chansons de geste. Actes du XVIe Congrès International de la Société Rencesvals pour l'Étude des Épopées romanes (Granada, 21–25 juillet)* (Granada: Editorial Universidad de Granada, 2005), pp. 123–34

Boyle, A. J., ed., *Roman Epic* (London: Ruthledge, 1996)

Bradley-Cromey, N., *Authority and Autonomy in L'Entrée d'Espagne* (New York: Garland, 1993)

— 'L'Entrée d'Espagne. Elements of Content and Composition' (unpublished doctoral thesis, University of Wisconsin, 1974)

— 'Forest and Voyage. Signs of *Sententia* in the *Entrée d'Espagne*', in H.-E. Keller, ed., *Romance Epic*, pp. 91–101

Brook, L. C., 'Allusions à l'antiquité gréco-latine dans *l'Entrée d'Espagne*', *Zeitschrift für romanische Philologie*, 118 (2002), 573–86
— 'Roland devant le monde sarrasin dans l'*Entrée d'Espagne*', in H. van Dijk and W. Noomen, eds, *Aspects de l'épopée romane. Mentalités, idéologies, intertextualités. Actes du XIIIe Congrès International de la Société Rencesvals* (Groningen: Egbert Forsten, 1995), pp. 209–16
Brugnoli, G., *Studi danteschi*, 3 vols (Pisa: ETS, 1998–1999)
Brundage, J., *The Crusades. A Documentary Survey* (Milwaukee, WI: Marquette University Press, 1962)
Brunetta E. et al., eds, *Storia di Treviso*, 3 vols (Venice: Marsilio, 1991)
Burman, T., 'Cambridge University Library MS Mm. v. 26 and the History of the Study of the Qur'ān in Medieval and Early Modern Europe', in T. E. Burman, M. D. Meyerson and L. Shopkow, eds, *Religion, Text, and Society in Medieval Spain and Northern Europe. Essays in honor of J. N. Hillgarth* (Toronto: PIMS, 2002), pp. 335–63
— 'Christian Kalām in Medieval Spain (Spain and the Mediterranean in the Middle Ages)', in L. Simon, ed., *Essays in Honor of Robert I. Burns* (Leiden: Brill, 1994)
— 'The Influence of the *Apology of al-Kindî* and *Contrarietas alfolica* on Ramon Llull's Late Religious Polemics, 1305–1313', *Medieval Studies*, 53 (1991), 197–228
— *Reading the Qur'ān in Latin Christendom, 1140–1560* (Philadelphia: University of Pennsylvania Press, 2009)
— *Religious Polemic and the Intellectual History of the Mozarabs* (Leiden: Brill, 1994)
— '*Tafsir* and Translation. Traditional Arabic Qur'ān Exegesis and the Latin Qur'āns of Robert of Ketton and Mark of Toledo', *Speculum*, 73 (1998), 703–32
Burns, R. I., 'Christian-Islamic Confrontation in the West. The Thirteenth-Century Dream of Conversion', *American Historical Review*, 76 (1971), 1386–434
Calonghi, F., ed., *Dizionario della lingua latina* (Turin: Rosenberg & Sellier, 1960)
Calin, W., *The Epic Queste* (Baltimore: The John Hopkins Press, 1966)
— 'Textes médiévaux et tradition. La chanson de geste est-elle une épopee?', in H.-E. Keller, ed., *Romance Epic*, pp. 11–19

Cardini, F., 'Il guerriero e il cavaliere', in J. Le Goff, ed., *L'uomo medievale* (Rome/Bari: Laterza, 1987), pp. 81–123

Cary, G., *The Medieval Alexander* (Cambridge: Cambridge University Press, 1956)

Carrara, E., *Da Rolando al Morgante* (Turin: Edizioni de 'L'Erma', 1932)

Chiri, G., *L'epica latina e la chanson de geste* (Genoa: Orfini, 1936)

Chittolini, G., 'Infeudazioni e politica feudale nel ducato visconteo-sforzesco', *Quaderni storici*, 19 (1972), 57–130

Cognasso, F., 'L'Unificazione della Lombardia sotto Milano', in *Storia di Milano*, 16 vols (Milan: Treccani, 1955)

Collodo, S., *Una società in trasformazione. Padova tra XI e XV secolo* (Padua: Antenore, 1990)

Comparetti, D., *Vergil in the Middle Ages*, transl. by E. F. M. Benecke (Princeton: Princeton University Press, 1997)

— *Virgilio nel Medio Evo* (Livorno, 1872)

Constans, L., '*L'Entrée d'Espagne* et les légendes troyennes', *Romania*, 43 (1914), 430–32

Coope, J. A., *The Martyrs of Córdoba. Community and Family Conflict in an Age of Mass Conversion* (Lincoln: University of Nebraska Press, 1995)

Corti, M., *Dante a un nuovo crocevia* (Florence: Sansoni, 1981)

— *Scritti su Cavalcanti e Dante* (Turin: Einaudi, 2003)

Cowan, D., *Modern Literary Arabic* (Cambridge: Cambridge University Press, 1958; repr. 2000)

D'Adda, G., *Appendice alla parte prima* (Milan: Tip. Brignola, 1879)

— *Indagini storiche, artistiche e bibliografiche sulla libreria visconteo-sforzesca del castello di Pavia compilate per cura di un bibliofilo* (Milan: Tip. Brignola, 1875)

D'Alverny, M.-T., 'Conaissance de l'Islam dans l'Occident médiévale', in *L'occidente e l'Islam nell'alto medioevo*, 2 vols (Spoleto: Centro italiano di studi sull'alto medioevo, 1965), II: 577–602

— 'Deux traductions latines du Coran au Moyen Âge', *Archives d'histoire doctrinale et littéraire du Moyen Âge*, 22–23 (1947–48), 69–131

D'Ancona, A., *La leggenda di Maometto in Occidente*, ed. by A. Borruso (Rome: Salerno Editrice, 1994)

Daniel, N., *Heroes and Saracens. An Interpretation of the 'Chanson de Geste'* (Edinburgh: Edinburgh University Press, 1984)

— *Islam and the West. The Making of an Image* (Edinburgh: Edinburgh University Press, 1960)

Davie, M., 'The Voyage of Saint Brendan. The Venetian Version', in W. R. J. Barron and G. S. Burgess, eds, *The Voyage of Saint Brendan. Representative Versions of the Legend in English Translation* (Exeter: University of Exeter Press, 2002), pp. 155–230

Dauzat, A, 'Tervagan', *Revue d'onomastique*, 4 (décembre 1950), 273–74

Dawson, C., *Mission to Asia* (New York: Harper & Row, 1965; repr. Toronto: University of Toronto Press, 1987)

de Mandach, A., 'Les Blasons des grandes familles padouanes dans l'*Entrée d'Espagne*', *Cultura Neolatina*, 2–4 (1989), 179–202

— 'Chanson de geste et araldique. Francesco Gonzaga da Mantova, le voleur de l'*Entrée d'Espagne?*', in P. and M. J. Schenck, eds, *Echoes of the Epic. Studies in Honor of Gerard J. Brault* (Birmingham Alabama: Summa Publications, 1998), pp. 161–73

— 'Le Destinataire de l'*Entrée d'Espagne* de Venice (Marciana fr. XXI): Francesco il Vecchio da Carrara?', in *AIV*, 148 (1989–90)

— 'L'*Entrée d'Espagne*. Six auteurs en quête d'un personnage', *Studi medievali*, 30 (1989), 163–208

— 'Sur les traces de la cheville ouvrière de l'*Entrée d'Espagne*. Giovanni Nono', in G. Holtus, H. Krauss and P. Wunderli, eds, *Testi, cotesti e contesti del franco-italiano. Atti del I simposio franco-italiano (Bad Homburg, 13–16 aprile 1987)* (Tübingen: Niemeyer, 1989), pp. 48–64

Delcorno, D., 'Eremiti e cavalieri. Tipologia di un rapporto nella tradizione epico-romanzesca italiana', in P. G. Beltrami, M. G. Capusso et al., eds, *Studi di filologia romanza offerti a Valeria Bertolucci Pizzorusso*, 2 vols (Pisa: Pacini, 2006), I: 519–41

Delisle, L., *Le Cabinet des manuscrits de la Bibliothèque Nationale*, 3 vols (Paris: Imprimerie impériale, 1881)

Dizionario Biografico degli Italiani (Rome: Treccani, 1979)

Dilke, O. A. W., *Statius' "Achilleis"* (Cambridge: Cambridge University Press, 1954)

Dionisotti, C., '*Entrée d'Espagne, Spagna, Rotta di Roncisvalle*', in G. Gerardi Marcuzzo et al., eds, *Studi in onore di Angelo Monteverdi*, 2 vols (Modena: Mucchi, 1959), I: 207–41

Dorigatti, M., 'Reinventing Roland. Orlando in Italian Literature', in K. Pratt, ed., *Roland and Charlemagne in Europe. Essays on the Reception and Transformation of a Legend* (London: King's College London Medieval Studies, 1996)

Doutté, E., *Mahomet Cardinal* (Chalons-sur-Marne: Martin Frères, 1899)

Duby, G. and M. Perrot, eds, *Histoire des femmes en Occident*, vol. II, *Le Moyen Âge* (Paris: Plon, 1991–92)

Everson, J. E., *The Italian Romance Epic in the Age of Humanism. The Matter of Italy and the World of Rome* (Oxford: Oxford University Press, 2001)

Faral, E., *Recherches sur les sources latines des contes et romans courtois du Moyen Âge* (Paris: Champion, 1913; repr. 1967)

Fauriel, C., *Histoire de la poésie provençale* (Paris: J. Labitte, 1846; repr. Geneva: Slatkine, 1969)

Ferrante, J. M., *Woman as Image in Medieval Literature. From the Twelfth Century to Dante* (New York: Columbia University Press, 1975)

Filoramo, G., *Islam*, in *Manuale di storia delle religioni* (Rome/Bari: Laterza, 1999), pp. 239–40

Finoli, A. M., 'Note sulla personalità e la cultura dell'autore dell'*Entrée d'Espagne*', *Cultura Neolatina*, 21 (1961), 175–181

Flori, J., *La chevalerie* (Paris: J.-P. Gisserot, 1998)

— 'Guerre et chevalerie au Moyen Âge (à propos d'un ouvrage récent)', *Cahiers de Civilisation Médiévale*, 41 (1998), 353–63

Flöss, L., 'Dall'epica al romanzo. Tecniche narrative e personaggi nei *Fatti di Spagna*', *Medioevo Romanzo*, 17 (1992), 61–97

Folena, G., 'La cultura volgare e l'"Umanesimo cavalleresco" nel Veneto', in V. Branca, ed., *Umanesimo europeo e Umanesimo veneziano* (Florence: Sansoni, 1963), pp. 141–58

—, ed., *Storia della Cultura Veneta*, 6 vols (Vicenza: Neri-Pozza, 1976)

— 'Tradizione e cultura trobadorica nelle corti e nelle città venete', in Folena, ed., *Storia della Cultura Veneta,*, I: 453–562

Folz, R., *L'Idée d'empire en occident du Ve au XIVe siècle* (Paris: Aubier, 1953)

Galent-Fasseur, V., 'Quand "Je" devient un autre. Un processus de conversion dans *L'Entrée d'Espagne*', in D. Boutet, M. Castellani et al., eds, *Plaist vos oïr bone cançon vallant? Mélanges offerts à François Suard*, 2 vols (Lille: Université Charles de Gaulle Lille 3, 1999), I: 273-83

Gautier, L., *Les Epopées françaises*, 5 vols (Osnabrück: Zeller, 1878)

Golubovich, G., *Biblioteca bio-bibliografica della terra santa e dell'oriente francescano*, 5 vols (Florence, 1906-13)

Gorra, E., *Testi inediti di storia troiana, preceduti da uno studio sulla leggenda troiana in Italia* (Turin: Trevirio, 1887)

Green, L., 'Galvano Fiamma, Azzone Visconti and the Revival of the Classical Theory of Magnificence', *Journal of the Warburg and Courtauld Institutes*, 53 (1990), 98-113

Grégoire, H., 'L'Etymologie de *Tervagant (Trivigant)*', in *Mélanges d'histoire du théâtre du Moyen Âge et de la Renaissance offerts à Gustave Cohen* (Paris: Nizet, 1950), pp. 67-74

Gribaudi, D., ed., *Storia del Piemonte*, 2 vols (Turin: Casanova, 1966)

Grousset, R., *Histoire universelle*, vol. II, *De L'Islam à la Réforme* (Paris: Gallimard, 1958-62)

Guénon, R., *Simboli della scienza sacra*, transl. by F. Zambon (Milan: Adelphi, 1997)

— *Symboles fondamentaux de la science sacrée* (Paris: Gallimard, 1962)

Gurevich, A., *The Origins of Medieval Individualism* (Oxford: Blackwell, 1995)

Haidu, P., *The Subject of Violence. The Song of Roland and the Birth of the State* (Bloomington: Indiana University Press, 1993)

Hillgarth, J. N., *Ramon Lull and Lullism in Fourteenth Century France* (Oxford: Clarendon Press, 1971)

Holt P. M., K. S. Lambton and B. Lewis, eds, *The Cambridge History of Islam* (Cambridge: Cambridge University Press, 1970)

Holtus, G., *Lexikalische Untersuchungen zur Interferenz. Die franko-italienische Entrée d'Espagne* (Tübingen: Niemeyer, 1979)

— 'Quelques aspects de la technique narrative dans l'*Entrée d'Espagne*', in Limentani et al., eds, *Essor et fortune*, II: 703-16

Huizinga, J., *The Waning of the Middle Ages. A Study of the Forms of Life, Thought and Art in France and the Netherlands in the XIVth and XVth Centuries*, trans. by F. Hopman (London: Edward Arnold, 1924; repr. 1976)

Hyde, J. K., *Padua in the Age of Dante* (Manchester: Manchester University Press, 1966)

Imbs, P., 'La Journée dans *La Queste del Saint Graal* et *La Mort le Roi Artu*', in *Mélanges de philologie romane offerts à Ernest Hoepffner* (Paris: Les Belles Lettres, 1949), pp. 279–93

Infurna, M., 'Note sull'edizione Thomas dell'*Entrée d'Espagne*', in C. Montagnani, ed., *Miscellanea Boiardesca* (Novara: Interlinea, 2010), pp. 25–37

— 'Per il testo dell'*Entrée d'Espagne*', in C. Donà, M. Infurna et F. Zambon, eds, *Metafora medievale. Il «libro degli amici» di Mario Mancini* (Rome: Carocci, 2011), pp. 121–37

— 'Rolando dall'eremita. Su un verso dell'*Entrée d'Espagne*', *Medioevo Romanzo*, 30 (2006), 167–75

— '*Roman d'Alexandre* e *Entrée d'Espagne*', in *La cultura dell'Italia padana e la presenza francese nei secoli XIII–XV* (Alessandria: Edizioni dell'Orso, 2001), pp. 185–99

Jackson, P., *The Mission of Friar William of Rubruck. His Journey to the Court of the Gran Khan Möngke 1253–55* (London: Hakluyt Society, 1990)

Jauss, H. R., *Toward an Aesthetic of Reception* (Brighton: Harvester Press, 1982)

Joly, A., *Benoît de Saint-Maure et le 'Roman de Troie' ou les métamorphoses d'Homère et l'épopée gréco-latine au Moyen Âge*, 2 vols (Paris: Franck, 1870–71)

Jung, M.-R., *La Légende de Troie en France au Moyen Âge* (Tübingen: Francke, 1996)

Keller, H.-E., ed., *Romance Epic. Essays on a Medieval Literary Genre*, Studies in Medieval Culture XXIV, Medieval Institute Publications (Kalamazoo: Western Michigan University Press, 1987)

Khol, B. J., *Padua under the Carrara (1318–1405)* (Baltimore: Johns Hopkins University Press, 1998)

Krauss, H., *Epica feudale e pubblico borghese. Per la storia poetica di Carlomagno in Italia*, ed. by A. Fassò, transl. by F. Brugnolo, A. Fassò and M. Mancini (Padua: Liviana, 1980)

Lazzarini, L., 'La cultura delle signorie venete del Trecento e i poeti di corte', in Folena, ed., *Storia della Cultura Veneta*, II: 477–516

Le Goff, J., *I riti, il tempo, il riso. Cinque saggi di storia medievale* (Rome/Bari: Laterza, 2003)

— *Tempo della Chiesa e tempo del mercante* (Turin: Einaudi, 1977)

Lelong, C., 'Olivier peut-il se passer de Roland? Remarques sur le devenir de l'éternel second dans le récits de la «Materia di Spagna»', in M. Possamaï-Perez and J.-R. Valette, eds, *Chanter de geste. L'art épique et son rayonnement. Hommage à Jean-Claude Vallecalle* (Paris: Champion, 2013), pp. 241–57

Limentani, A., 'L'Art de la comparaison dans *L'Entrée d'Espagne*', in *Actes du VIᵉ Congrès International de la Société Rencesvals - Aix-en-Provence, 29 Août – 4 Septembre 1973* (Aix-en-Provence: Université de Provence, 1974), pp. 351–71

— *L'"Entrée d'Espagne" e i signori d'Italia*, ed. by M. Infurna and F. Zambon (Padua: Antenore, 1992)

— 'Epica e racconto. Osservazioni di alcune strutture e sull'incompiutezza dell'*Entrée d'Espagne*', in *AIV*, 133 (1974–5), 393–428

— M. L. Meneghetti, R. Brusegan et al., eds, *Essor et fortune de la chanson de geste dans l'Europe et l'Orient latin. Actes du IXᵉ Congrès international de la Société Rencesvals pour l'Étude des épopées romanes (Padoue-Venise, 29 août –4 september 1982)* (Modena: Mucchi, 1984)

— 'Raimon d'Avinho con provenzali e catalani nelle rime dell'*Entrée d'Espagne*' in M. Jorba, ed., *Estudis de llengua i literatura catalanes oferts a R. Aramon i Serra en el seu setantè aniversari*, 4 vols (Barcelona: Curial, 1980), II: 277–89

Lot, F., *Etude sur le Lancelot en prose* (Paris: Champion, 1918)

— 'Les Noces d'Erec et d'Enide', *Romania*, 46 (1920), 42–45

Lukács, G., *The Theory of the Novel. A Historico-philosophical Essay on the Forms of Great Epic Literature*, transl. by A. Bostock (London: Merlin Press, 1978)

Mackie, C. J., *The Characterisation of Aeneas* (Edinburgh: Scottish Academic Press, 1988)

Manaresi, C., 'Le origini della famiglia Cavalcabò', in *Miscellanea di studi lombardi in onore di Ettore Verga* (Milan: Castello Sforzesco, 1931), pp. 198–99

Mancini, A., 'Per lo studio della leggenda di Maometto in Occidente', *Rendiconti della Reale Accademia dei Lincei. Classe di scienze morali, storiche e filologiche*, 10 (1934), 325–49

Maranini, L., 'Motivi cortesi e anticortesi nell' *Erec et Enide*', *Saggi di umanesimo cristiano*, 3 (1947), 3–20

— 'Motivi lirici e psicologici dell'amore nell'*Erec et Enide*' (Pavia: Tipografica ticinese di C. Busca, 1947)

March, J., ed., *Dictionary of Classical Mythology* (London: Cassell, 2000)

Marchesan, A., *Treviso medievale* (Treviso: Tipografia funzionari comunali, 1923)

Marcon, S., 'L'*Entrée d'Espagne*, manoscritto marciano Fr. Z. 21 (=257). La storia e l'aspetto materiale', in *La Entrada en España. Poema épico del siglo XIV en franco-italiano* (Valencia: Ediciones Grial, 2003), pp. 291-318

Mazzatinti, G., 'La *Fiorita* di Armannino giudice', *Giornale di Filologia Romanza*, 3 (1881), 1-51

— *Inventario dei codici della Biblioteca Visconteo-Sforzesca del castello di Pavia* (Milan: Brigola, 1875)

Meneghetti, M. L., ed., *Il romanzo* (Bologna: Il Mulino, 1988)

Menéndez Pidal, G., 'Còmo trabajaron las escuelas alfonsìes', *Nueva rivista de filologìa hispànica*, 5 (1951), 363–80

Metlitzki, D., *The Matter of Araby in Medieval England* (New Haven and London: Yale University Press, 1977)

Meyer, P., *Alexandre le Grand dans la littérature française du Moyen Âge*, 2 vols (Paris: Vieweg, 1886)

Misrahi, J. and W. L. Hendrickson, 'Roland and Oliver. Prowess and Wisdom, the Ideal of the Epic Hero', *Romance Philology*, 33 (1979–80), 357–72

Monfrin, J., 'Humanisme et traductions au moyen âge', *Journal des savants*, 148 (1963), 161–90; repr. in *L'humanisme médiéval dans les littératures romanes du XIIe au XIVe siècles* (Paris: Fourrier, 1964), pp. 217–46

— 'Les "Translations" vernaculaires de Virgile au Moyen Âge', in *Lectures médiévales de Virgile. Actes du Colloque organisé par l'Ecole française de Rome (Rome, 25–28 octobre 1982)* (Rome: École française de Rome, 1985), pp. 189–249

Monteverdi, A., 'Un fragment manuscrit de *L'Entrée d'Espagne*', *Cahiers de Civilisation Médiévale*, 3 (1960), 75–78

Moos, P. von, 'Les Collationes d'Abélard et la "question juive" au XIIe siècle', *Journal des Savants*, 2 (1999), 449–89

Mora-Lebrun, F., *L'"Enéide" médiévale et la chanson de geste* (Paris: Champion, 1994)

— *L'"Enéide" médiévale et la naissance du roman* (Paris: PUF, 1994)

Nitze, W.A., 'Erec's treatment of Enide', *Romanic Review*, 10 (1919), 26–37

Nolting-Hauff, I., 'La tecnica del dialogo', in Meneghetti, ed., *Il romanzo*, pp. 282–97

Novati, F., 'I codici francesi del Gonzaga', in *Attraverso il Medioevo* (Bari: Laterza, 1905)

Otis, B., *Ovid as an Epic Poet* (Cambridge: Cambridge University Press, 1970)

Owen, D. D. R., 'The Principal Source of *Huon de Bordeaux*', *French Studies*, 7 (1953), 129–39

Padoan, G., *Il pio Enea, l'empio Ulisse* (Ravenna: Longo, 1977)

Palermo, J., 'L'"Hector et Hercule franco-italien". Chant épique ou romans courtois?', in Limentani et al., eds, *Essor et fortune*, II: 729–36

— *Le Roman d'Hector et d'Hercule. Chant épique en octosyllabes italo-français* (Geneva: Droz, 1972)

Paratore, E., *Nuovi saggi danteschi* (Rome: Signorelli, 1973)

Paris, G., 'Notice sur l'*Entrée d'Espagne*', *Romania*, 10 (1881), 455–56

Parodi, E. G., 'L'Odissea nella poesia medievale', in *Poeti antichi e moderni* (Florence: Sansoni, 1923)

— *Poeti antichi e moderni* (Florence: Sansoni, 1923)

— 'I rifacimenti e le traduzioni italiane dell'*Eneide* prima del Rinascimento', *Studi di Filologia Romanza*, 2–4 (1887), 97–368

— 'Storia di Cesare nella letteratura italiana', *Studi di Filologia Romanza*, 4/2 (1889), 237–501

Pastore Stocchi, M., 'Le fortune della letteratura cavalleresca e cortese nella Treviso medievale e una testimonianza di Lovato Lovati', in A. Mazzarolli and E. Castelnuovo, eds, *Tomaso da Modena e il suo tempo. Atti del convegno di Treviso, 28 agosto – 1 settembre 1979* (Treviso: Stamperia di Venezia, 1980), pp. 201–17

Pellat, C., '*Mahom, Tervagant, Apollin*', in *Actas del Primer Congreso de Estudios Árabes e Islámico. Córdoba 1962* (Madrid: Maestre, 1964)

Pellegrin, E., *La Bibliothèque des Visconti et des Sforza ducs de Milan au XVe siècle* (Paris: Service des publications du C.N.R.S., 1955)
Peron, G., 'Cultura provenzale e francese a Treviso nel medioevo', in Brunetta et al., eds, *Storia di Treviso*, II: 487–544
Petit, A., 'Le Traitement courtois du thème des Amazones d'après trois romans antiques. *Enéas, Troie* et *Alexandre*', *Le Moyen Âge*, 89 (1983), 63–84
Procter, E. S., *Alfonso X of Castile. Patron of Literature and Learning* (Oxford: Oxford University Press, 1951)
Propp, V., *Morphology of the Folktale* (Austin: University of Texas Press, 1968)
Quint, D., *Origin and Originality in Renaissance Literature. Versions of the Source* (New Haven: Yale University Press, 1983)
— *Epic and Empire* (Princeton: Princeton University Press, 1993)
Rashed, R., ed., *Encyclopedia of the History of Arabic Science*, 3 vols (London: Routledge, 1996)
Raynaud De Lage, G., 'L'*Histoire ancienne jusqu'à César* et les *Faites des Romaines*', in *Les premiers romans français* (Paris: Droz, 1976), pp. 5–13
— 'Les "romans antiques" dans l'*Histoire ancienne jusqu'à César*', *Le Moyen Âge*, 63 (1957), 267–309
Renzi, L., 'Il francese come lingua letteraria e il franco-lombardo. L'epica carolingia nel Veneto', in Folena, ed., *Storia della Cultura Veneta*, III: 563–89
— 'Per la lingua dell'*Entrée d'Espagne*', *Cultura Neolatina*, 30 (1970), 59–87
Rinoldi, P., '«*Qui volt honor conquere sor son felons vesin / apraigne d'Alixandre la voie et le traïn*». Riflessioni sull'*Entrée d'Espagne* e il *Roman d'Alexandre*', in C. Montagnani, ed., *Miscellanea Boiardesca*, (Novara: Interlinea, 2010), pp. 39–59
Roncaglia, A., 'L'Alexandre d'Alberic et la séparation entre chanson de geste et roman', in *Chanson de geste und höfischer Roman. Heidelberger Kolloquium (30. Januar 1961)* (Heidelberg: Winter, 1963), pp. 37–60
— 'La letteratura franco-veneta', in E. Cecchi and N. Sapegno, eds, *Storia della letteratura italiana*, 9 vols (Milan: Garzanti, 1987), II: 727–59

Rosellini, A., *Codici Marciani di epopea carolingia* (*Ricerche bibliografiche*). *Dispensa prima* (Udine: Cooperativa Libraria Universitaria Friuliana, 1979)

Ruggieri, R. M., 'Dall'*Entrée d'Espagne* e dai *Fatti de Spagna* alla "materia de Spagna" dell'inventario gonzaghesco', *Cultura Neolatina*, 21 (1961), 182–90

— 'Il titolo e la protasi dell'*Entrée d'Espagne* e dei *Fatti di Spagna* in rapporto alla materia della *Chanson de Roland*', in *Mélanges de linguistique romane et de philologie médiévale offerts à Maurice Delbouille*, 2 vols (Gembloux: Duculot, 1964), II: 615–33

Runciman, S., *A History of the Crusades*, 3 vols (Cambridge: Cambridge University Press, 1954)

Said, E. W., *Orientalism* (London: Penguin, 1991)

Scholem, G., *Alchimia e Kabbalah* (Turin: Einaudi, 1995)

— *Zohar. The Book of Splendour* (New York: Schoken Books, 1995)

Segre, C., 'Quello che Bachtin non ha detto. Le origini medievali del romanzo', in *Teatro e romanzo* (Turin: Einaudi, 1984), pp. 61–84

Settegast, F., 'Die Odyssee oder die Sage vom heimkehrenden Gatten als Quelle mittelalterlicher Dichtung', *Zeitschrift für romanische Philologie*, 39 (1918), 267–329

Southern, R. W., *Western Views of Islam in the Middle Ages* (Cambridge, MA: Harvard University Press 1962)

Specht, R., 'Cavalleria francese alla corte di Persia. L'episodio dell'*Entrée d'Espagne* ritrovato nel frammento reggiano', in *AIV*, 135 (1976–77), 486–506

— 'Il frammento reggiano dell'*Entrée d'Espagne*. Raffronto filologico col codice marciano francese XXI (257)', in *AIV*, 136 (1977–78), 407–24

— 'La Tradition manuscrite de l'*Entrée d'Espagne*. Observations sur le fragment de Châtillon', in Limentani et al., eds, *Essor et fortune*, II: 749–45

Spitzer, L., *Classical and Christian Ideas of World Harmony. Prolegomena to an Interpretation of the Word 'Stimmung'*, ed. by A. Granville Hatcher (Baltimore: Johns Hopkins Press, 1963)

— '*Tervagant*', *Romania*, 70 (1948–49), 397–409

Sturm-Maddox, S., '"*En fer en cortoisie retorner li villan*". Roland in Persia in the *Entrée d'Espagne*', in B. K. Altmann and C. W. Carroll, eds, *The Court Reconvenes. Courtly Literature Across the Disciplines.*

9th Triennial Congress of the International Courtly Literature Society, University of British Columbia (Vancouver, 25–31 July 1998) (Rochester, NY: Boydell & Brewer, 2003)

— '"Non par orgoil, mais por senefiance". Roland Redefined in the *Entrée d'Espagne*', *Olifant* 21: 1–2 (1996–97), 31–45

Suarès, C., *The Cipher of Genesis. The Original Code of the Qabala as Applied to the Scriptures* (London: Stuart & Watkins, 1970)

— *The Sepher Yetsira. Including the Original Astrology according to the Cabala and Its Zodiac* (Boulder: Shambhala Publications, 1976)

Tabacco, G., *Egemonie sociali e strutture del potere nel medioevo italiano* (Turin: Einaudi, 1974)

Tester, S. J., *A History of Western Astrology* (Woodbridge: Boydell & Brewer, 1987)

Thomas, A., 'Les Manuscripts françaises et provençaux des Ducs de Milan au château de Pavie', *Romania*, 40 (1911), 571–609

— *Nouvelles recherches sur l'Entrée d'Espagne, Chanson de geste franco-italienne* (Paris: Thorin, 1882)

Toesca, P., 'Le miniature dell'*Entrée d'Espagne* della Biblioteca Marciana', in *Scritti di varia erudizione e di critica in onore di Rodolfo Renier* (Turin: Bocca, 1912), pp. 747–53

— *La pittura e la miniatura nella Lombardia. Dai più antichi monumenti alla metà del Quattrocento* (Milan: Hoepli, 1912)

Tolan, J. V., *Medieval Christian Perceptions of Islam. A Book of Essays* (New York: Garland, 1996)

— 'Peter the Venerable on the "Diabolical Heresy" of the Saracens', in A. Ferreiro, ed., *The Devil, Heresy, and Witchcraft in the Middle Ages. Essays in Honor of Jeffrey B. Russell* (Leiden: Brill, 1998), pp. 345–67

— *Petrus Alfonsi and His Medieval Readers* (Gainesville: University Press of Florida, 1993)

— *Saint Francis and the Sultan. The Curious History of a Christian-Muslim Encounter* (Oxford: Oxford University Press, 2009)

— *Saracens, Islam in the Medieval European Imagination* (New York: Columbia University Press, 2002)

Tomaševskij, B., 'La costruzione dell'intreccio', transl. by G. L. Bravo, in T. Todorov, ed., *I formalisti russi* (Turin: Einaudi, 1968), pp. 305–50

Torraca, F., 'L'Entrée d'Espagne', in *Studi di storia letteraria* (Florence: Sansoni, 1923), pp. 164–241

Ugolini, F. A., *I cantari di argomento classico con un'appendice di testi inediti* (Florence: Olschki, 1933)

Ugolini, P., 'Sistema territoriale e urbano della valle padana', in C. de Seta, ed., *Storia d'Italia - Annali*, 11 vols (Turin: Einaudi, 1985), VIII: 159–240

Vallecalle, J.-C., 'Roland sénateur de Rome dans L'*Entrée d'Espagne*', in *Romans d'Antiquité et littérature du Nord. Mélanges offerts à Aimé Petit* (Paris: Champion, 2007), pp. 769–79

Varanini, G. M., 'Istituzioni società a Treviso tra comune, signoria e poteri regionali', in Brunetta et al., eds, *Storia di Treviso*, II: 135–211

Villey, M., *La Croisade. Essai sur la formation d'une théorie juridique* (Paris: Vrin, 1942)

Villoresi, M., *La letteratura cavalleresca. Dai cicli medievali all'Ariosto* (Rome: Carocci, 2002)

Viré, F., 'A propos de Tervagan idole Sarrasins', *Cahier de Tunisie*, 2 (1953), 141–52

Virolleaud, C., 'Khadir', *Bulletin des Etudes Arabes*, 49 (1950), 151–55

— 'Khadir et Tervagant', *Journal Asiatique*, 241 (1953), 161–66

Viscardi, A., 'Arthurian Influences in Italian Literature', in R. S. Loomis, ed., *Arthurian Literature in the Middle Ages* (Oxford: Oxford University Press, 1959; repr. 1979), pp. 419–29

— 'La cultura milanese nel secolo XIV', in *Storia di Milano* (Milan: Treccani, 1955), V: 570–634

Vivanti, C., 'La storia politica e sociale. Dall'avvento delle signorie all'Italia spagnola', in *Storia d'Italia*, ed. by R. Romano and C. Vivanti, 6 vols (Turin: Einaudi, 1974)

Warren, F. M., 'The Enamoured Moslem Princess in Orderic Vital and the French Epic', *PMLA*, 19 (1914), 341–58

Webber, R. H., 'Towards the Morphology of the Romance Epic', in H.-E. Keller, ed., *Romance Epic*, pp. 1–9

Wilmotte, M., *L'Épopée française. Origine et élaboration* (Paris: Boivin, 1939)

— *Le Français à la tête épique* (Paris: Renaissance du Livre, 1917)

Wittig, J. S., 'The Aeneas-Dido Allusion in Chrétien's *Erec et Enide*', *Comparative Literature*, 22 (1970), 237–53

X Congresso internazionale di scienze storiche, Roma, 4–11 settembre 1955 – Relazioni, III: *Storia del medioevo* (Florence: Sansoni, 1955)

Zaddy, Z. P., 'Pourquoi Erec se décide-t-il à partir en voyage avec Enide?', *Cahiers de Civilisation Médiévale*, 7 (1964), 179–85

Zambon, F., *La materia di Francia nella letteratura franco-veneta*, in *Sulle orme di Orlando. Leggende e luoghi carolingi in Italia (Ferrara 25 luglio – 6 settembre 1987)* (Padua: Interbooks, 1987), pp. 53–64

Zankler, G., *Realism in Alexandrian Poetry. A Literature and Its Audience* (London: Croom Helm, 1987)

Zarker-Morgan, L., co-director with David Bénétau, FIOLA (Franco-Italian On-Line Archive) <http://www.loyolanotredamelib.org/fiola/>

— 'The Narrator in Italian Epic. Franco-Italian Tradition', in H. van Dijk and W. Noomen, eds, *Aspects de l'épopée romane. Mentalités, idéologies, intertextualités. Actes du XIIIe Congrès International de la Société Rencesvals* (Groningen: Egbert Forsten, 1995), pp. 481–90

INDEX OF NAMES

Abelard 162, 167
Abraham 45
Achilles 74-81, 103, 199, 200, 205
Adler, A. 47
Adolph (king) 224
Adorno, F. 140
Aebischer, P. 221, 254
Aeneas x, 8, 51-53, 57, 59, 60-61, 63, 65-67, 71, 75, 78, 80, 92, 98, 237
Alan of Lille 163
Alberic de Besançon 87
Alberico da Romano 246
Albertini Ottolenghi, M. G. 228
Albertino da Mussato 5, 227
Albertus Magnus 159, 233
Alexander the Great x, 48, 51, 79, 86-94, 99, 218, 219
Alexandre de Bernay (Alexandre de Paris) 51, 87, 88, 92
al-Djabal du Djabal Nusairi 165
Alexandre du Pont 166, 173
Alfonso X of Castile 156
Allegra, G. 113
Alphandery, P. 164, 169
Altmann, B. K. 176

Alvar, C. xii
Anchises 67
Andenna, G. 231, 242
Anderson, W. S. 57, 71
Andolf, S. 193
Angelica 63, 188
Anguigueron 33
Anseïs 62, 64, 186, 189
Antenor 68, 71, 75, 215, 226
Antiope 81
Apollodorus 83
Apollonius Rhodius 85
Appelt, H. 244
Argonauts 85, 86
Aristotle 87, 88, 156
Armannino Giudice 59
Armstrong, E. C. 87, 180
Arsanne 27
Arthur 18, 32, 33, 38, 94
Arthur, D. 193
Asín Palacios, M. 157
Asor Rosa, A. 6
Aude 15, 62, 114, 149, 186, 187, 188
Auerbach, E. 121, 124, 200
Ausonius 84
Averroes 156, 159
Azzolini, M. 230, 231

INDEX OF NAMES

Bacharuf 181, 208, 209, 210
Badalì, R. 71
Baebus Italicus 80, 84
Bakhtin, M. 3, 110
Banchi, L. 59
Bancourt, P. 92, 119, 120, 155, 163, 165-76, 190, 199, 211
Barbieri, R. 21
Baron, H. 20, 121
Barron, W. R. J. 44
Bartholomew of Cremona 213
Bartoli, R. A. 44
Bartolo da Sassoferrato 20
Bauer, C. 173
Baumgartner, E. 41
Bédier, J. 52
Benecke, E. F. M. 86
Benedetti, R. 88, 218
Bénétau, D. 153
Benoît de Saint-Maure 8, 9, 51, 63, 70, 72, 74, 76, 77, 79-84, 92, 93
Berengair 104
Bernard de Ventadour 247
Bernard of Anger 84
Bernard of Clairvaux 8, 61, 102, 105, 113, 115, 197
Bernardo del Carpio 15
Bertrand de Born 247
Billanovich, G. 68
Bisaha, N. 161, 203
Blachère, R. 167
Blanks, D.R. 155

Boccaccio 9, 83
Boehm, L. 173
Bohort 44
Bologna, C. 6, 217, 220, 228, 240, 249
Bonacolsi (family) 217, 224
Bonaventura da Bagnoregio 213
Bonner, A. 162
Bono, B. J. 8
Boort 45, 197
Bostock, A. 95
Boyle, A. J. 8
Bradley-Cromey, N. 3-7, 15, 55, 217, 218, 223-25, 227, 239, 244
Brambilla Ageno, F. 8, 60
Branca, V. 17
Brendan (St.) 21, 44, 49, 204, 205
Brezzi, P. 219
Brugnoli, G. 78
Brugnolo, F. 237
Brunetto Latini 157, 163, 172, 220
Burgess, G. S. 44
Burman, T. E. 156, 162

Cacus 56, 57, 71, 79
Calin, W. 10, 21, 42, 47
Calogrenant 38, 39
Calonghi, F. 105
Cardini, F. 40, 112, 197, 205
Carrara, E. 54, 226
Carroll, C. W. 176

INDEX OF NAMES

Cary, George 87-89
Castelnuovo, E. 226
Castruccio Castracane 220
Cato 23, 45
Cavalcabò (family) 230, 231, 232, 234, 236, 241-43; Cavalcabò (Cavalcabò Cavalcabò) 242; Guberto, 242; Guglielmo, 231, 241, 242; Marsilio, 242
Charlemagne v, xi, 1, 7, 9, 15, 20, 21, 23, 24, 29, 31-36, 43, 46, 47, 49, 57, 64-66, 68, 69, 85, 90, 92, 94-96, 103, 105-08, 110, 111, 113-15, 120-39, 141-45, 147, 149, 150, 151, 153, 154, 178-80, 183, 187, 189, 193, 194, 206, 209, 210, 212, 215, 219, 222, 225, 237, 238, 240, 248-50, 255, 256
Chiri, G. 52
Chittolini, G. 221, 230, 242
Chrétien de Troyes 22, 23, 28, 33, 38, 39
Cicero 67
Cigni, F. 44
Clamadeu 33
Clement V 112, 140, 164
Cognasso, F. 219, 222, 224, 230, 232
Colker, M. L. 87
Collodo, S. 226
Comparetti, D. 52, 86
Constans L., 8, 53, 58, 70, 71, 76, 77

Corti, M. 10, 157, 203, 204
Cowan, D. 232
Curtius, E. R. 52

Daniel, N. 155, 162-64, 169, 192, 199
Dante Alighieri 1, 7, 8, 9, 10, 12, 15, 57, 75, 78, 84, 140, 156, 163, 172, 194, 203, 204, 206, 226, 227, 236, 240, 242
Dares 9, 51, 70, 72, 75, 76, 78, 79, 83
Darius 88, 89, 90
Dauzat, A. 170
Davie, M. 44, 204
Dawson, C. 213
De Boer, C. 9
de Mandach, André 4, 55, 216, 239
Dedalus 86
Delisle, L. 228
Della Torre (family) 224
Desiderius 68-69
Di Ninni, F. 249
Dictys 9, 51, 63, 70, 72, 76, 77, 83
Dido 60, 61, 62, 63, 66, 92, 188
Dilke, O. A. W. 80
Diodorus Siculus 83
Dionés 21, 25, 31, 40, 55, 60-63, 83, 89, 90, 93, 95, 100-02, 117-19, 175, 182, 184-88, 190, 210, 212, 246
Donatus [Tiberius Claudius

Donatus] 58
Donadello, A. 39
Doutté, E. 172
Duparc-Quioc, S. 166
Dupront, A. 164, 169

Eçeler de Bordelois 141
Egidi, F. 23
Eisenhut, W. 70
Emerson, C. 3
Estout (Estous) 17, 95, 96, 100, 102, 114, 118, 130, 138, 132, 136, 139, 141, 148, 179, 180, 183, 200, 201
Euanthius 255
Eulogius of Cordova 169
Eumenidus 218
Everson, J. E. 54, 55, 58, 59, 85, 224, 240
Ezzelino da Romano 227, 238, 243, 246

Fabris, G. 216
Fanfani, P. 59
Faral, E. 52, 83
Faranda Villa, G. 71
Fassò, A. 237
Fauriel, C. 84
Febus 18, 25, 26, 27, 69, 70, 73
Feilitzen, H. von 193
Fernàn Gonzalez 15
Ferragu xi, 14, 17, 19, 32, 55, 74, 75, 79, 95- 97, 102-06, 108, 113-15, 126-28, 155, 162, 169, 171, 173, 174, 180, 190, 191, 193, 194, 196-206, 209, 210, 229, 232, 234, 235, 239, 242, 248
Filoramo, G. 168
Finoli, A. M. ix, 246
Folena, G. 17, 226
Folz, R. 127, 140
Fonseca, C. D. 61, 244
Francesco il Vecchio da Carrara 239
Francis (St.) 157, 158, 212, 213
Frasetto, M. 155
Fredrick II 238
Fulgentius 8, 64, 67

Galaad 18, 24, 41, 44, 45, 46, 49, 197
Gales de Vormendois 23
Galvano Fiamma 220, 237
Ganelon 64, 120, 121, 142, 191
Gautier, L. xiii, 60, 183
Gawain 28
Geophanais 179
Gerardi Marcuzzo, G. 2
Gherardo da Camino 226, 238
Gil, J. 169
Gilgamesh 47
Giovanni da Nono 5, 55, 216, 239
Girard de Roussillon 148, 149, 199
Girart de Vienne 53, 149, 161

INDEX OF NAMES

Goliath 56, 193, 194
Golubovich, G. 158
Gonzaga (family) 53, 70, 215-17, 220, 222, 243; Feltrino 222; Luigi I 243
Gorra, E. 72, 76
Granville Hatcher, A. 186
Green, L. 220, 237
Grégoire, H. 170
Gregory, T. 140
Gresti, P. xiii
Gribaudi, D. 219
Grignani, M. A. 44
Grousset, R. 165
Guenevre 31, 33
Guibert de Nogent 167, 168
Guido da Pisa 59
Guido delle Colonne 44, 51, 63, 72, 74, 76-78, 82, 85
Guillaume 15
Guiraut de Bornelh 247
Gurevich, A. 256

Hagen, H. 58
Haidu, P. 29
Hector 51, 57, 70, 72, 73, 74, 75, 76, 78, 79, 82, 98, 103, 199, 218, 221, 237
Heijkant, M.-J. 252
Hendrickson, W. L. 111
Henestor 26
Henry VII 224, 230, 241
Herbert 135, 136
Hercules 26, 56, 71, 72, 73, 79, 237
Hermann, P. 213
Hermannus Alemannus 156
Hill, R. 198
Hillgarth, J. N. 162
Holquist, M. 3
Holtus, G. 3, 5
Homer 9, 70, 77, 80, 83, 84, 103, 200, 255
Hopman, F. 155
Hugo von Trimberg 84, 87
Hugue de Blois 141
Hugues de Payns 119
Hult, D. 38
Huon de Bordeaux 47, 117, 206
Huygens, R. B. C. 168
Huizinga, J. 155
Hyginus [Gaius Julius Hyginus] 84

Icarus 86
Imbs, P. 21
Infurna, M. xi-xiii, 218, 223
Isoré 33, 130, 131, 139, 178, 179, 180, 190

Jackson, P. 158, 213
Jacobus de Voragine 173
Jason 47, 71, 85
John of Damascus 163
John of Salisbury 8
John XXII 219, 224
Julius Valerius 83, 92

INDEX OF NAMES

Jung, M.-R. 53, 73, 77

Khol, B. J. 226
Krauss, H. 5, 237, 243, 244

Laborderie, N. 193
La Du, M. 87, 90, 92
Lambton, A. K. S. 168
Lancelot 17, 21, 28, 31, 33, 39, 197
Laomedon 73, 85
La Penna, A. 71
Lavinia 63, 64, 93
Lazzarini, L. 226
Le Goff, J. 21, 40
Lelong, C. 111
Lepage, Y. G. 166
Levine, R. 168
Lewis, B. 168
Limentani, A. vii, 4, 5, 15, 16, 26, 27, 52-55, 57-60, 69, 76, 83, 86, 98, 101, 163, 164, 176, 198, 206, 215-18, 225, 232, 239, 240, 245-47, 252, 253
Lionés 102, 117, 118, 182, 189, 191, 210, 211
Lonnet, A. 234
Lot, F. 28
Louis X 173
Louis XII 228
Lovati, L. 5, 17, 226
Lucan [Marcus Annaeus Lucanus] 70, 71

Macareus 84
Macrobius [Ambrosius Theodosius Macrobius] 67
Machaire (St.) 45
Mackie, C.J. 80
Maçon [Macon] 82, 83
Magnani, A. 44
Malcuidant 26, 40, 182, 183, 184, 189
Malgeris 129, 130, 132, 137, 138, 179
Manaresi, C. 231
Mancini, A. 173
Mancini, M. 237
Manganelli, G. 39
Marcabrins 94
March, J. 83, 231
Marchesan, A. 218
Marco Polo 165, 166, 207
Marcon, S. ix, xii
Marsile 23, 92, 123, 128, 129, 134, 137, 199, 209, 210
Marsilius of Padua 39, 140, 220, 226, 227, 239, 242, 249
Martì, R. 158, 159, 163
Mazzarolli, A. 226
Mazzatinti, G. 59, 228
Meek, M. E. 78
Meister, F. 70, 72
Meneghetti, M. L. 20, 28, 41
Menéndez Pidal, G. 156
Mengaldo, P. V. 9
Metlitzki, D. 186, 194
Michael Scotus 156

INDEX OF NAMES

Michelant, H.   87, 89, 91
Miguel de Cervantes   113
Misrahi, J., 111
Monfrin, J.   53, 59, 63, 69
Monteverdi, A.   2, 221
Mora-Lebrun, F.   8, 9, 58, 64, 67
Morhault   18, 25
Mudarra   15, 111
Mohammed [Muhammad]   83, 100, 117, 156, 160, 162, 167-73, 175, 207, 209, 211, 212
Müller, M.   173
Mussafia, A.   249
Mynors, R. A. B.   55

Naime   121, 129, 131, 135, 136, 143
Nardi, B.   9
Nederman, C. J.   140
Niccolò da Casola   220, 224, 240
Niccolò da Verona   220, 249, 251
Nicholas   90, 91
Nolting-Hauff, I.   20
Novati, F.   222

Ogier   24, 29, 82, 105, 114, 126, 131, 143, 166, 193
Oliver   36, 74, 100, 103, 104, 111, 112, 118, 120, 131, 139, 141, 149, 151, 182, 183, 187, 201
Otis, B.   8

Ovid [Publius Ovidius Nasus]   x, 8, 9, 51, 57, 70, 71, 72, 80, 84, 85, 86, 167
Owen, D.D.R.   47

Paciocco, R.   213
Padoan, G.   75
Paratore, E.   78
Parodi, E. G.   53, 54, 59, 83
Pastore Stocchi, M.   226
Paul (St.)   44, 45, 205
Pauphilet, A.   18
Pausanias   83
Peleus   85, 86
Pélias   26, 30, 40, 42, 75, 76, 90, 95, 100, 101, 104, 118, 175, 182, 184, 188-91, 193, 210
Pellat, C.   170
Pellegrin, E.   228
Penthesileia   81-83
Pepoli (family)   240
Perceval   22, 23, 28, 33, 44, 45, 112, 185, 197
Peron, G.   226
Peter the Venerable   158
Petit, A.   83
Petrarch [Francesco Petrarca]   17, 83, 127, 220
Petrus Alfonsi   163, 173
Philip IV   127, 140, 146
Philip of Savoy-Achaia   219
Philip of Valois   219
Plato   67

Plotinus 162
Plutarch 87
Polifemus 84
Polyxena 63
Possamaï-Perez, M. 111
Pozzoli, F. ix
Priam 75, 78, 81, 82
Procter, E. S. 156
Propp, V. 11
Pseudo-Callisthenes 87, 92
Pseudo-Dionysus 162
Pseudo-Longinus 255
Pyrrhus 80

Quilichinus of Spoleto 87
Quint, D. 13
Quintilian [Marcus Fabius Quintilianus] 255
Quintus Curtius Rufus 87
Quintus of Smyrna 83

Ramat, R. 17
Ramon de Penyafort 159
Raymond Lull [Ramon Llul] 113, 161-63, 205, 212
Rando, D. 226
Rashed, R. 232
Raynaud de Lage, G. 53
Renaut de Montalban [Rinaldo da Montalbano] 225
Renzi, L. 5, 17, 217, 243, 247, 249
Riccoldo da Montecroce 159, 160, 163

Richard the Norman 106, 138, 146
Robert of Anjou 219
Robertini, L. 84
Rodrigo 15
Roger IV 53
Roger Bacon 156
Roland ix, x, 4, 7, 10-21, 23-36, 40-44, 46, 48-52, 55, 57, 60-66, 69, 73, 74, 76, 78, 85, 88-21, 123-33, 136-55, 162, 171-83, 185, 187-94, 196, 197, 199, 200-03, 205-13, 218, 222, 223, 225, 229, 239, 243, 246, 248-54, 256
Roncaglia, A. 14, 17, 87, 217, 218, 220, 243
Ronchi, G. 165
Rouguier, M. 193
Rudel, J. 247
Runciman, S. 164, 165
Ryan, W. G. 173

Salomon 106, 134, 135, 136, 138, 146, 149
Salverda de Grave, J. J. 8
Samson (biblical character) 210
Samson (hermit) 43, 46, 47, 49, 50, 69, 251
Sansonet [Samson, son of the Sultan of Persia] 44, 90, 95, 102, 119, 120, 178, 180, 182, 183, 191, 211, 250-54
Sapegno, N. 14
Scaffai, M. 77
Scholem, G. 233

INDEX OF NAMES

Scolari, D. 87
Segre, C. 41
Selmer, C. 10, 44
Settegast, F. 84
Servius [Maurus Servius Honoratus] 58
Simeoni, L. 20
Simon de Fraisne 170
Smyser, H. M. 193
Southern, R. W. 155
Specht, R. xii, 212, 221
Spitzer, L. 170, 186
Statius [Publius Papinius Statius] 70, 71, 80
Stendardo, G. 240
Sturm-Maddox, S. 176
Suarès, C. 233

Tabacco, G. 20, 221, 223, 224, 230, 242
Tempier, S. 159
Terence 255
Tester, S. J. 233, 235
Thierry 121
Thilo, G. 58
Thomas Aquinas 159
Thomas of Celano 157, 213
Thomas, A. ix, xi, xii, 52, 60, 176, 183, 224, 225, 228, 245, 247, 257
Tiois 133-35, 176
Todorov, T. 95
Toesca, P. 221
Tolan, J. V. 155, 158-61, 166-67, 169, 173, 191-92, 203, 213
Tomaševskij, B. 95
Tomaso da Modena 226
Torraca, F. 45, 216, 253
Tristan 17, 18, 24, 25, 39, 60
Trovo, C. 162
Turpin 29, 112, 120, 204, 215, 228
Turquis de Tortolose 137

Uc de Saint-Circ 247
Uc Faidit 247
Ugolini, P. 231
Ulysses 9, 10, 84, 203, 204, 206

Valette, J.-R. 111
Vallecalle, J.-C. 111
Vasoli, C. 140
Verra, V. 140
Villey, M. 168
Villoresi, M. 225
Vincent of Beauvais 173
Viré, F. 170
Virgil [Publius Vergilius Maro] 8, 52, 53-55, 57-59, 64, 67, 70, 80, 84, 86
Virolleaud, C. 170
Viscardi, A. 19, 23, 39, 47, 220, 222, 228, 242
Visconti (family) xi, 5, 6, 68, 69, 216-21, 224, 225, 228, 230, 231, 236, 237, 240-45, 247; Azzone (Azzo) 220, 237;

Galeazzo 220, 222, 226, 231, 241, 242, 245, 247; Galeazzo II 228; Gian Galeazzo 241; Giovanni 221; Luchino 221, 231, 237; Matteo 68, 219, 220, 222, 224-26, 231, 237, 245
Vivanti, C. 217, 221, 230

Wahlund, C. 193
Walter of Châtillon 87, 88
Warren, F. M. 185
Webber, R. H. 11-13, 15, 111

Wenceslaus (emperor) 241
Wilmotte, M. 52
Wunderli, P. 5

Yeandle, F. G. 53
Ysolt the Blonde 24, 25, 39
Ysolt of the White Hands 25, 60
Yvain 38, 39

Zambon, F. 4, 67
Zankler, G. 255
Zarker-Morgan, L. 6, 98, 153, 216

Milton Keynes UK
Ingram Content Group UK Ltd.
UKHW040920020224
437147UK00004B/184